THE COLD

Eric Del Carlo

"To my wife Samala Ray,
who saw this coming the whole time."

CHAPTER ONE

There is a Girl Upon a Hill

There she goes, again. My days are episodes of sleepwalking, for the most part. At age forty, and considering the state of humankind these days, I can't fault myself much for carrying on as if by rote. I am better than some others; more functional, at any rate, contributing something to this final pantomime of normal society. I come to the firm, to the office. I participate. I behave as if the financial matters at hand still have an absolute, inviolable relevance. It is how I saw myself when I studied econ and finance principles in school. So I have gotten what I paid for. I am who I am. I am Kyle Norris. And here I am.

But...there she goes.

She comes off the stepped peaks of Powell Street as it descends toward Market. The flat intersections are like ramps for her; she gets airborne every time. She is sleek, bent low over the handlebars. The bike seems light, spun from some polymer maybe. Her legs chug. Her hair--reddish dark--is chopped short, uneven, and the irregular tufts of it dance all about her head.

She is a cold. I'm sure of it. She is not on the old side of twenty. I am an old, of course. And we can usually tell at a glance when a youngster (youngster, such an old man word) does not belong to the same human set as ourselves.

The trim, active, vital body; the derring-do of the bicycle's trajectory and speed. Splitting the lanes of robotic traffic. Cables cars still run on Powell. They will run right to the end, I imagine. Some final gray-haired oldster, one of the last hundred thousand in the country, perhaps the last of a handful who will dwell in this city. She or he putting the rattling anachronistic coach through its brave, tired paces. Up the hill--clickclickclick— and down to the turnaround— dingding the bell with a clatter of cogs and toothed metal. San Francisco will not lightly give up its cable cars. They are too embedded in the local culture. Too precious.

But there is no cable car in sight now, and anyway my attention is focused on her. My eyes track her. There is a thrumming of effort or exertion or excitement in my veins. I have come to this corner, just above Union Square, specifically to watch for her.

She is a courier, not on any fixed route, but I have seen her on Powell before and wished to see her again and so have set up my hunting blind. I stand back from the edge of the sidewalk, almost up against the plywood wall, denoting another building undergoing renovation or some failed, surrendered place which has simply been walled up.

I don't want her to see me. Or don't want her seeing me see her. I'm successful. Her head doesn't turn as she passes me, barely squeezing her brakes at the intersection.

She has high cheekbones below cheap sunglasses, a tight jawline, a succinct nose; I see a flash of mouth and decide on the spot that it is a sensual mouth.

Her breasts are rounded and ripe, and—I also decide—inviting. Her young buttocks are lifted from the saddle seat as she slides away from me. The canvas courier bag flaps against her tidy, healthy form.

When she is completely out of sight, I let out a partly held breath and draw a long, slow one. I am steeling myself for a return to the office. I have overrun my lunch hour somewhat, but no one will care. None of this matters.

None of it.

CHAPTER TWO

Union Square

Walking diagonally through Union Square, I notice the two colds. Quite unmistakable this time. Fifteen-year-olds. Boys both.

The city's Financial District is painstakingly familiar to me. Years I have spent here. Going into the office, coming away from it; meals, shopping, sundry errands. I know the streets, the buildings, the cracks and crumbles. Streets need repaving. Sometimes they get repaved, but there is less hot tar work like that going on in this precinct than even just five years ago. No less need for the repairs and upkeeps; but the effort, the simple will, is perhaps not so easily mustered anymore.

Union Square. Another San Franciscan landmark, more or less. A movie was shot here, some long while back, but a significant film, one cited by cinema scholars as among the best of its category and era. Something about surveillance. Gritty driven characters caught up in some kind of intrigue. I can see the actor — an unhandsome face full of personality. It can be strange watching old movies. All that old tech. The bloated, improbable automobiles. And the sure and certain knowledge that even the most cold-eyed sociopathic figure on the screen possesses more emotion than any cold.

The two in Union Square. A plaza with some greenery, a monument at the center. The fifteen-year-old colds stand together.

They are dressed in the simple androgyny most colds effect. There is, I believe, no statement whatever in this style of wear. Colds do not make statements. The garments are a little loose on the bodies. Here and there they have been mended, not carefully.

I watch the pair but don't ogle. I'm not even sure if they arouse my curiosity. Too far away to eavesdrop, I note when one speaks. Minimal lip movement. There is a lengthy pause, then the other responds; or says something wholly unrelated. Cold conversation can be blunt, cryptic, dull. They pass utilitarian information one to the other, usually.

They don't look my way as I cut my diagonal through the plaza. It's a weekday, midday, but the two aren't in high school classes as I would have been at that age. The colds aren't made to attend school. They are, in fact, outside so many of the strictures which fenced me in during my adolescence that some part of me envies them. What if when I'd been fifteen (twenty-five years ago!), nobody had given me any adult crap about my behavior and responsibilities? There would have been freedom in that. I could have strutted and rutted and maybe died in a drunk driving accident, leaving behind the proverbial beautiful corpse.

Except that I never thought of myself as beautiful. Not ugly, not even homely, but beauty was never mine to claim on any level. And as an uptight horny teen, I lacked the guts I would have needed to be the cock of any walk. I doubt I would have gotten laid my first time any sooner than I did.

The two teenage colds continue their intermittent mutters. But now I see they aren't enacting their scene in total isolation. A third player impends; he's an old man, seventies, with a bitter face, sitting on a bench behind the boys, leaning forward, bony elbows on rickety knees, a look of malevolence flushing his otherwise pasty face.

You can see it coming. The old man is about twenty yards away from the boys. He is broadcasting his hatred at full frequency. The forward-leaning posture is prelude to him rising from the bench in order to come ambling furiously at the teenagers; and he does this now, a shambling gait full of the miseries of age, bloodless hands clenched into fists at his sides.

I slow my steps. I am still well away from what will soon be the scene of action. The oldster will try to pummel the colds. He might land a single fragile blow. Then the colds will simply retreat, outdistancing the old man. They won't return the look of hate. They won't try to ascertain why the old man is attacking them. They'll know; or they won't care.

But I am wrong about the scenario. I misjudged, left out yet a fourth key player. A uniformed officer comes sailing in from an obtuse angle. She has a hard, impatient expression, and she grabs the old man right under his left armpit, jerking him up, practically onto his toes; and she snarls something at him. It sounds, what little I can catch on the chilly afternoon breeze, vulgar and personal.

The old man bows his head with the abundant sadness of a denied child.

I pick up my pace. Back to the office. I have dinner with Maureen tonight; she specified the restaurant, but I can't remember it now. No matter. It's in a text.

The moment of street theater is behind me now, as I hurry on. I glance back once, but the two colds have vanished.

CHAPTER THREE

What Cannot Be

There are events which should never have happened, according to a collective human appraisal. Conditions that should never be suffered. Calamities are too ridiculous or outre to accept.

Kyle Norris, aged forty, was born into the frantic aftermath of 9/11. There was never a time in his life when the Two World Trade Center towers stood upright and intact; but he seems to have been aware, from a very young age, of their absence, in a way as tangible, say, as the presence of the Golden Gate Bridge in the city of his birth.

He was perhaps infected with the collective disbelief about the attacks on the New York site. No, not disbelief; shock; shock so potent, it expressed itself in a profound inability to fully absorb the trauma. Because the blow should never have happened. It—should—not—have.

Pearl Harbor must have felt like that, on some level, for a good many people. Also: assassinations of game-changing people. Wars or pseudo-wars which shouldn't ever have been entered into. The stock market crash of 1929. Presidents who should never have attained office yet did.

Impossible things, which nonetheless brutally proved their possibility by simply occurring.

Kyle Norris, like all in his age bracket, watched the arrival of the colds with all its slow motion horror. This, surely, could not happen. Was not happening. Should not be remotely possible within the framework of accepted reality. The colds shouldn't be among us. They shouldn't be replacing us. It is unacceptable that this phenomenon exists. Humans revolt against the actuality.

The colds can't be.

But the colds...are.

Therefore they are an affront, a direct attack on our properly configured view of the world. The colds are--what?--a Biblical judgment? A curse? Something wrong or something ancient, some horrible accident?

But there the colds are; there they have been, persisting in the face of all incredulity. Beings such as they are should not be. But are. They should not have sprung from the human race. Yet they did. Kyle Norris has stood witness with all the others, all the olds.

Disbelief has availed the olds nothing, except perhaps a lingering soul-deep sense of consternation. Or maybe it's more mechanical than that. Perhaps acceptance of the colds is as inconceivable as contradicted data fed into a computer. The ones and zeroes will not ever make sense; won't ever be tolerated.

It is the shock of the towers coming down, the dread into which infant Kyle was born. Though that event seems, frankly, rather petty at this distant point, viewed from beyond the cosmic line which divides the sentient species of the planet into olds and colds, the disaster felt unacceptable at the time. God or some other galactic timekeeper should have the responsibility of resetting the scenario.

The colds should not have happened; and so we shall wipe them off the board and replace the emotionless pieces with proper feeling ones, so to restore normalcy.

But this does not, of course, happen. And it has not happened for these past twenty years, which is half of Kyle Norris' lifetime.

CHAPTER FOUR

A Civilized Meal

I thumb up the text I got earlier from Maureen, and there is the name of the restaurant. It is a place we haven't been to together before and one I haven't visited at all. I am not a gastronome. Food isn't the primal thrill for me that it seems to be with others. I'm not talking about gluttons; merely people who rhapsodize about meals past as though recalling great lovemakings. Eating to me isn't quite the blunt act of refuelling, but it is nearer to that than to the transportive, transcendental experience some find it to be.

So. Dinner with Maureen. A seemly orderly date, staged in a properly romantic setting. I guess that the eatery is upscale. Maureen likes pricey food, wine with some history to it. The finer things, she says.

The meal should be a prelude to our latest carnal grappling, once the niceties of dining and digestion are seen to. Pleasant conversation, perhaps some hand-holding across the linened tabletop. I'll tell her she looks lovely tonight. I will smile, be attentive.

Maureen and I have been seeing each other for some five or six weeks. She is a junior partner at a firm of lawyers. I met her at a round-robin business luncheon; crowded table; people from my office talking over one another, working out some legal snarl with the suits from her office. We did not sit next to each other. She approached me as we were all rising, the meal and business finished.

"Hello. I'm Maureen Mccotter."

"Kyle Norris."

"Are you single, Kyle?"

"I am, Maureen."

That was our meet-cute. I don't ding it in any way. This is a very common approach these days. Time is running out, and few are interested in the hunt any longer. We went out the following evening. The night after that we went to bed together—her place, a steely jewel of a condo, monochromatic bedroom decor. She was adroit in bed, her slightly meaty body quite pliant. She didn't speak during sex, but she liked to make noises: riding ah's and oh's up and down the octaves. There was never any mistake when she orgasmed.

I walk to the restaurant. It is three and a half blocks away, still well within the bounds of the Financial District. The dystopian architecture of gleaming black towers. And nestled among those giants are steakhouses, Thai joints, cider bars, karaoke places.

Even if I had a vehicle, I would walk. I am pent up from what seems an inordinately long day at work. The air is chilly but refreshing. July in San Francisco. A reliable 55. Wind blowing, down from far-off Twin Peaks or up out of the Bay; I can't tell which. It tousles my hair, and I breathe through these minutes, unable to recall now a single thing I accomplished today at my firm. I shuffle money about, sometimes extravagant amounts of it. Very likely I did that today. But it doesn't matter.

No one needs a car in San Francisco. This was true even in my boyhood. As a grade schooler I went everywhere on public transportation. Busses, light rail, the underground Muni and BART, all of it better maintained than now. But even now, in this era of waning civic preservation, a private vehicle is unnecessary. The self-drivers are everywhere, and they are free. California is a progressive state and San Francisco practically a bastion of socialism. I'm okay with that. I don't mind people not having to pay for everything. Let the local government lend a hand. Nanny state? Fine. Big Brother? Not likely. Nobody cares enough anymore to want to establish a totalitarian realm.

I skirt Market Street, the broad main artery cleaving the city in twain. I make it down to Kearny, on foot. The wind tugs my tie out of my suit jacket, and I tuck it back in and go in under an awning of kaleidofabric, which displays restless colors; and I wonder if Maureen has chosen a place with a little funk, a bit of bohemian verve.

But no. The restaurant is coolly shining leather upholstery, strategic brass fittings and a severe-faced wait staff. No youngsters working the tables. Certainly no colds. Maybe they've got a few in the kitchen or running the chugging dishwashing units. In some states—Midwest, mostly—eateries have to display notices if they employ colds. Salt of the earth folk need to know if a cold is handling their food.

Maureen is already there. I can see her at a table. She waves. But I tell the starched person at the reception podium who I am meeting for dinner, and he murmurs, "Very good, sir," like we're in a period English drama; and I have to follow him as he escorts me to my destination.

I smile at Maureen and bend to brush her cheek with my lips before taking my seat.

She is a comely woman, her hair dark and straight and long. Her features are proportional, with the exception of a somewhat hawkish nose. The eyes, those are her best asset—vivid, watchful, playful.

Though as I look down at the menu, I cannot recall their color. This seems strange and amusing and—

Something's off with her tonight. We have had a few disagreements in our weeks of seeing one another. I sense a tension.

We order. The waiter is in his thirties. The restaurant is half full. What the hell is wrong with Maureen?

I make conversational feints, bloodless stuff. She can give me back soft formless answers; I'll keep the jabber coming, just to fill the time. But she doesn't even do that. Mmm, she says. Shm. Likes she's swallowed her lovemaking ah's and oh's.

I'm mildly annoyed. Obviously I am not tremendously invested in this woman. Oh, I like her just fine; she is decent, intelligent, responsible. But I would be lying if I said any real sparks ever jumped between us, even at the zenith of our sexual antics.

Even so, I have diligently kept up my end of the innocuous charade that is our relationship. I am continuing to do so, even now, at this table; while from her the emanations of tension increase. She is doing something with her mouth I've never seen her do before: rigidly pursing her lips, then pulling them back into a line so flat and unyielding it might have been drawn with a ruler and mechanical pencil.

Our food comes.

I dig in without enthusiasm.

And Maureen says, "Kyle..."

Suddenly I know — the instinct hot and bright — what she will tell me. The news she has for me. The unfortunate thing she must say.

I don't prompt her. I have done enough, I feel. So I continue to eat, which perhaps makes her somewhat uncomfortable but too bad about that, say what you're going to say, lady.

"Kyle..." A little tremble this time. Stop saying my name, for Chrissake. I chew and gaze blandly across the table, until: "I have met someone."

I chew on. I wash it down with a swallow of the sparkling water I ordered as a beverage. Finally I take pity. "You and I are through, then?" I don't put any side on the question; just cue it up nice and neat for her.

Maureen is my age, our birthdays separated only by a couple of months in fact. She has aged well: good skin, those eyes (which are blue and clear), face firm. A handsome forty year old female.

But right now I have the image of the girl on the bicycle in my head: her youthful and physical femininity. And Maureen Mccotter is a pale example of the sex in comparison.

"Yes...Kyle," she murmurs. "I'm afraid we are."

I have to backtrack to my original question. You and I are through, then? Well, there it is. A bouillabaisse of low-key emotions go through me. A mild stomach drop, as on a not too scary roller coaster. A meager pang of hurt as I wonder if she has slept with this other; but of course she has; she has met him and all which that denotes. I also feel a breezy relief to be severed from her.

I could laugh. But I don't. I say, "I enjoyed our time together. And I wish you well." I mean both these things, in the same modest way of those other feelings just now.

She smiles.

We finish out the meal, and it is very civilized. A final kiss, just this side of chaste; then she goes out of the restaurant ahead of me.

Someone at the dark-wooded bar is complaining loudly, in tones of near hysteria. It's not uncommon. People let loose all the time, over the pettiest things sometimes. Something goes wrong? Pitch a fit. Didn't get exactly what you wanted at store? Throw a tantrum. You're an old. Use your emotions while they are still the coin of the realm.

I step outside. The wind is singing through the old telephone wires. My body had geared itself tonight toward some sexual release. At forty years of age I haven't yet encountered much of a dip in libidinous energy.

But my body will go disappointed tonight. It doesn't worry me. It can handle it.

CHAPTER FIVE

Our Queen

When the fact of the cold phenomenon was first established—amidst that ultra-potent wave of shock and disbelief—one positive effort emerged from the mayhem: find the last human child born. Yes, other far less constructive activities were undertaken as well. Daycare centers were firebombed; pregnant women were hacked apart on the streets of Calcutta, Christchurch, Jersey City. These were indeed atrocities.

But there was also that mania for a time: the seeking of the final child born on earth with the capacity to generate emotion. Find that life fertilized at the absolute last possible nanosecond, that final twinkling before all breeding changed, just this side of the razor's edge. Who was that child? It must exist.

The search was like a worldwide egg hunt and perhaps as demented as the riots and slaughters which had preceded it; but there was a kind of giddiness to it. The prevailing mood was one of noble undertaking. People would abide for a time as the colds slowly replaced them, and great deeds might still remain in some of those people; but the search would surely be the last decent human thing they would take on as kinsmen, joined by the mere ability to traffic in emotion.

And it was accomplished. Through painstaking tireless

relentless searching, through the scouring of records of hospitals, clinics, midwives, from tropical shore to bleak steppe. The little girl was discovered in the Balkans. She was then elevated from the meanness of her native environs. She was fed feasts and draped in finery. A glorious palace was built for her and her family in the Albanian city of Tirana, on the eastern outskirts, beneath the spreading shadow of Mount Dajt. And the little girl was made a queen.

She lives still in the palace, receiving envoys and ambassadors and heads of state to her court. She is called only the Queen. She has grown so suited to her role that many believe she carried some latent blue blood stock in her veins all along. The world loves its Queen. She is the last of the olds.

CHAPTER SIX

Of Clay and Wattles Made

I catch a self-driver back to Potrero Hill. It's dark and overcast, but the moon is up there somewhere, silvering the atmosphere. Potrero Hill is where I live. The compact quietly murmuring vehicle lets me off on my street, at my doorstep, then goes on its ghostly way. I rent the bottom level of a venerable Victorian. I have no upstairs neighbors anymore. They were a couple from Columbia. The house is of such solid composition that there was very little noise leakage from above; and I presumably didn't bother them with any of my recreational sounds. We had a relationship of simple greetings: Hello, Emmanuel. Good day, Mariana. And they said, usually: Hola, Kyle. First names basis but no follow-up. Never ask how the other was doing or what might be going on in their lives. A pretense of friendliness, then. But what was the harm? We lived for several years in peacefulness.

But they moved away. And no one else moved in. And so the second level of the house is, I assume, barren, a series of empty rooms probably configured much like my level. Once, housing was at an absolute premium in San Francisco. You couldn't find a vacancy for love or blood money. Now people leave, and new residents do not manifest. It is common to see furniture abandoned at curbs. I don't know where the people go. Maybe they are opting for bucolic lives, getting back in touch with nature.

But I am not going anywhere. I enter my home, the cabin I have built there, of clay and wattles made. Maureen Mccotter is with another. She is no longer my lover. Our breakup meal feels as if occurred three weeks ago, even while the food is still in my stomach. I recall, suddenly, her canceling a date with me last Friday or Thursday. Perhaps that is the occasion she first lay with her new paramour; I imagine a somewhat fevered tangling, her body and emotions running wild, orgasms lining up one after the next, her spirit consumed by this other.

She told me none of this at the restaurant. I didn't want to ask her for details. What would they matter? All this happened three weeks ago. I'm over it.

I lose the tie, the suit. I floss. Brush my teeth. All the familiarities of my living space soothe me. I like my home. The neighborhood too. There are views of the Bay and the skyline. The district retains a certain funkiness. Gentrification has not quite sterilized every corner of the city. Here one can find a quaint shop, there a spot to hear live music. One can envisage an artist struggling righteously in these environs.

I don't struggle. At one time in my life—the Pre-Cold Era, of course—I fancied I might grow up to be a musician. As a teen I could rake out a few convincing chords on a friend's guitar. The name Kyle Norris had, I thought, a certain rock god potential. In rhapsodic moments I could see the sweep of my fame: the first album coming out of nowhere, singles climbing the charts, the live shows, getting bigger and bigger, until stadia roared with pleasure and hysteria; then maybe a celebrity marriage or two, some flirtation with drug abuse, just for laughs.

But no. I am instead Kyle Norris the financial man. He wears a suit and reports more or less dutifully to an office. He makes a good salary, and he is comfortable; and those distant chords of adolescence do not ring any longer in his head.

What would he have sung about, anyway? Odes to Sissy perhaps. But the fans would get tired of that. I don't listen to much modern music—not because it's new or unfamiliar or any of the timeworn reasons a man of middle years might not like the current crop of musical output. I simply don't like what people sing about these days. It's mostly about the world which is slipping through our fingers. It is about the colds. And I don't want to hear that in my music.

So I listen to music that is full of juvenile longing and heartbreak, and triumph and optimism as well; and it doesn't do much to move the needle on my mood one way or the other. I turn on my sound system now and go to fix myself a drink.

I settle into a chair in my living room. I start to raise a toast to Maureen, wishing her well; but the noble gesture is undermined. The image of the girl on the bicycle intrudes. And that picture stirs me on some level that is not so near the surface.

Her courier bag. Her chopped hair. Her taut young butt. She is a cold, and I would guess her to be nineteen, perhaps even twenty. It would put her in that first wave of the colds, the initial children born lacking all emotional capacities. She is lucky not to have been killed, for that was when the violence was at its worst, once the fact of those children's nature was documented.

I have generally dated and had relationships with my contemporaries; that is, when I was a gawky sixteen years, the first girl who would kiss me and let me feel her up was also sixteen; Sissy was a junior at the university at the same time as me; and on through to Maureen, she who has gone to greener pastures.

What would it be like to lay with a twenty-year-old? I remember the experience from when I was twenty, though I didn't get a whole lot of tail in college. Enough that I felt vaguely on par with the other burgeoning adults around me, not quite enough to extinguish the embarrassed sense that I should be having more sex. I was away at school, after all. Humboldt State University, a many hours' drive north from San Francisco. I was free of parental control. This was my moment. Why didn't I romp and frolic to the limits of my carnal capacity?

Because I wasn't very good at it. I don't mean the mechanics of intercourse; I was okay at that, even showing a little flair now and then. The first time I made a woman come with my mouth I was so proud I wanted to strut back and forth across campus, proclaiming my prowess through a megaphone.

But now I am forty. I have not put on weight. Clothes that fit me ten or fifteen years ago fit me still. Part of that is my mild indifference toward cuisine, part the modest but steady amount of exercise I get in the form of walks through the downtown and around the picturesque streets of Potrero Hill in my free time.

So, I have kept off the obvious decays of the body. My drug use is almost nonexistent, and my drinking is a meager habit. I look all right, even naked, for forty. I'm still a recognizably masculine specimen of the species. For forty.

But a general softening has occurred, subtly, over the years. It is an infrastructural thing, where the beams still hold the edifice outright, but they have worn a little. My feet have grown, and I wouldn't be surprised if I had lost a quarter or half inch of height. I'm pleased with my physical stamina and glad to be without arthritic aches or any chronic distresses whatsoever.

How, then, would it be to lay this slightly careworn body down beside the trim, tight, ductile form of a twenty year old girl? She is a hale being. She must burn endless calories on that bicycle, climbing those murderous San Franciscan inclines. How limber she must be. A snare drum layer of flesh over tense arrangements of muscle, limbs like tubes of hard meat, but possessed all over of a springiness, an athletic vibrancy. She must be a strapping girl.

I want her. Goddamn but I want her....

The courier bag flopping against her abdomen as she flies off the hills. There's a logo on it. She works for a delivery service.

CHAPTER SEVEN

Downtown

My firm doesn't employ any colds, but there are colds in the building. I do my work on the thirty-ninth level of the forbidding edifice, and occasionally a cold will be in the elevator. One is present today. Male. Eighteen years of age, I'd say, if my appraisals can still be relied on; the older I have gotten, the more people under thirty start to merge into a vague age category of Youthful Adult. But there is no mistaking this one's age: he is definitely twenty or under. That is The Line. When olds stopped and colds started.

I am alone with him from floors thirty-nine to thirty-one. I lean against a wall of the elevator, feeling the faint hum of its workings. My gaze goes over him, unhurriedly, without much in the way of lurid fascination. He has acne on his jawline. He wears a light blue dress shirt with two noticeable wrinkles crisscrossing the back, khakis and a tie inexpertly knotted at his throat. I can wrangle a tie knot with the best of the army of suits occupying downtown San Francisco. Windsor, full and half; Four in Hand; Hanover Knot or Balthus Knot; whatever the prevailing idiotic trend. My camouflage is intact, my plumage in full glory.

The cold does not seem aware of me—or of anything. He doesn't fidget, doesn't watch the numbers light up, which is the only thing to do in an elevator, unless, like me, you're eyeing your fellow passenger.

If I were staring at another old, I would be a creep. But looking at this cold makes me...what? Justifiably curious. Morbidly conscious of his presence.

He probably performs menial services in an office. Not a custodian, maybe a drone, a cubicle dweller, set to repetitious tasks. Do people—by people I mean olds—talk to him at his office? Does anyone greet him, even just as a perverse exercise in vanishing civility? Possibly. He might have attained a kind of mascot status among his emotionally capable coworkers.

The chrome doors ding open on level thirty-one. A man in his sixties in a pinstriped gray suit steps on, looking up and seeing the youngster. I watch, with a little private amusement, as the reaction rolls up his doughy body. He stops in the middle of his step, an awkward pause, precarious, and I figure he will back gracelessly out of the car. But no. He comes all the way aboard, scuttles to one side, and the doors shush shut, and we resume descent. His head turns, flaccid face showing dismay; he looks to me, not at the cold, who stands between us in the middle of the elevator. Still leaning against the wall, I shrug lazily at the old man. Don't try to enlist me into your abhorrence, pops. The kid ain't bothering me.

* * *

The downtown set is dressed; the dramatis personae strut and fret. I was a business major at my university, but I was not without a soul. In me was an abiding appreciation for the arts. I read literature, even when it wasn't required by my courses. I enjoyed nearly all of it, understood most of it. It was fascinating when fellow students would read something I had read for fun; for they were frantically searching for symbolism, motifs, all the literary telltales which were to bring forth the scholastic truth of the work. Whereas, I: Yeah, it's a book about a guy hunting a whale; not bad.

And so our players...

Two women, one a head taller than the other, standing on the broad sidewalk arguing heatedly in what sounds like Korean. The thirtyish man I wait next to at a crosswalk; tears stream down his calm set face. A male on a skateboard, slewing through the foot traffic, stripped to the waist and painted densely with tattoos. Someone is playing a guitar, and I pause and look around for the source; a busker, bearded, my age, the musician I might have become; making jangly chords as he sits on a marble ledge; he's not bad; if he had an open guitar case or a hat, I would throw him a few anachronistic dollar bills, but he's just playing to be heard so I hear him for a minute and give him an appreciative nod and go on my way.

(Lunch is sashimi in an automated eatery. My chip is read when I walk in, and I'm levied whatever I order. No human staff visible. The food comes up in a tiny lift set in the middle of the table. Maureen hated these places. Maureen? Maureen? Who's she?)

I turn off Market Street and head up O'Farrell. Ahead, two men in their late twenties, in suits, hail each other, then come together into an ardent embrace; as I pass them, they are kissing passionately, tongues flashing. A young woman—but an old—is wandering with a bombed-out dazed look on her face; some strenuous drug experience underway. Further on a homeless man roots in the trash; Christ, the end of the world is nigh and San Francisco still has homeless; he's got that encrusted look, and why doesn't someone just give him one of the empty residences evidently sprinkled all through the city.

Just before encroaching on Powell Street I come upon a sight that is not uncommon...but one which never fails to chill me:

A woman, in the waning segment of her twenties, not dressed in business apparel but sporting a comfortable ensemble of ochers and light purples; hair in a tidy coiffure, makeup amplifying a sturdy face. She walks along the sidewalk with a bundle to her bosom. Her gait tells me something. How she holds the bundle—with such care—tells me more. I see she is speaking to it, a swaddled shape, and I can imagine her cooing words. They are awful. I also hear the gurgled responses which must—must—emanate from the false package.

I hitch in mid-step, like the old man on the elevator. Only, I don't go further. I don't want to catch up with this woman, who is gaily carrying her "infant" through the streets. I step out into the traffic on O'Farrell. All the self-driving vehicles will stop; I see them doing so. But there might be one rogue car among the flow, some diehard motorist who finds connection with the past and maybe even misplaced hope for the future in the act of driving. He might run me down. But I will not come abreast of the woman with the fake baby. These are monstrous devices, more gruesome the more convincing they are. I will not look upon the synthetic face, the eyes of preprogrammed innocence.

The horror stays on me until I reach Powell. Then I turn the corner and look up the sloping street and see a cable car coming down. Dingding. But I look for something moving swifter than that, something with aerodynamic elegance, a thing of pedals and gears, powered by wiry youthful legs.

Perhaps I'll wait outside the Westin St. Francis. And see if she comes vaulting along.

* * *

I stand by the old, ornate, wrought-iron light poles outside the hotel. Suddenly, out of nowhere—a kind of literal, soul-curdling nowhere—I hear a baby's cry. I feel the chill again. But it lasts only a second or two; I realize I have heard the macabre scream of a sea gull. Jesus, I should know better: a native San Franciscan. It was seeing the woman with the counterfeit infant earlier that has done it.

Because of course there are animatronic babies. Androids don't exist outside science fiction; but these limited yet convincing (if you dearly want to be convinced) doll versions are available. That thing the woman was googoo-gaga'ing at no doubt could make sounds back at her—gurgles, giggles, razzberries. Its synthetic mouth would move and purse and maybe even blow bubbles, so long as you remember to refill the spittle tank. The thing likely had a rechargeable heating unit nested inside it, so that the clever polymer skin would have warmth. Maybe its fingers wiggled; maybe its little chubby legs kicked.

A chill. A bone-deep chill. The only children born for the past twenty years have been cold babies.

I look up Powell, watching for the bike. Automated vehicles, neatly aligned. I lean on the light pole, like I leaned against the elevator wall. Am I tired, lazy? I hold out my palm and glance up into the sky, as if testing for rain. It rains a lot more in the city than it used to, torrentially in fact when it has a mind to. It floods here like it didn't when I was in grade school and high school. Just a little climate crisis, something we're leaving for the colds. Miami should be underwater before we olds are through. No doubt I'll live to see a few more memorable hurricane seasons.

There is a glaze on my brain. Colors and sound and odors register, but they barely have surface value for me today. It's another day of sleepwalking.

I zone out, standing next to the ornate light stanchion. Traffic murmurs past. Suddenly there comes a dart of movement and a just as abrupt jerk of halting. A bicycle and rider stop not ten feet from me. A young body, trim and able, in nondescript clothing. But this isn't the girl, my girl. Still, the male is a cold; I can tell even in this glimpse, the lack of emotional vibrancy glaring somehow. He has braked inches from the back fender of a self-driver which has itself halted for some obstruction.

The boy-cold has a dispatch bag slung like a bandolier over his narrow shoulder. I am looking right at the canvas face, as if it is being deliberately presented to me. There is the logo. Rendered in blue and white. Sherwood Messengers. The first capital letter stylized in the shape of a bow, the remaining letters constituting the shaft.

Sherwood Messengers. The girl with the chopped, dark red hair carries this same bag.

An instant later the traffic flow resumes, and the messenger flits away like a starling.

CHAPTER EIGHT

Homo Sapiens Frigidus

Switzerland was the first nation to categorically forbid breeding. The legislation went on the books: it was now a crime--a punishable crime--to deliberately conceive life. Why, Kyle Norris has occasionally asked himself, is it surprising that the Swiss were the first? In his latent white privilege way he wonders if it wouldn't have been more palatable for a country like Boliva or Syria to initially advance such a hefty law. That decree should belong to a nation-state which could be comfortably thought of as alien, backward, reactionary. But no. It came out of the cantons of the Swiss, fourteen years ago. Six years after the arrival of the colds.

Similar edicts went forth, in other countries, including the United States. Reproduction was a criminal act. It could, after all, only produce more of the cold. Colds were, if not enemies, then a diametrically opposed species. Homo sapiens frigidus. They were human without being human. We must not add to their number.

But the injunctions are nonsense, of course. Millions of babies continue to be born every year. The colds themselves breed, producing their own kind; just as colds also come of fecund couplings between olds. Only colds are born. No more olds. But some olds try to breed anyway. The drive is powerful in some, a primal need overriding all else. Some, surely, even believe that their child will be exempt. They pray frantically or soak themselves in lamb's blood or what have you, desperate to create another normal child, one able to generate proper emotional responses.

There are a few nations which have not enacted the prohibitions. Iceland, for one. People may breed more colds there if they desire. Seems appropriate, Kyle thinks in his consciously offhand manner. He is also of the opinion, though he doesn't share this with anyone, that the anti-breeding legislation is so much sour grapes. Right or wrong, by science or magic, olds are losing their place as the dominant species. A violence has been done to the race, yes; but it is a quiet violence, on the genetic level; and to fight it with these laws strikes him as crass. More than most olds perhaps he has accepted the phenomenon of the colds, and softly acquiesced to the inevitability which their arrival entails. The olds will gradually die off, and only colds will be left. It's fact. It is done. Live with it.

* * *

The colds are a punishment from God. Or god. Even the most atheistic of the olds has likely entertained this possibility. What better way to lay some righteous wrath on a species of one's own making than to force them to be the instruments of their own extinction? And what sin is humankind guilty of? Hell, take your pick. Slavery, slaughters, the host of religious massacres which have spattered the pages of history with crimson and entrails; the injustices, the deceptions, the great groaning greeds which have brutalized whole populations for the opulence of a few. Genocides, the Crusades, the delusional Vietnam War. Or even more basic failures: a lack of true compassion, the callous impulses still abiding in the human breast. Perhaps humanity was given a set measure of time to work out its kinks. It came up short. And so The Line was drawn.

Kyle Norris tried on religion like a borrowed suit some years after the phenomenon was confirmed, about the time Switzerland was framing its anti-reproduction statute. It was a stretch for Kyle. He didn't come from a religious family. Mother never spoke about God; there was some mention of his father having been some brand of Protestant as a boy. (Methodist? Calvinist? He doesn't recall, and now the information is lost for all time.) Without any preconditioning he walked one day into a church. There was no service in progress. It felt like he'd entered a museum. Many other people sat alone or in small silent clutches in the lacquered pews. Faint incense tickled his sinuses.

He sat, then knelt. He put hands self-consciously together to make a steeple. And he thought hard. He tried to open a line of communication. He prayed.

And it was a strangely transportive experience. His head cleared some. A glimmer of optimism came to him. He had spoken into the vast yawning unknown, hoping to contact some sort of divinity. Maybe he'd grazed it, and some of the celestial love had fallen upon his weary self. Certainly the knowledge that the colds were coming weighed daily on his soul, especially in those days, when the horror of it was still relatively new.

Eventually, though, he realized that what he was doing was closer to meditation. He was blundering into simple mental alignment exercises. When he "prayed" his breathing changed. It was like the grab-bag Eastern philosophies he remembered from his college years, in the forested city in Northern California; a lovely hippie burg; rife with herbal medicine, acupuncture, yoga. Even Sissy had dabbled in meditation. Sissy Anspaugh, lithe legs folded into the lotus, hands in the proscribed position, face serene as still water...that face, that face he knew--

Kyle Norris didn't pursue religion after he got wise to himself. Even the rudimentary meditations went away after a while. He got out of the habit. He had his career; let that stand in for a faith, a dogma.

* * *

One can use humor. "Is there no cure for the common cold?" Everyone tells that limp joke. But in point of fact no cure exists for the colds. They can't be altered; what they lack cannot be instated. Neither is there the comfort of a cause...though cold comfort that would be. See that? Haha.

If it had happened gradually, it would have been easier. It would still be a ghastly phenomenon, but the slow motion factor would mitigate some of the sense of outraged disbelief. If a cold had been born here and there, even batches of them, they would have started out as curiosities. Humans would have marveled, but they also would have, very likely, gotten used to the idea. Children born without any emotional structures whatsoever. Then a greater percentage of births with the same results. Even when the numbers began to tip to favor the colds, a cushion of acceptance or at least acknowledgment would already be in place. The event might be viewed slowly, soberly as an evolutionary process. Perhaps, someone learned would likely argue, humans were always meant to develop beyond emotions. The history of the race after all might be said to be a chronicle of beings distancing themselves from their animalistic instincts. Why not all emotion-based responses, then? What did hate and anger and vindictiveness ever bring anybody? Love too. A messy business, that. (Yes, the argument would grow strained, even shrill, but it would continue to be made.) Humans should be without feelings. It is the logical end point of evolution.

But the change didn't come with succoring gradualness. It chopped down all at once, a mighty cosmic cleaver severing the breed into two distinct kinds. One instant there were humans; the next, colds and only colds were issuing from wombs. It wasn't immediately obvious, of course. A cold infant will make baby-like noises. When the phenomenon was first suspected, it emerged as a conspiracy theory about a wave of autistic children. Some sociopathic plague. But the children weren't sociopaths; they did not register on the autism spectrum.

And no matter how much testing was done—some of it no doubt black site slicing and dicing--no answer was found. The labs came back with nothing. Science failed. Or, just as likely, science could not be applied to the cold phenomenon.

* * *

The suicide rate is up. Murders have dropped in the nation. That is, old-on-old homicides. Colds still get killed, and the perpetrators are always olds. No cold has ever taken the life of another cold, anywhere in the world, according to all available data. Why would they kill one another? But they aren't utterly passive. They will defend themselves when they recognize a violent situation and are left no avenue by which to flee.

Colds cannot vote. They aren't entitled to educations. Federal camps house them if they wish to avail themselves of such facilities. Many of the oldest of the colds have entered the work force, taking menial jobs--the sort of labor the youngest of the olds, those twenty to twenty-five or so, might have been expected to do under normal circumstances. But that bracket of olds generally disdains all conventions. They aren't eager to become wage slaves; they rarely attend college; campuses across the country are going to seed. They have only known a world where the colds exist, where they themselves are a final precious commodity: the last true humans born. If they're full of themselves and glutted with smarm, perhaps there is some justification for that.

Colds can't marry, though it's doubtful they would take advantage of this institution. Marriage is an emotional commitment, after all. But the ACLU and Amnesty International and other bodies have, after some delay, come forward to press for minimal rights for the cold. It is illegal to perform coercive anatomical tests on them, for instance. That had to be enacted. People in general have shown infinitely more compassion for their house pets. Many parents rejected their inhuman offspring when it became apparent what they were: hence the fed camps, where the children could simply be warehoused. Some families remained intact, however; human parents raising a cold child, going through the routines of diaper changes, buying successive sizes of clothing as they grow. But what do they talk about? How do they interface in any meaningful way? A cold doesn't play sports. A cold doesn't have a favorite food. A cold doesn't appreciate art.

The cold: how have they responded to these abominations inflicted upon them? As they have to all things--dispassionately, rationally, realistically. They do the most sensible thing in any given circumstance to assure their well-being and survival.

Their best bet, it is believed by some olds, is to lay low. Kyle Norris, an old aged forty years, subscribes to this opinion.

The colds should take what the olds dish out and wait for them to pass from this earth.

Which is what they appear to be so sensibly doing.

CHAPTER NINE

Alice Is Her Name

Days of sleepwalking. Even at my desk. Seeking investment vehicles, interpreting trends, reading the tea leaves of the securities market. I have said none of it matters; but I can still act as though it does. Nevertheless, I often feel at one remove at least from all this financial mishegoss. (Careful with the cultural appropriation, Kyle. You don't have the cred to fling around the Yiddish so flippantly.) The world economy continues to function after a fashion, and the economic health of the U.S. remains relatively sound. The system works because everybody still more or less buys into it. Money has meaning. Abstracts are concrete. Credit is tangible, believable. Debts must be paid; transactions are still honorable.

Fiscal smoke and mirrors, of course, but I'll go along, doing my bit. I'm good at what I do. Not great but reliable, dependable. Occasionally I demonstrate flashes of thrilling imagination. The firm likes me. They keep me around. I don't cause trouble.

I have my little private space, with all the computer equipment I need to do my work. Things, in general, don't work as well as they used to. There is a slow, steady undermining of infrastructure. Communications are sluggish compared to when I was a youth. There are also fewer airlines, fewer trains on the cross-country rails. Things fall apart, you bet they do. And no, the goddamn center definitely does not hold.

A call comes straight in to me at ten past two. I don't often have to deal with direct human voices. I mostly prefer my workdays that way.

"Yes, Kyle Norris here."

"By God, still there. Kyle. Kyle, it's Lester." An unexaggerated baritone.

A little shock prickles me. "Lester. Wow. This is a surprise." Lester Crofft worked at this firm. He allowed himself to be headhunted by another company about two and a half years ago. We had been not quite chummy but very affable with each other while we both worked here. I learned a few strategies from him. He wanted me to go with him when he left; said we'd make an effective duo. He might have been correct, but I had no need--still have none--to make any lateral career move or even any further advancement. This is the rut I have chosen, and I will not be dislodged from it.

He catches me up on his life, just a thumbnail sketch. I'm not sure if anything major has changed for him. I am also not certain why he has called. We didn't try to maintain a friendship after he left.

"I'd like to see you," he says.

I blink. Lester Crofft, better than a decade older than me, stocky, big-handed. Does he have romantic intentions in mind? Is that why he wanted me to go to that other company with him? The notion only bemuses me.

"What's this about, Lester?" I ask neutrally.

"Just lonely for your company, Kyle. Thought about you the other day-- Never mind. No specific motive here, pal. I thought I could have you over to the condo. I'll cook a lavish dinner. We'll uncork some wine. I'll let you pick a night, and if you don't pick one, it's okay."

I ruminate through a moment of silence. I have no reason to be rude to this man, no reason really to reject his invitation. But neither is there any strong incentive to go see him. What could we talk about but work? And I don't especially like talking about what I do.

"Well, I've got your number here, Lester." I feel strangely guilty for being so noncommittal.

"That's fine, then, Kyle. Fine. I'll hope to hear from you."

Little click from my earclip as the voice from the past vanishes.

* * *

* * *

The place is over on Clay Street. It's a bit of a hike. I could hail a driverless, but this is part of the discipline: if it is walking distance, walk it. I am maintaining appearances. I might already have put on unsightly middle-aged weight, but I haven't. I do the small things, do them consistently. Sustain this good habit, avoid that bad one.

It's a grim little depot when I find it. The underground level of a former parking garage, I think. A shuttered dry cleaners and an open Pakistani eatery flank it. Standing at the top of the ramp, I watch bicycles whizz in and out. The couriers are colds, every last one. Colds don't goldbrick, and they don't go on strike. They work these low-tier jobs because no one else wants to. It's sensible that they take such jobs. It is realistic.

The squawks of dispatchers' radios reverberate out of the grotto. I have come only to reconnoiter. This is my first time seeing the nerve center of Sherwood Messengers. She works here, though she isn't any one of the riders I see coming and going. Those unlined faces and pristinely trim youthful bodies. I look for her chopped dark red hair, afraid I might see her. It's too soon. This is recon. Recon only.

But I find myself starting down the concrete slope. There is flaking plaster on the walls, and it all smells of damp stone. Like a flooded tomb? I don't know. Why am I entering this place? Too soon. Too soon!

None of the mounted colds stop me or even acknowledge me. The below-ground level is a low-ceilinged space. The riders come in, leave their bikes lying on the ground, and retire to benches along one wall; empty bags bunched in their laps; and they sit and gaze in that way that isn't quite vacant but which doesn't lock on anything. Or else, in a few cases, they talk in pairs. It's that seemingly disjointed way of conversing, with spurts of speech and lengthy silences. Even unable to hear a word over the dispatch blares, the talk seems eerie.

The outgoing couriers spring up when some name or code is announced over the garage's crackling speaker system. They grab a bicycle--apparently at random, no one assigned a specific bike--and pump their way up the ramp, presumably to go grab a small package or sheaf of deadtree from one place and deliver it to another. This is still a legitimate service. Not everything in the world can be transmitted through the network ether. In a way it is nice to know that there are still corporeal objects to be transported in real space/time.

I am anomalous standing there in my business suit. My clothing costs money. What the colds wear might almost be picked from rag piles. Still no one accosts me. Nobody asks what I'm doing here, where I plainly don't belong.

I look up at the mounted speakers. The voices have some emotion in them; they belong to olds. I hear impatience. I can understand impatience. Am I on somebody's security monitor right now? I look around further.

There is a door marked private. It seems as good a place to start.

When I knock, nothing happens. I wait, try again. Just what the hell am I going to say to whoever--if anyone--answers?

The door, sheeted in dented steel, pulls inward. An old stands there, in a shabby sports shirt. His hair is white and overgrown. His thick forearms are covered in coarse dark hairs.

He looks me over, and I see he is leery. Maybe he thinks I'm an inspector, some person of authority who might suddenly complicate his life.

Without any introduction or preamble, I say in a cop voice from the old movies: "A girl who works here. Dark red hair, chopped uneven and short. High cheekbones, wear sunglasses, comes down Powell a lot."

His somewhat chunky face works as he thinks. I imagine he is considering slamming the door on me or at least asking me who I represent. But--I also imagine--he has been in trouble before. Sherwood Messengers probably gets the job done; but I would bet the place is rife with code violations. I wear an expensive suit. I might be the Man.

His features go still. And I know that he recognizes my description. Now he has what I want. Will he try to leverage this information for something?

"What...what about her?" He doesn't have the energy to try to hustle me. He doesn't really care why I'm here; he'd just be happier if I went away.

"Her name," I say in the same flat tone. As if not telling me would be a grave error. (Seriously, what the hell am I doing? I never planned to take this step. I haven't asserted myself like this in years.)

"Alice." He licks his lips nervously. "Okay? That's all I know. It's all these, uh, kids are required by law to give me. A first name, something to write on a timecard."

I let out a breath, audibly. I nod curtly. Then I turn and walk away, amazed and a little aghast at what I have just perpetrated.

But my prize--oh, my prize! A name. That name: Alice. I know thee by thy title, fair sweet Alice.

CHAPTER TEN

Icer

Norris considered what he had done. What he was doing. For this surely was a process, an unfolding and escalating situation. He had gone to the girl's place of employment and constrained information about her from one of her superiors. Maybe the white-haired man was one of the dispatchers heard on the garage's speakers; maybe a supervisor, maybe the owner of that puppy mill. Norris was still dismayed at his own conduct. So forceful. Almost truculent. It hadn't just been Norris' expensive suit. The man with the white hair had sensed his vibe, his determination. He wanted the girl's name, and he wanted it now!

And so he had it. Alice. He turned the name over and over in his mind when he reached home that night on Potrero Hill. The name had texture. He put it to his lips, to sample its flavor. It seemed to have color for him: the a was green, the i a licorice black, the e a robin's egg blue. As a teenager he'd been much more aware of this mild mental quirk of his which assigned hues to vowels; but now the associations came back to him, vividly, with renewed spirit. Alice was a kaleidoscopic name to him.

He took a shower and made himself a simple filling dinner. He opened up the back door and replenished the water bowl at the bottom of the two wood steps. He also refilled the stainless steel food bowl. At the rattle and tinkle of dry cat food, one of the neighborhood strays came cantering across the unkept back yard. Fluffy black fur, lustrous blue eyes. She allowed Norris to pet her, dutifully rewarded him with a purr, then had at the tiny starfishes of feed in the bowl.

Norris wasn't in the mood for alcohol tonight. He was still high from today's accomplishment and still mentally examining his deed for its full meaning. He brewed a cup of chamomile tea, somewhat surprised to find it in his cupboards. He didn't recall having a taste for the stuff. Had he gotten it because Maureen liked it? Maybe it had been favored by a previous lover. He hadn't had a gruesome slew of paramours over the past few years, but he'd done well enough; and the solo stretches hadn't been especially lonely.

He put on music— old school jazz, just for a change— and sat in his deep comfortable chair in the living room. He hardly ever sat on his couch when he was alone, but it was part of the room's ambience, and he would miss it if it wasn't there.

The chamomile was fragrant. It seemed to have a soothing effect with his first sip.

Alice.

Alice...

What, he wondered, would it be like to lie naked with her? For, surely--come on, Norris!--that was what all this interest and investigation was about. It was raw, primal lust. Don't try to cast it as anything else, squire. He had seen her several times now; she had piqued his attention from the first. He remembered, even now, that initial occasion, how he had jerked to a halt on the sidewalk, how someone had jostled him from behind; then, there, flying down Powell; and how he had gaped, like a struck adolescent, and how his head had swiveled of its own will as she shot past, and he had stared and stared after her. Later he would mask his interest, even as he deliberately sought her on the same street. He didn't wish to be seen as the middle-aged man gawking at the pretty young thing-- particularly when that object was a cold.

But today he had taken it a step further. He had gone into Sherwood Messengers and virtually strong-armed the girl's name. And now he could bask in his achievement. Or be embarrassed by it. (What, after all, was he doing?) It was apparent, though, that this scenario wasn't over. He wouldn't stop at having acquired her name.

Alice. Alice. What did that tell him? What could he do with just her name?

Lie naked with her. How would that be? She was twenty; he was willing to wager that fact. The cold side of twenty. Just shy of The Line. Norris had of course lain with a twenty-year-old before. His time at Humboldt State University hadn't been entirely sexless. He had dated; he'd had a few one-off encounters of a carnal nature. And there had of course been Sissy. She and he had both been twenty. The memory of her lush firm collegiate body was burned permanently into his very being. He could, if he wanted to torture himself, rhapsodize interminably about her physicality, which would, inevitably, bleed into his past fervent feelings for her. He could go on a bad trip of nostalgia regarding Sissy Anspaugh.

No. Not tonight. Other matters were pressing, for once. He wanted Alice. He didn't care that she was a cold. Or perhaps he did. Surely he did! That factor was a major one, an overwhelming one, for Chrissake. Was he a perv now? It was an established kink, of course. Olds who desired colds. You heard about such things online. Icers, they were called. Chill chasers. Was Norris an icer? Should he apply for membership in one of those internet clubs? No. No. Something in him had simply responded to the girl. It had happened at that first sight. That was...romantic. Wasn't it? The age-old thunderbolt. So what if he was twice her age. Literature and movies were strewn with older men hooking up with sweet young angels. (Of course, many of those enterprises were written by aging, sagging males desperate to create fictitious universes were an aged drooping man might draw the attention of an enticing wisp of a female half his years.)

Norris knew where she worked. He knew her name. This was actionable information. His goal was to be with her, in the sexual sense. This wasn't a reaction to Maureen breaking up with him. He had spotted Alice on her bike while he was still with Maureen Mccotter. He'd said nothing to her, of course. Maureen wouldn't have had a sense of humor about that.

He could be with a cold, if he wanted it badly enough. It was another open dirty secret that colds worked as prostitutes. It was illegal, of course; somehow the United States had never rehabilitated its stodgy laws regarding sex work. But in the big cities, like San Francisco, one could prowl about and find a youngster willing to trade sex for money. Colds were pragmatic, above all else. Lawful labor wasn't always available, so they earned their livings as they could.

But he didn't want a body, any body. He wanted her body. The body of Alice. And he had taken the first meaningful step in acquiring it. It gave him a little tickle of pride as he drank down the last of his tea. He had done something today. Broken through the lethargy. The world was slowly sinking all around him, and he was going down with it. But he had at last made an effort, had raged against the machine. And he felt the small icy thrill of that.

CHAPTER ELEVEN

To Market, To Market

I wake up a half hour before my bedside alarm goes off. Sudden, implacable consciousness, like a switch has been thrown. Eyes spring open. I sit up. No dreary dregs of sleep trickling through me. I am refreshed.

Why is this? Where is my normal sleepwalking mode? I brew coffee, a good dark strong concoction. Appetite prickles me. Again, unusual. I rarely awaken hungry; but this morning I make eggs, smear jam on toast, enjoy my merry little repast. I still have the extra time on my hands from my premature awakening. What to do? I know. I'll go into work along a different route. Shake up the status quo. What the hell. I'm not quite giddy--that would be disturbing--but I am possessed of a certain lightness today, it seems. Perhaps I shouldn't poke and prod the feeling too much. It might well dissipate, as so much mental vapor.

Dressed in my natty monkey suit, I leave the house. The sky is lit, the atmosphere still. I head downhill at a brisk pace. I feel the steady draw of air into my lungs; my pulse thumps firmly at my carotid. I feel hale, physically. My body is working as it should--limbs, ligaments, joints--and there is some strange quiet joy in that.

I take in the familiar scenery. I like Potrero Hill, my neighborhood. My childhood was spent in a small aging house on a face of Twin Peaks. (San Francisco is as hilly as it is reputed to be. Swells of land scattered willy-nilly across the peninsula on which it is situated. Twin Peaks are mounds of upthrust terrain at about the city's center point; and yes, as a boy I didn't fail to view the two knolls as giant breasts.) Where I live now has more character than my boyhood environs. I walk east. At a curb stands a dining table, blond wood, rather expensive-looking. A block farther on I pass a credenza tipped on its side. A few people are out and about, mostly morning joggers. I wonder if any of them experience the same pleasantly restless vigor which affects me today.

I walk on. There are busses I might already have caught, but I keep going, down into Dogpatch. Here the landscape is industrial-chic. The bars and eateries are hip. This is the shoreline, running along a deep edge of the Bay. A light rail passes along this stretch, and it's time I actually made my way more deliberately toward the office. I wait on a platform. The train comes sighing along, and I board.

At the next stop there comes a bustle and a flurry. A gaggle of young-olds piles aboard, stumbling, giggling. They are dressed in costumes: harlequins and fairies, dominos and gossamer wings. Their shrieking laughter sounds counterfeit to me, but I understand the effort they are making. These are twenty-two, twenty-three-year-olds, among the youngest of the olds. They have likely been partying all night, ingesting this or that substance to stimulate or contort their senses. It is a busy frolic, a determined escapade. There is a certain ruthlessness to their behavior, something vaguely sociopathic; but again, I understand them at a base level. They have only ever known a world where they are the last true human beings. The colds have ever been with them, and so it falls on these young-olds to expel as much emotion as possible. They cavort. They gambol. They raise a racket on the sleek commuter train. It is conceivable that they might turn violent. I am one of the only other passengers, but I smile and nod at them, and they look through me and go staggering toward the rear of the coach.

And I make my way downtown.

* * *

The physical vim I feel doesn't translate into productivity at the firm. I find this out almost immediately on arrival at the office. The thirty-ninth floor is abuzz. A hint of flop sweat in the air. Something with the markets. Some dangerous upsurge or plunge or migration of capital. We are a tiny island here. There are twenty thousand other little specks flecking the investment seas, and each island is wary of the other, and each can, under certain conditions, cause panic in its neighbors. Such seems to be the case today. I go to my station and try to plug in--mentally, even emotionally--to the whole system; but the game feels especially nonsensical just now. We could, if we wanted, cancel it all right this second: just sweep the entire economic apparatus into history's dustbin. Money is an abstract. Or at best a conspiracy. This chit has worth. Because we say so. You will trade labor for it; your survival will depend on the number of chits you accrue.

What will the cold economy look like, once they have assumed the majority and will have surely begun to arrange and manipulate the world in their own inimitable ways? I have asked myself this question a number of times. It is a heavy ponderable. I have worked in the financial sector most of my adult life; I've got a prideful stake in it, despite all my disparages. Others no doubt wonder what will become of their walks of life when the colds rule the roost. What will become of politics? What will art be? (I suspect there won't be any, of any sort. The colds as yet have created nothing which remotely resembles art. Theater, fiction, music, dance: gone.) And...economics? It too may simply vanish. An economic system is a practicality, a means ultimately of keeping a population in line. But it also has personality, emotional underpinnings. Money makes for greed. The colds aren't greedy. Neither do they indulge in any of the other seven deadly sins. But they are not, of course, moral creatures.

The work finally pulls me in. I must reroute and safeguard those of the firm's fortunes which have been entrusted to me. It's a slog at first. I work through lunch. Then, somewhat surprisingly, I fall into a series of successful moves. Instincts emerge, like talons. I am robust; I am clever. I steer my capital away from the hazardous market zones. It is as though I am soaring, and I see the turf below clearer than others who are scrambling ineffectively on the ground.

Finally I sag back into my chair. I am fairly spent. Things have settled down somewhat around me; I see a relieved face or two. Major crises have been averted, then. We're all still in the clear. Hip hip.

No lunchtime stakeout of Powell Street. I have put in a day's work. I've justified my salary. One of the firm's partners stops by to give me an atta-boy. I accept it with good grace. The office is predominantly male, and rather too white; tinges of Old Boy Club. Most are my age and older. College attendance nosedived when the cold phenomenon was established. Fewer people pursuing degrees, in anything. I think of the young-olds on the train this morning, red-rimmed eyes, speedy and spastic with drug use, wearing those ridiculous costumes, as if you could put on gaiety like a cloak. They don't want a job like this. They don't want to work at all, and many don't. It is the same in all the serious professions. Very few new neurosurgeons, architects, opera stars. No one wishes to put in the time. More, there isn't much motivation to do so. This is last call for the human race. Those adult children in the fairy wings and checkered tights will be the final feeling people, before the colds take it all for themselves.

* * *

The day has been too taxing, and I have given too much of myself to it. Today I will not go to the Sherwood Messengers garage, there to seek Alice or perhaps only to find out more information about her. I let it go, for now. But I am not done. I'm not giving up on her.

On Market Street's broad sidewalks I happen upon a scene: a stout man in his sixties in sweaty clergy garb, crying out in a carnival barker's voice. He has, it seems, proof of God's existence and wants to share it with any and all. He doesn't have much of a crowd. He's rather too piercing, and the somewhat crazed look in his eyes is off-putting. He does have a prop of sorts. It is a cold. A stolid adolescent boy. He stands alongside the preacher, just out of gesticulating range. Hands at his sides, slumping posture. Here's the proof! exults the clergyman. Here! Look! Know! See the work of God. Okay. I'm seeing. I see the cold. The preacher explains that only God could have made such an empty vessel. Only God could have taken away the human soul, all at once, in every corner of the globe. God is the only answer to the now age-old question: where the fuck did the cold come from?

It's not the craziest argument I've heard. It has a logic to it.

But I don't even have to slow down to have gotten the religious old's message. Logical, yes; but also very simple. God is the culprit because he is the only one not in the room where the crime was committed. The preacher must be paying the boy. There's no other explanation for his participation. Yet I am reminded of an antediluvian organ grinder and his monkey.

I pass through the line of the boy's vacant vision, and my skin prickles uncomfortably, just for a moment.

CHAPTER TWELVE

This is How We Feel

What is emotion, anyway? asks Kyle Norris. Asks every old no doubt, even the most frivolous drug-addled young-old. The Queen herself has surely asked herself this in her composed royal chambers. The olds were imbued with emotion, in the timeworn tradition; but the colds were denied it, and that is the new way, the final way.

But...what was left out of them? What, exactly?

An old's brain assigns emotions as a means of survival. The bang of a gunshot is quickly associated with danger, with fear. But the clap of sound, when next heard, might only be thunder, with refreshing rain to follow; but the old flinches at first anyway.

The cold do not make these associations on any level but the perceptual. They learn what a gunshot means, and they know it is best to leave the scene immediately--but they are not afraid.

Survival has value to a cold. It also has value to a banana slug.

Emotions are assembled in the limbic system, and they are pleasant or unpleasant. Physiological displays often ensue: sweaty palms, racing heart, a veritable symphony of facial expressions. The colds do without this rigmarole. They learn that fire burns and that it is hazardous to be nearby an uncaged lion. This is, seemingly, simply information which they absorb.

But. Again. What is emotion? Is it pure neurochemistry? Do

disparate emotions reside in segregated precincts? This Jim Crowing of the brain is unlikely. Amygdala, frontal cortex, insula, hippocampus: they are all in on it, harboring fugitive feelings in mammals, in primates, in humans.

Still, just neurotransmitters? That is the only thing at play, nothing more. Where is the poetry of the process? some olds might ask. Kyle Norris might even ask this, given a reflective enough mood. (But how does he achieve this mood? What gives him the feeling? Maddening! Ludicrous! It is the eye trying to see itself.) Feelings, perhaps, should be richer than their chemical components. They should be considered to have greater value. Shakespeare broke hearts. He has done so for hundreds of years. It isn't simple luck that olds weep for Lear and curse Iago; those responses aren't--shouldn't be-- mere accidental groupings of brain signals.

(Shakespeare. You had to bring up Shakespeare. Shakespeare, my feeling friend, will be gone, just as soon as the last old's mortal coil has been tidily shuffled off. Titania, Prospero, Polonius, Cordelia, Cassio, Laertes, Puck and Dogberry, Macduff and Pistol and the Ghost of Hamlet's Father. They will all go silent, and remain in that hush forever and ever. For the colds will not speak those lines again; they won't read the words; they will let the plays rot, in all their papery forms. Computer storage will become corrupt too, in time. The play's the thing, yeah, you bet. But not if no one watches. And no one will be watching for there shalt be naught to see, sirrah.)

The colds do not feel. The colds do not feel. This has become the central fact of the world. The brain processes of these creatures are mysterious, eerie, distinctive from the olds'. When the phenomenon was confirmed, people looked to science to solve it. Yes, The Line had somehow--terribly, grotesquely, impossibly--been drawn, but surely it could also be erased. The brain was a body part, after all. Neuroscience was a science; and science had cured all sorts of things, ailments and disasters which had previously been seen as insurmountable. So teams were funded. Whole armies of medical and scientific minds were enlisted to the cause. The budgets were extravagant. Finally science was on par with military spending. The human brain--the human soul--required saving, and scientists were now on the spot to do so. No excuses would be accepted. Failure wasn't an option.

Except it was an option. Colds were tested; they were studied; they were likely vivisected as well. Nothing of value was learned, save this: the phenomenon could not be undone. Every being born would continue to be born cold.

So the olds of the world, who are slowly dwindling with the implacable passage of time, wonder about emotion itself. They consider it in its most abstract essences and as tangible chemical interaction, and some expend as much of this emotional energy as possible. Kyle Norris occasionally navel-gazes with the rest of them. He ponders feelings in general. He ponders his own. He has been invested with emotion all his life, and he has a laundry list of memories where his emotions went to extremes. Like everyone--every old--he has known fear, anger, epiphany, envy, the whole maudlin bag. Those emotions have been real within him. He doesn't doubt this. But these days, these past many years in fact, he finds himself far less demonstrative than before. His quiet reaction to his breakup with Maureen Mccotter is a good example. That was an opportunity for some serious emotional display. He could have overturned that restaurant table, gone on a self-righteous tirade. He didn't. It would have been undignified. But it's more than that: he wonders sometimes if he himself were born with a tincture of the colds' lack of emotional ability. Perhaps he was a precursor, a first case, or part of an initial spasm of cold-like humans born to the world. As a boy he was soft-spoken, with watchful liquid eyes. As a teen he was unsentimental, driven by little more than the cardinal drives of lust. And as a fledgling adult? Ah. His college years. Good years. Productive ones. But college had also meant Sissy Anspaugh, and whatever else you want to say about Kyle Norris and about Sissy and about their intersection, know this: he loved her. He loved her. It was deep, and it was true. And it was made all the more substantive by the fact--fact-- that for a time Sissy loved him back.

But, hey, that was twenty years ago. Before the cold had begun to arrive.

And now Kyle is experiencing a renewal of sorts. He is engaged again. He has an interest. Her name is Alice, and she is a bicycle messenger; and she is a cold, and half his age; and she is the age Sissy was during their time of glory together, before it all went to hell.

CHAPTER THIRTEEN

A Girl for Hire

I am flushed with adolescent misgivings. I don't fight the sensations; rather, I shove up the rusty gates and let everything in. The emotions are present. Feel them. Be grateful you have them, you goddamn reptile. They do harken back, though: these are teenager feelings: taut desire, a primal longing, and spread over it all like autumnal sunlight is a bright chilly naked fear. If she rejects me, I will be undone.

Jeopardy. I am invested in something that can have consequences. It has been some while since this last occurred. For quite a time--years--I have risked very little. Certainly I haven't opened myself up to heartbreak. (And I'm not now; get serious; this isn't love. It is not.) I have stuck to the median of things. No excesses, no extremes. It's not that I haven't occasionally enjoyed myself or even been softly thrilled by something. I might read Yeats or happen on an old David Bowie album that I find transportive. The experience stirs my soul. I see beyond myself; I see, maybe, the world in its fundamental holy form. For a time. But the revelation fades. It must fade. That's okay. You remember it, even if you no longer feel its hot immediacy.

I am dawdling. Again there is a teenhoodedness in my vacillations. I'm a bony overexcited fifteen-year-old trying to compose the perfect text message to a girl named Jacomina. She is out of my league. I don't even have a league, as yet. I'm festeringly virginal. I haven't even yet hooked up with the sixteen year old girl who will let me palm her tits. Jacomina is an ideal. Statuesque, poised, very pretty in the face, her skin grades richer than my Caucasian-mutt coloring. I send her a text, a neutral respectful invitation to meet me after school for tea at a coffeehouse frequented by a college crowd. It is a carefully chosen locale. It might hint at my own sophistication, my hidden depths. Skinny Kyle Norris drinks tea amongst college students? Hmm. I need to rethink him. But of course she never responded to my message, never ever, and in the halls of our high school she showed me not a flicker of recognition or acknowledgment. And why should she have? And why did it feel like a stone hand was crushing my heart?

Yet still I dither, though I've arranged my plan in my mind. It is lunchtime once again. I have left the office, gone down in the elevator. At the foot of the black obelisk of the office building I now stand. My heart is beating loud and steady. Finally I tap my earclip, and my phone contacts Sherwood Messengers. I tell the voxsynth what I want. I'd been halfway hoping for a human voice, so that I might explain my request if necessary. But the workaday AI handles my order, debits my credit account, and tells me delivery is underway.

The sky is gray, and the street is gray, and there is windborne grit; but flashes of graphic color pop out all around me. Someone strides by in a long lavender coat with a fleecy scarlet collar. A square of window across the street is royal blue, splashed with a neon yellow message. A drone flits past above the street poles, glassy red body, shiny even in the foggy daytime.

I wait for my delivery. Simultaneously, I feel anticipation, that same teenagey squeamishness, and a healthy dose of adult self-loathing. Because I know this is a creep move.

After a time I see the darting movements, like a predator swimming out among the staid rows of driverless traffic. The bike shoots, it dashes, it is controlled by a mind making split second decisions. She pedals hard, and she cuts across the front of a vehicle, fishtailing the rear tire so that it will clear the front bumper, just barely.

She bounces up onto the sidewalk and avoids pedestrians with the same narrow caution. Her eyes, behind the plastic sunglasses

(sunglasses? even with the overcast?), flick up to the building's address. She's where she is supposed to be. Fingers squeeze, and the bike's brakes halt her sharply enough that the back tire lifts briefly.

My throat is tight.

Nonetheless, I call in a convincing masculine tenor: "Alice."

Her high-cheekboned face registers nothing. There is no snap of reaction. But I sense a silent mental click, and an instant later she looks straight at me. And I look at her. Dead on. I am closer to her than I have ever been before. All the familiar telltales of her person are present: logoed dispatch bag, irregularly barbered hair in a dark red that shades toward glossy black. Her breasts are ripe and promising, as before. She is sleek, sound, with slender legs that must be all muscle.

I realize that her clothing is not quite the standard cold raiment. That is, she wears a tatty long-sleeved sweatshirt which appears more secondhand than nondescript. Her leggings too are unusual for a cold, not carelessly baggy trousers; rather, black jeans of some stretchy fabric. They mold her rump pleasingly.

I am stirred by arousal. Yes, it's all a creep move; because in this scenario I'm the creep. A wannabe icer. An amateur chill chaser.

But I have legally contracted for her presence. I have arranged for her to deliver herself. To me. And so she has done. And now she waits, without a trace of impatience, to see what comes next.

I cross to her and stand by her and her bike. People go around us. I don't look at them. I don't care what facial cues they might be giving me. Shoot daggers. Wonder why I'm accosting a twenty year old girl and draw your own lurid conclusions. Colleagues from my firm might be going past, but I pay no attention. My focus is intense. I have observed this female for a while. I might never get her this close again. My eyes stamp her memory hard into my mind. Her jaw looks tight, almost clenched. But there is a general elasticity about the rest of her, running throughout her body. She must be in peak shape. All those hills, the nonstop cardio of her workday. I breathe her in (creep! creep! creep!), savoring her aroma, which is not at all scrubbed clean, nor even particularly hygienic. She smells unwashed. A tablespoon of perspiration could probably be wrung out of that sweatshirt. But her complexion is clear, face unblemished. I imagine she has armpit hair, unshaven legs. Her nethers must be fragrant, an untended womanly odor, a bush sticky with--

Christ, Kyle, are you trying to disgust yourself?

"Alice," I say again, and again there is no automatic flicker of response to her name. Colds aren't even like dogs in their reflex reactions. I say, "I wish to hire you. Not as a messenger. As a companion. For me. For one month. I will pay whatever rent you pay. I'll provide meals. You will engage in--in--" Goddamnit, Norris, you've come this far! "--in sexual congress with me at least, say, half a dozen times. I might like to have you stay over at my home from time to time. Or perhaps more often. We will go places, engage in recreational activities. I won't abuse you. I won't harm you. If this arrangement turns out not to be agreeable to me, we will break off relations, though I'll continue to compensate you monetarily. And no matter how it goes between us, we will terminate the agreement at the end of that month's time."

She is still astride the bike, one foot up on the pedal, the other en pointe, acting as a kickstand. She has leaned back from the handlebars while I have spoken. Still no expression on her face, of course. Her bicycle isn't like the other bikes I saw going in and out of the Sherwood subterranean lair. Hers is better quality: lightweight frame, more elegant in design. Sitting on it, she seems to belong to it.

I have finished my pitch but haven't prompted her to reply. Is she considering my offer? Shouldn't a cold make up its mind instantly, once the facts have been presented? Will you come have tea with me, Jacomina?

"Do you accept my proposal, Alice?" I ask. Risk. Jeopardy. Potential...hurt? Yes, hurt. I'm all in here.

She says, "This can't interfere with my job." Very little inflection in her voice; almost--but not quite--a monotone. Hers is a contralto, hint of rasp at the back of her throat maybe. A lovely voice, I think.

"It won't. I promise." I feel a soaring in me. She hasn't outright rejected me!

She reaches into her jeans pocket. "Chip my rent."

I fumble out my own credit chip and in a daze tap in the amount indicated and transfer it over. I can barely believe this is happening. An ecstasy of unsettling magnitude is building in me. My system isn't used to such heavings.

She takes a last look at her chip, then says, "I accept the terms."

She leans onto her handle grips, ready to sail smoothly across the sidewalk and back out onto the street. I admire the slope of her, from shoulder blades--prominent with the sweatshirt now pulled tight across them--to her buttocks. I am overwhelmed even glimpsing that backside, knowing--knowing--I will see it uncovered, laid bare, in all its succulent glory.

Nice job, creep. You just literally bought yourself a piece of ass.

Her head comes up, and I feel her eyes, behind the cheap smoked lenses, lock on mine. Intensely. As if this is the final part of a blood oath. She says, "I'm off work at six thirty."

"I'll meet you at the garage."

She zips away.

I am limp, of a sudden. Drained. I actually stagger back half a step, unsure if any passersby overheard enough to recognize the exchange for what it was. Today I told an artificial voice that I wanted Alice to come visit me; I described her. Alice came; just another delivery to her, perhaps. I propositioned her in stark cold-blooded terms. Companionship for money. Sex for money. The transaction is illegal. We can have no contract between us. She is relying on me, then. And I have already come through to some extent: I have paid a month's rent on whatever hovel she calls home. I can afford the expenditure. I sit atop a comfortable financial cushion.

Holy shit...I did it.

Am I crazy? Am I a bona fide icer now? Maybe I'm just a Nabokovian obsessive, an old school pervert, a pederast (except that she's of legal age). A forty year old man lusting after a woman who is aged twenty. Is that so amoral? So outrageous. So very far outside the sphere of normal longings. I don't think so.

Except that she's a cold. If I had any iota of doubt before, it has been obliterated. She is on the young side of The Line. She might have been among the first hundred thousand colds ever born. The first ten thousand. Whatever: she does not perceive the world as I do, through emotional filters. She has no heart, in the poet's sense. She is without a soul.

And I desire her as I have not desired another being in a long, long time.

My spirit is all vertigo and rapture, derangement and excitement. I turn and totter back into the office building. It is some hours until 6:30.

CHAPTER FOURTEEN

This is Our Date

I am, suddenly, living in real time. It's disconcerting. Minutes drop away, one after the other; time is finely tooled, a precise engine now. I cannot drift off into fog. No sleepwalking today. Alice has changed it. Or I, through the medium of Alice, have changed how I engage with time and life and the wider reality around me.

But I perform through the rest of my workday. I'm even more conscious and conscientious of my labor. The work isn't more or less interesting than before, but it seems to have an authenticity, if not an importance, which it has lacked.

Earlier, I purchased myself a relationship, and at half past six o'clock this brisk summer evening it will commence. How should we start? I could take her straight home with me. Cut through the preliminaries (what preliminaries; she's a cold!) and hop right in the sack. I have no doubts that she will be pleasing in shape and tone. In fact, she will be stunning. She'll dry my mouth, flutter my stomach and stiffen my joint. I would be excused for weeping at the sight of her nude form.

But do I want to take that golden prize all at once? Perhaps not. She will not respond. She will not feel my same anticipation, but I can draw the process out myself, delay, delay, let the juices come to a simmer, let the yearning approach a critical peak. I could pretend that we are dallying, flirting, tentatively testing the carnal waters. Maybe we kiss. I feel a rush. My loins are aglow. I kiss her again, more deeply. The rush is more a torrent now. But still we don't go forward all the way. We savor, knowing that our first screw can never be unscrewed; thereby we are desperate to get it just--

We. We. No, Norris. This is purely an I scenario. You're in this alone. She is a prop in your soliloquy. This isn't a masturbatory event. It is, instead...well, I'm not sure a modern vocabulary exists for what this will be. Or if it does, you don't hear it in polite circles. Maybe only dedicated icers could describe the relationship I have entered into.

She has, in effect, trusted me. Even though trust has an emotional tinge to it. Her analytical faculties evaluated me, and she has decided to rely on me. But should I rely on her? What if I go to the garage and she disavows any knowledge of me and our squalid arrangement? I would have no recourse. Even proof of our initial transaction--my paying a month of her rent--wouldn't help me. It would only build a case that I had illegally solicited her. I see, creep. You're chasin' the chill. No, there's no law that says she has to give you your money back. People like you make me sick.

Colds don't subscribe to any morality. They aren't "good." But do they lie? Do they deceive? I could see one lying to save his or her skin--say, disclaiming their true nature to an angry mob. Yet the complexity of chicanery necessary to get Alice to lie to my face seems beyond a cold. It seems beyond her.

As if I know her. As if she has attributes which other colds do not. Careful, old man. That's a deep rabbit hole. Go down it at your peril.

I get off work earlier than she does. I'll have a little time to kill. Should I buy her flowers, a small gift? Here, Alice: a token of my affection. Do you understand that word? Affection. It is what I feel for you. Or perhaps what I'm telling myself I feel at this early stage of things between us. I meant what I said before, that I will break this off if I don't like it. That could happen. This transactional alliance of ours might be a sour experience once it is truly underway. I might want to bail out quickly. But I'll continue to furnish you with meals, as though we were having them together. Shelter and food: these I supply you with for the prescribed month.

I am excited and sick. Sick and excited. What in the name of fuck am I getting into?

* * *

Creep. Creep. Creep. I keeping saying it, in my head, desensitizing myself to the term. I don't really have anything to be ashamed of in all this. I'm not doing this to a person, after all. A person would have told me to go to hell if I'd offered to pay her rent and buy her meals in trade for companionship which included access to her body. Rot in hell, creep. Fuck you, creep. But Alice is a cold. She has no hangups about the swap because she has no hangups, period.

When I'm out of the office, I stop at a walk-in bar and order a drink. A martini. I don't know that I've ever had a martini in my life. The drink is gestural. A businessman's drink, symbol of success, privilege. I closed a deal today, Joe. Big account. The rewards will be...

Well, we'll see what they are. We shall see.

I sip my beverage. I try to imagine the next two hours of my life. Then I head out for Clay Street. The depot. The home of Sherwood Messengers.

* * *

Distorted dispatch voices squawk in the garage like feuding birds. It's so low-tech. Why aren't all the kids on a wireless network? Maybe this way is cheaper. It seems a shabby business, after all, this Sherwood Messengers. I wonder why Alice works here. But it's a stupid thing to wonder. She is a cold, and this is a cold sort of job, the kind of gig someone might pick up in his first summer after high school. You'd have a hard time finding a young-old who would take this job. Twenty-two-year-olds these days just want to drug and screw. I can't blame them.

I walk down to the lower level and am ignored, as I was previously--or almost ignored. One of the colds looks toward me, the motion uncharacteristically sudden. I don't flinch, but a mild chill crackles over my skin. He is sitting on a bench, and I am certain, for an instant, that he recognizes me from last time and that my reappearance is cause for concern. It is not an emotional response; it is simple caution; and colds know caution. They are leery and watchful, because they have been given reason to be. They are a separate people from us, and they have their own sad, beleaguered history. Welcome to the world, children. Persecution is the price of admission.

There are fewer messengers about and more bikes lying on the ground. They must just leave them there. The aesthetics of that bothers me. It seems willfully careless. But to these colds it is surely just practical. The bicycles are all in the same mediocre repair.

I sense the gliding motion an instant before I turn. She comes down the ramp, and there is that extra grace she somehow exudes. She brakes smoothly, dismounts, looks at me. I say nothing; I might even be afraid to speak. We have a verbal contract between us. I don't want to disrupt it.

She crosses to a timeclock I haven't noticed before. Others are clocking out as well. It is 6:30 precisely. She puts her thumb to the smudgy scanner. She comes back to her bike, and with deft movements I can't quite follow she folds the thing up. It's magic; it's origami. The pedals tuck flat. The frame doubles over on itself, parts interlocking, until there seems nothing more than two spoked tires pressed together. There is a strap suddenly attached to it, and she slings this over her bony shoulder. She gazes wordlessly at me. She is still wearing the sunglasses.

"Are you hungry?" I ask her.

Again there is that silent mental click, like a grace note. She doesn't respond immediately; then: "I could eat."

I blink. It's a colloquial rejoinder. You hungry? Eh, I could eat. But she has said it without lilt, without any underlying wryness or other emotion. She has simply considered my question and answered truthfully. At least, that is how it seems to me.

"Then let's go get a meal," I say. I start toward the ramp, and she follows half a step behind. I consciously slow so she can catch up. Side by side, up the slope, her with her folded bicycle slung on her back.

I picked a place earlier today, while wondering if we shouldn't just go right to my bed. It is a Thai restaurant, an automated place, with the food coming up through the tables. Some part of me wanted to take her to the posh eatery where Maureen told me our time was through. Get that maître d' or whatever he is to say Very good, sir when I walk in for a table with my cold. Draw some horrified stares. Give a few patrons indigestion.

The Thai place is only one block away. We walk together and say nothing. I imagine she is content not to speak. I imagine...no. She isn't content. Contentment is an emotional state. She is simply not motivated to say anything. I haven't prompted any response from her. A dozen questions pop into my head, but I don't put any of them to her. We reach the place and enter. It is warm in here. About a third of the tables are occupied; not an upscale crowd; I'm the only one in a suit. I gesture to a table, and Alice sits down, tucking her bike under her chair.

The menu in on the tabletop, beneath a laminate. I say, "Why don't you take off your sunglasses?"

"I wear them in the daylight." The almost flat tone. Yet something seems to lie under the structure of her words, a phrasing that isn't completely dulled. It is July; sunset comes around 8:30.

"I'd like it if you took them off." Not a command. Will she comprehend the implied suggestion? I wait. I watch.

The pause of mental processing. Her hand comes up, and she tugs them off. Her eyes are green, the dark lashes long.

"You have lovely eyes," I say. I hear mutters around us. Perhaps just other eaters conversing, but I sense that we are causing a minor disturbance.

She doesn't respond to my comment. What do I expect her to say: Thank you or You have nice eyes too.

Something absolutely astonishing occurs to me just now, and I say, "My name is Kyle Norris, by the way." Realizing in retrospect that I didn't offer my name when I made my proposition to her. But she accepted anyway. I could be anybody to her, any old who had just paid her rent.

She gives me the shallowest of nods. Acknowledgment. A human gesture? Maybe. Maybe she has gotten into certain habits in the course of her job. She makes her deliveries; she interfaces with olds. Perhaps mimicry is part of the survival instinct.

She points, indicating what she wants to eat. I can only wonder how she chooses. I make my own choices and place the order. My chip has already been linked to. The debit goes through, and minutes later the food comes up to us. It is decent fare, the sort of passable food I am most comfortable with. She eats...not quite mechanically. Certainly there's no sign of epicurean delight on her pretty face, but she flicks her pink tongue tip into the corner of her mouth to pick away a tiny shred of pork. (The sight of her tongue excites me.) There seems some kind of base fulfillment in this for her, though I can't quite pinpoint what makes me think so. Eating when one is hungry is probably just a positive experience. Knowing that she isn't paying for this meal is another small boon.

"How long have you worked at Sherwood Messengers?" My own tone is conversational. I try to sound interested because I am interested, both in whatever she might tell me and how she'll say it. Needless to say, I have never before sat down to dinner with a cold. Doubtless very few olds have.

"Started seven months ago." She swallows before she speaks. Doesn't talk with her mouth full. Good manners? And her reply: she didn't need to say Started or ago; could have just said Seven months. She isn't using the bare minimum words, not speaking like a robot in some old science fiction movie.

I almost ask if she likes working there. A stupid question, an old's question. I say, "Your bicycle is different from the others there. Does it belong to you personally?" No one else left the garage on one at 6:30.

"Yeah." Another colloquialism. Not a formal Yes but a laid-back Yeah.

"Why did you buy it?"

"'Cause it's better." 'Cause! An elision. Almost slang.

"Better how?"

"Goes faster. Climbs hills easier."

"And that makes your job easier?"

"Yep."

Holy Mother. Yep. The flippant affirmative. How did she just decide to use the term? Yeah one moment and yep the next. I am amazed. I'm also, on some level, delighted. She is giving more than I expected from her, from any one of her kind.

I realize as well that this isn't really a dialogue. I am putting queries to her and analyzing the results. Even so, there is a ghost of coziness to this moment. We are two living beings supping together. There is something primal and good about that. Of course, the other dynamic--me being forty and her being twenty--makes the scene a bit less savory. But that algorithm too has a tradition behind it. Lots of middle-aged men before me have tried to charm girls half their age. The custom shades toward the pathetic, but in bygone days at least both parties would have been wholly human.

I ask Alice why she wants her job to be easier. She says so she can do it better than others and thereby have a greater chance of hanging onto her employment. I recall that her only caveat about our arrangement was that it not interfere with her job. She's serious about being a bike messenger, then. Does she, in some colorless way, take pride in the work? I can't say. But there seems to be some unforeseen depth to her. She isn't, I am starting to believe, just a sum of instincts and survival programming. Or perhaps she is only those things, but they are more sophisticated operations than I would have anticipated. Her interactions with the world have a life onto themselves, so to speak. Maybe. Maybe.

We finish up eating at the same time, right to the forkful. In another situation--say, on a real date--this would be charming. But we exchange no coy smiles, as we would if the simultaneity indicated an emergent connection between us. It just means we eat at the same speed.

So. We have been out to dinner. A recognized courtship ritual. Now do I see her to her door, wherever that might be? Hope for a kiss at the threshold. No. Because there are no rites to this, no stations to observe. I can tell her that she is coming home with me tonight, to be bedded; and were I to say so, I believe she would indeed come along.

But I merely rise from the table, and she gets her bicycle and follows me out. The sidewalks are nearly empty. Thin traffic on the streets. The Financial District is in ghost town mode.

"I'd like to see you tomorrow," I say.

Not a question but she responds anyway: "I'm off at six-thirty." She still has that mild rasp in her voice. I find it sexy, but it doesn't change my mind about sending her away alone tonight.

"I will meet you at the garage. Is Sherwood open weekends?" Tomorrow is Friday.

"Nope."

Nope! Endearing, somehow. I say, "We'll do something on Saturday. In the day. Let's talk about it when I see you tomorrow evening. Good night, Alice."

I turn to hail a driverless. She is already unslinging the bike off her shoulder and snapping the magical frame back into its working configuration. When my back is to her, I hear her say, "Good night, Kyle."

CHAPTER FIFTEEN

Assessments

Norris felt. Alice did not. That was the rock-bottom truth, the inescapable stony layer of the thing. He could spade around in the surface dirt, flicking about this clod and that, but whenever he might try to go down to the heart, he would encounter this same rocky stratum. Tonight had been...well, amusing. Captivating, even. She had held his attention throughout the meal, and their conversation had not been as stilted as he would have imagined. On any first date he would surely have asked about work. Alice was a bike messenger. She was intent on holding her position. She had even gone so far as to invest her earnings in a superior cycle. Such information wasn't exactly spellbinding, but he'd found it interesting. It meant she thought ahead. Maybe her deliveries were made half again as fast as the other couriers. She was, in a sense, dedicated to her career, even if there was no emotional impetus behind that dedication, just cold logic. Ha. Cold logic. What other kind would she have? They had plans for tomorrow. Norris felt a stronger anticipation than he had ever felt for a forthcoming date with Maureen, even on those occasions when he had been certain they would have sex. He could be laying Alice right now, here in the bedroom of his Potrero Hill home. His mind started to cobble together suitable images. A few eager mental snapshots of Alice, along with some free range pornographic visions--

But no. He didn't wish to fantasize about her. He wanted it to be new when it happened. And it would happen. He had invested in her; her rent was paid; she owed him. But perhaps his hesitation about fantasization ran deeper. It might, just might, be that he didn't want to cheapen her with his thoughts. He didn't leer at women on the street or make suggestive comments to females who came through the office. He also didn't think it nice to violate a woman in one's mind. Why should it be different if the female was a cold? An interesting question, one that had an answer: the cold wouldn't be offended. Even so, that left him alone with the moral burden. He could choose to undress her in his thoughts, to run his hands over her bare taut youthful body, or he could refrain from doing so. He had chosen restraint. Did this mean he respected Alice, even if just on an abstract level? Perhaps. Perhaps. Maybe he didn't want to feel like a fool, like a sad aging billy goat. The whole situation was rife with unexpected dilemmas and discoveries. What a fraught thing was underway. He had embarked on an impossible relationship. Norris felt, and Alice didn't. That was unresolvable. It wasn't a chess match where one was black, the other white. The sides weren't even. There wasn't even a common field of play. They were meeting someplace blunt and unnatural. And yet...and yet. She had charmed him during dinner. Without meaning to, of course. Without intent, no doubt. He found her exotic, in a way. She didn't come from some fanciful culture; she didn't speak in liquid tones of a foreign tongue. Cold culture was perhaps no culture at all. But she was, nonetheless, different. Different from himself, to be sure; but also perhaps--perhaps--different from other colds. She was the only one with a new bike at the garage. She dressed slightly differently than the others. (Why? Because the clothes were more comfortable on her body and allowed her to ride more efficiently? Or did she, somehow, just like them better, even though "like" would never enter into it.) This was as close as he had ever gotten to a cold. When the beings had first started to appear, he had been leery of them, as had everyone else. Back then they'd been children--eerie, emotionless children. You rarely saw any out in public. The time of violence was underway and would only get worse. Norris' apprehension toward colds had always seemed a natural response. It was certainly shared among the old. Granted, some political groups were belatedly advocating for cold rights, but no one was saying the creatures should be wholeheartedly embraced. What would be the point in that? Love a cold: why? It was a dead equation, a wasted effort. Norris' mother, when he was twelve years old and well into his phase of pubescent stoicism, had grown frustrated with his willful impassivity one day and had snapped at him, "It's hard, Kyle, loving someone who won't love you back." He hadn't let it show, but the words did sting, especially since his mother rarely even raised her voice to him. Afterward for a time he had attempted to be more demonstrative, but his own signs of affection felt clumsy and false. And what about now? Did he feel some ghost of affection toward Alice? Did a few of his synapses snap with a dormant warmth with regard to the girl? Maybe it was purely lust, along with a dash of lurid curiosity. He wanted to fuck her, yes. But he had also wanted to take her to dinner, and he had done so. It's hard, Kyle, loving someone who won't love you back. Yes. Yes, of course it was. But he didn't love Alice. It would be madness to love her.

CHAPTER SIXTEEN

Immortal with a Kiss

I meet her at 6:30. It's almost routine now. Leave the office, kill a little time, then wander over to Clay Street and pick up my gal. The normality is its own kind of strangeness. But these are strange times, are they not? The human race is going extinct, so we should be allowed our peculiarities. Grown people walk around carrying mechanical babies that gurgle and laugh, and yes, it's creepy as hell, but nobody stops them from doing it. Plainly they are trying to cope. So. I am coping. In my own way.

She wears the same clothes as yesterday. Her dark red, ill-barbered hair is disarrayed, with a hank of it sweat-plastered to her forehead. After she folds up her bike and punches out on the timeclock, I reach out and with a fingertip brush the errant hair back. It is the very first physical contact between us. She doesn't flinch. Gooseflesh rises along my forearm, beneath my suit coat.

I say, "I picked another restaurant. I hope you'll like it."

"It'll be fine."

I hope you'll like it. What a thing to say to a cold. I want to chuckle at myself. My self-loathing feels well in check tonight. I am committed to this.

I walk with her to a staffed diner. It's a few cuts above greasy spoon, a place I've frequented for lunch previously. But they have a dinner menu. We take a small table toward the back, and a mid-twenties waiter materializes. I'm a little surprised he has such a job or any job at all, considering his age. He is more likely to be out cavorting with his young-old contemporaries, getting loaded and partying like it's the end of the world. But maybe he wants to work, to contribute, to take part in normal activities. His gaze flicks across Alice's face. He knows what she is, but he probably encounters all types here. He maintains an imperturbable waiterly front and neatly takes our order.

"How was work today?" I ask Alice. Again: pretty much an asinine question.

There is that audible processing pause, then she says, "It was productive."

"How many deliveries do you typically make in a day?"

Thinks about it. "Eighteen average, I guess."

She guesses! I feel that same odd rush of excitement as when she used slang yesterday. Do colds really guess? Does guessing require a certain low-level emotionalism?

"Eighteen. Wow. Is that more than the other messengers?"

"Yeah."

Yeah again. A smile tugs the corners of my mouth. "It's because your bike is faster, right?"

"Right."

It is almost a conversation. Information exchange of friendly trivialities. Were I to see a transcript of our tête-à-tête, it would probably read as ordinary, conventional. But this is an old talking to a cold, and there is no getting around that. Everything that passes between us is colored in strange charged hues.

Our food comes. As yesterday, there are others in the restaurant, and I am aware that they are aware of us, of our unorthodox pairing. Look at that sad fuck on a "date" with a frosty. You hear about icers, but honestly I've never seen one before....

But no one stares belligerently. Nobody gets up and accosts us. I'm not sure what I would do if that happened, if the situation turned hostile, even violent. Certainly I'd make an instinctive effort to defend myself. Really, though, I can't remember the last physical confrontation I was in. And would I defend Alice as well? Say if some fellow old just couldn't stand the sight of us one instant longer and smashed a catsup bottle and came at us--at her--with the jagged neck. For a few overbright seconds I see it vividly. I even assign the action to a man sitting alone at the counter; I have caught him glancing at us. He moves in on the attack, his dripping improvised weapon in hand. I lunge out of my seat, sweep Alice aside with one arm and sail my fist into the man's throat. My punch goes deep, and the effect is instantaneous. He is out of the fight, gagging, falling to the floor. I stand over him, making sure he is through. Staying between him and Alice. Protecting my woman.

The scenario pumps adrenaline into my blood. Colds, I know, live under this sort of threat every day. Now I have made myself vulnerable. I have bought into that dangerous exposure. It's like being a part of a "mixed" couple in a racist region and era. On my own I am ordinary. But by pairing with an undesirable I take on the taint. I am subject to the same prejudices.

But before I can get too high up on my horse, I silently remind myself that I have hardly been a champion for cold rights or even decent treatment for the breed. Yes, I sincerely felt revulsion at the violence done to these people across the globe. That seemed a descent into barbarity, perhaps into final human madness. Once aroused, it seemed we might just turn to slaughtering one another, crazed with blood lust, carrying on until the world was dead. But my abhorrence didn't carry over to standing up for the colds in any way. I enlisted in no causes, signed no petitions. I didn't even really give thought to what treatment they might deserve, simply as living things. Those federal camps didn't bother me. They even seemed like sensible facilities, a way to safeguard cold children abandoned by their horrified parents. Sure, there were occasional reports of abuse at these places, but those incidents had to be the exceptions. Besides, with the world in such a state of existential chaos there were bound to be missteps and hardships.

Across the table Alice eats more robustly than last evening. She has taken her sunglasses off without my asking her to. I wonder if she is hungrier tonight, if she missed a meal earlier. I watch her jaws work, note the even line of her white teeth. Does she brush and floss? Could be. Colds have survival instincts; that is well established. Alice thinks ahead. She may be inclined to preserve her health as best as possible, which could include a regimen of dental hygiene.

We eat. We finish. I give the waiter a healthy tip. Alice takes her folded bicycle from under her chair, and we go out. The man at the counter, who I fought in my imagination, starts to look our way; but he halts the motion, gives a small shrug, and concentrates on his plate.

We're out on the sidewalk. Few pedestrians about. The temperature has dropped, and I can see my breath in a plume. It is Friday night, and most everyone has deserted the Financial District. Tomorrow is Saturday. I will see Alice tomorrow, in the day. I probably should have discussed arrangements in the diner, but I find I am nervous.

"I'll come pick you up tomorrow. At one in the afternoon. Where do you live?" Her green eyes are vague until they focus suddenly on a point of my face. She recites the address. The northern waterfront. Cold housing. Cheap metaceramic structures. A lot of decaying tourist terrain was taken out to make room for these buildings. Tourists don't come to San Francisco anymore.

She stands there, holding her bike by its strap. She is waiting. Am I done? Do I want anything else?

I do want. I bring my hand up. I slide my fingertips lightly along her jawline. Her skin is amazingly smooth. Applying soft pressure, I tilt her head two degrees. As I begin to lean in, I say in a whisper, "I'm going to kiss you."

It will be like kissing a mannequin. She will not respond. A kiss can mean nothing to her. My lips come up against hers. My nervousness is again adolescent in its intensity. I am close to trembling. Without warning her mouth comes alive. She presses with her lips. Her head moves against my fingers. A rushing warmth seems to emanate from her: raw, urgent, sexual. Her lips open, and I feel the darting of her tongue. I am stunned. Also fiercely inflamed. Desire is a bonfire's heat licking up my body. My tongue meets her, and we tangle. I am aware of her body's sweaty aroma. She is almost pungent, but those odors and pheromones are in me now, sucked in by my nostrils, as our kiss continues, a wonderful, probing, energetic kiss. Our mouths stay sealed together, ever moving. She is reacting. She is reacting!

We break for breath. My lungs are at a gallop. My heart pounds. I haven't taken her in my arms, haven't pressed my body against her. She would feel the swelling at my groin, and I might find her stiffened nipples needling me through her sweatshirt. Every iota of me is alive and animated. This is arousal beyond the mere carnal. This is excitement of some further profound magnitude.

Or maybe it's just that I haven't kissed a twenty-year-old since Sissy Anspaugh.

I step back from her. Her green eyes seem to shine now. Her breasts rise and fall with a telltale rapidity. I think that passersby gasped while we kissed, but the street is a blur to me. I say nothing more to her. Blindly I stumble to the curb to grab a self-driver. The night around me sings a high sweet song of memory and awakening.

CHAPTER SEVENTEEN

Warehouse for Living Things

I try to sleep late. I bob in and out of sleep, turning over in my
big bed, pulling up the covers, willing myself back into
unconsciousness again and again. Rags of dream find me. A motif
recurs across several episodes of slumber: a romantic rendezvous is
imminent, and I must get ready; but I keep losing items--my credit
chip, the shoes I mean to wear--and the stress roils me. But there is a
sweetness too to that tension. It's partly that adolescent feeling again.
The high bright anticipation, the hormonal overdrive mixed with fear.
But now I have the memory of Alice's mouth moving against mine, the
quick dashes of her tongue. I am warmed by what has already passed
between us.

But...why did she kiss me so yesterday? I wouldn't have
thought colds would kiss at all. What is to be gained by a kiss? Colds
have sex drives. Their needs constrain them now and then to engage
in intercourse. They of course produce cold babies. (Those babies are
as illegal as any others in this and many other countries, but I am
thinking of biology now, not legality.) Still, I wonder if there is cold
foreplay. I consider how these matings might occur: what ritual, if
any, precedes the event? Do the two colds make their decision with
obdurate pragmatism? A cold male and a cold female sit down at a
table in a bleak little room and present their case to each other. We

must continue to breed. Agreed, it is the imperative of our species-- any species. Our physical traits are good, our health sound. Our offspring would be acceptable members of our race. Let me pour you a glass of champagne, darling, and you dim the lights.

This last bit stimulates my mind enough that I am drawn into wakefulness for the final time. I've slept past 9:30. I get up and shower. I scrub and scour myself. I shampoo my hair thoroughly. At forty my locks are not as rich and full as once they were, but I have no obvious signs of outright hair loss.

After, I wipe steam from the full-length mirror fixed to the back of the bathroom door and give my image a long, critical view. Not a bad body. Not a sagging, broken down middle-aged one, anyway. I'm hardly the masculine ideal, but I was never one who wanted rock-hard abs and vein-corded biceps. I am recognizably male, reasonably free of body fat, maintaining a decent muscular tone, and I've got a member of respectable size. (Sissy, when we were in our happiest and most frolicsome period, used to like telling me I had a big dick while we were screwing. I never got tired of hearing it.) Finally I go out to the bedroom to dress. No suit today. No hint of stolid businessman vogue. In my grade school we wore uniforms: the boys in white shirts, blue corduroy pants, pastel blue sweaters. Every day after school when I got home I would rip these glad rags from myself, full of pent-up rebelliousness, eager to reclothe my scrawny little form in jeans, in T-shirts, the attire of the liberated.

I put on a pair of black jeans, narrow in the leg. I step into a pair of sneakers. I'm reaching for a casual sweatshirt when I realize that I am dressing like Alice. Chuckling, I grab a red and yellow striped pullover instead. I'll take a jacket along as well, the eternal San Francisco precaution; the climate can turn swiftly, and you might get chilled to the marrow if you haven't brought along an extra layer.

Today I shall drive. I thumb up a rental agency and arrange for a vehicle to self-drive to my doorstep. There's no logical reason to want a car. It is simply so I can sit behind the wheel, control the thing, feel...what? In charge of the moment. Manly. It's more adolescent folly. I remember in high school how there had seemed a direct correlation between manhood and having a driver's license. I shrug. Alice will not be any more impressed when I show up driving a vehicle. She won't be impressed at all, in fact, in any way. Then again, I hadn't expected her to French kiss me last evening. She isn't usual; but frankly I don't know what is usual for a cold, not really.

I make breakfast. Grapefruit. Cottage cheese. Yogurt. Everything soft and calm, nothing particularly filling. I can have all day with Alice. We can go where we like--or where I like, anyway. I wonder what she normally does with her time away from work. What is a cold's weekend like? The question has the tenor of a Zen koan. It sounds like a riddle, something designed to make you think past the immediate conundrum. Of late I am thinking about the cold, more perhaps than I ever have before. I am involved in a cold's life, and it may be that before the night is through I will have bedded a cold.

My car arrives. I go out to inspect it, smiling at the thought of piloting it myself. One o'clock is taking its sweet time.

* * *

I leave early, so to assure myself that I can handle the car. My driver's license is up to date, of course, but I have been ferried around by self-drivers for some time now. That too is a form of sleepwalking, I suppose, being lulled about the city's somnolent hills in ghost vehicles, speaking to no one, eyes aglaze in the back seat.

Coming down off Potrero, heading westward this time, I pick up 101, the freeway, and take it to 24th Street. Then up through the Mission District. There is a little life here, some lingering Latino heritage behind the aggressive gentrification. People are out and about, crossing the street at random points, assured the driverlesses will stop. A few faces peer in at me, the man with his hands on the steering wheel of a vehicle. Curious looks. Maybe a little rancor, even. What's this asshole trying to prove?

I might ask myself the same thing. I might. But I don't. My commitment to this endeavor remains. If I appear foolish, so be it. If I disgust others by courting a cold female, they will have to live with it.

There is music from the sidewalks, salsa beats and pounding house bass. Grocers are selling fruit. Customers take their goods away in knotted mesh bags. It is Saturday, and the sky isn't too overcast; and perhaps there is still some hot blood pumping through the city's veins. My confidence in my driving grows. All the sense memories are in place, but even so it feels new. My sneakered foot gooses the accelerator, applying a lover's gentle pressure. As I climb 24th's vertiginous incline, which will take me up into Noe Valley, I bear down on the gas. The electric engine gives a modest heave, but I feel like a charioteer, all brawn and might, at one with my conveyance, driving it forward with pitiless joy.

Noe Valley is full of old expensive homes, though I'd be surprised if a percentage of them weren't vacant, as in every other quarter of San Francisco. 24th Street is the main east-west artery through the ward, and traffic crawls the rather narrow way. People are out here too, but everything is a little more prim. Olds stroll and window shop and pause to converse on the corners. It's an insular neighborhood in its way. The same familiar faces, seen over and over. There are well-attended churches, and events are sometimes held, staid block parties and fundraisers. I see no less than three police patrol cars. If there are any colds about, they aren't making themselves conspicuous.

I cruise the strip. As a boy I would come down here sometimes, visit the shops, kill time with school chums. We had so much time on our hands, back then, and it had to be dealt with one way or another. Ahead are the looming mounds of Twin Peaks. The little family home up there, where I spent that boyhood, has since been gutted and revamped, a story added to it, modernized to a fare-the-well. I put it on the market when my mother passed away and socked away the cheerless capital in my bank account. I doubt I will ever buy property. There are those who rent and those who own, and I am of the former disposition.

At Castro Street I turn north, climb the monstrous hill, up to the plateau, down the far side into yet another neighborhood, this the storied Castro District itself. Onetime gay mecca. A self-appointed precinct, reserved once for the liberated queer souls yearning to express themselves publicly. It retains that legacy, of course. Rainbow flags are everywhere, but they memorialize now. One needn't live in or visit a particular city sector to assert one's sexuality anymore; it wasn't even especially true when I was a boy.

Nonetheless, some flamboyance still abides in the Castro. I am surprised to see a line of monks crossing through the intersection ahead. Heads down, deep cowls concealing faces, hands clasped in solemn supplication. Traffic stops. Suddenly music booms, and the robes are flung open, revealing male bodies. Some are naked; others are clad scantily in wisps of lingerie. The men dance campily to the hammering beats. They waggle their genitals with, well, gay abandon. It is very throwback, very much the kind of thing which might have once shocked the squares. But today it only incites applause and cheers. In moments the music cuts out, and the column of monkish exhibitionists are ambling away, presumably to reenact this spectacle at the next intersection. I smile after them.

And so I go, through the city. The different sights, the different landmarks. Haight Street. The Western Addition. A city of kitsch and history. It is all so precious--sometimes cloyingly so. But here I dwell. And will go on doing so, no doubt, to the end; or to my end, anyway. I won't be the last of the olds. That fate will befall some unlucky bastard, maybe even the Queen herself: crippled and senile, the last human born and the last to expire.

My roundabout tour at last takes me toward my destination. I have timed it right. It is just coming up on one o'clock in the afternoon.

This used to be Fisherman's Wharf. It still is, but some of the old rotting sights have been torn out. Even San Franciscans can't hold onto every last little bit of historical minutiae. A few of the restaurants were razed, a block or two of tacky tourist shops leveled, so to make way for housing for the cold. The city uses colds in its labor force. Not every business hires them, but enough do to justify quartering them within the city limits.

I guide my rental past the first square of buildings. The metaceramic facings gleam dully in the wan daylight. They are dismal structures. Not ugly, just characterless. Warehouses for living things. There are no architectural frills, really no deliberate symmetries at all. These are, at best, simply shelters. The 'ceramic coloring is a careless mix of grays. No lawns, no flower beds, no landscaping at all. They are three-storied, the doors spaced closely. Each unit is probably tiny, perhaps claustrophobically so.

Homes for colds...

I see a lone individual emerge from a door and go walking swiftly in the direction I am coming from. Youngster. Late teen, maybe. Dressed nondescript, head down like those pornographic monks I saw. A cold out on an errand. Otherwise, the buildings are utterly still. I realize with a start that they have no windows, only narrow slits. It all looks too much like a prison. But no one guards the site; no razor wire is strung. No doubt some olds in the city would prefer it that way, even those making use of the colds in their workplaces. Ghettoize the young fuckers. Seal 'em in, like it's Warsaw 1940. Let them out only with working permits. Police the hell out of the area, so they don't slip away willy-nilly. Hold it there, frosty! Show me your papers, boy! Don't make me club your little skull open.

I come to the second block of metaceramic housing. It's no better--no different whatsoever--than the first. But this is where Alice lives. I have paid her rent here for a month. That month is mine. She is mine. She has already let me kiss her. She has even kissed me back, with seeming enthusiasm. Things can only escalate between us.

Or maybe they will end abruptly. I have had relationships go sideways on me without the least warning. Sometimes you're seeing it one way, and she's seeing--

But: I have never paid for a relationship before. And Alice so far has honored our bargain. I choose to believe she will continue to do so.

I slow, then pull into the curb. A great deal of muck has dried here from the last rainstorm to hit the city. I shove open the door and step out; and when I don't immediately see her, something lurches in my chest. But a figure comes out from a wedge of shadow at the front of one of the grim buildings and walks straight toward my car.

It's her. It is her.

I take several steps toward her. I stop. My face is contorted by a grin. I am happy to see her. Perhaps I am overjoyed.

"Hi," I say.

"Hi, Kyle." She greets me. Why does she greet me? What sense is there in a greeting, what emotion?

She wears a different sweatshirt than the last two times I saw her. This is gray, hooded, a little snugger on her. I note how it cinches her youthful waist. She moves with that easy fluidity. She is limber and nimble.

She stops in front of me. She doesn't have on her sunglasses, and her eyes squint a bit in the diffuse sunshine. Not letting myself hesitate, I bend a little--I am three or four inches taller than her--lean ahead and swiftly and soundly kiss her cheek. Once more I inhale the aroma of her and feel a prickling down my spine.

"You're free for the whole day?" I ask.

"Yes." The not quite toneless voice.

"Good. Come on. I rented a car. We can go places." Again I don't pause. I do as I have planned and take her hand and lead her to the curb. Her grip isn't limp; she holds me back. I first held hands with a girl in grade school. The event meant the world to me. My heart skittered crazily, and my breath came short.

My heart rate is noticeably up and my breathing quick as I walk hand in hand with Alice to the car.

CHAPTER EIGHTEEN

Supporting Players

Kyle Norris' life is not a soliloquy, not a one-man performance. He has had plenty of support, right from the start, as has most every human being ever born. Maybe the colds even have cliques and individuals on which they center their attentions.

Kyle Norris was born of man and woman. His parents planned to have him, wanted to have him, and when he became a reality, they carried on faithfully in the care and feeding of him. The two remained married until their deaths: Dad went when Kyle was thirty-two and gainfully employed at the firm at which he still toils; Mom died two years and five months later. Both lived into their seventies, had relatively sound health until the last few months of their lives. Kyle paid for in-home nursing, and both parents experienced the quiet dignity of dying in their own beds. Though Kyle saw much of them in their waning weeks, he wasn't present for either's death. Had he been, he tells himself, he would have sat at bedside and held the fragile hand and listened carefully and with vast sympathy for any final words. He would have closed the eyelids with infinite gentleness. He would have done these things. Had he been there.

As a boy he ran through a series of best friends, all male. They shared secrets and speculations and urgently tried to figure out how much of what they heard from others--grownups, especially--was bullshit and how much plain fact. There seemed to be a new best friend every year when he was in grade school. Each of these players made his impact.

In high school there was, above all, Philippa Charpentier. She was the one who kissed with her tongue and finally let him grope her breasts. She was extremely exciting. Many firsts were achieved with her, though he was not released of his seething virginity by her. That occurred in a one-off incident that was equal parts terror, clumsiness and white-hot joy. It happened at a party, in someone's bedroom. The girl never acknowledged afterward what had happened between them, and he told no one about it. Ecstatic about no longer being a virgin, he was nonetheless also fairly sure that he'd been used in a way he couldn't entirely explain to himself.

Later in life, when he had a career, other performers entered. The office manager of his internship: Mr. Geoff Hardaway. Later, a rival: one Denise Thorpe, who inadvertently taught him a little boldness. There was of course Lester Crofft, his hail-fellow-well-met colleague. (Lester, who had resurfaced so unexpectedly the other day, that call into the office, the offer of dinner. Kyle is still considering whether or not to contact him.) Along with these workplace characters there are the women he has known during the same span. Maureen Mccotter is a good representative of the friendly yet tepid relationships through which he has navigated throughout those years. Yes, Maureen will do nicely as an archetype. Cut and paste her a few dozen times.

And now? And now? Does Kyle Norris have yet another significant player in his life, someone who is making an impact? Perhaps. Perhaps. But we do not deal in the present here, and he must work such things out in real time, left to his own devices and without the luxury of hindsight.

But wait! you cry. A part of the narrative is absent. A glaring part. Kyle's college years. He thinks of this time, sometimes, as his heyday, the best years of his life. It was that last segment of normal reality, of humans being born of humans, before the supply of emotion to the species was so brutally choked off. The Line had not yet been drawn. And Kyle Norris was in his prime, intellectually, passionately, sexually. His world gleamed with a lacquered richness, harboring a deep alluring texture. Everything was possible, all but the impossible things, but they were few.

One person stood alongside him at that pinnacle of things. One absolutely key player. She was Sissy Anspaugh. She comes into his thoughts now and again. She still has a certain meaning. She stings and beguiles; she is elation and regret, bitterness and bleached-out optimism. And she may never entirely go away.

He really must speak at length about her sometime.

CHAPTER NINETEEN

Guided Tour

"See? There?" I am pointing, over the stone wall made to look like an old English hearth. Alice goes up on tiptoes, and the gray sweatshirt rides up her back. A crescent of pale skin is exposed just above the waist of her jeans. I see two knobby vertebrae before I wrench my gaze away.

"Which one?" she asks. I am pointing into a cluster of houses on the lower face of the peak. I tell her the color of the roof. She says, "I see it."

"That's the house where I grew up. Well, sort of. It's been remodeled almost out of recognition, but that is the location of my childhood. I lived there until I went away to college."

I watch her face. We are standing side by side at the Twin Peaks lookout, which offers a panoramic view of the northeastern section of the city, the main cable of Market Street where it starts in the Castro before cutting its way all the way to the Bay. Buildings gleam in the distance; great sheets of window wink with sunlight. Clouds scud overhead, but flashes of blue sky come through. The wind is brisk up here. San Francisco is a windy city. If the temperature is low enough, the wind can knife you to your marrow.

Having dutifully observed my boyhood home, she comes down off her toes. There is a parking lot attached to this lookout point, which has a few of those bulky public telescopes mounted on swivels along the stone wall. A few other vehicles occupy the lot's slots along with my rental. Two other couples are taking in the vista: a man and woman of late middle age, both bundled up against the wind; and two males of that nebulous Youthful Adult age, arms casually around each other, murmuring, laughing, looking like they have a good thing going.

If any of them has given us dirty looks, I haven't noticed. Then again, I have not been watching closely.

I lean back against the wall and cross my arms. I smile at Alice. "What would you be doing right now if you weren't here with me?"

Her green eyes seem to go out of focus but come right back. "I'd go out to buy groceries. Or sleep."

"Sleep? In the daytime?"

"Yes."

"You mean you...nap?" The notion seems fanciful, somehow.

But she says, "I nap." I hear a subtle emphasis, as if she is making an assertion. Colds nap, old man. Get used to the idea.

The smile spreads wider across my face. I wonder vaguely what I might be doing if I hadn't made these extraordinary arrangements with this girl; but the thought has no interest for me. My weekends are generally as bland and unchallenging as my workweeks. I feel very much...here. Present. In the moment. I stand on Twin Peaks, and I am with Alice; and we have the whole day ahead of us.

Something occurs to me. "Do you know how to read?" I ask.

"Yeah." (She just used yes a mere moment ago; why does she use yeah now; how does she decide which to--)

"Where did you learn?"

"At my facility."

"Your...camp?"

She nods this time. A nod! She fascinates me. I am boundlessly curious about her. I have obviously never before been so drawn to a cold. But now that I have overcome any initial misgivings, I am almost comfortable around her. It is as if she had a disability or deformity, and I had adjusted my ableist-centric thinking to accept her as "normal."

We are walking bundles of prejudices, we humans. So it seems. I wonder if we would have evolved into something more inclusive and accepting, given the time.

I am intrigued by the facility she mentioned. A fed camp. There are several in the Bay Area. Most were put up hastily on the grounds of razed shopping malls. Early on they drew droves of protesters: some groups wanted the colds put into total quarantine, as if their condition could be spread; other factions demanded the children be liberated; and probably more than a few reactionary nutjobs wanted every frosty executed on the spot. But the protests petered out, though the facilities remain. They continue to take in those babies illegally born.

"Who taught you at the--the facility?" I ask.

"Programs. They played on the walls for hours each day. You could watch or turn it off."

"You watched."

"Uh-huh." (Oh God, a new slangy affirmative!)

"Do you read books now?"

"I've read books."

"Do you read novels?"

"I've read a novel."

I want to gawp at her. For a breathless instant I absolutely cannot wrap my head around the possibility of a cold reading a novel. Fiction. Something entirely made up. What would motivate an emotionless being to peruse a work of fiction? What would she think to gain from it? My sense of reality--or at least my understanding of colds in general--seems to wheel underneath me.

"What..." I have to pull in a breath. "What did you think of the novel?"

The pause. It's too indistinct a question, I realize. Though I have said "think," I really mean "feel." What did you feel about the novel? Useless to ask her.

She says, "I thought it was a novel." For some reason I'm glad for the cryptic, inanimate reply. A tautology, if I remember what that term means. If she had said: "I enjoyed it," how would I have reacted? Probably faint dead away.

She shifts her stance, and the wind snatches a few blades of her unwashed irregular hair and stripes it across her left eye. Before she reaches for it, I do, catching it on my finger and combing it back into her dark red hair. The sun shines directly between the clouds, and the red looks almost purple among the glossy black locks. She doesn't recoil when I do this. I don't repulse her because...of course I don't. I can't repel her. But she can be wary of me, even if she shows no signs of it. I am an untrustworthy old because, well, all olds are untrustworthy. Is that a tautology too? Hell if I know. College was a long time ago.

I ask, "Have you ever been out to the beach, seen the ocean?"

She shakes her head. A gestural negative. She lives in San Francisco, nearby the waters of Fisherman's Wharf, but she has never gone to the Pacific shoreline, stood on the sand, though it is mere miles away. There must have never been a motive for her to do so.

"I'd like to take you," I say. Then more decisively: "I'm going to take you there."

We hold hands again on the way back to the car. The late middle-aged couple has vanished, but the two men still stand together in a lasting embrace. If they are aware of the two of us, they give no indication, and I certainly feel no need to look in judgment on their partnership. The more affection in the world, the better off we will be as we dwindle away.

* * *

Alice said reading programs were available at the facility where she grew up. The (residents? inmates?) colds there could watch these programs or not. She seemed to imply that some chose to watch--and thereby learned to read--and others did not. That means that in a group of given colds placed in what were probably uniform circumstances, some might make different decisions. But how the hell can that be? If survival and basic logic don't decide, then what is left to drive the decision process? Preference. But preference requires personality. The cold don't have character. Emotions haven't shaped them. One cold shouldn't elect to learn how to read while another doesn't. They are not, of course, a hive mind...but they aren't exactly individuals, either.

The questions dance on the head of a pin. A steely spiked pin, as icy as a winter grave.

* * *

* * *

I grab my jacket. She zips her hoodie up to her throat. We crunch across the broad sand-strewn sidewalk and go down the weatherworn cement steps. The beach is wide and brown, and it is a trudge to the water. The wind comes in fiercely, and harsh sunlight bounces off the sea. Alice slips on her sunglasses as I squint into the fiery light. The salt air is invigorating. I breathe it deeply. I am a human, an old, freighted with all the time-tested emotions--although perhaps not in the usual quantities--but even I, who should be able to motivate at will, haven't bothered to go out and look at the ocean in some time.

Alice reels, catches her balance like a tightrope walker, takes a few more steps, reels again. I realize that she has never walked on sand. The farther out we go, the damper the sand becomes and the less sure her steps. It must be like encountering snow for the first time, as an adult: a heretofore unexperienced terrain, something one may know about but which one has never dealt with firsthand. She hasn't dealt with sand before. I take her elbow; I give support; I move with her, and we make our way. Her strides grow firmer. I am watching her gain her sand legs, acquiring a new skill, and it suddenly moves me on some level. My throat tightens, and I remember how tears tasted when I was a boy.

The ocean has grown louder and louder all this while. It is a steady, cyclical sound. A dull deep roar that subsides into a foamy sigh every time. I feel tiny drops of spray on my face. Alice touches her cheek with two fingers and gazes down at the fingertips. I see no obvious expression on her face, of course, but her brow has an extra line, as if she is concentrating or frowning.

Ocean Beach, which is where we are, isn't a beautiful beach. The sand is rife with splinters of driftwood and shattered bits of sand dollars. The tideline is slimy with jellyfish and glistening ropy kelp. The spumes of foam look like dirtied surgical gauze.

Here we stop. The breakers come in, tall and rolling, and arrive with a great aquatic thud. Alice has her hands in the pockets of her hoodie; she gazes straight out. I watch the waves, watch her sidelong. It is like when you are showing someone you care about a great movie they haven't seen before: as much as you yourself enjoy the film, you also want to watch the other's reaction, knowing how indelible that first experience is.

Christ, I think with a small awe, she's never seen this before. She has seen the Bay...but never the raw heaving might of the sea where it strikes the land. Her mind--however that mind operates--is absorbing this sight, this experience, and it is happening only because I brought her here.

Right, creep. And the only reason she came along is because you've purchased her time and can effectively order her about like a paid escort.

But that self-loathing voice isn't strong in me today. I am enjoying myself, enjoying the girl's company. Look what we've done. I have taken her sightseeing, shown her the house I grew up in (that is kind of intimate, huh?), and she even shared some details about her upbringing. This is the sort of information exchange I would expect on a first few dates with any woman.

I continue to observe her sidelong, hoping she doesn't notice. I want--desperately, I realize--to ask her what she thinks of the Pacific Ocean. But it is that same imbroglio: I'm not asking what she thinks but what she feels. And I can't ask that. I cannot.

The sea is green and gray and black, gold where the sun strikes it directly; everything but blue. This isn't a swimming beach, but there are other people on it, in the distance. Tiny shapes, like desert mirages. A dog is energetically fetching the stick its human continually throws. Someone a half mile down flies a kite. Olds. Olds play with their dogs. Olds send kites up into the wind, for no logical reason.

I am about to suggest we head back to the car. But she says, still looking straight ahead, "Why does the water curl like that?"

For the past few minutes she must have been trying to figure it out, I realize. This is a day brimming with realizations for me.

"The moon does it," I tell her. "The pull of the Earth's moon." Then I try to explain it in further detail. I am getting it mostly right, I think, though it has been a long time since I was in a science class.

I leave her to watch the incoming waves a while more, presumably integrating her new knowledge with the visual evidence itself. I wonder if she really grasps the semi-abstract concepts of gravity and inertia. Maybe everything is face value with her, with all her kind. They observe physical phenomena and accept whatever explanations they are provided. Perhaps one could tell a cold child that Santa Claus rules the planet and mermaids caper in every ocean. Unless the child learns otherwise, it might go on accepting that. Or it is just as plausible that the cold are born wary of us, a survival instinct laced into their frigid genetics, and that they don't believe a thing we tell them. They just go along. Because they are waiting. Above all else, they are waiting for us to pass from this world.

When I think she has finally had her fill of the oceanic panorama, I start us back to the rental. She walks a little better on the sand this time. I intend to show her a few more sights. Then I will take her to my home.

CHAPTER TWENTY

Home Again, Home Again

I show her a few of the attractions in Golden Gate Park. We eat a couple of hot dogs from an autovendor. I look up at just the moment when a man on old-school rollerblades slews past, giving us--giving me--a look of blunt disgust. Middle-aged old fraternizing with a cold. The man has a wiry physique, and veins garnish his thick upper arms. I'm glad when he keeps going. I don't want to fight him if he insists that I do.

An icer, then, must be prepared to face some societal backlash for his predilections. Maybe I should start carrying a shockstik. Or just not go out in public with Alice.

Screw that. I've said it before: I am committed to this. I won't spend this month in hiding with her.

I take her a couple more places, then in the waning afternoon we journey together to Potrero Hill. She has deliberately watched me several times as I operate the vehicle. Perhaps she has never been driven by another person before. I think maybe I'll teach her to drive. There is time for it. Weeks are ahead for us. Already I am past the threshold where I might terminate our arrangement prematurely, as I explained to her in my initial proposal. This situation is agreeable to me. I like her company. I enjoy her presence. Today has been a very winning day.

And the day isn't done.

The Victorian where I live has a patch of lifeless lawn out front and a path of lavender paving stones bisecting it. I lead Alice along it to my door. Again I am intensely in the moment. Every instant seems to crackle with internal life. I pick out the chirp of a cricket. The reflection of a tree is on my front window. The breeze is turning chill, taking the temperature down to the San Franciscan median of 55.

I step aside, and she enters, and I close the door quietly behind her. She is now a guest in my home. The house retains heat rather efficiently, and it is still warm inside. I wonder if the line of her shoulders is a bit tense. She might be ready to spring away from me if I make a violent move. Yes, I have taken her to dinner twice; yes, I have acted harmlessly; but I am an old, and all might be pretense. This whole routine I have engineered might be leading up to a vicious assault, a savage rape, here in the comfort of my very own abode. It would do no good to tell her that this isn't so. She studies my behavior. She decides, through her own processes, how much she can trust me.

Trust. Come on, Norris. Stop using words of emotion.

I am about to offer to take her sweatshirt, like any gallant lord of the house would, when she says, "I need to pee."

It's not exactly a swear word, but it startles me nevertheless. I would have expected a cold to say urinate for some reason. For some preprogrammed, old-thinking reason. Alice isn't what I thought a cold would be like. Maybe I was right to fixate so on her. Maybe I sensed, even just seeing her on her bike, vaulting off the hills...something.

I point her to the bathroom.

While she is in, I take the cat bowls from outside and wash them out in the kitchen sink, then fill them with food and water, respectively. Two of the local felines are waiting when I return. For strays they are well-mannered. As they wait patiently, I fetch a saucer and divide up the dry food so they can eat at the same time. They are a calico and a white ring-tailed. When I started leaving out food and water three or four years back, I would also keep the back door open for an hour or so, in case one of the strays wanted to come in, look around, see how the other half lived. But no cats ever entered the house, so far as I knew. I stopped doing it. In hindsight it seemed a weak effort, a bid without proper commitment. If I wanted a cat to live with me, I should go get one. Pet adoptions have been booming since the inception of the Cold Era.

As I step back in through the door, I find Alice standing in the kitchen, observing. She radiates no sort of subliminal or bioelectric presence, and I try not to start too sharply. My hand on the knob; the door is still open.

"Have you ever seen cats before?" I ask. The two are eating rapidly. I can hear the flecks of cat food crunching in their teeth.

"'Course." Did I just detect a subtle edge there? As in: of course I've seen cats, fool. I wouldn't mind if she called me fool. I wouldn't mind any overt emotional display or telltale that wholly belied her presumed nature...because I seem to sense that she is already unusual of her kind.

I say, "I was planning on making us dinner. I'll put on some music. You're warm enough in here, yes? Let me take your sweatshirt."

* * *

I do something with pork, frying it up with rice, bamboo shoots, green onion and soy sauce, and do something else with a few strips of tender beef. I give these a caramel glaze and serve them with hot cashew halves and mushrooms. I also make salad and whip up a passable dressing.

I don't have a dining room, but the kitchen is spacious, accommodating the square pale table at which Alice and I sit. I pour her a glass of cranberry juice and iced tea for myself. She eats with knife and fork. There isn't much delicacy about it, but it is civilized enough. Her napkin remains in its scrolled brass holder on the table. I don't tell her to pull it out and drop it on her lap. I am observing. She chews with some vigor, jaws working hardily. When a line of dark juice dribbles from the right corner of her mouth, she wipes it with the back of her hand. She eats the pork, the beef, the salad at the same deliberate speed. Though this is a more elaborate meal than I generally cook for myself, I can't ask her anything about it while she is eating. There is emotion in every question: do you like it? does it taste good? Pointless. But I wait until she has finished; and then I ask, "Are you full?"

She nods, and for the barest instant she looks a little dazed, as if maybe the rich meal has done something more than merely quell appetite and supply bodily fuel.

I finish my helpings and set down my utensils. We haven't spoken during the dinner.

I say, "You should go take a shower." I can see the pit stains on her shirt. The greasy spot is still on her face and the back of her hand. Her erratic hair looks stiff.

"Okay," she says as she stands. I don't stand. I tell her again where the bathroom is, just off the bedroom; but I am not going to follow her in. I simply want her clean. Colds evidently don't prioritize hygiene. I hope she knows enough to use the soap and shampoo she will find.

I wait until I hear the water running before I clear the table. Earlier I had put on music. Bartók. Because what do you play for a cold guest in your home? I watched to see if she responded to it. She didn't. She didn't even seem aware of it as anything more than ambient sound. I shut it off. I can smell her odor--not unpleasant--on the air; but I'm still glad I sent her to the shower.

As I am standing there, it strikes me, the full impact of it: I have a cold here, a girl, a girl I very much desire. I have fashioned this mad situation. Such an effort. Such a risk. I cannot predict the consequences I might face. I shiver. There is magic here. And lunacy. And some other element that--

"Kyle."

I blink. The water has stopped running. She has called me from the other room. I detect--think I detect?--a tiny tremor in her voice. I go to the open door into my bedroom. The light isn't on within, but the bathroom door is open, and the light in there is lit, and steam billows into the bedroom, cottony clouds of it, and Alice, utterly unclothed, stands in the backlit steam. And she is astonishing. She is miraculous. She has toweled her hair, but it is still damp. And I remember a minor sexual fixation I once had for naked women with wet hair. Dark strands cling to her left cheek. Her face is in shadow, but I still see it. Her eyes are wide and steady, focused on me. Her lips are slightly parted. Her breasts lift as she breathes; that breath is a little quickened. Her breasts, also, are high and tight. And gorgeous. Her nipples are extended. Her waist is narrow. Skin is taut over her hipbones. Strong thighs, muscled calves. The pubic triangle, a dark thatch, is as damp as her hair. She is youth. She is vigor. She has called me in here, but it may be for something purely nonsexual. She may not regard nudity as anything significant.

Alice--and yes, there is a tremor, a small quaver in her voice--says: "We should fuck."

Time slows there in my bedroom; it grinds to a perfect halt.

* * *

I show her the pill, tell her what it is for before I swallow it. She knows what it is. Turns out the science to demobilize sperm was easily discovered once medicine devoted a serious effort to it. The male birth control pill.

In a haze of lust and wonder I shed my clothes. She lays down first upon my bed, and I follow. I take her into my arms--or really, she squirms with some urgency into my embrace. The feel of her. The smooth, soft skin. She is as wiry as expected, a sensual limberness. Will we kiss again? Yes. Yes. Her mouth on mine. A slavering kiss, tongues loosed. It is like before but even more passionate. (Passion? Does she feel passion?) A strong bodily reaction is underway within her. She moves energetically against me. Her hand roves. God, her touch! She reaches boldly--boldly! how can anything she does be bold?--for my cock, fingers closing and squeezing. A moan escapes my lips, spills onto hers. I caress her breasts. Emboldened myself, I slip a hand betwixt her tight thighs and find her slick and ready and waiting.

The symphony begins. Bassoons. Slow deep kettle drum, a steady march. A flute, the notes butterflies of sound. Now the strings enter, a hint of riptide in their collective power--

No. No, it's not music. It is not anything rarefied or abstract. This is flesh. This is animal want. She is gloriously responsive. I enter her, and she writhes and wriggles. Every part of her seems alive. She says nothing; certainly doesn't call out my name; but as we proceed, chugging along, I am keenly aware of each orgasm as it overtakes her. She is evidently quite susceptible to sexual climax. I feel like a goddamn stud as I take her through her paces, maintaining an admirable control over myself.

But that control won't last eternally, and I don't want it to. She is soft against me, with a thrum of trim muscle beneath the skin. I sally at her once more. Her hips buck. She makes little sounds of exertion. I throw myself into it, seeking the end point of the pleasure that has been building so sweetly inside me. My blood pounds. There is heat in my eyes. Suddenly everything is rushing; time has come unglued and is tumbling ferociously toward a zone of feverish light and roaring cascades.

I come hard. It is a great terrible joy. Alice, I think, shares a last orgasmic quiver with me.

Then she is still.

And I am still.

The rumpled covers. The cooling flesh. The scent of sex on the air of the bedroom. I cannot ask her qualitative questions. To evaluate a thing one must feel something about it. But here I am helpless. I must ask. The impulse is born of a masculine insecurity which I have never entirely shaken over the course of my adult life.

I lick my dry lips. I audibly draw a breath. And I ask: "Was that okay for you?"

She shifts. Our bodies still touch. She says, "Sex is necessary." Perhaps this is the only answer she can give me.

* * *

I tell her I am taking her home. She doesn't object, of course. I could go again; I could. Middle age hasn't sapped me of vitality. And I certainly feel a good deal of physical enthusiasm toward the girl. But let it rest at one screw for now. We have consummated our relationship or our transactional partnership or whatever the hell this thing should be called. The single experience was special. My being is still humming with the thrill, the exquisite pleasure.

She follows me to the car, and I ferry her wordlessly across the nighttime city. There are carousers in the streets, mostly young-olds, drunk and drugged; but a few older olds are out making mischief, raging against the dying of the light. Streetlights are out here and there. Sometimes whole blocks are in relative darkness. Last year several power outages hit the area. In the end perhaps the whole system will go down, unless colds are trained to understand and handle the equipment. That, however, presumes they would be willing to do so. It might be they plan to let all our machines expire. When we go, we can take our noisy civilization with us. They could have something quieter in mind for when they inherit everything. Something simpler, perhaps. It might even be better, a way of life we olds with our messy emotions couldn't grasp.

Does Alice know what the future holds for her kind?

I take her to the grim block of housing units. I tell her when I will pick her up tomorrow. We kiss before she gets out of the car, but I still don't know what a kiss means to her. She may just be tailoring her behavior toward my wants: after all, I have paid for this service. A part of me doesn't care if it is all a fake. The illusion is a happy one, and I've just had the best sex in quite some time. Besides, I have been in other relationships which were rote experiences, nearly empty of any genuine feeling.

But another part of me wants the kiss to be real, wants the girl to be authentic. And as I watch her cross toward her building, I can believe she is something more than survival instincts and unfeeling patience.

CHAPTER TWENTY-ONE

When the Music's Over

Murders are down. That is, old on old murders. Those who feel don't commit homicide against their own kind so readily anymore. Old on cold killings do still occur; but after the mass slaughters of yore these statistics seem pale, almost blithely inevitable, as though the colds can expect this death toll as the price for being permitted to exist at all.

So, fewer murders. But a general rise in violent crimes. Not muggings, not anything where one might seek criminal profit. These are assaults, often crimes of passion, spur of the moment episodes. It seems a part of the new emotional ways of the old: the hair-trigger responses, the extreme use of feeling, no matter how petty or paltry the catalyst. If one is going to exhibit a convulsive temper whenever something untoward occurs, one can expect to occasionally take that display to a physical level. Your steak was overcooked when you ordered rare? Attack the waiter. Someone grabs a driverless you were hailing? Go at them with your bare hands. Generally these incidents don't lead to homicide. Police intervene. Citizens will step in and pull combatants apart. The fighters will be dazed, bleeding from their wounds, astonished at what they have done.

Suicide too is at an all-time high. It is something of a sacrament now--or it soon will be. Many states have decriminalized the act. It is more and more often viewed as a personal choice, one to be made with thoughtfulness and carried out with solemn dignity. Commercial pills to facilitate the deed will likely be made available in the coming years. The drug companies will price them competitively.

No wars are currently being waged anywhere on the globe. This might seem astounding, but militaries the world over have been depleted for some years, even in countries which still enforce national service. Desertions are commonplace. Armies hemorrhage soldiers as fast as they can conscript them. The historic hostilities among nations carry little weight today. What good is it to conquer an ancestral enemy? The cold are engaged in the ultimate conquest. They will win everything, in the end. It makes meager sense to give one's life to warfare or even to the starched traditions of military service. So, occupying troops have been withdrawn to their homelands. Missile silos go dark. The sword grows dusty on the shelf.

There are other statistical data. People still marry; they still divorce. Some religions enjoy an uptick in recruitment, but the gains and losses seem faddish, as if the creeds are mere styles.

And, of course, babies are still born, although far fewer than any time in modern history. In a generation the world population has dropped by an estimated billion people. Yet every child born is a cold child, no matter its parentage. And enough are created that the species--the cold species, anyway--will certainly go on.

Eventually, eighty or ninety or more years from now, someone somewhere will be the last human person alive. The very last. It is the juvenile science fiction scenario of The Last Man on Earth. She or he will not know of this unique solo status. But in a room, in some necropolis of the future where the rest of the dead olds lie in bony heaps, that final being's fragile life signs will flutter and stutter and give a last desperate surge before the close comes, before darkness takes the vision and the heart will pump no more. The body will lay in the dust and slowly become dust itself. It will be surrounded by whatever comforts this person gathered. Pictures of loved ones, long departed. A handwritten love letter, carried for decades in a wallet, brittle and discolored with age. There is a bed, where the person has died; a blanket, green and white, a Navajo print, gift from some forgotten friend. On the nightstand a little music box sits; inside a ceramic ballerina, chipped, but still ably performing en pointe. The simple mechanism will play a tinny melody if only the tiny metal handle protruding from its side is turned a few times. But it will not be turned, by anyone. The sentimental music will not play. Not ever again.

CHAPTER TWENTY-TWO

Balling

Sunday. I pick her up earlier than yesterday. She is waiting outside the metaceramic barracks of the cold. She wears what she wore the previous day: gray hooded sweatshirt, jeans. But wait...a different shirt. It bears a floral pattern, red and white and lime. So colorful. So startling when worn by a cold.

Hand in hand we walk to my car. I will probably keep the rental all month. I can afford it, though it is an extravagance. It feels good to be spending my wages on something; not just rent, bills, necessities. Why have a prestige job like mine if you're not going to indulge a little now and then? I know others who work in my office that throw their money into art and stamp collecting, who spend immoderate amounts of capital on rare books. Probably there are a few with high-priced drug habits, others who perhaps splurge on prostitutes. It might be there is a fellow icer or two employed at my firm. A brother creep. So you're not so alone as you imagine, Norris.

But the tormenting voice is weaker by the day, it seems. I deposit Alice in the passenger seat and shut the car door. I skip across to my side, feeling chipper, pumped full of energy. I'm wearing gym shorts and a sleeveless sweatshirt. Not very strategic attire for San Francisco and its cruel ever-shifting weather. But I have an athletic day planned for us, at least to start with. And I am counting on physical exertion to keep up my body temperature.

I get the car up to speed. The electric engine seems as potent as I feel, pouring on the environmentally friendly horsepower. It is illegal to run a fossil fuel-burning vehicle inside San Francisco's limits.

We approach a stoplight which has just turned red.

I say, "I'd like to teach you how to play basketball today. Or one on one, anyway."

"I know how to play."

"Really?" A high note of surprise in my voice; and a little disappointment as well. I wanted to show her the game.

She says nothing because my Really? is a null question to her, surely. I'm only questioning her answer, not asking for further specific information.

So I ask. "Where'd you learn?"

"Facility. Exercise yard. Sometimes the guards played us."

A number of followup inquiries occur, but the light goes green, and the self-driver behind me--evidently programmed with San Franciscan driving attitudes--starts honking. I accelerate. Basketball with the camp guards? That sounds...amiable. Maybe the abusive conditions I heard about at those facilities are exaggerated. Or outright anomalous.

There is a basketball rolling around in the footwell of the seat behind me. I don't shoot hoops as often as I walk or run for exercise. A few playgrounds are within easy distance of home on Potrero Hill, but I take us to Russian Hill, to Greenwich and Hyde Streets. It is an outdoor court, with nice views all around. I am still acting as ambassador, showing her around my hometown.

Two sinewy women, olds, are thwacking a ball back and forth over the net of the tennis court, but both ends of the basketball area are empty. I have a coin in my shorts pocket. She calls tails in the air-- evidently also familiar with how coin tosses work--and has the ball when we start. I am taller than her. I thought I would have more advantages, such as knowing how to play the game. I had meant to be magnanimous, to patiently explain the rules, then to elucidate the finer points of strategy. But she dribbles hard, right at the outset, and moves like a rabbit. Immediately I'm off-guard. She barely telegraphs any move. Those green eyes shift and dart, but there is no commitment to read in them. She is playing the game--and playing it very damn well--but she isn't caught up in it. She doesn't care. No competitive spirit.

Which makes it all the more disheartening when she scores eight points before I make a decent layup. She is a surprisingly good defender, given our size differential. I wonder if she played this hard--and yet this indifferently--in her camp.

I can tell it has been a while since I last played. I feel the strain in my calves. My arms grow heavy. But I throw my body into it, willing myself toward a second wind. After a time my fadeaway jumper comes back to me, and I am lining up my shots with increasing precision. She has a harder time blocking these. Sweat has broken out all over me. Her forehead shines, but otherwise she appears barely taxed. She has taken off the sweatshirt to play, and her breasts jounce pleasingly inside the floral top.

She wins the first game. I compete hard in the second. Plainly she needs no instruction. I like how our bodies bump, especially as I know her physical terrain. She is as limber on the court as in bed, and I grin at the salacious little thought. She ducks past me on my left, and I can't quite get a hand up to block her shot. She rims the ball in. As I retrieve it, I notice two young-olds--twenty-somethings--watching us from the edge of the basketball court. The two women playing tennis have vanished. I didn't see them go.

The two watchers are male. They are both a little slack of feature, as if they have been partying all night. I stand where I am, methodically dribbling the ball. I am between them and Alice. They appear...curious? Hostile? Once again I think I should be armed. If I am to go around in public with a cold, I ought to be prepared for the worst.

"Excuse me..." one of them says. "Is she--uh, you know."

I stare back. At least I should make him ask properly.

But he says, "Is she?" His tone is guileless.

I give in. "Yes."

"Wow," says the other, only innocent wonder in his voice. "I never seen one of, um, them play a sport. She's pretty good."

"She is," I agree. I remain alert, but these two are only fascinated. Alice and I resume play. I can feel the two males watching the whole while, and it is a little disconcerting; but I'll take slack-jawed wonder over belligerent prejudice any time. Still, by the third game, which I win, I have had enough of this particular exertion. On the way off the court I nod to our two spectators. They gaze at Alice, awe in their red-rimmed eyes. They have seen something new today.

I take her to the car. My body is awake, alive. The exercise has fomented deeper physical urges in me. I want her. I want her badly.

* * *

Sex is necessary. It has stayed with me, that simple pragmatic declaration of hers. I have thought on it, naturally. I think she means that a cold body, like an old body, has its built-in needs which must periodically be satisfied. The bladder fills; the bladder must be relieved. Sexual tension accumulates and thereby has to be alleviated. Her physical responses inform me--rather unmistakably--that she experiences bodily pleasure from the act. But this doesn't necessitate an emotional joy as well. Her orgasms are physiological events, things of flesh and tissue and healthy functioning organs: nothing more. So I remind myself.

She will do what I tell her to do; but I am careful not to issue outright commands. This is for my own sake, I think, far more than for hers. I wish to maintain a pretense between us. A willful illusion, one I can halfway believe in at any rate.

So I manage somehow to merely suggest that we shower together when I bring her to my home.

She is a slippery glory beneath my hands. The hot water feels good on my exerted muscles, but that is hardly the most agreeable part of the experience. I lather her lovely gleaming body, soaping buttocks, cupping her choice young breasts. No hint of sag; life has taken nothing from her yet; she is in peak condition. Quite unlike flabby old Maureen Mccotter. Ah, put that name finally from your mind, old man. I do so. Alice's hands move over me as well. She isn't fastidious about it. She washes me, sliding her hands into my armpits, soaping the back of my neck. But she also grasps my stiffening member and not simply for purposes of cleaning. I touch her similarly. Soon we are hurriedly rinsing away a stream of bubbles.

Her hair is still wet. The bedroom is light; it is midday. She lies on the bed, leaning back on her elbows, knees raised but not together. I drink in the sight of her, a sensual visual overload. She is...lovely. It seems improbable that a woman should exude such desirability. If I have felt this yearning before, it has been a long since it touched me so deeply. Now, here at the tender age of forty, I am on fire with passion. I stand at the foot of the bed, rock hard, eyes blazing. She gazes back, only a kind of animal lust animating her features; otherwise she is blank. Merely waiting to see what I will do.

I climb onto the bed. Her strong silken thighs slide along my shoulders as I move into the desired position. My head in place, I hunker between her outspread legs. And I taste her. I devour her. Faint soapy residue and the strong flavor of feminine nectar. Her responses gather. I eagerly drive her onward, my tongue stretching and straining. Her thighs clench the points of my shoulders. She jams herself against my mouth and grunts. This is followed by a dwindling growl and the slackening of leg muscles.

Face wet, I lie down alongside her. I pant happily. It is such an intimate act, I have always thought. My eyes drift closed.

The mattress shifts as she moves. A serene haze has come over me; but it is dispelled as I realize what she is doing. When her mouth makes contact, my body jumps, a single startled electrical jerk. Then I settle in and bask in the sublime pleasure. I do not open my eyes, even though I would like the images for my memory. But I am keenly aware of the tactile reality of her cinching lips, her flattened cheeks. Her tongue is eel-like in its speed. I sink down and down into the bliss. I make no move; let her do the work. And when I am finally catapulted upward, borne on the upswell of my climax, she doesn't pull her mouth fussily away.

We lay again, side by side. This is a day like no other. I feel the soft crackle of magic in the air. It is early afternoon, and I want to drowse.

I am not her first lover. That much was plain yesterday; perhaps it was obvious from the first time we kissed. She is touched by experience. This doesn't entirely surprise me. Colds must have sex lives of some sort. But her oral talents...these are unexpected.

I murmur, "Where did you learn to do that?"

Her voice, like mine, has thickened some with oncoming sleep. We will nap together. She says, "The facility. Some guards gave privileges if you blew them."

My eyes snap open. I gaze bleakly at the ceiling of my bedroom.

There is so much I don't know about her, about the life she has led. Now isn't the time to interrogate her. But I will know her better. I would wish to come to know Alice thoroughly. So I promise myself as we both subside into slumber.

CHAPTER TWENTY-THREE

A Rolling Stone

In a sense Norris was being cautious. Not in the greater sense: not in the execution of the overall scheme he was enacting with the girl. No. That was quite reckless. But in the smaller particulars his innate wary nature showed itself. He had not let Alice stay overnight at his home that first night. It was too soon for that, even though that "too soon" was a measure which existed only in his mind. She would stay if he told her to. Her only stipulation was that she reach her job on workday mornings. That was part of the deal: this partnership could not interfere with her duties as a bike messenger. He respected that.

That Sunday, after their afternoon sex, they dozed for several hours. Norris awoke refreshed and cheerful. He planned to cook dinner for the two of them again. But first he wanted to try an experiment.

She came awake as he got up from the bed. Her green eyes opened, and she seemed immediately aware of her surroundings. He stood there a moment, naked and halfway erect, and followed the sleek line of her body with his eyes. She had slept on her side, atop the covers, and he found the notch of her waist, between lowest rib and hipbone, to be breathtaking. But it more of an aesthetic appreciation than a renewed surge of desire. And besides, his hard-on was already wilting. They didn't need to fuck every minute they were together, after all. A little pacing was called for. A little caution.

For his experiment he told her to dress and come into the living room. He queued up a song on his sound system and instructed her to listen closely to it. It was an old tune, one of those rock and roll staples anybody who'd listened to the radio for the past fifty years would know. He set it playing. Up came the wash of organ music, almost blaring, then in crept piano, guitar, drums, until at last the exaggerated nasally lyrics surfaced.

Norris watched Alice. She didn't flinch at the sounds, but something in the subtle set of her comely features told him this wasn't a pleasant experience for her. Her eyes narrowed as the singer read/sang his lines. The song was unusually long for something of its genre. She didn't nod along with the rhythm; didn't show any sign that the melody was reaching her on any sensitive level. What was it, then? Just noise, with words strewn through it?

He shut off the system when the song had completed. He had thought about what question to ask her. "What do the words mean?"

She said nothing. It was a longer pause than she normally took. Finally: "It's fiction."

"Yes. What else?"

"Story of a woman who falls on hard times."

"And who is telling the story?" Norris felt a quickening of excitement.

"The singing man."

"Yes." He quietly bit his lip. "Does the man believe she is getting what she deserves?"

Her eyes shifted; she seemed to retreat without making a move. He had the feeling she was reviewing the lyrics in her head. "I don't know for sure." The rasp in her voice was suddenly more pronounced.

"Guess."

Again came the subtle beleaguered look. "Yes."

He hid the grin which tried to move his mouth. "Yes, the singing man thinks she deserves her fate?" he asked, wanting absolute clarity.

She nodded, just once, the motion almost curt. If she were an old, he would figure he was starting to seriously irritate her.

He said, "What about the chorus? The words that get repeated over and over throughout the song. 'On your own,' 'a complete unknown.' What does that mean?"

"What it says."

"By why the repetition?"

Another processing pause. He saw a minute vein jump at her temple. She said, "I don't understand the redundancy."

An honest assessment, he thought. "Who is the rolling stone, then?" Maybe she would see the metaphor, grasp that the freely tumbling stone was the woman whose life was so out of her control.

The green-eyed gaze was as flat as ever. "Stone is a what, not a who."

He gave her a dismal smile. The song he'd played her brimmed with emotion, with poetry and vibrant imagery. She could only hear the words, only take them at their face value. All else was lost on her.

Norris put together their dinner. Tonight he made pasta, with more salad and a helping of butter-soaked garlic bread. Alice ate what was put before her. He wasn't disappointed with her. The experiment had been its own sort of success. He had gotten her to listen to and, to some extent, to analyze a song. He imagined that not many people had tried that with a cold.

When the meal was done, he drove her back to her quarters. They kissed good night in the car, then she got out. He returned to his own home, poured a glass of thick red wine, and played and replayed the same song, alternately singing along with its jaunty lyrics and soberly brooding on its cold-blooded perspective. It was a hell of a piece. A masterwork. And now, just maybe, it would linger in the memory of a single cold even after every old who would care about the song had slipped away into darkness.

CHAPTER TWENTY-FOUR

The Coming of the Cold

When he had completed school and had his business degree in hand, Kyle Norris returned home. To San Francisco, city of his birth. But also to the family home, the small house on a slope of Twin Peaks. It had been understood that it would be this way. He didn't have a job in the financial sector waiting for him. He would have to compete. While he was doing so, his parents would host him. It wouldn't be like it had been living there during high school, of course. Though he'd had few rules as a teenager, now it was an unspoken but acknowledged fact that he was a man, an adult, and was merely lodging with this aging married couple who just happened to be his mother and father.

He had seen them fairly regularly during his years at HSU; they would come up or he would travel down to the Bay Area on school breaks; but even so, his parents remarked repeatedly on how much he had changed. He looked so mature. He acted different, in a more sophisticated manner. His humor was urbane, almost debonair; he didn't used to be funny like this or, really, at all. When he spoke to them, he looked them in the eye. He had a new presence, an aura of confidence.

Kyle wasn't quite sure what they were seeing. Sure, he no longer acted like a kid. He had no reserves of manic energy. Everything seemed on a level for him. But that wasn't, he thought, maturity. That was what the scorched earth breakup with Sissy had done to him, even though it had occurred some time ago. Over a year, in fact.

If he seemed confident, it was because he had withstood true anguish. If he was funny, it was because he finally grasped gallows humor. He didn't know that he looked especially different. The face in the mirror seemed much the same to him, year after year; but he supposed his features now conveyed a certain weariness which could be mistaken for adult character. Again, this was all because he'd now had his ass quite thoroughly kicked, and that, so they said, gave a person character. Great. Sissy had given him character.

Though Humboldt State University wasn't intrinsically a business school, he had made a few connections in the financial field. He got in at a firm as an intern. The office manager, Geoff Hardaway, was an easily exasperated man with a thinning head of curly hair. He expected the best from everyone at all times. Kyle fairly threw himself into the work, which was within his capabilities. He never panicked, the way some of the other interns did; and this swiftly endeared him to Mr. Hardaway. His fellows, who he saw sometimes for a beer after work, grilled him on how he kept his cool when being told to do ten things at once. Kyle would shrug and say he just took his tasks one at a time, but that wasn't it. The truth was simpler: he didn't care if he failed at this.

It was something he could admit only to himself. Certainly his parents didn't want or need to hear that from him, after they had forked out for four years at a university for him. But he again had Sissy to thank for his dismal attitude. Everything had gone pale after her; and color seemed reluctant to come back into the world for him.

Yet this indifferent outlook of his actually served him well in his internship. He operated without fear. When he did something wrong, he didn't try to hide it. In this way he learned from his mistakes and bluntly applied his new knowledge next time he met a similar problem.

He worked well because he was not emotionally involved in his work. Nor in much else in his life.

At the end of the internship period the firm hired him. He was the only one to make it. He never saw any of the other interns again.

Now he was earning a salary. He had also worked during his college days, at various restaurants scattered through the quaint but semi-bustling town where the university was located. He had bussed and waited tables; it was a grind, and it impinged on his study time, but it put tip money in his pocket so that he didn't have to rely on his folks for every dollar in his possession.

This new job, however, was a wholly different kind of employment. Now, like it or not, he was a grownup. The firm couldn't just grab any random kid off the street and set him to do this work. It required all the knowledge he had so diligently amassed at school. It also needed a certain knack, a penetrating fluency in the language of finance. None of the other interns had had that quality. Kyle Norris did, though in modest proportion. Still, it had been enough to get him in the door.

He continued to apply himself in the same uncaring manner as before. None of this much mattered, but that didn't prevent him from behaving as if these fiscal affairs were matters of life or death. Gradually it became a game; and he played it ploddingly but not ineffectively. He was a reliable tool to the firm. His work wasn't brilliant, but it was consistent and more than competent.

Funds accumulated in his bank account. He went apartment hunting, which in San Francisco was a nightmarish, almost Kafkaesque undertaking. It was profoundly difficult to find any living space, even at the exorbitant rents being demanded of would-be lessees. But he didn't get frustrated. Like all else, this too was of a pale significance. So what if he couldn't find a decent place to live? What did it matter?

But this was important. He realized it slowly. He needed to get on with his life. It was a damaged life, to be sure, a life to be lived without Sissy Anspaugh...but he still had to go and live it. Enough with this prolonged bout of moping. Enough of thinking nothing really mattered.

The revelation supplied him with a rush of energy he hadn't experienced in some long while. His spirits didn't lift, but the mere presence of a greater vigor gave him some kind of illusion of cheerfulness. He wasn't trying to fool himself. But he found he was able to give more of himself, to his job, to his hunt for a place to live. It had been fine staying at the family house; he'd had no difficulties with either his mother or father, and they had seemed genuinely glad to have him around the house again. But they too must have recognized that he needed to move on, to forge something independent for himself.

Thus he scoured apartment listings and asked everyone he knew through work of any impending vacancies. He really didn't care what part of town he ended up in. San Francisco had once been a wildly diverse city, but steady gentrification was homogenizing it. To hear the aging natives tell it, the Mission wasn't the Mission anymore, and the notorious Tenderloin had lost much of its druggy charm, and this district and that had gotten whitewashed to a fare-thee-well.

Then somehow the miracle happened. He managed to be first in line for a one-bedroom unit in a lackluster apartment building in the Marina District. In a frenzy, over the course of a single weekend, he boxed up his earthly goods and transported them to his new home. The apartment was utilitarian but not squalid. He went out and purchased kitchen supplies and necessary furnishings. It was quite the undertaking, but his renewed stamina saw him through.

It was while he was relocating his entire life that he first heard about the strange babies.

The news popped up on social media. At first it seemed like background noise, not much more substantial than a reshared meme. But he must have paused at some point, resting his aching muscles and scrolling on his phone. He had given the news item a look. Something about a wave of odd behavior in a whole swath of newborns. Disease? he wondered. No. This was something more subtle, less quantifiable. The babies were simply acting...odd.

He didn't at the time take any great note of this. Curiosities occurred regularly, in all realms of life, and social media spread them like brush fire. Next week it would be something else.

At the moment he was an independent person for the first time. It was almost as though his life were starting anew.

* * *

But the news intensified and grew more widespread. It was now no longer a fringe theory or potential disinformation campaign: newly born children were exhibiting aberrant behavior. They were not responding in recognizable ways to their parents, to stimuli, to their environments. These babies would suckle at their mothers' teats, but they did not laugh; their elastic little faces didn't break into spontaneous happy expressions. They were often quiet. They seemed almost...watchful. Which some of the baffled parents found chilling.

The phenomenon was also pervasive. Reports came from every state, then from the rest of the world.

Kyle was still at his firm. He was even excelling there, in his own modest manner. Dependable Kyle Norris; not a daredevil, no, but he had sound instincts backed by some very credible business knowledge. He must have been paying attention in his classes at that Northern California stoner college he went to.

He was aware of the news, of the rising tide of uneasiness. Much speculation was put forth as to the nature of this strange happening. Many suggested that this was, for want of a better term, some sort of behavioral plague. An epidemic of autism-like impediment. These children, so new to the world, seemed to be lacking. Even the earliest indicators of socialization were absent in them. They expressed no discernable wonder, no joy, no hysteria. They were indeed quiet little beings. Subdued. Passive, even. They were not as babies should be, as babies had always been: noisy, needy, expressive.

Kyle dwelled in his small Marina District apartment. He had started seeing a woman, named Anaya, who he had met while out socializing with his co-workers. She was easygoing, intelligent, undemanding; and he was enjoying having a steady physical relationship with a female again. It had been a long time. Far too long, in fact. He made no comparisons between Anaya and Sissy. Indeed, the less he thought about Sissy the better. He had surrounded himself with all the trappings of a new life. And if it felt sometimes as though he were just playing along in something illusory or even false, so be it. He was living this new fake life as best he could, and it was, by any objective reckoning, a success.

But the world surrounding his new successful life grew more and more fraught. The impossible phenomenon was emerging as an inescapable reality. Something was wrong with the children. All the children, the world over. This could not be. But it was. The first true panic took hold. Even in his insulated existence Kyle felt it. The air seemed to have an extra bite to it, something deeper than the normal vexing San Franciscan chill. The atmosphere felt charged. Fear. Anger. Incredulity. People struggled to respond. How was one to deal with this situation? There seemed no seemly reaction. And what of these wretched parents, who found themselves yoked to these taciturn offspring who were nothing like the babies they had been expecting. How should they behave? These weren't the children they had sought to create. The parents' love appeared to mean nothing to these creatures.

It's hard, Kyle, loving someone who won't love you back. It popped into his head one day, that thing his mother had once said to him, designed to convey her frustration--and probably to hurt him a little also, as he had been more or less unwittingly hurting her with his semi-sullen stoic demeanor. But all that was behind them. He now had a good relationship with his parents. He communicated regularly with them, took them out for dinners occasionally, and was forthcoming about events in his life. He told them about Anaya. That was something of an irony. In school he had been deeply involved with Sissy for an extended period. It had even seemed, for a time, that they might one day get married. Yet his parents had never met her.

His mother and father were also aware of the bizarre global phenomenon. They seemed even more perplexed by it than some, as if it belonged to some modern trend which they couldn't quite grasp. Whenever he discussed it with them, they appeared hopeful that this time he would somehow explain it to them in terms they could comprehend. Father had lost some of his muscle mass and moved more gingerly than he had used to. Mother appeared to be developing a slight stoop. They were getting old, Kyle realized. The world probably would have seemed daunting and bewildering without this cold phenomenon; with it, reality was something alien, even dangerous.

The cold. Yes. People were starting to call them that. The babies. They were colds. Which meant, logically, that everyone else must be an old. Colds and olds. The concept was given terms. And so too came The Line, for it was growing gruesomely apparent that this horrible thing had happened all at once, dropping like a guillotine blade, dividing the two sentient species currently inhabiting the planet.

When the nomenclature was in place, the violence truly began. Somehow language gave permission. It started as random rioting. People were fearful. They were horrified and furious. The need to express this profound dismay reached critical mass. Bricks were thrown, cars set afire; sections of cities were looted. The mayhem had no direct purpose. These weren't protests, not in the traditional sense. There was, after all, no party to complain to about the colds, unless one wanted to take it up with God. When that particular fact sank in, the churches were stormed. Rioters defiled the sacred places, demanding that a supernatural being few of them believed in show his goddamn face and set things to right. Barring that, he at least owed humanity an explanation.

Kyle carried on as best he could. Like everyone else, he had difficulty accepting this new reality. But rather than succumbing to violent disbelief, he found himself more prone to wry bemusement. Surely all this was some fantastically elaborate hoax; surely some cabal or agency was screwing with the world, just to see how far they could take such a thing. It was Welles' War of the Worlds broadcast writ absurdly large and updated for the social media age. Sooner or later it would all crumble. Kyle waited, ready to be in on the last laugh. After all, he hadn't personally seen one of these cold babies. Maybe they didn't really exist.

The police presence in San Francisco was stepped up to extreme levels. Overnight, it seemed, officers in tactical armor were visible everywhere, sporting assault rifles and other military weapons. MRAP vehicles grumbled sinisterly through the streets, as if this were some overseas war zone. Other cities were on fire; in other places pregnant women were now being murdered. Not here. The San Franciscan authorities weren't having it. They would turn the town into a lockdown before they saw it senselessly harmed.

So Kyle went to his work amidst all this militaristic panoply. But the disquiet still hit every level of society. Items started to disappear from supermarkets. At first it was certain brands, then whole categories became scarce. You couldn't find olive oil anymore; tofu vanished for some reason. It got worse. Just about every kind of pork product ran out and was not restocked. People wondered about mass starvation, about total social collapse.

Naturally, the financial markets were in a state of chaos. Fear drove the stocks. Corporate entities crashed and burned every day. Kyle plied a steady course, adjusting to the new paradigm but remembering that an uneventful day of trading could be a good day. Several of his fellows at the office, including people senior to him, looked to him for guidance.

Somewhere along the line Anaya bailed out of his life. She decided, quite abruptly, that she was moving back to where her parents lived, which happened to be an obscure hamlet in Montana. She left without giving him a chance to say goodbye to her face to face.

Across the nation, around the globe, there was a time of blood and terror. Massacres came. Attempts at genocide. But the cold could not be annihilated because the cold were the products of the old, and no matter what, people wouldn't stop breeding. It was the deepest instinct in the species. Babies were being born each day, droves of them, despite the warnings, despite the prohibitions being proposed in some places.

Time wore on. And somehow, by some bleak miracle, humankind adapted itself to this new order of things. The federal camps were inaugurated. The unwanted cold children were taken off any parents' hands who wished to surrender them. Great research projects were undertaken, but a few scientific minds were already proclaiming that no solution would be forthcoming. This was a metaphysical problem and an unsolvable one. Emotion had been switched off in the human race, and that was that.

Kyle Norris plodded on through his life. He stayed at his job and eventually had enough capital to move to more comfortable lodgings on Potrero Hill. Comfort became important to him; no extravagant comforts, just the small steady things. He liked his new home. He liked the neighborhood. His job was a tolerable exercise, one he felt he could do indefinitely. The markets restabilized to some extent. Normalcy didn't return because it never would; but a certain white-knuckled calm returned to life in general. People got on with their lives, even knowing that this was the finale for their kind. Olds were on their way out. Colds were arriving.

Kyle would eventually feel as if he were sleepwalking. It was not so uncomfortable a state to live in. He might have stayed in it permanently, in fact; but one afternoon, walking about the Financial District after eating his lunch, he spied a spry girl on a bicycle leaping off the slopes of Powell Street, and this would change his life as nothing had before. As no one had before. Almost no one.

CHAPTER TWENTY-FIVE

And the Stars in Her Hair Were Seven

"I arranged for the place to stay open," I tell her. She has put her folded up bicycle in the rental's trunk.

Today it was strange to be back at work, after the weekend with this girl. I still feel the glow: the sweet afterimages of her body, the tactile memories. Christ, her mouth...

But I am not taking her directly back to my place. When I proposed this contract to her, I said we would engage in sexual intercourse. But I implied it might not be too frequent. I realize now I was hedging my bet both ways. I wanted the bargain to be agreeable to her, in that she wouldn't have to service me day and night. But I'd also been leery of our consummation. It could well be that despite my surface attraction toward her, she might repel me in bed; I might find the touch of her distasteful on a profound level. Flesh backed by no emotion. Would it be much different from lying with a life-sized doll? But I hadn't known what her bodily responses would be like, how vital she was physiologically and how marvelously similar that was to a healthy human female's reactions.

We pull up at the hair salon. The closed sign has been flipped, but a light is on inside. I tap on the glass. Someone unlocks the door, and Alice goes in ahead of me. Dwight offers me a tight smile. He is roughly my age, with both arms sleeved in tattoos. His ears are quite thoroughly pierced, and God knows what other studs adorn his body. But he is an able barber, capable of delivering the conservative businessman's haircut I have been getting from him for years.

Dwight eyes her uneasily, but I'm paying him fifty dollars for this. He indicates a chair, and she sits. Once in it his professional nature kicks in. He drapes a nylon sheet over her, cinches it at her nape. He examines her head of hair critically. He seems about to say something to Alice but catches himself. A cold has certainly never come into his salon before.

"Who's been cutting this?" he mutters.

"Me," Alice says.

Again he almost addresses her. But he shoots me a look instead. "How do you want it?"

He gets the dynamic, then: I'm paying for this, I'm probably paying for her, so I get to call it. There is no obvious disgust on his face, but it might be right under the surface. I tell him the style I want for her hair. Anything will be better than her self-inflicted asymmetrical 'do, of course. A haircut is a thing of vanity. She is without vanity. No doubt she has just been chopping at her hair whenever it starts getting in her eyes, thus interfering with her job performance. I wonder if she even has a pair of scissors or if she has just been using some bladed instrument. I wonder further if she got haircuts as a child, in the camp. It is easy enough to picture a boot camp barber in there, shearing the kids like sheep on a bi-monthly basis. No care given to the process.

I am still shaken by what she said about giving blowjobs to the guards to get favors. How widespread was that abuse? How many times did she decide the tradeoff was worth it?

In the otherwise empty salon I watch Alice get the first real haircut of her life. Dwight is vastly efficient, quick but not hurried. He snips with scissors, buzzes with shears. Her hair comes into shape, all the disarray and mismatched lengths swiftly vanishing. Her hair will be short, feathered, stylish.

Alice's hair is not like Sissy's hair. Both are red, but Alice's is deep and dark, no lighter than thick wine even in direct sunlight. Sissy's head of red, on the other hand, was a strawberry hue. It was also wavy, abundant, lush, where Alice's is straight and much finer. The two have red hair, but they are not the same, not in any way. I must be careful not to compare them.

Dwight blow-dries away all the loose bits of hair. He daubs a bit of gel into her new tidy locks, causing the hair to stand up. It gives her a vaguely avian look. Dwight's own hair is a gaudy crest of purple, practically a plumage. He gives his latest job a final critical look, then nods solemnly to himself.

But he still asks me, "Well?"

I smile. To Alice I say, "You look lovely."

She looks back at me, blinking slowly. My compliments must mean nothing to her: they are mere indications that I am satisfied with her company.

As we leave the salon, I catch Dwight giving us a last glance. He sees my hand on her arm, guiding her out the door. Something flickers on his features. Not disgust. The opposite: as if to say if you're happy with her, why not enjoy yourself?

Yes. Why not, indeed?

* * *

I take her to my home. We engage in intercourse. It is rather varied tonight. I discover a reserve of stamina and let the session play out slowly, enjoying her this way and that way, delighted again that she comes repeatedly, her bodily pleasure unmistakable.

After, I get up to make dinner. As I chop vegetables and meat, it occurs to me that I haven't had sex three nights in a row in a long time. Even when I've been seeing someone steadily these last few years, I never scheduled three consecutive nights of sex play. I simply--and literally--haven't been up to it. I tell myself I haven't experienced much if any diminishment to my libido as my middle years overtake me, but that evidently is just the sort of bullshit middle-aged guys tell themselves. Of course my game has dropped off. Three nights in a row would have been easy for my thirty-year-old self. Hell, in the decade before that--say, in the era of Sissy Anspaugh-- three times a night was more like it.

So I let myself preen a little as I dump everything into the wok. The meat and veggies crackle noisily in the hot olive oil. Alice has woken me: out of my sleepwalking, out of my stupor. Her youth and beauty are the jolt I have needed, without knowing I have needed it.

She has in a way returned me to my own younger years, when I too was vital and vibrant. Before the human race was handed its extinction notice.

I call her when the meal is ready. She comes padding into the kitchen naked. A shock of raw desire takes the breath momentarily from my lungs. She sits at the table, utterly unself-conscious. Well, what the hell. If she wants to eat nude, let her.

I put her plate before her. I dig into my own portion, but I can't help eyeing her. Her exposed breasts are mesmerizing. Her haircut is extremely complimentary. At any time in my life this girl would have turned my head; I'm sure of it. I am not wrong to be so captivated by her.

"I'd like you to stay overnight here," I say.

She drinks some of the juice I have poured her. She says nothing because I haven't asked a question.

I clear my throat. "Will you stay the night?"

"Yes."

Under the terms of our verbal agreement she doesn't have much choice, but her answer sends a bright little thrill through me nonetheless. I have told myself it is too soon to have her sleeping over, and I can tell myself that again, but it will do no good. This thing finds its own momentum. We are underway, Alice and I. Our relationship will not be stopped, not before our month expires. A great deal, I truly realize for the first time, might transpire between us in that span.

I do not know where we will go. But I can't give her up. I cannot.

* * *

We lie next to one another in the dark. I will drive her to work tomorrow morning. I have asked if she needs to stop off at her home beforehand; she has said no.

When I turned off the light, we kissed a final time. The kiss didn't lead to anything else, but if I had again felt the urge and were able to summon the necessary tumescence, she no doubt would have accommodated me. I must remember that: she is only accommodating me. Even if, according to her, sex is necessary, she isn't necessarily interested in having it with me. Then again...who knows with a cold? One cock is much like another, in the end. Suddenly I wonder if there are queer colds. I recall that vaguely prejudicial hackneyed saw: homosexuality isn't a choice. I never liked that. Dig a little in that and what it's really saying is that if it were a choice, no one would choose it. Screw that idea. If someone actively decided to be gay, I would be all for it.

But a gay cold. Sexuality may or may not be a choice, but it seems there must be some emotion tied to it, something hardwired at the biological level. I look over at Alice. I can't see her in the dark, but she's there. What if she is a lesbian? I might be buying sexual favors from someone who has little to no use for my particular moving parts.

I hear her breathing. Her breaths haven't yet started to slow, to steady out.

"Alice. The other day, after I, uh, went down on you...why did you blow me?" I hadn't asked her to do it.

"'Cause I figured you wanted it. When you people do something, you usually want the same thing back."

I ask nothing else. My eyes are wide in the bedroom's darkness. It is a sensible answer she has given me, but that isn't what has so startled me. It is those words....

You people. It must be how she categorizes us in her mind. Perhaps all her brethren think the same way. Olds. You people. A separate kind. That is how they see us. Just as we see them as Other.

We do not nuzzle together in the bed, but I am aware of her presence alongside me throughout the night. Even when dreams come, she is still there.

CHAPTER TWENTY-SIX

Behind This Mortal Bone

An ineffable domestic sweetness arrives with the morning. We wake together to the alarm I have set. I tell Alice she can use the bathroom first, and when she gets out of the bed, I put my hand where she has lain and feel her lingering body heat.

I brew coffee, and when she comes into the kitchen--still undressed--I start to ask if she wants some; then: "Have you ever had coffee before?"

She shakes her head. She rubs a knuckle against her right eye, just like anyone waking a bit reluctantly in the morning. I try not to think of her as a child getting up for school. Her nakedness would make that unseemly. Then again, on some level the unseemliness of this whole situation is unavoidable.

But the cozy domesticity prevails. I pour her a cup of rich dark roast, explaining that it is a mild stimulant. She sips with caution. I go to have my shower, briefly toying with the idea of inviting her along. But that would spoil the illusion of sweetness. I find her company here in my home at this early hour a genuine pleasure.

Once I'm done, I tell her she should shower. Plainly this isn't part of her normal morning routine. Cleanliness is not a priority with her kind. Nonetheless she goes along. Obediently. I cannot entirely forget that she is essentially complying with my commands.

I make breakfast, and when she emerges, we eat at the kitchen table. She has dressed, but her short styled hair is damp. She looks gorgeous. I lead her back into the bathroom when we have finished and show her how to use the hair dryer.

I don't want to go to work. I don't want her to go. This scene is so very precious. I can imagine having her here, day and night.

But employment calls, for both of us. I solemnly promised that our arrangement wouldn't interfere with her job, and I must make good on that. So, off we go.

* * *

It strikes me suddenly: I am taking this too fast. I have slammed our relationship into a high gear, almost from the start. Three nights running we have had sexual intercourse. She was my overnight guest last night. I want her to stay over again tonight. I thirst for that. I long for it.

But...is it wise? Wise, even within the profoundly unwise framework of this prostitutional arrangement. I had envisioned taking this slower, letting my desire for her build. But she is so delectable, so very enticing.

I fear I will ruin it. I should stand witness to the rise of my own passions; I should savor the gradual experiences between us. This is a marathon, not a sprint. We have a month. Several of those days have been used up already, but many more are to come. I must make intelligent use of that time.

At the office I impulsively call Lester Crofft. He picks up immediately, like he has been waiting for me to contact him.

"Kyle," he says before I can speak. "I do hope this is good news."

I smile a little. "Well, if your offer a meal is still in effect..."

"Of course! What night do you like? Hell, I can lay out a lovely spread tonight. How about that, Kyle? Tonight. Come to the condo tonight!" He sounds almost childishly enthusiastic.

I am still in an impulsive mode. "Why not. Tonight, Lester." He gives me the time and place. I am not particularly looking forward to this, but it will serve as a distraction. I can pick up Alice after her work, buy her dinner, and tell her that tonight I have another engagement. I start to wonder if she will be disappointed, then roll my eyes at myself. Christ, am I ever going to fully realize I'm involved with a cold?

It will, I perceive, make me feel good on a certain level. I can show her that I have a social life, even if I really don't. Lester Crofft is an anomaly. After tonight I might not have contact with him for another two and a half years. Who knows?

I do my work. The office seems to move in slow motion around me. No one here knows about Alice. I can only guess how they would react. My superiors at the firm are a cautious conservative lot. They might even think my relationship with the girl to be unwholesome, deleterious, the kind of thing which could reflect poorly on the company. They might quietly take me aside one afternoon and with great grave ceremony tell me that I must terminate my dalliance.

I allow myself a chuckle. Let 'em fucking try.

* * *

The automated eatery is almost empty. I can't tell if the sterile industrial decor is meant to be ironic or not. Alice eats a stir-fry of vegetables and beef, while I nurse a cup of flavorless green tea. I have told her I will be visiting a friend tonight and so will drive her home when she is done dining. It has actually given me no pleasure to impart this news; I would rather be spending another night with her. But I promised Lester. And on some level I also recognize that this break is probably healthy for me.

On impulse--because this is, it seems, a day of impulsive behavior for me--I ask, "What is the date of your birth?"

She tells me, and I feel a twang of surprise. She is twenty years old, yes, as I suspected--knew--all along. But her birthday is amazingly close to The Line. She really was among the first colds. It is a wonder she didn't get snatched up as a secret test subject when the government broke all its own rules to try and find a cure for coldness.

I take a ruminative swallow of tea. "You're lucky to be alive, you know that?"

She says nothing. I have invalidated the question by including the word lucky. Colds don't have luck, good or bad.

I ask, "What do you think your life will be like when you're my age?" The question startles me. I haven't wondered this even in my own mind before.

She chews. She seems to do that invisible frown thing, an expressionless expression. "How old are you?"

"I'm forty." I am ready to restate the question. Now that it's been said, I'm quite curious about her answer, though I don't expect she'll really give me one.

"When I'm forty, I'll be forty." A Zen koan reply. From someone just a brief scattering of days older than her, the riposte would have been laced with snideness. But hers is more a computer's response, the only answer the data on hand will support.

But I can't seem to let this go. I press: "At age forty do you think you'll still be a bicycle messenger?" I'm asking her to forecast. It is probably a wasted effort. Prediction has an element of emotion to it, I would hazard.

"Unlikely," she says, and I am surprised yet again.

"Why not?"

"Tough job. Bodies wear out."

My God. She does think about the future, at least in these flat terms. I had come to believe colds lived only in the moment, reacting to events and their environment; nothing planned, nothing foreseen, not even the flagrant eventualities like aging.

Somehow it warms me to think she has even this much depth. I start to formulate more questions along this line. Maybe I can learn more of how she perceives the world.

But she says abruptly, "Are you tired of me?"

I blink. Does she understand the concept? Again, from another person, from an old of any age, this would be a charged question, particularly coming from a woman with whom I was involved. It was the sort of prickly question designed to set off a fight.

"What?" I say, stalling.

She doesn't repeat herself. She knows I heard her. I vacillate, which is ridiculous. I can't hurt her feelings.

But I dodge anyway. "Why would you ask me that?"

"You don't want me tonight."

"That's not true. I do want you. But I have this social obligation, is all...." I reach across the table and take her hand, squeezing it, as if that will convey my feelings, as if my feelings are things she can genuinely understand. I silent rebuke myself again. Well, my icer friend, this is what you signed on for when you began this.

I withdraw my hand, and she resumes eating. Strangely I feel we really have just had a fight--or at least a short snapping exchange. I'm both bewildered and amused. There is nothing in my dating history to prepare me for these circumstances. Yet instinct tells me to reassure her some more.

"I'm very attracted to you, Alice. Every moment we've spent together has been better than the last. I've even wondered if I am too caught up in you. But I care less and less about that. And more and more about just being with you."

She finishes her meal, but her eyes are on me the whole while. Her pretty face is as neutral as ever, but some--surely unreliable-- intuition informs me that I have said the right thing.

* * *

I feel a wrench when she gets out of the car, but the kiss we have just shared lingers on my lips. Why have I agreed to dinner with Lester when I could be taking this luscious young woman home with me? But it is too late to cancel. Lester deserves better than that. For whatever reason this meal seems to have some significance for him, and the thought of socializing with him isn't especially disagreeable, though I doubt I will make a habit of it. My days of having close friends are behind me. I make do with acquaintances.

Alice enters her building, and I pull reluctantly away. As I cross the city, the night streets are surreal. I pass a car burning at the curb; flames roll out through the glass-less windows, along with oily black smoke. Several onlookers watch at a distance. I assume one of them has called emergency services. No other vehicles are parked near the burning one. I'm left with no clue as to how the fire might have started.

A few blocks farther on a woman crosses the street in front of me. She is topless. Her breasts are ample, but she isn't as firm as Alice. Teeth gleam in a feral expression on her face. She appears like an animal on the prowl. Or in heat. I slow to make sure I don't come too close to her.

When I reach Lester's building, the sky opens up and rain cascades down. It is one of those huge sudden deluges, the sort of rainfall San Francisco rarely got when I was a boy. Now all kinds of eccentric weather conditions prevail. There were three straight days of snow two years ago. Unimaginable for the city, except that everything is now imaginable and possible. If locust swarmed the town, nobody would even blink.

Lester Crofft lives in one of the quasi-futuristic residence towers out toward the Bay Bridge. It is a soul-less black obelisk, gleaming in the night just like the topless woman's teeth. If Lester has a condominium here, it is an expensive one. Such structures used to house the tech boys of Silicon Valley. They were the city's aristocracy. But new ideas don't come out of Silicon Valley anymore. No one cares about research or innovation any longer. It will be enough if humanity can keep the lights on until it's so close to the end that it won't matter.

The tower has a good security system, and I am let through in due course. Belatedly I realize I haven't brought anything with me. A bottle of wine would have been appropriate. I have lost my socializing mojo, it seems. Well, screw it. Lester will have to make do with just the pleasure of my company. I go up in an absolutely soundless elevator which also conveys no sense of movement whatever.

Lester greets me at the condo door, and to my dismay I am immediately drawn into a smothering hug. Lester and I have never embraced before.

"Kyle! Kyle! How wonderful."

After a second's resistance I give in to the engulfment. Lester is a few inches taller than me and half again as heavy. Tonight his round face is lit with merriment. He finally ushers me inside. The condominium is spacious. The basic decor is chrome and mirrors, but he has evidently lavished all sorts of softening touches on the place: paintings, tapestries, lacquered furniture, plush pillows everywhere.

The air is warm with the smells of garlic, hot oil and spices I can't begin to classify. I look around the large living area, which abuts the open kitchen. One wall is a long sheet of reinforced window glass. The rain spatters frantically there, but this place feels like a protected aerie, safe from any storm.

Lester pours me a glass of wine, tells me to make myself comfortable on a great slab of a couch. He asks about the office. It is a fertile enough topic to keep the conversation going awhile. Many of the people he worked with are still at the firm. It's harmless gossip. I still don't know why he has invited me here; but the wine is tasty, and the cooking aromas are pleasant, foretelling a sumptuous meal.

In the kitchen Lester bustles about. He too is drinking wine, and I would guess this isn't his first glass. But he is jovial, almost vehemently so. When he laughs, which is frequently, it is a roaring guffaw.

By the time I finish my wine, I have resigned myself to whatever is happening here. Recent years have plainly de-socialized me. If the world were still the world which I knew as a boy and young man, I would worry about my isolation. But the cold have come, and the world is bent nearly out of all recognition; and detaching myself seems a useful response to my environment.

Lester cheerfully refills my glass. What the hell. The rental can drive me home. I am feeling real pangs of appetite. Normally I would have eaten by now, one of my unadventurous meals, prepared quietly at home. Hunger builds as Lester continues to clang about with pots and utensils. It becomes vaudevillian: a sketch about the extravagant meal that never arrives, leaving the guest to starve.

Just as I am growing genuinely impatient, he delivers armloads of bowls and plates to a massive expanse of dining table. I come when I am summoned. The spread is staggering, a Roman feast. I won't be able to consume a tenth of it. There are two elaborate meat dishes, several mounds of vegetables, all of it seemingly saturated in butters and sauces. Lester lifts his glass. "To friends dining together!" Again: what the hell. I drink to the occasion, caught up in it as I am.

The food is superb and unconscionably rich. If Lester eats like this regularly, it is no wonder his fiftyish body is so stocky. I indulge myself, taking helpings of food glazed with exotic flavors. Every mouthful is an epicurean delight. I eat more than I expected to, and when I finally can't lift another forkful, I am in a warm stupor.

We retire to the living area. The rain is still coming down, a deluge. There will be flooding in parts of the city. Lester produces an embossed snuff box of marijuana and proceeds to load an ornate pipe. He asks if I mind, if I would like some. I say no to both questions. Even in college in Humboldt County, a traditional region for marijuana agriculture, I never got into the swing of pot. It lifted and dilated my thoughts, whereas if anything I wanted to quiet my mind, burdened as it was with absorbing the complexities of economy and finance.

Lester sucks in the smoke in the timeworn manner. He is still as jolly as when I walked in the door, but there is still that underlying manic quality to his cheerfulness. I sink back in the cushions and sip wine from the new bottle he has opened. I get the sense we might soon arrive at the purpose of all this. And suddenly I am convinced there is a purpose, something ulterior.

He relaxes from his first few puffs. Lester Crofft, more successful than I, as evinced by the costly trappings of his home. Had the old world continued in its customary vein, I would envy him. Even his name is more sensible than mine. Kyle Norris has a faint ring of frivolity about it. Lester Crofft conveys reliability and maturity.

I realize I am breathing in the secondhand smoke.

"Say, Kyle. Do you ever think about...dying? About death?"

I gaze at him a moment. "One cannot avoid thinking about such things." My answer is cautious to the point of cowardice. But the question has made me instantly wary.

Lester grins. Or more precisely he shows his teeth; this, I see, isn't a grin. "It's on my mind. A lot. I feel...tenuous. Do you understand that feeling, Kyle?"

"It comes with being mortal." I try to put a little English on it, spin some drollery into my reply.

He doesn't respond to it. "I'm serious. I'm very, very serious. Even right this second...I feel like my life force could just end. I could snuff out like a candle."

"Are you feeling unwell? Have you seen a doctor?" Now I'm trying to be reasonable; but I sense the brink he is on, see the mortal terror in his eyes now. The dark round face is pinched with fear.

"I've been examined," he says with a dismissive wave. "My health is more than acceptable for a man my age and weight. That's not the point."

"What is the point, then?" I don't want to have this discussion, but the only way out of it may be through it. Besides, this man fed me like a prince this evening. I can listen to his troubles. For a little while, anyway.

He sucks in more smoke, but it doesn't mellow him. His agitation is growing, if anything. "It's this. If the cold can come as they have, then how do we trust anything? Any norm. Any law of physics, even. I am healthy, according to medical science. Sure, I should eat less, get more exercise. But my organs, I'm assured, are all in fine fettle. I'm not due for a stroke or an aneurysm. I can expect to live for a good number of years. But what is that good number? In twenty years I'll be well into my seventies. That is dangerously old. That is the age of fragility, of disrepair, of decay. And I have no guarantee that I will even reach it. I am tentative, Kyle. I am momentary. In the pit of my stomach there is fear. My heart beats, and I am intensely aware of those beats. And each one might be my last. Such a delicate machine, the heart. Durable, yes, a wonder of physiology. But I could squeeze it in my hand and make it cease. So I am breakable, extremely fucking breakable. What if my breathing stops? Just...stops. It's an involuntary function, but it doesn't entirely feel automatic, does it? You can, after all, hold your breath. Perhaps my body will decide on its own to shut down my lungs. I am so very conscious of the air that I breathe. There are pangs and aches and tiny spasms in me. Any one at any moment might herald the coming of true bodily calamity. My anatomy is set for a spell of riot, to garble a James Joyce quote. And think of death itself. The ending. The absolute finality of it. All lives will one day quit. Death is a yawning abyss, gobbling us one by one. Have you thought on death, Kyle, really thought? Our bodies, no longer functioning. Our brains, without electricity. Our memories just so much dead synaptic goo, never to be revived. People might remember us when we die. You, for instance, just might remember me after death has claimed my being, but my consciousness will be forever lost. I. Will. End. It is so terrible an idea. A sadistic truth. And it could happen at any time, any goddamn second....Oh...oh..."

He doesn't cry. I think he is past weeping. The mortal dread has enveloped him. He is a pitiable sight, seated across from me, mounded into the chair, pot pipe forgotten in his hand, face twisted with fright. There is nothing I can say to comfort him. I think he knows this as well.

We all die, Lester. We are all transient. Everyone realizes this on the profound level eventually. Curiously I was more acutely aware of my mortality when I was seventeen than I am now. I felt some version of the fear he feels. It was a consuming thing, but I managed to move beyond it. Maybe the vitalities of youth helped.

And maybe in ten or twelve years I too will be like Lester, eaten alive by thoughts of death.

He does make one lucid point, though: in a world where there are the cold, how can we rely on anything?

I sit there in his living room, in the fractured silence into which he has descended, and listen to the rain as it baptizes the whole city.

CHAPTER TWENTY-SEVEN
A Night Full of Rain

Norris drank too much that night. Lester Crofft's ramblings on his personal mortality had of course soured the evening, but both men carried on after a fashion, digesting the ample meal and swilling more of Lester's fine wine. Norris asked about his former co-worker's social life. Was he seeing anyone romantically? It seemed a relatively safe topic. What Norris was curious about was if Lester had anybody else to talk to about these matters. Did he have a friend, a confidant, or had he unearthed Norris as a last resort, calling him in like a reliever late in the game?

Lester, having unburdened himself, appeared drained. But he kept up the pretense that Norris himself was trying to maintain: that this was still a benign social occasion, a dinner between onetime close associates. Lester made mention that he was currently between romantic attachments but implied that he had a wide and varied social circle. Perhaps he had already run through his obsessively morbid diatribe with all those others.

"How about yourself, Kyle? Seeing anybody?"

Norris' head swam with the wine. The rain was still coming down. He gazed off into the distance. "Yes. Her name is Alice. She's...much younger than me." A corner of his mouth curled in a mischievous smile. Lester had made him uncomfortable with his self-indulgent tirade about mortality. Norris could similarly unsettle him, most likely.

"Alice. Pretty name."

"A pretty girl."

"Is she--"

"She's a cold."

Lester didn't react. After a moment he reached for the pot pipe and loaded the fancy contraption of royal blue ceramic with a fresh plug of weed. He drew meditatively on it. Finally in a neutral voice he asked, "Just how young is she?"

"Twenty."

"Well, at least she's legal age." He breathed out a blue plume. "What is she like?" There seemed to be no edge, no judgment in the question.

Norris wondered at himself. He obviously hadn't planned to blurt out anything about Alice. But now that he had spoken, he felt the urge to follow through. "She's dynamic in bed. Fiercely orgasmic."

Lester's brows lifted. His head tilted at a wry angle. "I wouldn't have thought that."

"Her body is like any other--except, of course, she's young and ravishing. What I mean is her physiology is what you'd expect from any healthy female old."

"But...her emotions?"

"She has no emotions." Norris said this bluntly, though it wasn't anything Lester wouldn't know, naturally.

"Then how do you relate to each other?"

"She answers my questions when I ask them, though her replies can be a little cryptic sometimes."

"But, uh, how did this relationship start between you?"

The smile returned more forcefully to Norris. He had come this far....."I am paying her rent on the condition that she be my companion for one month."

This time Lester's round face showed surprise. "Well," was all he managed.

There. Norris had now unburdened himself. He certainly hadn't felt any confessional impulses when he had arrived at the stylish condominium, but there was a strange grim relief at having disclosed this information to another person. He wasn't carrying on in secret with the girl, after all. But now he had declared what he was doing. It made it realer somehow.

He studied Lester, pitying the man some. Here he sat, listening fearfully to every gurgle and groan from his own body, dreading an inevitability which might indeed be decades in the future. Something in the absoluteness of death had poisoned him. It would likely continue to rob him of whatever vitality and pleasure his life might yet hold for him. He was a participant in his own deathwatch.

"Kyle..." Lester set down the pipe with a thoughtful look on his features. "Do you have feelings for the girl? For this Alice?"

Something caught in Norris' throat. He struggled a moment to clear it, so that his voice came out strained; but his words were resolute: "I feel for her. I can't help but."

* * *

The rental car, in self-drive mode, took him home. He felt foolish sitting in the seat, grinning helplessly and inanely at the passing cityscape. He would have a hangover tomorrow. What a bizarre night this had been. It was entirely possible he would never hear from Lester Crofft, not ever again. Both men had divulged something deeply personal, even precious, and the mutual knowledge might be too potent for them to ever face one another once more. But it didn't much matter. The present world was painted in meaningless colors, built on aimless beams, and it was a great labor to attach significance to anything.

Yet...Alice mattered. Of all the pieces of the world, the twenty year old cold had substance for him. She was the being around whom his existence was coalescing. He wanted her. He wanted her tonight. And he was nearly drunk enough to order the car to her housing unit, so to fetch her back to Potrero Hill. His bed would be lonely this night.

But he retained sufficient restraint to let the vehicle ferry him all the way home. He stumbled out into the rain and staggered up the line of lavender paving stones. He hung onto the door frame a moment before finally gaining access. The apocalyptic downpour had fairly soaked him, and he wondered if he would succumb to a cold as well as a hangover.

"What if I get a cold?" Norris asked the empty rooms of his

home. Again he grinned idiotically, disgusted by his own drunken behavior but for the moment helpless to it. "What if I get a cold?" he repeated. "Oh, wait! I've already got one!"

His laughter rang hollowly. He was glad Alice wasn't here to see him in this state.

CHAPTER TWENTY-EIGHT

When Tears Come No More

There once was a boy named Kyle, who was uncertain of his feelings.

He knew he was equipped with emotions. He knew which ones he was experiencing when they were upon him. Some cartoons made him laugh; a ghost story or even the dark of his room got him scared; he'd been angry and bored and sad, and understood those feelings when he was in the midst of them.

But he wasn't always certain they were the right emotions. More to the point: his feelings didn't always seem strong enough. So, maybe he was doing something wrong.

His early classmates and boyhood chums appeared ferocious in their emotional states to him. Sometimes the intensity of their likes and dislikes dismayed him--which was itself an emotion but a strangely muted one, almost contemplative in nature. (These were not the words in his vocabulary. Kyle was somewhat precocious but not obnoxiously so.) He often felt his feelings didn't measure up. It wasn't just the expression of those feelings, he gradually came to understand. It was the sentiments themselves. He felt, but he felt...cautiously. Stingily, perhaps. Emotional energy was not an unlimited resource within him, he sensed; so he spent it judiciously. He might chuckle but not bray with laughter. A given moment might call for him to be afraid, but he refrained from cowering or whimpering or biting his fingernails in the exaggerated way in movies. Such displays struck him on some level as undignified.

There were no obvious reasons for his curtailed behavior. Both his parents were warm and open. The extended family of cousins, who showed up sometimes on holidays, was equally affectionate. Young Kyle was doted on by elders who dutifully pinched his cheeks and ruffled his hair and declared themselves delighted to see him. His responses to these overtures were, generally, tepid.

He wasn't hostile. He just couldn't seem to find the same emotional frequency to which most others appeared to be tuned. So he went through motions and mimicked and tried to give himself feelings by exhibiting all the surface behavior he saw around him. He felt awkward doing it--but not terribly awkward. He couldn't summon even that intensity.

As a young teen he lost the ability to cry. Tears simply wouldn't come anymore, no matter the provocation. Nothing in the real world was sufficiently tragic enough to induce weeping in him. Tear-jerking films and television shows stirred him more than reality but still not enough to actually provoke a single tear.

His very patient mother would call him on all this one day. She would utter a hurtful string of words which would stay with him for the rest of his days, words he didn't try to refute.

When he became an adult and went away to college, he would eventually encounter true sorrow, what would become the central tragedy of his life. But even then--even then--it wasn't enough. It wasn't of adequate strength to tear out all his wiring. He was hurt by what happened, yes; but he was also numbed by it, and that desensitization was a more familiar response than outright grief, and so he embraced it instead, and he returned to San Francisco after school a hollowed out automaton. More sophisticated than before. Better abled in the mimicry which allowed him to, say, build a better relationship with his parents than he'd had before.

But these were still emotions half felt, sentiments not given their free rein. Because Kyle didn't know how to do all that. As a man he was still something of the boy who was uncertain of his feelings.

CHAPTER TWENTY-NINE

Lovers

She is my lover. She's also my faithful dinner companion. There is an intimacy we share, whether or not Alice can feel it. The physicality of sex and supping is real.

We converse over meals and before and after intercourse. I have learned how to ask her things--how not to, really. Carefully I avoid any emotional values. I don't inquire into her feelings about any matter, because there will be no feelings. But I am able to coax responses from her which transcend the robotic. She tells me things about her life, where she shops for food, how many designs of bicycle she looked at before purchasing her lightweight foldable model. I try to probe deeper, hoping for insight into her decision processes. She does not want things. She needs them--food, clothing--and obtains them. The fast bike gives her job security, so she can continue to earn money and thereby buy her necessities.

But for this month she also works for me, in a sense. Well...more than in a sense. Remember, creep. You bought this girl.

When I want her to do things, I have also learned to frame my words so they sound more like suggestions. This is surely more to assuage my own discomfort. Ordering her about like a lackey would bring me no pleasure. I am with a cold, but I wish the trappings of a normal emotional relationship. And so I maintain these little pretenses.

I plan for the coming weekend. I can't remember when I last so looked forward to free time. We will go out of the city. It will be an adventure.

Meanwhile I pick her up after her work. We dine, then I take her home, where she stays overnight. I can't imagine not having her in my bed now. No longer do I feel pointless caution; this isn't moving too fast; it is in implacable motion, and I will ride with it to the end. I relish the moments. I enjoy her easy nudity in my house. I like holding her in the night. We do that now, in bed, nestling like love mates. Sometimes the feel of her arouses me in the small hours, and we quickly and efficiently consummate.

I continue to observe her, noting the little things. It is no surprise that she doesn't wear makeup. Neither does she shave any body hair. None of this bothers me. I have changed her hygiene habits, at any rate. She now starts each day with a shower. She is also already in the habit of brushing her teeth. This is a maintenance matter no doubt. She means to preserve her physical self. Good teeth facilitate eating; eating sustains life. One logical point leads to another.

The cold aren't smarter than us. Studies have shown this. A lack of emotion doesn't boost intellect, it seems. But Alice appears bright to me. She has demonstrated analytic capability. She excels at her job. Granted, she is only a bike messenger, but there is probably not a better one at Sherwood Messengers. She can't be proud of this fact, but I can be proud for her.

On Friday, with another workweek behind us, I take her to one of the automated eateries we have frequented. My mind is racing with thoughts of the weekend. Across the table she methodically devours a plate of calamari as I gaze rapturously at her, oblivious to anything else.

This proves to be a mistake. We aren't alone in the restaurant, and I belatedly realize that the mutterings registering on the fringes of my hearing have been decidedly hostile.

My spell is broken when a voice calls out, "Like it on the chilly side, do you?" Ugly laughter follows. The voice isn't alone. I turn and see three males sitting together. Two look large, certainly bigger than me. All three are younger, but all are olds. And they don't like the spectacle of me dining with the girl, apparently.

"Aren't you afraid your dick'll freeze off?" More laughing, laced with cruelty and menace. Perhaps these men work construction jobs. It will be no contest if they decide to come over to me. I fear for myself, yes; but worse is my fear of what they might do to Alice. I lock eyes with her, get ready to tell her we need to bolt out of here.

She turns toward the corner table where the three men sit. Loudly she says, "He fucks me better than any of you limp pricks could ever manage!"

The trio freezes, sharing the same stunned expression. Then as one they erupt into laughter, a different sort of laughing, the self-effacing kind. They'd gotten it wrong: the old guy wasn't with a cold; she must be one of the extreme young-olds, just this side of The Line.

I hide my own expression of shock. She did not speak like a cold just now. There was mockery in her tone. She even wore something of a scowl on her face.

She defused the situation. Some part of me still wants to flee the place, but pride--hell, honor--seems to demand that we stay and finish our meals at our own pace.

The three toughs are done before we are, and they troop past our table, chuckling. One of them winks lewdly at me, probably envious that I'm laying so young a thing.

You should be envious, asshole. The thought feels triumphal.

* * *

I wake beside her. Sleep hasn't come easily for me. My mind is busy, and that excitement has even invaded my dreams. The weekend! At last!

I slip out of bed and make coffee. She has coffee in the mornings now. I will make us a light breakfast to follow. We can snack in the car as we travel.

She wakes around nine. Showers. Comes out for coffee. Bare padding feet, bare gleaming body. I smile at her. I am still amazed at how she behaved at the eatery last evening. Survival mode. She must have perceived the threat the three men posed. She diagnosed the situation, understanding what was making them so upset. She then defused everything by mimicking an old. Acting. Acting. It is one more function I wouldn't have thought a cold capable of demonstrating. It seems to involve too many abstract layers. Yet I saw it happen. She is extraordinary. She must be extraordinary.

"I have something for you," I say. She follows me into the bedroom, and I lay out the clothes I have bought for her. They are stylish. They are brightly colored. They are new. I have included an array of panties. Up to now she hasn't worn undergarments, and I am not quite equal to the task of explaining how or even why a woman might wear a brassiere. But her breasts are high and tight and in no need of support.

She looks to me. "Which do you want me to wear?"

I shrug. "It's up to you."

She turns back to the bed. She takes up the closest pair of panties, steps into them. She reaches for a fashionably cut pair of jeans, also the nearest at hand. I figure she'll put on the first top her hand finds, that this apparel is all equal and thereby indistinct. But she pauses, and I watch, startled and pleased, as her green eyes tick back and forth for several seconds. She is deciding. I wonder how she is deciding.

When she takes up a top in purple and gold stripes, I gasp silently. The panties and jeans are the same hue; the top's colors are a nice compliment. Is it mere coincidence that she chose so?

"Why'd you pick those?" I can't help but ask.

She answers immediately, "To please you."

"Me?" It is a vapid response, and she says nothing. I regroup. "Why do you think those particular clothes would please me?" I am saying please, an emotional term, but she has used it first. Perhaps she can navigate it when it is not being applied to her.

She doesn't shrug, but some subtle shift in her stance makes me think she has. "I see how you dress."

It seems all the explanation I'm going to get. I examine her words and find worth in them. She has observed my own color combinations. She chose according to the palette she has seen on me. Remarkable. This is a basic grasp of aesthetics, I think. I, evidently, prefer certain tones and blends, and she has imitated these. Her attempts to please me are logical. This relationship is beneficial to her. She won't do anything to upset it.

You've got her trained well, creep. Congratulations.

But the buoyancy of the day won't be denied. It feels like a holiday to me, a boyhood one, where travels out of the city seemed like exotic excursions to wondrous lands. I have gotten a travel bag for Alice's new things, along with toiletries. After our quick bite to eat I take the bags out to the car. It is a gray and grim July day in San Francisco, but today we are leaving the city, and the places to which we are journeying may indeed be as wild and romantic as the boy in me is anticipating.

* * *

It has been some time since I have been outside the city. Longer still since I've driven any distance with another person in the vehicle. It stirs memories: a few relatively long distance road ventures with my parents; later, excursions with friends at college. School break road trips, a carful of gleeful howling maniacs looking to blow off steam. There had been youthful magic in those jaunts.

Sissy and I once drove up over the Oregon border one weekend. No reason. Neither of us had been over that particular state line, and it was something to do, a way to share time together. I remember the windows down, her hair blowing. She drove, and I grinned at her practically the whole way....

Alice sits in the passenger seat in her new clothes. I have explained that these are a gift to her, that nothing further is required of her for them. She has not said thank you, but I wouldn't have expected it from her, of course.

She looks good in the outfit. With the haircut she is not so obviously a cold, though the cast of her eyes has the telltale remoteness and her expression never really changes. I've picked up Highway 1, the coastal road. The day has become bright now that we have left San Francisco behind. She wears her sunglasses. She seems to be looking out at the coastal scenery, which is quite lovely.

I don't play the radio, content with the electric thrum of the car. The driving engages me, a physical operation, almost athletic after so many trips in self-drivers. A few people in oncoming vehicles gaze curiously at me.

About fifteen miles south of where we started the road locks up, half a dozen cars in a still line; ahead, a California Highway Patrol vehicle, rollers on, siren quiet. There is an ambulance on the scene as well. No urgent activity. We wait. Soon enough an oversized rescue drone lifts into view, having been down among the rocks of the long cliffside which falls toward the frothy swells of the Pacific. The red hovering vehicle carries a long rubbery sack in its collecting arms. I don't need to ask what has happened. I only wonder where the person left the car.

I turn to the passenger seat. "Do you know what that is?" She doesn't answer; I haven't been specific enough. I might mean the drone, the police vehicle, anything. "The black bag. Do you know what it contains?"

"Can't see inside," she says.

"No, you can't. But it's only used to bear one thing. Can you deduce what that is?" It is a little like a macabre version of the license plate game I remember playing as a kid: a fun road diversion. Say, kiddo, can you guess what's in that body-sized bag?

The wash from the rotors blows grit over the waiting cars, but nobody honks a horn or demonstrates any sort of impatience. The solemnity is almost palpable.

"Person?" Alice says, but she speaks without her usual flat certainty, and so it does sound like a question.

"What kind of person?" I encourage her.

She pulls off the sunglasses. Her gaze goes to the ambulance. "Hurt. Or dead."

Now the drone's arms are lowering the bag, and the med techs are taking it. They bundle it into the rear of the ambulance, and a few more minutes elapse as they no doubt confirm that the body is indeed lifeless. I am grateful they do this out of sight, having no desire to see the battered and broken corpse. It's a hell of a drop down the rocky face.

The ambulance and CHP cruiser pull out together. Our little line of traffic resumes. I say, "That person almost certainly committed suicide. By jumping."

She is silent. I haven't asked her anything.

I continue to navigate us down the coast road, heading south. "People kill themselves more often than they used to. Do you know why that is?" She has intelligence. She can figure things out. Has anybody tried to talk to a cold like this--really tried? Perhaps my relationship with her has a deeper purpose. Maybe I will fathom the colds better through all our intimacies.

"My kind doesn't commit suicide." Curt, decisive statement.

The phrase sends a small shock through me, something cool and tingly. My kind. It is like when she referred to olds as you people. She knows full well, then, that we are two separate breeds of being. We might as well be different species.

What she has said is doubtlessly true: colds don't kill themselves. Suicide is a decidedly emotional act. But that she has said this so definitively is in part what has chilled me. It is almost as if there are rules for the cold, known to them all. They don't kill themselves. And if there can be rules, then it might follow that there is, after all, an agenda. They may have a collective plan, a broad blueprint for the future, which is, of course, a cold future. One where the olds are gone. We will age and die, or else helpfully off ourselves in a variety of ways, clearing the planet for cold domination.

The cliff jumper back there...that old just gave away a tiny piece of this world to the heartless children.

* * *

Santa Cruz is the destination, and we arrive in relatively short order. Summer is in effect here, true Californian summertime. The sun beats down, brightening the buildings. The ocean smells different here, with a tropical undertone. Things seem in good repair, except for the streets, which are buckling. They are buckling in San Francisco as well. And in St. Louis, Pensacola, Trenton; and surely in Paris, undoubtedly in Johannesburg, reliably in Frankfurt. All the streets, slowly giving way. We can't seem to mix up the tar fast enough anymore, nor find those to slather it into place.

I check us into a motel that is on the seamy side but which appears deserted, though still operational. An ancient crone in reading glasses pushes a key across the counter, gawping in wonder. I don't think it is Alice's presence that disconcerts her. She is just surprised that anyone has stopped in here. People don't travel much, not recreationally.

The room is dusty, tidy, passable. I suggest/command to Alice that she change into the swimsuit I included among her gifts. She does so, while I get into a pair of trunks, a T-shirt and sandals. She puts on a denim skirt as well. I have told her where we are going, and I know she will not feel the same rush of joy I experienced as an eight- and nine-year-old when my parents would take me down to the Santa Cruz Beach Boardwalk.

I drive us there. Of course the seaside amusement park isn't what it was. The venerable roller coaster still stands, but it was taken out of service years ago. The broad boardwalk is mostly empty, but here and there a few tanned olds stroll, usually in pairs. There are still attractions: a couple of thrill rides, a miniature golf course. Vendors sell hot dogs because the setting seems to demand it.

Alice puts her sunglasses back on. I should get her a better pair. The lenses of these are scratched. I walk with my arm around her. She leans into me. "What's that on your hip?"

I clipped it on at the motel. She must not have seen. "It's a shockstik." I purchased it this past week, having in mind the near-incident with the three burly males at the automated eatery. You can't obtain guns anymore, so an electrified baton is the next best thing. I have never owned one before. "Don't worry," I add. "I'm not expecting trouble." Stupid words. I have just told a cold not to worry. And trouble will come if it so wishes.

The Beach Boardwalk is more museum than carnival these days, it seems. But it doesn't dampen my mood. I am enjoying myself. The sun's warmth is pleasant. The promenade goes on some distance, a ticky-tacky array of leftover recreations, a family-friendly park gone to seed.

It abuts a wide swath of beach, naturally, and I lead her down onto it. She walks better on the sand this time, in her own pair of flip flops. This isn't like Ocean Beach in San Francisco. The breeze is fragrant and warm. Others are out here on the sands as well. Saturday at the beach, a timeworn Santa Cruz tradition. I receive one hostile look. It comes from an oiled, muscled male, not much younger than me; one of those middle-aged olds who has put all his life's energies into sculpting his physique. I have no doubt he could break me in two, but the shockstik on my hip, under my T-shirt, would alter the outcome of any contest between us. I am glad when he doesn't rise and stride after us but merely spits contemptuously into the sand.

Down near the water she drops her skirt, and we wade out into the water. It's not a swim. I hold her hands, feeling her sway and reel with the gentle movements of the surf. The water is tepid. Here is yet another experience she might not otherwise have had if not for me. I gaze at her face, at the sunlit highlights in her hair. Nameless emotions move within me; or maybe not so nameless. I am touched by her. I have arranged this whole scenario--the dynamic of lovers frolicking at the beach--and I cannot help but to respond as if it were, on some level, real. Real in that her hands in mine meant attachment; real in that she would gaze back at me with fondness and desire; real in the sense that this isn't all forgery.

We only go out up to our mid-thighs. The shockstik is waterproof, but I wouldn't know how to teach her to swim. So we hold hands and dance in the careening waters. And I grin, and she does not.

Later we will return to the motel. Sex will ensue. She will have her mechanical ecstacies. I will empty myself of pent-up lust. I have my contraceptive pills with me, of course. Someone at my office, in casual conversation, once remarked to me that such pills made him feel "unmanly." It seemed such a throwback attitude that I couldn't stop myself from countering with: "Would bringing a cold child into this world enlarge your masculinity enough?"

But before we return to the hotel, I will take her out to a meal. And before that we return to the boardwalk. I take her on the merry-go-round. It must be utterly senseless to her, traveling in a literal circle atop an artificial horse. But let her have the experience anyway. I am giddy with the summer heat, with the blaze of sunshine and the bracing stench of sea air.

One last thing before we quit the park. The haunted house ride. It scared me as a boy, though I tried to hide my fear. This time I face it bravely. Alice and I ride in the clattering little fiberglass car, her thigh pressed against mine. The place is filled with all the shopworn fake horrors. Monsters pop out at us. The tunnels ring with tinny screams of terror. These are probably the same props from my boyhood, eternally springing from their niches to frighten willing park-goers.

But something new is at the end of the ride. It has to be new. As our car rattles on its track toward the exit, a final horror appears. It isn't a ghoul, not a vampire leaping from its coffin. It is a boy and a girl, realistic mannequins both. Children. They merely stand there, in full view, of the same height, staring straight at us as we pass.

Their faces are expressionless. Their eyes are dead. They are a pair of colds.

CHAPTER THIRTY

Her Home is on the Deep

I get us back to San Francisco around three, Sunday afternoon. The rains haven't come back, but the gray sky is thick and the city has a sodden feel to it.

Sleep was a coquettish tease with me last night. In our amenably cruddy motel room in Santa Cruz, Alice fell asleep readily after our spirited session of physical passion. I expected to slide easily into a cottony unconsciousness as well; but that didn't happen. Instead, my mind set itself to wandering and wondering. I recognized this mental state. It was a limbo, one where I wouldn't be able to quiet my brain enough for slumber, but also one where nothing would come of my brooding. I would solve no riddles, reach no conclusions. I had suffered from this same condition my first year away at school, when I realized on a true gut level how strenuous my studies were, how adult a version of an educational institution the university was, as opposed to the low-stakes arena of high school. For weeks, even months, I questioned whether or not I could actually be a college student. And so my exhausted mind kept me awake into the small hours, vexing me with these worries but providing no solutions for my situation, other than the drably obvious: knuckle down, focus, study harder.

In that motel bed, lying alongside the somnolent naked girl, I pondered different matters, of course. I wondered about Alice. About her status as a cold. Not a very original line of contemplation, granted; every day every old on the planet probably thought about the colds to one degree or another. There was no escaping them. But now I had a nearer perspective. I was closer to a cold than I had ever expected to be. Surely my intimacies with this girl gave me some measure of insight, even if my observations were strictly mechanical. I knew she used the bathroom. I had given her a taste for coffee. It wasn't that she liked coffee now; it was likely that she found the stimulation helpful.

I could almost picture her folding her caffeine habit into the course of her normal workday. Stopping off at a kiosk. Standing in line with a bunch of downtown olds, who would be looking askance and scandalously at one another. Placing her order at the counter. Would she leave a tip, as she'd seen me do?

But what was simmering rather uselessly in my head was a broad question: what comprised cold culture? Was it a culture? Culture required shared experiences. Surely the colds had that. They also had suffering and beleaguerment, ingredients which seemed quite significant to making a rich cultural stew. But I couldn't say if that were enough. The cold were unique. They were beings stripped of all emotional workings. Cold culture would never celebrate a day of observance each year, marking some momentous event or honoring some individual, because colds wouldn't celebrate. It was unthinkable. And what event could be sufficiently meaningful? In order for something to possess meaning, it must first be felt. And who could the holiday's honoree possibly be? There could be no cold heroes, could there? The colds could esteem no one. Therefore, they could elevate no one to heroic stature.

But I wondered at how deep that went. It was like peering into a stygian chasm. If one knew a single cold, it might be that one knew them all. Lacking emotional capacity, they might default to a baseline sameness, where individual variations were so slight as to be insignificant.

Yet...there I lay beside a single cold. She was my lover. We had our own shared experiences. I had just given her Santa Cruz, the ocean once more, that ride through the fright house.

So, my musings went nowhere and served only to rob me of an hour or two of sleep. I took a more direct route back to the city, eschewing the coast road.

Now the gloam of summer fogginess saps a little more of my poise and energy. I'm tempted to switch the rental over to self-drive in the city, so to deliver us back to Potrero Hill. But a thought occurs. I have wondered about her culture, if one exists.

"Alice, I'd like to see your living space. Do you have any objection?" It is the roundabout way I have with her, the desires I express without making them explicit demands.

She doesn't respond. Silence has come to mean acquiescence. Perhaps the notion of her objecting is too emotionally charged for her to make comment. So I wend us through the city, to the quarter of the cold. The row of loveless metaceramic structures. I park at the crumbling curbstone.

She seems to move a little jerkily as she gets out. Surely I am imagining it. She bangs shut the car door with more force than needed. A muscular miscalculation, nothing more. Surely.

I follow as she crosses toward the nearest building. As we approach, I see the dismal swirls of gray which go into the overall coloring. I note too how the skin is blistered in patches. Truly, a cheap construction job. These outer walls probably went up in a day.

She thumbs the scanner and elicits an approving ding. The door is narrow. I step through sideways, expecting something wider beyond. But the constriction persists down a scarcely lit corridor, past a double row of doorways. The doors are spaced impossibly close together. They can't indicate individual quarters.

I halt behind her at one such door. This building's interior reminds me of the choked dimensions of a submarine. She opens the door without touching the scanner inset beside it; maybe it's broken; maybe she doesn't lock her interior door. I'll ask her when we are inside her space.

But stepping within, my gut clenches. I can't quite believe what I am seeing. I have a closet in my home that is bigger than this entire place. The unit is perhaps four strides long and two wide. My head brushes the ceiling. Cabinets line the uppermost part of the side walls. Lower, on the right, is a cooking rig: basically an old-fashioned hot plate; a tiny sink is alongside. A lone light hums overhead. There are no furnishings. Where is the bed? Where is the toilet?

Alice taps the cabinets. "Clothes," she says, the rasp somewhat more prominent just now. "Food." Indicating a cooled larder. "Bathroom," she says and bends to yank a contraption out of the wall on squealing wheels. It barely qualifies as a toilet; more like the waste bucket they might give a prisoner, though there is plumbing attached. "Bed," she adds, as she toggles something in the floor with her foot. A bubblebed starts to rise, hissing and swelling. She lets it expand enough so that I see it will eventually take up two-thirds of her area. Then she toggles it back down. She points to a hook at the far end. "That's where I hang my bike."

She faces me. She has volunteered all this. I am still awash with sickening surprise. This is how the cold live--the lucky ones, the independent ones, the ones with gainful employment who have left the federal camps. And this is what I am paying for. A month's rent on this...this box.

She waits without waiting, standing there, leaving the next words or action to me. She isn't ashamed of her home. Because she can't be. And yet something seems to stir in her green eyes. There is the faintest trace of a vexed gleam present. I have forced my way in here, and she doesn't want me here. Her displeasure is like an emanation, and I can feel it pushing me back out the doorway.

But I am just imagining this. I am reading what isn't there, because of my own guilt, which is suddenly quite acute, as it was when this first started between us, this thing, this arrangement, this relationship. And now you're here, creep. You've invaded her home. Does all this turn you on? Why not kick on the bubblebed and give her a jolly bounce right here. Right here!

"Thank you for showing me," I mutter, ducking out. Fleeing the scene. The corridor strangles me as I hurry down it.

* * *

I cook us dinner that evening, but it is just opening cans and heating the contents on my stovetop. We don't talk as we eat. I can't seem to summon even the pretense of conversation. I don't ask her if she deliberately leaves her living unit unlocked. Maybe no cold would steal from another. Maybe she knows there is nothing of value to take. Her bicycle--the only costly item she possesses--is always with her.

But I don't ask. I don't wish to speak of her living space. I remember when those structures were first proposed. There was a great deal of hue and cry, of course. This is San Francisco. Our first impulse is always to protest. People didn't want housing set aside for colds. Such a thing would drag down the property value of every adjacent precinct. Good ol' Nimby. Not In My Back Yard. Most olds might suffer a cold to live these days, but that doesn't mean we want them to have permanent shelter within the bounds of our beloved metropolis.

If you could see those units, how they are living...

Ice cube trays, some people called those buildings. I had thought that was just a cold dig.

I stream some news but can barely focus on world and local events. Besides, nothing new ever really happens anymore. I try to watch some scripted shows, old half hour comedies--nobody makes new comedy television shows any longer--but the familiar jokes and situations feel hollow. These are programs from another world, before the cold. One can't find the humor in our current circumstances; or if one can, it is only the blackest of comedies we are in. The joke's on us. We get the pie in the face every time now.

When we get in bed together, I take Alice in my arms. I caress her; I kiss her. But I do not rise. The hollowness has worked its way into me. She gamely tries to arouse me, but the familiar responses are absent tonight. I tell her she can just let it be. Hell, I don't have to screw her every night, do I? And she surely doesn't need this constant onslaught of sexual attention. Sex is necessary. Yes. So she said. But the pawings and gropings and impalements she has been receiving from this forty-year-old are not entirely necessary.

I am nonetheless shamefaced about the whole thing and glad of the bedroom's darkness. We do not cozy up together. I leave her to sleep on her own, not nestled against me. I turn away. I stare blindly at the wall. Another night of bad sleep won't do me any good, but I may be doomed to lie here for the next few hours, my mind churning uselessly. And in the morning we both have to go to our stupid jobs.

CHAPTER THIRTY-ONE

Hangover Morning

The following morning Alice informed Norris that her period had begun. He had been apprised of her cycle; it was inevitable that these days would arrive at some point in their month together. He had laid in tampons, in amongst the other toiletries reserved for her in his bathroom. He felt a certain relief: he would not be expected (would not expect it of himself) to perform sexually with her while she was menstruating. Therefore, he needn't worry about further failure. One flaccid showing did not an impotency make, he knew. Knew in his mind, as a physiological fact. Yet last night's limpness lingered in his spirit. He felt ever so slightly...unmanned. It was a juvenile reaction, particularly since Alice would never say anything about it, probably thought nothing about it, patently felt nothing about it.

He tried to recall, in detail, the other times in his life when he had malfunctioned in the sack. It wasn't self-torture. Really, he was looking for comfort. If it had happened before, during different times with different women, then he couldn't pin his failure to Alice, or to her status as a cold, or to himself as an old who was belatedly experiencing misgivings about lying with a creature such as herself.

So it was with relief, rather than chagrin, that he dredged up a handful of incidents of non-performance. Sometimes a situation simply misfired: the wrong mood, a poorly digested meal, any number of randomly off-putting factors. Hell, he recollected with a grim smile, one time with Sissy he'd been unable to sustain an erection after a particular song had played on the radio. He associated the song with a girl he had seen the previous year, a brief ugly affair that had served to demonstrate the intense incompatibility between them in all spheres save the sexual. She'd been a great lay and terrible for him in every other aspect. And just hearing that song--he couldn't recall now why he had associated it with her; they'd certainly never had anything to call "their" song—had kept him from achieving anything better than quarter-mast stiffness. And that was with Sissy, the woman he was mad about, the fine red-haired girl who turned him on so fiercely and engaged his emotions in ways that—

No. Norris caught himself before his mind ran away with the catalogue of Sissy Anspaugh's attributes. In the twenty years since they had parted ways, he had thought on her in depths which truly were self-torturous. No need to start on that this morning as he drove Alice to Sherwood Messengers, then himself to the black obelisk where his firm did business.

As feared, he hadn't slept well the previous night. Nor had his wakefulness answered any questions which might be vexing him. Alice--more pointedly, Alice's kind--remained enigmatic to him. An impenetrable being, despite the numerous times he had penetrated her. Get it? That was what used to be called blue humor. He shook his head tiredly, settling in at his work station, letting routine take him over. Sleepwalking. That was what he needed this morning. Some of his patented zombie-like by-rote sleepwalking habits.

Monday mornings at the office were traditionally hangover mornings. Norris had considered slipping out of bed last night to indulge in a nightcap or two, but alcohol as a sleep aid had always been a dicey proposition for him. Booze might put him out, but he was just as likely to lose sleep hours by waking prematurely and than not being able to fall back asleep again; and those closer-to-the-alarm-clock hours were usually the ones he filled up with his REM sleep. Not sleeping and not dreaming was a recipe for next day disaster for him. He'd had this fact driven home when he was away at school. After Sissy was gone, he had tried, rather affectedly, to become a serious drinker. It hadn't lasted long, and it hadn't worked. But it had established, apparently for all time, the cycle of unstable slumber if he tried using the stuff to help him gain unconsciousness.

But others here at the firm--respected members of the team, even--sported outsize drinking habits. Alcohol and drug abuse were of course much more prevalent in the Cold Era. One could hardly blame anyone for indulging in a little mind-altering, even to the point of immoderation. No one, the common wisdom went, needed an excuse to get doped up, not when there were so many reasons to do so.

So people showed up with sore heads and trembling hands, unapologetically bleary-eyed after a weekend of chemical mayhem. They eased into their work. The market was often quiescent on Monday mornings. No one wanted to deal with volatility.

Norris today was a bit dazed and irritable, and the telltales of these behaviors fit with the overall pattern on full display among many of his colleagues. He didn't much care for the office coffee, but today he helped himself to a cup. A co-worker stood by the dispenser, leaning back against the wall, face visibly drawn, tiny bird prints in red visible on his eyeballs. He regarded Norris dully, seeming not to recognize him for a second or two. The man's name was Ikenberry. Norris couldn't remember when he had been hired on, but he had certainly been here long enough to know who Norris, and every other long-tenured person here, was.

"Hey. Norris."

"Hey." He wasn't eager to chitchat. Best just to mire himself in his work.

But Ikenberry put up a hand when Norris made to step past. "I got to ask." A mischievous and adolescent look touched his features. Dropping to a whisper: "Who is she?"

Norris only stared, a frown pulling his brows together. "What?" He honestly didn't know what the man meant.

Ikenberry looked both ways, leaned forward. This was conspiratorial, but he wanted Norris to know he was on his side. "The girl. I didn't know you had the icy itch."

The vulgarity tightened his stomach. Right behind that response was a more eruptive one: fear. Fear that he had been found out. He hadn't told anyone--besides Lester, who he'd told drunk and who worked in another workplace--about Alice. He didn't intend to ever speak of her here in the confines of the office. Alice was his secret, as far as the firm was concerned. She was nobody's business here but his own. He resented...no, was repulsed by Ikenberry's leering insinuations. This, then, was to be locker room talk, a subset of discourse he had no use for. If Ikenberry wanted to hear him brag, he was going to be disappointed.

But he did seem to know. How? The answer came as soon as Norris had posed the question. He had been taking Alice to restaurant's throughout the Financial District. It was, despite its size and busyness, a fairly insular community. Folks had eyes. They also had tongues. Was Norris already the stuff of unrestrained gossip?

"I don't care for that sort of talk, Ikenberry." He kept his tone low, non-confrontational. Perhaps he could evoke some shame from this man. Most people, when they realized they had caused offense, tended to back off. The alternative was either to threaten Ikenberry or make some lewd comment about "the girl," thereby embracing his identity as the office icer. Or perhaps only yet another member in the firm's chill chasing community. For all Norris knew Ikenberry himself went after cold tail every chance he got.

Ikenberry got a disappointed look. He shrugged and walked away. Norris returned to his station, to his numbers, to his financial stratagems and monetary hocus pocus.

But now someone at the office knew. Or thought he knew. An accusation might follow, and a witch hunt could ensue. Management might not be thrilled with having an icer working here on the thirty-ninth floor.

CHAPTER THIRTY-TWO

Elsewhere

Kyle Norris, perhaps, has a slightly above average imagination. His IQ has always charted higher than the median, and he feels this intellectual capacity must feed, at least obliquely, a robust creativity. He thinks his mild affinity for the guitar substantiates this theory. He may, of course, be full of shit.

But he at least possesses the creative competence to play what if? from time to time. Lately, since taking up with Alice, he has posed himself a fanciful question: what if he had initiated a relationship with a cold in some other locale, some other city? San Francisco is so integral to his rhythms, even his identity. Love it or loathe it, this is where he has spent most of his life, and the city's familiarities are his daily backdrop. Here is where his relationship with Alice is playing out. San Francisco must be influencing that entanglement, if only indirectly; the city sets a mood, provides certain charms and exasperations. It is, whatever else, still a rather picturesque town.

But...what if Kyle were romantically engaged with a cold somewhere else? There were so many different places in the world, many other customs and environments.

He might be with a cold girl named Alice in New York City. Yes. Let's keep calling her Alice, no matter what face she might wear in these alternative imaginings.

In New York Kyle is a Wall Street predator. He plays the game harder here because that is how it must be played. The aging traders are gladiators, and it's not a worthwhile day unless you go home with blood under your nails. The cold camps in New York are located on a string of barges. A cold whose name is Alice busses tables at an Asian fusion restaurant favored by the personnel in Kyle's office. He, like the Kyle in San Francisco, makes the proposition to her--rent and food for companionship, including sexual relations--and she accepts. The young-olds in New York have revived the concept of the street gang: they wear colors, they claim turf, they knock heads with rivals. It is purposeless, of course. They don't deal drugs because every narcotic, or its equivalent, is available over the counter. And they don't run guns because guns are over in the U.S. But they cause a good deal of disruption, hassling citizens, vandalizing property. Kyle takes Alice around the town, cockily daring anyone to give him the stink eye. (This Kyle is far more assertive and quick to anger than the San Franciscan rendition.) One evening he is escorting Alice to the theater to see an acclaimed Eugene O'Neill revival. He is curious what she will make of it. He is curious about many things with regard to this girl, and this interest in her borders on serious infatuation, even as he tells himself repeatedly that this is a doomed and, frankly, ludicrous romance. As they walk together, a passel of these gang members sees them. Kyle wears a shockstik, openly displayed. But one of the twenty-somethings says something anyway, a silly ribald comment. Kyle might have just kept walking. He turns, calls out the young-old, who must answer for honor's sake. A duel of sorts ensues, and when it is clear that the middle-aged guy knows how to use his 'stik, the other gang members jump in. They beat Kyle; beat him too thoroughly; he dies on the sidewalk as they flee. Alice stands over the body a moment, then walks away.

The Kyle in New Orleans manages a restaurant. He is smart with numbers and keeps the books nicely balanced. There are strip clubs in the French Quarter, where this eatery is located, which feature cold dancers exclusively. He doesn't meet Alice at one of these. Instead, she is a food delivery cyclist (though her bike isn't as fancy as that of the Alice in San Francisco) who brings him fried oyster po' boys at four a.m. when he can't sleep. After a time his growing fascination with her gets the better of him and he makes the proposal.

She accepts it, and they become lovers. She effectively moves into his apartment on Dauphine Street, a brief distance from his restaurant. He is determined to make the most of their month together. New Orleans, and the French Quarter in particular, is a great drunken madhouse brimming with jazz, rich food, absurd traditions. No one seems to have much of a problem when it becomes common knowledge that he is shacked up with a cold. Pleasure and decadence go hand in hand here. He revels in her body, her youth. He wants to delve this woman, to know her as no old has ever known a cold before. She has no feelings, no; but there must be some intellectual equivalent to human emotion somewhere within her. It shatters him when he can't find these proxy sentiments. When their month is done, he releases her and starts on a serious drinking binge. Now he is just one more careening drunk, no longer even able to do his job with any real competency. He waits to be fired and broods and broods on the girl named Alice.

Kyle in Chicago, a rather high-strung version, kills himself when the affair has run its predetermined course.

The one in Vancouver, Canada...

(He realizes, after a time, that each of these Kyle Norrises differ from himself in one crucial, inescapable way: none of them has Sissy Anspaugh in his past. The notion strikes with a gong-like profundity deep in his soul. It seems quite remarkable that any Kyle Norris anywhere should be going through his life without having known and experienced that particular human female. But it is true. In these alternate scenarios he grows up elsewhere. His romance with Sissy never occurs. She goes to Humboldt State University, having arrived there from her Upper Midwest home state, and has experiences and lives her life without ever having involved herself with Kyle. Extraordinary. It is like imagining a star winking out all at once in the night sky, never to shine again.)

Overseas now. The Kyle in France. The Kyle in Frankfurt. The one in Rome. More exotic--to him, anyway: Johannesburg, Tirana (where the Queen, the last old ever born, lives), on into Russia, to China, to Japan. Kyles, even if the Western name no longer really fits. And Alices, over and over. Some menial girl who he plucks up and makes his whore. Always the transaction. Always the pragmatic acceptance on her part. Each time his fixation, his feelings, deepen. He grows obsessed. There is never enough time to plumb the depths he senses— delusionally?— inside her. But the time is forever fixed. He has one month, no longer.

And so the Kyle in Rio de Janeiro and the one in the hills of Columbia and the Icelander Kyle--they are all led through their paces; and they all come to sticky ends, more or less, though some of the tragedies are less grandiose than others.

In San Francisco the original Kyle Norris (though isn't he just another interpretation, a derivation, even?) is by now deep into the pattern. Despite himself, he is acutely curious about the girl. Despite his best efforts, his feelings for her continue to metastasize.

CHAPTER THIRTY-THREE

The Chess Game

While Alice is on her period, we do nothing sexual. It seems a natural pausing point. I don't want to compel her into servicing me; and besides, frankly, I begin to feel that I have overextended myself on the carnal front. I am no kid anymore. My libido has shifted into middle-aged mode. My body probably doesn't need this much stimulation and release. Such would certainly explain--justify?--my lapse the other evening, when I lay sullen and limp, brooding into the night. Do yourself a favor, Norris. Give your willy a respite. When the menstrual tide has receded, you might have at her with renewed vigor.

But I see her every evening, of course, and she still spends the night at my place. It would, at this point, be unthinkable not to have her there.

The days take on a pleasant, if fanciful, sense of domesticity. It is a bit like a painting done in pointillism; it only appears real when viewed at the proper distance. I know that these quiet moments with Alice in my home do not indicate the cozy comfort between lovers. She is quiet because I almost always must prompt her to speak. When I gaze at her and she gazes back, her eyes don't brim with affection as mine do. She is simply taking in visual information, probably watching to see if I will do or say something. By now she must have concluded that I am not a danger to her, that I'm unlikely to rape or beat her; though this doesn't mean she has necessarily dropped all guard around me.

Hell, if I were a cold, I wouldn't trust any old completely.

(If I were a cold...Oh, my. There is something I could navel-gaze about for a prolonged period. Imagining myself as one of the cold. It may be evident by now that I tend toward the introspective, the internal monologue. I don't know that my thoughts are particularly insightful, but I am simply trying to keep my human vessel afloat as I navigate the treacherous waters of this final segment for my species.)

During our sexual timeout I teach Alice the game of chess. I have a very nice board in emerald and ivory squares. The pieces are pewter and done up in some Medieval style I've never been able to pin down. I think the set was passed down to me from some great uncle when I was still in grade school.

Alice understands each piece's movements when I explain them. But she has no comprehension of classic openings and responses. She opens randomly at first, advancing her rook pawn or bringing out a bishop in an almost chaotic fashion. I have to adjust to this anarchy, but my steady hand and sensible strategy put her down every time.

I pause and stream a tutorial for her. She watches my flatscreen. She has been taught basketball; I believe she can learn this as well. Really, I estimate she is capable of absorbing knowledge on just about any level. Put her in a classroom and she could compete intellectually at the college level.

But what school would encourage a cold to attend classes? Besides, educational institutions across the breadth of the nation are quietly shuttering, one by one. The young-olds don't show much interest in higher education. Right now there is probably some hallowed ivied academy where a doddering robed professor is croaking out lessons to a cavernous classroom attended by three students. Or by none.

After the tutorial Alice's game transforms. She appears to see the sense of advancing the middle pawns first. She uses her knights in more traditional sequence. Thus we play a more recognizable game of chess.

Yet while I see this immediate improvement, I grow aware of a kind of flatness to her play. She isn't setting up for any particular advancements, not launching any real gambits at me. Her game is mostly reactive. She watches what I do and tries to counter me, even when she is in a position to go on the offensive. She doesn't seem to think multiple moves ahead. She is merely trying to hold me off, keep me at bay, perhaps wear me down, let me collapse from exhaustion. Then maybe she'll move in to pick over my bones.

It is how I have long imagined the cold as a whole will deal with my kind. Allow the olds to dwindle, to lose their grip on the world; then move to take over, and enact whatever agenda these emotionless beings may have somehow concocted.

So. Chess uses up one of our sexless evenings.

The next day, after our respective workdays, I make good on a promise half-made to myself: I take Alice to teach her how to drive. She seems nonplussed by the idea--or as perplexed as a cold can be, given the emotional nature of that state. She asks, "Why?" when I tell her I want to teach her how to operate my car. I don't really have a good answer for why I wish to do that. In amongst all the erotic antics I have engaged in with her, I suppose I have—solemnly, soberly--been attempting to expose her to aspects of this world she might otherwise have missed. The ocean. Good home-cooked food. Music. That haunted house ride in Santa Cruz. Now I want her to sit behind the wheel of a vehicle, one which requires her to control it. This may be a skill that will serve her one day. There is no saying how the future is going to play out. I have estimated that infrastructure will continue to break down in the coming years. Perhaps the self-driving vehicles will all give up the mechanical ghost at some point. Knowing how to pilot an unwieldy conveyance like this one could save her life someday.

So, in the broad empty parking lot adjacent to an equally empty square of city park, I talk her through the physical operations. I show her all the basic controls. It is a slow patient instructing. When the time comes, I confidently switch places with her. Under the darkening sky she puts her hands at ten and two and gently gooses the accelerator. The rental jerks and lurches, but she moves it forward and later into a tentative turn. She is, I suppose, no different from long generations of teens taking the wheel for the first time under the tutelage of an older instructor.

Inevitably she acquires the elemental knowing of operating the car. I don't take her out onto the streets; she doesn't have a driver's permit, of course. But inside an hour she can maneuver adroitly enough through the lot. She now has a new skill. It's something else she likely never would have gained if not for me.

The next night I take her out for some live music.

It is down to the Dogpatch for this, the enclave of bohemian liveliness at the foot of Potrero's unhurried eastward slope. I go for a little age inappropriate chic on my part: a black leather coat cut snugly at the waist, an open weave shirt unbuttoned to my sternum, jeans the color of charcoal, and buckled square-toed boots. Alice still looks good in the brightly hued clothes I have given her. When we get to the club, I take her in, her hand in mine. The shockstik is clipped to an inner pocket of my coat.

But we encounter no immediate hostility. They are charging a cover at the door, and the show is about to start. The place is crowded. I check Alice to see how she is reacting to all the jostling elbows and the close atmosphere, but she looks like she could be standing alone on a deserted street corner...except that she acknowledges me with her green eyes. Which makes me melt a little. They are lovely eyes. I have told her so. I have given her many compliments on her appearance. She hasn't returned me one. Why should she?

The floor is planks; the ceiling is beamed. I see age-dulled brass fittings about. There is something vaguely nautical about the place. I hadn't expected a turnout like this on a weeknight when I searched online for local acts. Then again, being late for work the next day or not going to work at all doesn't carry quite the penalties as before. Employers know they can't hold total sway over their workers' lives anymore. Said workers are just as likely to tell you to go fuck yourself as toe the line. The great perspective has shifted: careers don't mean much; living is deemed more important.

The lights dim, and a gasping expectation races through the crowd. I haven't seen this band perform before, but I feel the anticipatory excitement anyway. It is something hardwired in, I think. Live music, when I went to experience it in college in the company of Sissy and others, was always a highly stimulating affair. The university town had clubs, and there was a good deal of local talent afoot. Giving in to the sensory overload of blistering guitars and pounding drums was a nice way to reset my hyperextended mental capacity, so that I was no longer seeing investment principles and market algorithms every time I blinked.

Alice nudges closer to me. She may be wary of the crowd. I wrap my arm around her shoulders. A protective gesture. A proprietary one also, no doubt. If any other icers in the joint had a notion of making a move on her, I would slam shut the door on that.

When the stage lights come up, the band is in place. The noisy jubilee commences. It is a rock and roll cacophony, the sound filling up the club. I can feel the music quaking through my body. They are a competent ensemble. This certainly isn't their first paid gig. I peer past the swaying bodies, the pounding heads, and pick out the individual musicians. I zero in on the lead guitar. The player is my age, wringing his instrument for all his worth. Once again I feel a wry wistful pang: here is the Kyle Norris not taken, perhaps, the alternate me, the one who had a greater musical calling--and surer talent--and pursued his way even as the world slowly crashed around his ears. He would play himself through the coming apocalypse for humankind, without regret or faltering. Music was all to him, nourishing his spirit and entertaining the masses in these small pockets.

But that is not the Kyle Norris who, with a shrug, sold out his soul and now lives comfortably without any of an artist's financial qualms. This Kyle Norris--me--can afford to purchase the attentions of a twenty year old female for a month; whereas my counterpart on the stage must settle for the ministrations of whatever groupie olds cross his path. Which of us deserves envying?

The band plays a loud lively set. They throw in a couple of covers, but most of this sounds like original music to me, constructed around an adept if repetitive block of chords. Nevertheless it gets my blood pumping, and I nod along with it. Alice, still under my sheltering wing, seems to be enduring the noise level. I watch her. Her gaze tracks the individual players, just as I did. She watches the drummer as her sticks fly. She trains her scrutiny on the tall bass player, standing stiff-legged, leaning back, fingers plucking thunder from his strings. Alice has probably never seen live music on this scale before. Another new experience. She might be pairing the musicians with the sounds their instruments make. Or she might be gazing blankly at the spectacle, waiting for it to end.

And eventually it does end. By the time the group has played their second encore, I am ready to get out of there. Outside, I spy a food truck parked a short distance away. I feel a murmur of appetite. "Let's check it out," I say.

Alice follows. My ears are ringing, and I've sweated through the back of my shirt beneath the leather coat. The night air is crisp.

At the truck I suggest she order something to eat. Suggest. I know this is a pretense. She virtually always follows my lead. She has a vested interest in keeping me happy. I might as well command her to eat.

The old man manning the truck appears alone in there. He is in his seventies, with spiky silver hair, a ferocious grin, and animation streaming off him like meltwater from high alps. He has a snappy line of banter, calling me "youngster," beaming at Alice, and setting about to prepare our orders with lightning efficiency. I watch him with envious dismay. This man is relentlessly alive. He is a force, an elemental. He is his food truck, and his truck is his empire, his pulpit. Here he engages with the world, setting it to right in his mind. The colds are coming? So be it. He hands Alice her burrito with gleaming teeth and an elfin twinkle in his crow's-footed eyes.

We stand on the sidewalk together, Alice and I, and eat. No one has hassled us tonight. I feel an inner peace, as if we stand inside the hush of a grace note. The night is vivid, the stars straining to reach us through the overcast, urgent with their messages of ancient light. The moment feels made for epiphany, but none comes to me. I smile anyway.

What did she think of the music? I can see no easy way to ask her.

"This tastes good, Kyle."

I balk. I almost drop my own burrito. "What...?" The air leaves my lungs before I can get the single shocked syllable out.

She doesn't answer. She must figure I heard, so no need to repeat herself. She continues to methodically wolf down her food. Yes. Yes, she must be enjoying it. Or appreciating it. Or experiencing it in some positive way which does not involve emotion.

Yet. Yet...what she just said. It tastes good.

My blood races again, like it did for the frenetic music in the club. But the buzzing in my ears turns to a sweet song of angels, and there are trumpets in there as well, and a cooling breeze blows off the edge of heaven, and in that breeze is a whispered promise: Alice is not a dead thing, not mere motorized flesh. Something resides within her. A heart. A spirit. A soul. I may yet have the opportunity to find out the full truth about her.

CHAPTER THIRTY-FOUR
Now O'er the One Half-World

And just like that, the month is halfway over. Kyle has quibbled with himself over the precise specifications of that month in which he and the girl are to maintain their physical and romantic relationship. How does one define a month, anyway? Is it from the date in July until that same date in the following month? Or is it a nice neat four weeks from the starting day? Some use thirty days as the shorthand for a month, even though calendar months vary. These are persnickety details, but Kyle has already decided what will qualify as the month between him and Alice. He has done this preemptively, knowing his own penchant for overthinking. He will not permit himself the luxury of vacillating when the end of their time together approaches. There is as well too much indignity in that, what would be a childish scrabble to buy just a fraction more time, like a small boy begging for ten more minutes of television. No. No. So he has fixed the termination date, and he intends to honor it. When the day arrives, the curtain will ring down and the theater will go dark, and he will walk away from this illusory spectacle of passion and tenderness. There shall be no compromise, no last minute pleas for clemency, no stays of execution. The finale is to be...well, final. He and Alice shall part. He and Alice shall part.

And they are now halfway there. From this point onward the

days ahead grow fewer than the ones behind.

164

CHAPTER THIRTY-FIVE

A1384-7K

"What is your full name?"

A pause in the dark--that processing pause, it feels like. "Alice."

"Is that all? No middle name, no surname?"

We lay together in the bedroom. Relations have resumed between us, and the hiatus did indeed benefit me. No need for the details. But the afterglow is delicate and perfumed, and she is all the softness in the world as she lies caged in my arms.

I remember the man at Sherwood Messengers, the one I strong-armed into giving me Alice's name. He said the colds working there only had to supply a first name.

"It's not a name," she says. The words are drawn out, laced with sleepiness. With not a little pride I think of how I have taxed her tonight. This old still has some spunk!

"What, then?"

"A1384-74K. Alice A1384-74K. That's my full name."

They hang in the darkness for me. Brute numbers and letters. Dog tag figures. The dehumanizing stamp they award prisoners. Perhaps even something they ink on an inner forearm. A1384-74K. Jesus.

I bite briefly on my lip. Euphoria has fled the room, but I still feel the bodily exhilaration of our lovemaking. I channel that energy into my abiding curiosity about this woman. I have refrained from interrogating her. But perhaps it is time to delve a little. After all, that time is running out.

"Do you know who your parents were?"

"I know their names."

"Can you tell me those names?" Again, this is that roundabout way I have with her sometimes, so that I can pretend she is doing something for me voluntarily. Right now the subterfuge strikes me as particularly egregious.

She says, with further heaviness in her voice, "Nora Felzien. Cameron Felzien."

I don't try to picture them; but the reality of the two names intrudes upon me, in an assaultive manner. Cameron and Nora Felzien. A married couple. A married couple who had a monster instead of the human child they were expecting. And when the truth of what their daughter was could no longer be denied, they did the only sensible thing. They cast out the cold demon child. Sent it away. Discarded it.

The camps. The goddamn federal camps. Where Alice A1384-74K would eventually learn that she could procure special treatment from the male guards by sucking them off. Was that the fate you had in mind, Cameron, when your wife was sweatily expelling your child in a white antiseptic delivery room? How about you, Nora--was there anything in those baby books you read about farming your offspring out to a federally run detention facility? I doubt it. But you surrendered Alice. You let strangers take her. Or else you delivered her yourself. It must have been in the time of true madness. The rioting, the killings. Maybe--just maybe--you risked yourselves by taking her directly to the facility. Some parental instinct might have lingered within you. But despite what unimaginable grief you experienced, or what feckless hand-wringing you put yourselves through, you did it. You fucking threw your daughter out of your lives and let the state raise her.

Alice Felzien. For the first year or two or three of her life she must have been Alice Felzien. Christ. The name reverberates in my skull, and I feel the vast awful collective guilt of the olds. It steals into me, from every corner of the darkened bedroom. We are the humans. We are the ones with feelings. And we are devils. We have committed endless atrocities against our own kind in the name of our emotional impulses. But such crimes as we have perpetrated on the colds...those will be writ large, in scarlet lettering, in the history books.

Or perhaps they will not be. Unless we write those histories, they won't be committed to print. I can't imagine the cold will bother. Oh, they'll remember us, after a fashion. So I guess. We will at least be an oral tradition for a time. The coming generations of colds might require explanations as to the state of the world. Where did these crumbling cities come from? What is the meaning of those museums stuffed with molding art? What is art, and why is it?

The colds will tell their children of us. They will find some way of describing emotion. The olds in these stories will be the monsters, creatures who looked like colds but who were possessed of deranged behaviors. They all shared an...infection. Yes. Emotion as plague; and every old born in the Pre-Cold Era was born already infected.

The cold. They won't even call themselves that, I realize there on my bed, with my lover in my arms. My people. It is what she said. Maybe they'll take up another name, even more straightforward. Human. The colds will be humans. They will pick up the title where we left it on the ground as we disintegrated into extinction.

Gooseflesh touches every part of me. I shiver, at the marrow, ever so slightly. Alice doesn't stir. Her breathing has deepened. She sleeps.

I cling to her, as alone as it is possible to be in the presence of another living being.

* * *

"Can I ask you something?" This is another of my feints, an unnecessary preface to a question I will ask anyway.

Alice, buckled into the passenger seat, gazes ahead and says nothing.

That's yes, then. So I ask, "What facility did you grow up in?"

She rattles off a number-letter stream. If the camps are officially designated this way, I've never heard of it before.

I try: "Where is the facility located?" We are coming into the Financial District from the east. I'm on 4th, about to cross Market with the next light change.

"Concord," she says, voice staccato, the natural rasp a little edged. Again I have the irrational sense that I am annoying her.

But I know her facility now. In Concord, California, it was the Sunvalley Shopping Center--or its leveled remains--where the cold camp was erected. The site is still operational.

"How long ago did you leave it?" I ask. The traffic light changes, and all the driverless vehicles around me surge forward in unnerving unison. I creep ahead as well, just a hair out of step.

Alice says, "Two years ago."

Eighteen, then. She has been on her own since age eighteen. I went away to college at eighteen, but I had a wide safety net spread beneath me. My independence was mostly illusory. Did she come straightaway to San Francisco?

Still so much to know about her. And the time in which to learn these details is slipping away.

I drop her at the depot on Clay Street, popping the trunk so she can retrieve her bicycle. When she has it slung over her shoulder, she comes around to the driver's side, leans in the open window, and gives me a kiss. It is a little firmer than usual, a bit more verve in it, though it doesn't feel like passion. More like, when you ask personal questions you rile me. But the kiss is also to say: you're worth the aggravation.

And those are the delusions I have willfully concocted this gray July morning.

* * *

I do just enough work at the office to keep the numbers moving, but I devote half my time to online research which has nothing to do with financial matters. Alice and I have only two weekends left together. These are the times when we can truly get away, leave the city.

The internet is sluggish. Or, really, it is just not the instant gratification juggernaut it once was. My searches time out repeatedly, but between bouts of actual investment business I locate information I am seeking.

Sunvalley still houses several thousand colds, despite the nationwide ban on breeding. I wonder, idly, if that prohibition will ever be lifted. Or will it, like so much else, eventually simply fall by the wayside, rendered moot by dwindling human numbers. When the cold become the majority, the olds will feel the constriction of their minority status. Will colds run for political office? Probably not. They are banned from voting, so they are probably forbidden from holding office, though I have never heard the statute quoted. We rigged the game against them as best we could. But they have time very much on their side. When the tables are inevitably turned and they are the dominant species, the old will likely plead for mercy, for justice, for compassion, even. Yes, we will sue for compassion from a breed incapable of delivering such. It will not be a dignified scene. It will be spectacle. The olds will be truly old by then. The young-olds will be my age, and everyone else will be slipping away into the true depths of middle age and beyond, into the calcified realms of elderhood.

I read everything I can about the Concord facility. It seems a typical fed camp, but I know I am not getting the full story. Even the few whistleblower articles I find don't get to what I suspect is the full depth of the corruption and abuse. Someone rich is probably getting richer off these facilities, because prisons have always been profitable. The banal depravity of the guards at the camps is another matter. I think of the abuse Alice was subjected to, and a brute masculine instinct makes me want to visit harm on whoever exploited her as a girl.

But the Sunvalley camp, like all the other federal camps, is subject to rules, at least on paper. The colds, despite their pariah status within society, do have certain rights. You might get away with murdering a cold--due to a lax police response, say--but you will still have broken the law. The crime will exist, even if all punishment is circumvented.

Alice has rights. Alice A1384-74K. Alice Felzien. I wish to help her to exercise certain of those rights.

I want to go back to her camp with her. I want to see where she started from, so to better understand how she sees this world. How she sees the olds.

How she sees me.

CHAPTER THIRTY-SIX

The Good That is Done

It is true that emotions are freely spent amongst the olds. And those volatile expressions are often public and can be quite negative. People scream at each other in stores, at restaurants. The disputes are usually petty, and they oftentimes escalate, which is why there is so much violent crime these days.

But Kyle Norris, who himself has never indulged in a public tantrum as a fully grown adult, has witnessed quite a number of emotional displays that are based entirely in kindness, in empathy, in pity. For every old overturning a table because his soup isn't piping hot, there might be a corresponding Samaritan who takes the opportunity to put some tenderness into the world's ebbing supply.

On a windy day a couple of years ago Kyle saw a businessman stumble on the sidewalk and drop his briefcase, which exploded open in a flurry of papers. The man yelped in anguish, and before the cry had cleared his throat, a dozen passersby were scrambling madly after those pieces of deadtree, snatching them out of the air, pinning them down to the ground with the toes of their shoes. Kyle was too far off--and frankly too stunned--to participate in the spontaneous gathering effort. But the operation, undertaken by complete strangers, was evidently a wholesale success. The businessman had tears in his eyes as he gratefully accepted return of his pages. More than one of his impulsive helpers embraced the man.

Kyle has seen other acts as well. A woman in one of the downtown automated eateries with her arm in a plastic cast, having a devil of a time wielding her cutlery and nearly weeping in frustration; and the younger woman who came to her table, who wordlessly and smilingly began to cut up the older woman's meat and feed it to her a forkful at a time.

People giving up an umbrella in the middle of a downpour because somebody else looked like they needed it more. Others handing over fistfuls of paper cash to panhandlers. Or when there is a sudden crisis: a mishap--someone falling down some steps, say, or a one in many millions fluke of a malfunctioning self-driver, resulting in an accident. Watch civilians on the scene jump in and try to help however they can until the professionals arrive. The impulse is there. To aid. To comfort. It is perhaps just as strong a propensity as that which accounts for such abrupt acts of selfishness and pettiness.

Of course, the good deeds have not been confined to quaint street scenes like these. The phenomenon is grander, more poignant, and it has often risked much more. During the most fervent period of global madness--the massacres of colds, the outright pogroms--some olds stepped up. They took in the rejected children by the dozens, by the hundreds. They offered shelter and protection against the bloodthirsty mobs. This occurred in virtually every nation. Olds with means, and even those with little more than an avid will, did all they could to see to it that their small clutch of the cold would survive, no matter what atrocities were committed in the name of fear and hatred. Not all of these noble champions were successful. Some died horrendous deaths, along with their would-be charges. But others did succeed, and whole swaths of the cold endured in billionaire bunkers, in barricaded inner city projects, on board cargo ships, in the mazes of urban subway systems; all of them shepherded by an old or olds who saw it as a moral imperative to preserve these alien children from the slaughter.

Kyle Norris has always admired these figures. The hero's story is often a satisfying one, and hearing of such feats, he is moved. He feels better about humanity in general. But he cannot, even in his most fanciful reveries, imagine himself taking on such responsibilities. He is no Tubman, no Schindler. He will smile on the good deeds but knows he doesn't have the capacity to take on the necessary risk and sacrifice. It is beyond him. He isn't cut out to be the hero.

But perhaps one needn't rescue a whole raft of persecuted colds in a flamboyant manner. Maybe it can be smaller than that, less grandiose. It might be that one need not even shield a single cold from the wrath of an angry mob. Suppose one were to simply try to make contact with a cold. True meaningful contact. Communication on the human level. A heart to heart connection. If an old--let's say Kyle Norris himself--could establish a link between the two species, that could be a worthy contribution to all the valiant human deeds scattered across history. He might be a hero in a very small story. And maybe no one else would ever know what he had done.

It would still count, though, right? He would have done something with his life, other than merely sleepwalking through it.

Right? Right?

CHAPTER THIRTY-SEVEN

Fire

The ululations of the fire alarm, while sufficiently loud, lack a certain urgency. It is a three-toned sound, ascending octaves; but there is a staid, measured quality to it, and so I sit at my work station through half a dozen repetitions of this clamor, feeling no acceleration of my pulse.

Fire alarm. I lean back in my chair, lift my chin, and try to smell smoke. There is nothing, just the slightly crisp, antiseptic air of the office.

"Are you coming, Norris?"

This is from one of the executives, striding past my desk. I leave my work screens on. I take nothing but my suit jacket. If everything I leave behind is reduced to ashes, I will have no regrets.

The same exec, above me in the firm's hierarchy, is standing at the elevators when I catch up to him. I am about to say something about taking the stairs, but then decide he must know what he is doing, since he is my superior. I will follow his lead, even if the elevator stalls out, fills with smoke and suffocates us both. I am glad to have the decision out of my hands. Besides, I don't want to walk down thirty-nine goddamn flights.

We pick up five others on the way down, then five more, then the car is at capacity. The alarm sounds inside the elevator as well. It seems to be making some of the others nervous.

Out on the street it is as if there is no emergency. The fire units haven't yet arrived, and the downtown backdrop plays at its usual pace. I glance at a man staring up at the tower. He is paunchy and in his sixties. I am just near enough to hear him mutter, "I hope it goes up like a Roman candle." Then I recognize him: he wore the pinstripe in the elevator when I rode down with a cold who worked in one of the offices; he was visibly shaken by the youngster's presence. Somehow him wanting our building to burn up makes him slightly less obnoxious.

I don't know how long this unexpected work hiatus is going to last. I welcome the break. The first of my last two weekends with Alice starts tomorrow, and my mind is on that more than my job. Before anyone from my office can say anything to me about when we should report back, I put my head down and shuffle off with my hands in my pockets. Nobody in management calls my name. I slip away, feeling like a schoolkid ducking class.

The temperature is up today, a good fifteen degrees above the median. There is some strange bite to the air nonetheless; not a chill but an undertone, something mysterious, perhaps another climate anomaly brewing. The cold, whatever else, very likely won't do the planet the damage we have done it. I imagine far less industrial activity in that future which belongs to our emotionless successors. Colds will not need goods on our scale; therefore, less manufacturing, which will mean less warming of the atmosphere. The cold might heal this world. Hell, maybe nature created the cold in order to save itself. It is a theory I've heard bandied about many times. I don't dismiss it. I don't really dismiss anything when it comes to the origins of the cold. They are such an unknown factor that virtually anything about them might be true. They live in a negative superstate in my mind.

But...Alice. Alice doesn't just live in my head. She is real. She is physical. There is nothing theoretical about her to me.

I walk along. The environs are familiar, of course, but I am not going anywhere. It is too early to eat lunch. I wonder if the remainder of the workday will be canceled, but I have a hunch that the fire emergency will turn out to be something relatively minor, the evacuation a mere precaution. Or maybe the tower will blaze and burn, like the two buildings in New York which set the emotional stage for my arrival in this world as an infant. But if this skyscraper goes down, it won't be a landmark event, a game changer; it will just be an accident, a mishap. No one will shed tears, so long as no one dies in the misadventure. My firm's data is surely secured, saved to some corner of the digital ether. A new office would open, somewhere in this same part of the city no doubt. I, along with my fellow well-paid drones, would report for duty, and life would resume. I would have gained nothing and lost nothing.

Ahead I notice police vehicles. They are parked helter-skelter across the middle of a block, as if they have just raced to the scene, disgorging officers. That in fact appears to be the case. I hang back but am near enough to see a dozen figures in police garb. They are wrangling a small group in far more colorful raiment, a posse of young-olds, it looks like. These are done up as circus clowns--or so they might have appeared hours ago, when this carousing spree of theirs probably began. Now they are ragged and torn, the baggy pants split, the colors striped with mud or blood, wigs askew and makeup runny. They have become apparitions, horror jesters, and no doubt their antics turned ominous some time ago. Have they hurt anyone? Did they murder a cold, just for the laughs?

However their binge of frenzied behavior has played out ahead of this moment, they are now spent; and the cops bundle them away into their vehicles. There are still consequences for actions. Some of these dumb-asses may end up doing time for whatever impulse crimes they have perpetrated. Imagine that. Witnessing humankind slowly ceding the world to the cold from inside a jail cell.

The scene clears, and the patient automated traffic resumes. I start to shuffle onward, but something has occurred to me, a quickening and uneasy thought. Did they murder a cold? Such things happen, even in a relatively peaceful town like San Francisco.

My steps begin to hurry. I cross at an intersection, dash to another. Two more streets up. I could hail a driverless, but I'm almost there now, my heart pounding a steady rhythm, cool sweat at my hairline. My race to Clay Street has allowed time for paranoia to build; so when I am jogging down the sidewalk with the entrance to Sherwood Messengers in sight, I have constructed several elaborate tragedies which involve Alice.

But then I see her. And the air turns crystalline around me, and joy streams in my veins. I see her. But she does not see me. I flag; I stop. She is half a block away. She isn't alone.

I squint, peering forward, even as I fade back a step, then sidle into the lee of a splintery telephone pole. I focus on the pair with an intensity that should have a machine hum accompanying it. Both colds are astride their respective bicycles. One--Alice's--points toward the garage, the other out to the street. So the two of them face each other. They are very near one another, each leaning toward the other. The cold aimed toward the street is male. His hair is a soft brown, probably finely textured, and very overgrown. It blows about his shoulders, which are only slightly wider than Alice's. He is slim and young and a cold and a male. And he and Alice are speaking; and there is a sense of intimacy between them. I can detect it even at this distance. Something in the muted body language. I have been around Alice a great deal. Perhaps I have picked up telltales I'm only halfway aware of. These two share something, beyond their status as colds and as bike messengers.

Alice's hand comes up. She touches the boy's face. I can't tell if they smile at each other, but of course they don't--they can't. They wouldn't. But the gesture is flagrantly intimate nonetheless. Had Alice kissed him full on the lips, I would have drawn the same conclusions as I come to now, in this perilous and tremulous moment.

They are lovers. Or, barring sexual familiarity, the boy is of special import to the girl, and vice versa. They have a relationship. They are together, in some respect.

Still behind the pole I watch them part. The brown-haired boy comes in my direction. I caution myself not to stare too conspicuously but can't help myself. I scrutinize him as he passes. His hair spills out behind him. He has a little patch of hair on his chin, a fuzziness on his cheeks. His clothes are standard issue cold: functional and nondescript. He doesn't wear sunglasses, and his eyes are big and long-lashed. His muscles work at a strong easy tempo as he pumps the bike up Clay, a dispatch bag flapping at his hip.

There is no emotion on his face. He is a good-looking kid, I have to admit.

Alice has gone down into the depot. I could stride down the street, go down the ramp, find her among all the other riders in that dank concrete hole. I could tell her what I had seen and demand an explanation. This would be my ultimate chance to pitch a public scene. Watch the old lose complete control. See him make an absolute spectacle of himself. It would be even more volatile and ridiculous than the usual such public tantrum, as he would be enacting this tirade before an audience of colds. His emotional display would not connect with any of them. They might understand his upset in a strictly definitional manner, on an almost binary level perhaps. The old is...jealous. Jealousy--though itself a mystery--produces these effects in olds. Olds. Your kind. And so they will watch, enigmatically. And Alice will gaze and occasionally blink, and be wary of my behavior in case I finally turn violent on her. If I did so, I wonder if her fellow messengers would intervene and defend her.

But I don't approach the garage. I certainly don't go looking for Alice right now. I beat a retreat. I'll go back and see if my office building is blazing like a torch. I doubt it, though. I smell no smoke on the air, only the scent of perfidy and hurt.

CHAPTER THIRTY-EIGHT

Her Stand

We leave the rental in a lot nearby the pier. I indulged in some debate about how to reach Sausalito--crossing the bridge or taking the ferry. The Golden Gate Bridge is a monument, of course. But in the past few years questions about its safety have come up. It takes quite a lot to maintain the massive suspension bridge. Spots of discoloration are visible on some of its international orange surface. That is the name of the color of the bridge: international orange. It groans audibly in the wind these days, like a rusty squeeze box. People still use it, but it only gets a fraction of the traffic it used to. Occasionally a mountain lion will come down from the Marin Headlands and bring everything to a halt as it wanders across the lanes. The big animals seem to know that something untoward has happened to humankind at large, and they are testing the resetting boundaries between their domains and ours.

Alice should experience the bridge, but I can't show her everything. Besides, a ferryboat ride across the waters of the Bay is another innately San Franciscan episode she should undergo. A voyage to the misty romantic realm that is Sausalito, a town on the northward side of the water whose purpose it is to be picturesque. The deck will rock beneath us. We can stand at the rail, feel the droplets of spray on our faces.

But it is chilly once we are out on the water, and I go inside and sit in a scratched plastic seat. Alice follows. We both have overnight bags. I bought her lingerie a few days ago, and tonight, in our cozy hideaway, she will no doubt play dress-up for my benefit. The thought stirs little in me.

I feel scoured, as if I have been scrubbed down to the bone. Jealousy has unmanned me, and I hate myself some for that. This is a heart-hurt schoolboy reaction. It's juvenile, almost infantile.

My time with Alice, our days and nights...they now seem even more fraudulent than before. I have manufactured this relationship. It is an artificial edifice, as I have known from the start. But now there is an added layer of deceit. She is not mine alone. The boy's face is burned into my mind. Boy? No, stop it, Norris. He is her age or no more than a year younger. Over eighteen, at any rate. An adult, by the traditional yardstick. If he were human, he'd be eligible to vote, to apply for any number of commercial licenses, to partake in life as a state-sanctioned grownup. My calling him boy does nothing to lessen him. His worth is determined by Alice, at least as far as it concerns me. He has some measure of her attention; he participates in her existence in some significant way. I feel sure of that. The way they stood so near, astride their bicycles; the touch of her fingertips to his face--

The shameful adolescent hurt rives me. I want to make some animal sound there in the sparsely inhabited passenger cabin, a fine high mewl of pain, but I remain silent. Of course I do. I won't subject myself to the indignity of a public display of these rancid emotions roiling about inside me.

"What is Sausalito like?"

I blink, utterly lost for a moment. I realize I have barely spoken all this morning. She has finally piped up. But what a question from a cold. What is Sausalito like? For something to be like anything, there must be emotional value attached to it. I think back on her comment at the food truck the other night, equally unlikely coming from a cold: This tastes good, Kyle. She was talking about her burrito. But how could a burrito taste good to her? Good implies a scale of caliber, and food is inherently passionate. Most people have fraught, emotional relationships with their food. Meals take on great significance. One might rhapsodize about a sauce one experienced years ago or a rack of lamb at a fancy restaurant. Alice bit into a burrito and told me it tasted good. That meant--somehow, by some unknown reckoning-- she took an emotional measure of it. A cold's judgment regarding food should fall into one of two categories: what is edible and what is not.

"You're not saying much, Kyle."

I haven't responded to her first question. Now this. Another remark which seems outside the sphere of a cold's ability to comment.

My throat is a bit tight. I deliberately unlock my jaw and say, "Sorry." As if she is a human girlfriend and I am trying to placate her while nursing my own bad mood. More deception, more pretending. She is my lover, yes; but only in the most mechanical terms. This amorous weekend I have planned, in aggressively quaint Sausalito, is puppet theater.

I glance around, almost hoping someone will be giving us a dirty look, but the other passengers take no notice of us. My shockstik is on my belt, under my jacket.

I say to Alice, "I'm just...preoccupied. Okay? Nothing's wrong."

But it is not true. Things are wrong. Things have gone wrong. And I don't know if I can do anything to right them.

* * *

It is another boardwalk, another view of water. This isn't the kitsch of Santa Cruz; rather, it's the studied charm that can only be Sausalito, a community tucked in below the Headlands. This place still receives visitors. Not quite tourists, since tourism is a fading concept, but Bay Area locals come here, convincing themselves they have gotten away from it all by crossing the cobalt waters of the Bay.

Sausalito does its best. I'll give it that. It is the forced smile which refuses to quit. The houses remain freshly painted, the streets in good repair. The water is always on, and the sewage never backs up. The businesses along the scenic boardwalk all appear to be flourishing. Or at least none are boarded up. There is a palpable sense of calm here.

But I am not at ease. I stroll with Alice at my side, and I point out the lights of San Francisco on the other shore. I name this building and that site--the venerable Transamerica Pyramid, Coit Tower--and she appears to take in this information. The night is cool without being chilly. We have already eaten, plates of seafood at a restaurant that looked like a gingerbread house from the outside.

I stop walking. I still have that flensed feeling, like all the meat has been taken off my bones. When Alice halts after another step or two and turns to look back, I gaze emptily over her head.

"You're just humoring me," I say. There are others out, ambling, couples in search of someplace restful and going along with the premise that Sausalito can provide that respite. All olds, no colds. No one is nearby us on the promenade. The splash and slosh of bay water is a white noise in the air.

Alice says nothing. She might not know what humoring is, even as she has practiced it with me these past weeks.

"You have been indulging me," I explain. "Letting me have my illusions about you. Encouraging me, maybe. The other night you said that burrito tasted good. Why did you say that?"

"Because it did." Staccato words, but the rasp is in her voice, lending it a suggestion of passion.

"It can't taste good, Alice. Goddamnit, it can't. Not to you."

I hear her draw a breath and let it out. "My taste buds are the same as yours, Kyle." Again it is as though I have riled her, as if she is holding in some potent expression of anger right now. But that can't be. More illusion.

"Those buds are the same, but you can't appreciate anything. You aren't permitted to say that something is good. Or bad."

"If you offered me a hamburger or a pile of horseshit, I would know which one to eat."

"Sure. Right. One is fuel for the body, which is all food can possibly mean to you." I hear the strain in my voice. It seems I might actually be on the verge of a wild emotional display after all.

She goes silent again. I finally lower my gaze from over her head. I lock eyes with hers. Some unnamed energy seems to dance in those green orbs. Despite everything I know, everything I am telling her here, some part of me can't shake the belief that emotion resides within this woman. Or a mockup of emotionality, some kind of compromise. Her species--and yes, damnit, she is a different species!-- may have formed, or may be forming still, a mental interface for coping with us olds. They do not feel, but we do, and for the time being they still have to interact with us. Perhaps the cold brains have, by necessity, opened new pathways. Interpretive nodes, processing centers. Whatever it takes to handle us; so that, for instance, young Alice in the fed camp knew enough to give a guard a blowjob in exchange for privileges. Or how she recognized that what I offered her--essentially, the same deal--was worth the effort on her part.

But by understanding us, humoring us, were the cold somehow taking on ghostly emotional characteristics? Like children getting into their parents closets and trying on the lurid oversized clothes.

It is too much, suddenly, to take in. I actually feel lightheaded. Alice's hand is abruptly about my right elbow. Her grip is strong.

"We should get back to the room," she says.

* * *

The room is a treasure trove of old-fashioned comfort. Furnishings in lacquered teak. Every hinge and knob is cast in brass. There are throw pillows--a whole arsenal of them--embroidered to a fare-thee-well. Tapestries, doilies, hooked rugs, framed watercolors on the pastel walls. This is a love nest and no mistake.

Fatigue weighs my bones, bones which might be all that is left of me. I take to a chair, shoving pillows off it. It creaks as I lean back, giving off an antique vibe. I am still wearing my jacket. The shockstik is clipped to my belt. Alice stands out in the middle of the belligerently romantic room. No real expression on her face. I can try to trick myself, pretend that emotional fires burn somewhere within her because she is different than other colds. But I may have passed some limit within me; I can't trade in any more bullshit. At best Alice's "emotions" might be the theoretical ones I just postulated: sham stand-in feelings, cutouts without centers, merely the result of dealing with the olds who have, so far, dominated their lives so aggressively.

As we olds die off, will subsequent generations of colds be free of even this shadow of human sentimentality? It is another interesting thought, that there might emerge generational divisions among the cold. But I'm sick to death of interesting thoughts, I find.

I stare with swollen eyes at Alice, where she stands and waits. She still knows this situation is in my hands. Even now I could tell her to change into the lacy lingerie and parade up and down; she would do it. Or I could tell her that we were through and to sleep on the floor;

in the morning we would go back to San Francisco and part ways forever.

Instead in a toneless non-accusatory voice I tell her what I saw yesterday, just outside her work. I go so far as to explain that I wasn't spying on her, that an odd series of circumstances came together to put me on the sidewalk at just that time.

"Who is..." I almost say the boy. But I manage, "Who is he?"

Alice pauses. Processing? Stalling? I don't know anymore. "His name?" she asks.

"Sure. Tell me his name."

"Carrow."

Carrow. A first name, a last? A name plucked from the ether? Again I don't know. Maybe Carrow's name is followed by a string of numbers and letters in a federal camp database. Or maybe he was among the few cold children kept by his parents. But that isn't what I am most curious about. I ask the question that goes to the heart of things: "What is Carrow to you?"

Is the question too abstract, too tinged with emotional value? Alice pauses again but then says firmly, "He's my stand."

It's my turn to lose a beat in our conversation. "Your...stand? What is that?" I have never heard the term as she seems to be using it.

Her hand shifts ever so slightly at her side. This looks like an abortive gesture to me, maybe one indicating frustration with communication between us. But that's more bullshit. It is my mental and emotional weariness reading into things.

"With my kind a stand is...that person you rely on above others. The one you might stay alongside. Into the future." Again her hand twitches by her hip.

I sink further into the chair, feeling muscles go lax. She may be having difficulty conveying this concept--she has probably never had to explain it to an old before--but her meaning comes across. And it astounds me. She is talking about a potential lifetime companion. One she might stay with into the future. A...fiancé? No. But perhaps the cold equivalent of one. A special relationship, comparable to--what? Marriage? It sounds as if commitment of some form comes into it. Alice and Carrow. He is her stand; she is his. Currently they rely on each other, whatever that means exactly. In the future they may deepen that dedication somehow.

I have wondered often what sort of world the cold would make for themselves, what kind of society they might construct. This might be a first true look at it. Carrow and Alice, drawn together by instinct perhaps, or by cold-blooded calculation. How, after all, would a cold choose a mate?

Is that it, finally? Has Alice already chosen her partner for life?

Then, what the fuck is she doing fooling around with me?

I slouch nervelessly in the antique chair. I am bones. I am not Alice's stand. I am not her future. I never was going to be.

CHAPTER THIRTY-NINE

The Misery of the Room

Jealousy had not been a factor when Norris and Sissy Anspaugh parted ways. No, that breakup had been too insidious to involve outside party complications. But he had nonetheless encountered the emotion before. Of course he had. He was a flawed being, like all the other flawed beings around him; and in the midst of the emotional havoc that was adolescence he'd felt the sting of romantic covetousness, of unrequited lust and like, the whole slate of tiresome envying which was sometimes mistaken for actual love.

So he knew the tenor of jealousy. Sawing at his heartstrings, it produced sound at a certain pitch. But the tune this time was played at a punishing volume. There was a whole orchestra behind it.

He envied this Carrow. He was jealous of him. What Norris had fabricated with Alice, Carrow had established in a real sense.

There was misery in the room of embroidered things and driftwood geegaws. Norris remained slumped in the chair, hating how depleted he felt. This was a teenaged boy's reaction to bad news. Hey, guess what? That girl you like doesn't like you back. Worse, she likes someone else. Ain't life just a kick in the teeth? You should sit and mope like nobody's ever sat and moped before.

Alice still stood, several feet away, green eyes flicking his way now and then. There were things he should ask her. It took some while to summon the strength to begin.

"Does..." pausing to swallow, "Carrow know what you have been doing with me?"

"Yes."

She wasn't deceiving her stand, then. That word. That term. Stand. It was, in its way, evocative. It was also something simple, what a sign language-speaking gorilla might come up with on its own to label a concept it couldn't find in its present vocabulary.

Carrow. How did Carrow feel about-- No. Carrow was a cold. The question had to be framed just so.

"Did Carrow resist the idea of your entering into a relationship with me?"

"No." Stark honest answers.

"Does he see the same benefit in it as you do?" Again, careful phrasing.

"Yes."

"Which is?" He sat up in the chair, tension snaking through him once more.

She paused and seemed, as before, somehow on the verge of making a gesture, giving him a shrug, without actually committing to it. She said, "Financial gain. You paid my rent. I can save two paychecks this month."

The transaction. He could still vividly remember transferring the amount to her chip, there on the downtown sidewalk. So much had happened since then, yet at the same time nothing at all had occurred. Their relationship was only that transmittal of funds and nothing more. Everything else had transpired in his head, perhaps in his heart.

"What do you intend to do with the money, ultimately?" That question might require too many steps to reach an answer. He waited, wanting--and not wanting--to know.

She said, "Carrow and I will both move out of our housing units, into an apartment."

A hollowness opened in his stomach. "You mean a real apartment. Like where olds live."

She nodded. He tried to recall if he'd seen her do that before. He decided he had.

So. Alice and Carrow, saving up to move in together, into a

decently sized living space, something much different from that frugal monk's cell she currently inhabited. Carrow no doubt lived in the same structure, or in one of the adjacent barracks, in a chamber just as cramped, just as bereft of comforts. They were planning a future together: cohabitation, mutual support. They were two compatible beings, evidently. Were they especially different from twenty-year-olds Norris had known in the earlier times of his life, before the advent of the cold? A pair of new adults, seeking to band together to get through this thing called life. Banking their money, waiting until they had enough to make their move.

And she was willing to let a forty-year-old paw her all over and teach her how to play chess and drive a car and direct her through a farce of romantic domesticity. And her Carrow, her stand, her lover in whatever sense that might be, went along with this strategy. Did he feel jealous of Norris? Certainly not. But on some level, some emotionless stratum, this cold must view him with dry contempt, with a bloodless disgust which was reserved for all olds. My kind. You people. And you people were dangerous to my kind.

A further question occurred. It worsened the hollow in his gut, made it a gnawing thing. But he asked anyway. "Have you done this sort of thing before? Traded your...your favors for financial reward."

"Yes." Another short cutting answer.

He wasn't even her first creep, then. Perhaps her time at the fed camp had conditioned her. She would feel no revulsion for performing sexual acts on olds. She had already weighed the matter and decided that the risk was worth the payoff.

Other icers had been with her. Chill chasers. And he was just one more of those degenerates.

A sideways thought intruded. Norris asked, "Has Carrow ever entered into similar arrangements?"

The green eyes went briefly but distinctly still. She said, "He has."

For some reason it made him feel incrementally better. Alice's boyfriend could be bought as a plaything just as readily as she.

But...Alice was using Norris, just as surely as he was using her. That was at the core, beneath even the livid layers of jealousy. Right now he couldn't locate the vestiges of the pretense he had been enacting with her. The scenario he had created was fully revealed as the ghost town it was, it always had been, peopled by nothing but shadows and the settled dust of hopeless dreams.

He drew a long deep breath and let it out slowly, deliberately. As he did, he willed energy back into his frame. He would not be the mopey adolescent. It didn't suit him. Alice had someone special in her life, and he was not that person. So be it. So. Be. It. But it changed nothing regarding their current contract.

Rising from his chair, he shed his jacket. He took the cylinder of the shockstik off his belt and tossed it aside. He tried out a grin, which felt like a rictus on his face, stretching muscles too wide. Alice regarded him with wary dispassion.

In a steady voice he said, "I brought lingerie along for you. I want you to wear it. I want to see you in it. It'll be like a live pornographic spectacle for me, you understand? Then when you've pranced about enough to my liking, I am going to screw you six ways from Sunday. Understand that, Alice? Understand me?"

* * *

She looked very good in the lace, in the stockings, in the garters. She moved unself-consciously for him, following his instructions. He couldn't help but be aware that he was essentially playing with a life-sized erotic doll here, putting her into this pose and that. Arch your back. Push out your breasts. He even had her purse her lips and make other pouty faces, but none of it showed in her eyes. They were like green glassy marbles during this exhibition.

And afterward, when he was thoroughly--if somewhat mechanically--aroused, he led her to the sumptuous bed which was adrift with kaleidoscopic quilts and eiderdown pillows. There he set himself to a lovemaking session to end all others; but he merely grunted and drove and sweated and toiled. And in the end it wasn't anything extraordinary, really. She got off; he got off. He was too tired to go again.

He told her to take off the Victorian Era harlot rags, and he pulled up the fancy covers and put his head to one of the less overstuffed pillows, telling himself that sleep was unlikely, that the events of yesterday and today would chase round his head, allowing no respite.

But he dropped quickly into a deep consuming slumber. He awoke once, in the small hours, to the sound of a cacophonous rattling. It was like a giant bag of teeth poured out onto a hard surface.

His half-conscious brain told him this was hail on the hideaway's roof. The temperature in the room had dropped precipitously. He groggily pulled another few quilts from up off the floor. Alice, alongside--but not touching him--shifted in her sleep. It shouldn't be hailing, some dim part of him said. Only yesterday in had been nearly seventy degrees in San Francisco.

Weather gone mad, he thought.

Whole world gone mad, he further thought.

And then he slept.

CHAPTER FORTY

'Stik

I wake in a lighter mood. Or, more likely, I have absorbed the bitterest sting of my jealousy. My adult self cannot sustain perpetual hurt of this nature. It feels too ridiculous; jealous of a boy; and yes, Carrow is in my mind something of a child, no matter that he is deemed a worthy mate by the woman who currently holds my affections.

So I push Carrow from the forefront of my thoughts, and concentrate on Alice, who is with me in the flesh. I treat her to a leisurely breakfast, then we poke about the shops on the waterfront.

I have her pick out a pair of sunglasses. They aren't the name brand to the cheap imitations she wears; rather, a pair with oblong, golden brown lenses that wrap tightly over her face. It is easier to see her eyes through them than with her other pair. I ask how they fit. "I can feel my eyelashes brush them when I blink," she answers. The woman at the register chuckles at this, a porcelain smile on her aging face. Maybe she thinks Alice is a young-old. Maybe she just wants our business.

There is one question I have not asked her, even with all that has come to light this weekend. I can't bring myself to voice it now. It stirs up too much inside me, roiling the silt of memories I have kept carefully dormant for some good long while. The question, as yet unasked, verges too closely into Sissy territory. My relationship with Alice is already too charged, too perilous, with this new information I have about her. I don't need to add the sins of my past to this particular present.

We go to the place where the ferry comes in. Sausalito's streets are damp with the melt of last night's hail shower. Today is mild, though nothing like the temperature spike in the city the other day. The boat is a growing dot on the dark water.

Alice says, unbidden, "I can't help running into Carrow at work." She scratches behind her right ear. "But I won't talk to him if you don't want me to."

She understands my jealousy, then, at least the mechanics of it--though the sentiment itself must be even more opaque than most emotions belonging to olds. But not only does she grasp it, she is taking steps to placate me.

I feel a smile trickle out onto my face. It puts a little meat back onto my bones. She doesn't care about me--because she can't--but this effort at appeasement touches me nonetheless. In an old this behavior would be "considerate."

To my chagrin I almost take her up on her offer. I could cut her off from Carrow, from her stand, for the remainder of our time together. Instead I say, "No. See him, talk to him. He's your future, Alice." I am merely your present, I add silently. And that present is running out.

We have one more weekend left. And then a handful of days after that, at which time our month will expire; and this relationship will terminate.

Goddamn, I'm going to miss her.

We stand, bags slumped at our feet, and watch the ferry approach.

* * *

Some kind of emergency lockdown is in effect at the San Francisco port. Armed police are on hand at the Ferry Building, where we are detained with the other disembarking passengers. Whatever is going on seems to have just happened. I don't get too anxious. It might be a bomb; it might be a prank. Perhaps someone has doused themselves with a flammable and set themselves aflame in the middle of the Embarcadero. I lift my nose and scent the air. No burnt meat smell. I shrug. I don't bother asking any of the cops. They never like answering questions, especially during a crisis. They stand about with their snub-nosed sonic rifles, black earclips feeding them updated information. The others who have come off the boat are equally blasé about the situation. Whatever the disaster is it can't be greater than the cataclysm we live with on a daily basis: having the cold among us.

I glance automatically at Alice. She is a cold. But she is not a calamity, not the bane of humans; at least, she is not that to me. I don't feel threatened by her, by what she represents. Maybe every other cold in the world still gives me the heebie-jeebies to some small extent or other, but she is a living being, invested with her own peculiar traits. She seems self-motivated. She learned to read, as a girl. She has secured her present and makes plans for her future. Was I so different at age twenty? I remember being inspired, determined to insure my future with a business degree. And maybe I even contemplated something long-term with Sissy Anspaugh. Maybe, back then, I had begun to think of her as...as my stand.

Conversationally--and impulsively--I ask Alice, "What do you want to do tonight?" It is not a question to ask a cold, but I have asked it anyway. Her responses have surprised me more than once.

She says, "Whatever you feel like."

Feel. It should be strange even hearing the word from her lips. She shouldn't be able to wield the verb as well as she does.

I give a little chuckle. "Suppose I want to do whatever you want to do." It's a little word puzzle I have built. I'm not being cruel; I am just vaguely curious how she might handle it.

Her eyes blink slowly behind the amber lenses of her new sunglasses. "Let's find that food truck again."

It's my turn to blink, only much more rapidly, as I process what she has said. The night we saw live music, down in Dogpatch, the burrito--the burrito she said tasted good. That is the food truck she is talking about.

Distantly I hear myself saying, "That could be fun...."

The corners of Alice's mouth move. They widen the flat line of her lips, upturning ever so slightly. She holds the expression for several seconds.

She is smiling. My cold lover is smiling.

A commotion arises within the venerable Ferry Building, another San Franciscan landmark. Has the crisis--whatever it is-- entered the building? I look around. No. People are just gathering their things and shuffling toward the exit. The police are waving everyone along. Evidently the emergency is no longer in effect.

I turn back to Alice. Her pretty face has resettled into its placid neutral mode.

* * *

We go with her plan. We try to chase down that same food truck. Fortunately there are apps and even chat groups devoted to the movements of local food trucks. In the big cities of the States it is as prevalent an activity as trainspotting in the U.K.

It's a game. Or it feels like one to me. So I give myself over to the sense of play. Why not? When was the last time I did anything truly goofy? Alice isn't giggling along, of course, but her attention is at least engaged. I can't remember what name was on the truck, but enough of a description remains in my memory. Some helpful soul on the network gives me the first vital information. With the name-- Coriolanus Cuisine--it is easier to track the mobile kitchen.

Alice and I jump in my rental. I haven't bothered unpacking from our Sausalito jaunt; I have just tossed my travel bag into a corner of the bedroom. That getaway at the romantic hot spot didn't turn out too well. Alice had too many surprises for me over the weekend. But we can still salvage Sunday evening.

Off into the twilight we go, heading crosstown. Somebody on the boards logged the Coriolanus truck at Haight Street where it dead- ends into Golden Gate Park. I get us there, goosing the accelerator a bit, flirting with the speed limit. What's the point of having power over your own vehicle if you don't push it a little?

But the t-intersection is empty. No truck doling out hot delicious foodstuffs to hungry passersby. I'm not really disappointed. This chase is enjoyable. I thumb up the app, report our lack of success, and ask after any other sightings. A moment later we receive a fresh clue.

Some part of me suspects we are being led a merry chase by a coterie of organized pranksters. But I don't particularly mind this joke being on me. The last strains of jealousy seem to be lifting from me. I cannot begrudge Alice a lover/companion who is her own age--and of her own kind, for Chrissake. She deserves that comfort, even if she would never call it a comfort. Now I will know that when she and I part, she won't be alone. She'll have Carrow. She will have her stand. And I just might have enough maturity and decency inside me to wish them both well, even as she slips out of my life forever.

It takes a solid hour to locate the truck. It turns up in North Beach, a historically Italian district; but ethnicity means nothing in a city which gentrified itself into a bleak sameness decades before the arrival of the cold. Coriolanus Cuisine is parked on the southern side of Washington Square. Across the tidy spread of green urban parkland Saints Peter and Paul Church looms. The same silver-haired man is in the truck, same drastic grin on his face. There is a line to reach the counter. Standing in it, I see the rust on the hinges of the metal awning that folds up from the side of the vehicle. There are a number of dings on the body of the truck, and one headlamp is patched with red tape.

But beat-up or not the old man is as lively as ever. I briefly hope he will remember Alice and me, but if he does, he makes no mention in his fast friendly badinage. Soon our food is prepared, paid for, and in our hands. Alice has gone with another burrito, but I take on a formidable chili dog. We stroll out onto the Square. Others are out and about, of course. North Beach, even these days, is rather densely populated, and quite a number of restaurants remain in business.

The dog is delectable, the chili hot, the onions crisp. I take big bites and chew slowly, savoring. This isn't just about the good food. This is another experience I will put into my book of mental keepsakes. The night Alice and I hunted the food truck. Hopefully she too will retain the memory; it will at least remain recorded in her brain's hippocampus--

Someone blunders into me, and as I stagger, trying to hold onto my chili dog, I realize with a surge of adrenaline that the collision was intentional. Derisive snickers from a gaggle of three or four individuals.

I manage to keep my balance, then shift and drop a foot firmly behind me. The group--they are a quartet, I see--has turned and appear to be considering a second pass. Young-olds? They look like a mixed bag. A couple mid-twenties, but at least one person in his thirties. A little band of roughs, out hassling whoever presents themselves for persecution. Evidently I have caught their attention. Alice too. She steps back from the group, flanking me. Her knees are bent, her posture wiry. She will probably--wisely--flee if any further menacing occurs. Colds have no need to save face. They will run from any fight. It is a sound tactic.

The faces leer. Bullies. The stamp of stupid cruelty is there, as prominent as a Neanderthal's brow ridges. I'm not even sure that my being in the company of an evident cold has drawn their rancor.

But the next move is made toward Alice. I am ready for it. I unclip the shockstik, push off from my back foot, and jam the stalk into the would-be assaulter's rib cage. The 'stik makes a satisfying crackle, and I can feel the charge streaming from it. The person--one of the mid-twenties males--yelps and manages to stumble backward. He gets only a step and a half before his whole body gives and he drops nervelessly to the ground. Luckily he got off the concrete path and onto a patch of grass.

I still hold my chili dog. Watching the remaining three cretins, I take another big bite. The shockstik remains at the ready.

The trio break their momentary paralysis and gather their fallen member. It is necessary to haul him away by his arms and legs. I return the implement to my belt, proud and pleased that my hand shakes not one iota.

CHAPTER FORTY-ONE

Weakness

The next day I still feel like d'Artagnan. I grin inwardly every time the sense memory comes: the juddering shockstik, the faint whiff of ozone. More, it is the great satisfying sense that I have stood up for my woman. A brute threatened her, and I brought him low. It's the most physically antagonistic act I have committed in a long time. I am glad I did it. I would do it again. But I hope the need doesn't arise. That moment could have gone south a dozen different ways. Any or all of the other punks might have been armed, perhaps with 'stiks themselves, maybe with blades. That would have been a sorry fate for me, bleeding like a stuck pig in Washington Square, the remains of a chili dog still gripped in one fist. I wouldn't have felt much like a swashbuckler then.

I am also probably lucky a cop wasn't on hand. What I did surely falls into some category of assault, even if it was defensive in nature. And a given police officer might harbor prejudice against me, since I would have been revealed as a card-carrying icer, out on the town with my age-inappropriate cold paramour.

Yet somehow that adventure of finding the food truck managed to be more exhilarating than our entire weekend of prepackaged romance in Sausalito. The confrontation with the quartet of roughs only made the escapade that much more invigorating.

And Alice was the one to suggest it.

I take the self-satisfied feeling with me to the office, after dropping off Alice. I don't see any sign of Carrow at the depot's entrance. It is some comfort to me to know that the two won't be sharing a bed until my time with her is through. Alice will be with me every night, right to the end. No chance for her and her stand to get up to whatever sort of carnal frolics--if any--they are accustomed to. It now seems rather ridiculous to me that at the outset of this arrangement I imagined I might only take her to bed a few times. Either I hadn't known how enticing she would turn out to be or I was aiming at some kind of aloof pose, thinking I could remain above the proceedings even as I initiated them. It was a hopelessly false effort on my part, for I am very much in this thing. Entangled. Embroiled. Devoured by it.

The hungover Monday pace at the office doesn't affect my work. I dibble and dabble. The numbers are unexciting, which suits me fine. I am not in an adventurous mood, as far as these matters of high finance are concerned. At the end of the day I doubt I will have left a ripple anywhere. Yet I also will not have risked any of the firm's capital. This has been a formula for job security for me for some time. Stay the course. No icebergs ahead. Steady. Steady.

I get a ping in the midmorning. A summons. It is from management, from a man named Archambeau. He is one of the executives, holding a title I can't recall at the moment. He would like me to visit his office, says the bland message.

Leaving my work station, I have no sense of what might be in store. I work my way through the maze of corridors, into the executive suite of offices. The decor improves markedly. Art adorns the walls. The lighting is somehow more luxuriant. I tap on the dark translucent glass of Archambeau's office door. It opens automatically with nary a pneumatic sigh.

The interior is almost lush, with deep-cushioned furniture and gleaming fittings. It is at once sterile and cozy, perhaps an artificial life form's idea of serenity. Archambeau's desk is broad, with an amorphously shaped surface. All sorts of monitors and readouts are embedded in the top; or more likely this is state-of-the-art holographic touch ware. Things wink and glow on the desk, but Archambeau isn't sitting behind it.

Instead he is stretched out in a kind of chrome-framed sling, the bedding a leather-like material. He sways slightly in his recumbent position. A big mug sits at hand on a lacquered stand, aromas rising with the steam that mix perfume with--I think--mango.

I hesitate in the doorway. This man's relaxed posture disturbs me. The firm's higher-ups don't make chitchat with me. I know I am not being groomed for a better position in the company. I don't want advancement. My niche is where I want to be, as much as I want anything having to do with this field. Once, long ago, the notion of finance genuinely excited me. But the world changed, and now the job is just my life raft. I need only keep it afloat.

"Kyle," he says. "Do come in."

Kyle no less. I enter, my foreboding increasing.

"And take a seat," he further instructs.

I sink into a square of cushion that threatens to swallow both my thighs. I say nothing because I don't know what the play is here. Archambeau lets that silence stand a moment. He is older than me by about fifteen years but looks to be in fine fettle. Trim, toned. Either he follows a serious health regimen or he is purchasing his fitness a sculpting treatment at a time. His lined face is at ease, confident; but I sense an underlying contempt aimed straight at me. Or else I have been assigning emotions too readily to others--even to those who can't possibly possess emotions--and I am in danger of second-guessing myself right into a corner.

Finally he says, "Bit of excitement the other day."

"How's that?" I ask, speaking for the first time.

"The fire. Evacuating the building."

Ah. Of course. Which sent me wandering the streets, to inadvertently spy on Alice and her boyfriend. "Yes. Exciting."

He takes up the mug and indulges in a long sip. I expect him to come to the point afterward. Instead: "Turned out to be nothing. Or almost nothing. Something on the sixteenth floor."

"Yes. I heard." I hadn't, actually. Or someone might have told me all about it when I got back to the building, but my mind was surely preoccupied with the sight of Carrow and Alice. I was in the first awful throes of jealousy.

"So," Archambeau says, "I'm going to be a little indelicate here and just come out with it."

Good. "Yes?" I'm still unnerved, but I want this over with.

"Okay." But he gives me another musing silence, swaying on his sling, before he says, "We all have our...weaknesses, Kyle."

He raises his silvered eyebrows at me, as if expecting a reply. I return him a nod. He could be going anywhere with this. For the first time I wonder if I'm about to be fired.

He goes on, "Your particular, well, weakness-- Actually, I'm reluctant to use that word. It conjures scarlet letters and stuffy morality, neither of which I'm qualified to trade in. I can say unconditionally that every person who works for this firm harbors some seamy secret. That isn't because this place is a hive of degenerates. It's because we're all human. You understand that much, Kyle?"

"I do."

He smiles, and I sense the contempt once more. A fraction before he speaks, I realize what he is going to say; and I close my eyes.

"Kyle...we know about you and the--the girl." He says it apologetically, as if he finds the intrusion into my personal life distasteful. Whereas the truth is much more likely that he finds what I do with my personal life distasteful. Repugnant, perhaps. Or, hell, for all I know he's a chill chaser too, with a passel of sexy young colds at his disposal, and the contempt he radiates is for himself as well. Maybe he intimately understands my weakness.

But I don't think so. He must surely have some kink in him. Probably a loathsome habit he indulges in in absolute secret. But it's not a taste for ice pussy.

Perhaps my co-worker Ikenberry ratted me out, though I can't think why he should hold any enmity toward me. Maybe he did it for laughs. Or maybe word of my liaison found its way up to management levels by any of a dozen different routes. I haven't been making my relationship with Alice a secret. If anything, I have perhaps been flaunting it. So much time spent together in public. Christ, how long did I figure I could carry on unnoticed?

There are two ways for me to go now: deny everything categorically or cop to it, coolly, without shame.

I say, "The girl is named Alice." I like how the words form in my mouth, the way they spill out, like tough guy dialogue from an old film noir.

Archambeau nods with infinite sympathy. "Yes, of course."

I don't let him settle into another silence. Suddenly I am impatient. "Is this going to get me fired?"

The notion appears to genuinely shock him. His eyes widen. "Do you want to leave us?"

"I'm still waiting for my answer." I shouldn't be lipping off like this. But I can feel the ghost of the shockstik discharging in my hand, the muzzle thrust against ribs.

He considers me, reevaluation in his eyes. "No. You won't be fired. But you won't continue with your relationship with this...person. I can cite you the clause in your contract, Kyle. We do have the right to intervene in this manner. Fraternizations which damage the reputation of the firm fall under the discretion and jurisdiction of the board of-- Jesus, man. No one is saying you can't live your life however you want. Personally I don't have a problem with your activities"--even as a look of disgust flashes briefly across his face--"but some of our clients would and do. They could make things difficult for the whole enterprise if it was known that one of our employees, in a critical position within the company, was gallivanting--"

"Gallivanting?" I interject. I don't even know why I object to the term.

"--carrying on so boldly with, well, a cold. As yet this is a matter contained within this office. But..."

He is still swaying. Abruptly he puts a foot down, halting the movement. Maybe he realizes how silly he looks in the position; maybe his attempt to make me feel at ease--if that is what he was doing--is at an end. In a fluid motion he rises, and I see he stands half a head taller than me. He straightens his suit vest.

Looking down at me, he says in a direct tone, "Just keep her out of sight. Like I said, it's your life. But you need to be more discreet. You get me, Kyle?"

* * *

I settle, slowly, almost gingerly, back into the familiar, ergonomically caressive chair at my work station. There is an expression on my lips, but I don't know what it represents. Have I been too long in Alice's company? Have I lost the talent for facial eloquence.

Then I remember the smile she gave me at the Ferry Building, just when the police lockdown lifted. Was it a real smile? What, exactly, do I mean by real?

I raise a hand and touch my mouth, as if I can read it like Braille. The shape feels vaguely like a smile, I decide. Perhaps a wry one. Or maybe it is the smile one makes just before a violent demonstration ensues, one which has nothing to do with happiness.

Tension snakes down my limbs. My fingers tighten on the chair's armrests. Something potent is stirring in me. Abruptly I remember: I once imagined this very scenario. Some superior at the firm taking me aside, telling me I needed to stop seeing Alice for the sake of my career. I imagined also how I would respond. Something along the lines of a conspicuously raised middle finger. Nobody was going to tell me to stay away from her. Nobody.

Yet I left Archambeau's office meekly and returned to the less luxurious regions of the thirty-ninth floor without a fuss.

But. But. I will not keep apart from Alice. I am not capable, at this point, of breaking away from her before our allotted time is through. So, what the fuck am I going to do?

Once I ask myself the question that plainly, the answer is manifest. I have scads of vacation time accumulated. I am no one's idea of a workaholic, but for the past several years I just haven't been able to organize any time off. I haven't known what to do with big chunks of empty time. Who goes on vacations anymore, anyway?

I go to my keypad. I draft a quick memo and send it on to the proper department. If they don't let me go immediately, it's possible I will simply walk out of this building and never come back.

CHAPTER FORTY-TWO

Wounded

Evidently I am valued. This is a happy surprise. My vacation request has gone through with an absolute minimum of bother. The firm's resource director buzzes me at my work station, asks a few cheerful questions, then thanks me for my time. By one in the afternoon my time off has been approved. After close of business today I need not report here again for two weeks.

My vacation time will cover all my precious remaining days with Alice. When I return, I will no longer be the potentially embarrassing icer on staff, the liability who might spook clients because of his perverted tendencies. I'll just be cautious and steady Kyle Norris again, the bloodless army ant who does his work and causes no consternation for anyone.

It takes a while for it all to sink in. Eventually I figure out why the company has been so acquiescent: they don't want to lose me. I sit before my screens and think about the abrupt departures from the firm I have witnessed over the past years. It hasn't happened often, but I recall personnel up and leaving, barely giving notice. Maybe they quit on impulse. Maybe it's tied to the many abandoned properties here in the city and all that sad furniture cast to the curbsides. People do things rashly these days, because the mechanisms which would normally keep them in place are...not so much broken, but revealed as inconsequential in the greater scheme. It is difficult to take job security seriously when a tide of inhuman monsters is slowly creeping in behind you. The old priorities lose their luster. It seems reasonable to indulge a caprice. Sick of where you live, where you work? Just walk away. Don't squander the remainder of your time doing anything or being anywhere that doesn't make you happy.

I won't squander these coming days with Alice. The thought injects excitement into me, and for a moment I am positively aflutter at the notion of the free slate ahead for us; then I realize that she still has her job, and part of our agreement was that this arrangement would never interfere with her work. Just because I'm free doesn't mean she is as well. She is an independent person, not some adjunct of myself.

Quietly I finish out my workday. I try to tidy up behind me, aware that I will return to these same numbers, these same financial tasks. But already, on some level, the job is a million miles away, and I am soaring over cool green landscapes with the sun on my face and my love at my side.

* * *

I go to pick up Alice from Sherwood Messengers. I sit in the car at the curb and wait for her to come out. If she wants to say a farewell to Carrow, I will nobly let them have their moment.

Finally she appears, climbing the ramp from the underground garage. Her bike is folded up like an origami crane and slung over her shoulder. As she comes out onto the sidewalk, I see that she is limping. I start, then fling open my door and hasten to her.

"Alice! Are you all right? What happened?" Worry streams in me like an adrenaline rush.

She halts. "Took a spill. Banged my knee." She indicates the left.

I look. It appears swollen. My concern amplifies. Got to get her to an ER, have a doctor examine--

"I've got a bandage around it," she explains.

"But--"

"It's fine, Kyle."

"But we should--"

"I have fallen before. I heal."

I stand there, still desperately wanting to do something. She gazes at me a moment; then: "Here. Carry my bike?" She shrugs it off her shoulder and holds it out to me.

It is about five yards to the car. She doesn't need me to carry the lightweight bicycle. But somehow she has figured out that it will calm me down, make me feel better. She has analyzed the emotionality of the situation, and come to an effective solution. She doesn't feel; but she recognizes my feelings. I wonder if it's like decoding the cries animals make at each other. It seems extraordinary to me that she is able to do this.

Gratefully I take the bike. It is even lighter than I guessed, closer to the weight of a kite. She must have spent quite a bit of money for it; but she had done so for sound reasons: to further secure her future as a messenger.

She limps alongside me back to the car. I eye her sidelong. What will she be doing when she is my age? Will she and Carrow still be together? I try to imagine their relationship ending--not, this time, because I am jealous but merely out of curiosity as to how such a thing might be effected. Colds breaking up with one another? Well, it wouldn't be a screaming match with recriminations spewed back and forth, the way it might go with a pair of olds. Two colds might instead have a brief, succinct conversation. Or maybe one simply said to the other, "We're done," and that was that. No fuss, no accusations.

She will still be beautiful when she is forty. Her habits are healthy, and she seems intent on maintaining herself. She'll likely retain her looks when she is fifty as well. I can foresee the crow's-feet, but her green eyes will stay have a certain brilliance. Her cheekbones will stay high and sculptural. At sixty she will still possess all her basic structural attributes. She might well still be trim, even taut. At sixty...

Yes. And when she is sixty, I have a good chance of being dead. Or else I will be eighty, and death--even if my own health sustains-- will be a hovering thing, a patient darkness which shall follow me wherever I go.

But if I yet live, come that far-off date, I will most surely retain my memories of Alice. Alice A1384-74K. Alice Felzien. She may be the last thought in my head when the black fog rolls in on me with great finality.

Or perhaps I'll hold the memory of Sissy Anspaugh in my mind, as that vast dusk takes me.

Or maybe it will be some perfectly trivial mental twitch which occupies my ultimate moment in this life. My neurons might feebly fire one last time to present me with a snippet of a television show I saw as a kid. Or a snatch of an earworm song I always hated. Hell, I might think of Gregory Peck or the color puce or a fragment of an economic principle I got out of a textbook long ago. Memories, at that late stage, will be flotsam and jetsam. I probably won't have the luxury of organizing a concluding thought.

I hold the passenger door for Alice and wince a little as she pulls her left leg gingerly inside. Then I put her bike in the trunk and hop in behind the wheel.

* * *

Naturally I insist on babying her. I am genuinely concerned about her knee. When I help her out of her jeans and gently unwind the springy gauze bandage, I see that some swelling has indeed occurred. The knee is bruised. I have her tell me about the mishap as I prepare an ice compress. It is not much of a story. Her front tire got caught in a narrow fissure in the street's tarmac. It was just wide enough to accommodate her wheel and hold it, while her momentum carried her over the handlebars.

"It's not the safest job you have," I mutter as I set the ice pack on her joint, applying soft pressure.

"It was a fluke, Kyle. I could go over that same patch a hundred times and it wouldn't happen again."

I move in an ottoman and lay her foot tenderly atop it. "I've seen you come off the hills on Powell Street," I add. "That is not safe."

She says nothing, but I assume it is her normal cold non-responsiveness when she hasn't had a question put directly to her. But I look up and find her eyes on me.

"You watched me." The rasp tickles her voice. There is of course no wonder in her tone, but I feel somehow the subliminal conveyance of her surprise.

"I..." I begin to say and trail off.

Without prompting, she goes on, "There was a man who would

stand and watch. I saw him several times. That was you...." This last is almost a question, but not quite. She saw me, on my lunch breaks, staking out a piece of sidewalk, hoping to see the girl on the bicycle with the wind-whipped dark red hair. Only now has she realized the man was me.

My face warms. I don't know if this is an "aw shucks" kind of chagrin or if I am actually embarrassed.

I say, "I'm glad you didn't hurt yourself worse."

"It is a part of the job, sometimes."

"I wish you could take time off too." I told her on the car ride that I was now on vacation time.

Again she looks straight at me; again there seems some hidden extra intensity to her gaze. She says, "My kind don't have jobs like that."

It is a broad sort of statement. Colds usually answer questions-- when they answer them at all--in a cryptic but specific manner. They address something tangible. Alice has just offered me something almost...philosophical. Her kind doesn't get the sort of jobs where one is entitled to vacation pay, sick leave, benefits. Colds work the shit jobs and everybody knows it, and I am being an asshole by murmuring about how I wish she could take time off. Like she doesn't spend enough time with me. Like I'm not using up every second of her life when she's not at her job.

But of course she says none of this. Maybe she doesn't fucking have to.

I remain kneeling on the floor, before her, applying more gentle pressure to her injured knee with the ice pack. The cold will keep down the swelling.

* * *

I drive her to work in the morning. It is strange not to be wearing a suit on a Tuesday. Her knee is better today. The limp has vanished.

Once I drop her off, I find myself adrift in the random conduits on the downtown. I pilot the rental. I turn down this street and that. The full empty day awaits me. Belatedly I realize I have made no plans for this alone time. I'm officially on holiday. I should take advantage of this opportunity.

But part of me is sick of this city, of its wiles, its attitudes and spectacles. There has always been a sense of privilege to the place. I was even aware of it as a kid, though it was a background hum, barely perceptible and difficult to interpret. But I remember adults telling me and each other: "San Franciscans are special people."

We are not, though. Or no more special than residents of Tampa, Trenton, Tucson or any other locality which has stood long enough to have gathered a few traditions and idiosyncracies to its bosom. San Franciscans--or a certain stripe of San Franciscan, anyway--take on a mantle of entitlement which no one, really, should assume. A few landmarks and geegaws don't add up to cultural superiority.

Still, I will surely never leave the city. I'll remain dug in, hopefully occupying the same ground floor in the same Potrero Hill Victorian, staying at my job until I can retire or until our financial system starts to crumble. And if the latter is the case, I will hole up in my home, holding out as long as I can, while outside the now majority mass of the cold begin to finally reshape the world in whatever image they deem best. I hope they won't see the logical need to exterminate us remaining olds. I would be happy--grateful--if they just let us quietly expire in our dens and warrens.

I laugh out loud, behind the wheel. I turn sharply and accelerate, getting myself out of downtown, heading home. I have woken early in order to drive Alice to work. Now I am going back to bed, to sleep the sleep of the just or the damned or whatever it is that I am.

* * *

It is a willfully idle day. I read some, listen to some music. I take a walk around the neighborhood. A piano is parked at a corner of an intersection. I don't know what the sanitation department does about junked items like these. I never see garbage trucks attempting to take away these bulky pieces. But they do eventually seem to disappear, as if reabsorbed into the urban fabric. Maybe people are snatching them up for their own homes. I remember a low-slung red velvet chair I snagged off the street in my college days. In my junior year I moved off the campus, into a tiny apartment. The red chair, a bed, a nightstand/

desk were my only furniture. I loved that place. I had to bust my tail to make rent on the money I earned at the restaurants I worked at, but it was worth it. It furthered my sense of independence. I started to think I could really make it in the real world.

I remember Sissy sitting in that chair, wearing only one of my long-sleeved white waiter shirts. She had her feet drawn up onto the front edge of the cushion, hands gripping her knees, so the shirt wasn't doing much to cover her essentials--which was fine with me. She was grinning at me; that is a part of the memory; and I of course was grinning back, so happy to have this lush, luscious woman in my life--

I am thinking a lot about Sissy lately. Or maybe this is the usual amount of thought I give to her in a given period and am only noticing it now more acutely, for whatever reason.

Perhaps I need to really think about her at some point. Clear the mental air. Delve the memory depths, perhaps to purge some of the stale atmosphere down there. Sissy was so long ago. So long. And what lurid circumstances caused us to part.

But if I am going to look inward and backward with some intensity, it is not going to be today. It's nearly time to pick up Alice. I get dinner prepped. A nice home-cooked meal tonight. How hollow it will be when she is no longer around, with me puttering about in here on my own, carelessly making my solo suppers. No doubt I will sit at the table and gaze mawkishly across at the vacant seat opposite. Cue the orchestral strings. Minor key stuff, with sad oboes thrown in.

I can't even summon a gallows chuckle at the image. It is too precise, too prescient. I will be sitting there. And I will feel the loneliness. There is no avoiding it.

I fetch Alice at the garage. No accidents today; so she tells me when I ask. She is wearing one of the colorful tops I got her. She will keep on wearing them once we have parted. The items are quality. But they will probably not get laundered often--maybe not at all. I don't remember her ever mentioning doing laundry. So, she will wear and wear the articles, and they will slowly fade from use and from the sun. Maybe a few seams will split, and maybe she'll sew them up. But the garments, one by one, will lose their vibrancy, until eventually they will perhaps be as nondescript as typical cold apparel.

Without prompting she asks what I did today. I'm not as surprised by the question as I would have been two weeks ago. Alice is a cold; but Alice has...personality? No, not quite. Perhaps she simply possesses quirks, at least within the scope of known cold behavior. She is capable, now and then, of emulating certain demeanors. But it must be pretense, mimicry. She asks about my day not because she cares, as a lover would, as a girlfriend, but because she wants to keep me interested and happy. So I have long since concluded.

But I keep up my part of the pretense. I tell her about my indulgently idle day. Soon we are home. I fire up the stove, and she goes to take a shower, again without prompting. Maybe she feels there is an advantage to her in clean skin. I wonder what Carrow makes of her cleansed state these days. Will she keep up these hygienic habits after she and I have parted?

I lay out the meal. The aromas are comforting, but really it is Alice's presence which gives the scene such a lovely domesticity. I could make this exact same food for myself, and eating it alone would be an empty experience, the mere consumption of food as bodily fuel.

Despite all the hearty meals she has eaten with me, she doesn't appear to have gained an ounce. She retains her taut, limber shape. It must be nice to have that youthful metabolism, coupled with the strenuous exercise regimen that comes with her job. I generally eat smaller portions than she does, trying to maintain my own weight and form. After she is gone, my meals will doubtlessly be less elaborate. I imagine I will experience a loss of appetite as well.

She eats. I have put on some music to accompany our dinner. It is some old jazz. She responds in no way to the sounds. They must be random bleeps and blats to her, less coherent than other music I have played for her. I can't even imagine trying to explain jazz to her; I don't know if I could explain it to myself. But I like it playing in the background as we eat.

As we finish, she reaches a hand across the table. She takes my right-hand fingers in hers and squeezes. The action startles me. She is looking into my eyes.

"Is there anything you want to do tonight, anything...special?" Perhaps I am halfway imagining that suggestive pause. But my mind is not conjuring the movement of her lips now, as the corners stretch. It is like the smile she gave me the other day, in the Ferry Building. This time she also closes her eyes partway.

My throat catches. "Special?" I whisper.

"Do you..." No mistake now; there is the provocative pause. "...want to fuck me in the ass?" Her mouth stretches even further.

I snatch my hand out of her grip. She has used vulgar language before, but this seems beyond the pale. Shock pushes me back in my chair. I have to clear my throat again before I can speak. "Why would you offer me something like that?" I'm not repulsed by the idea, but that she would volunteer such a thing is unfathomable to me.

"To make you happy," she says. She keeps up the smile, but she doesn't have it quite right. It is the structure of a risque leer, but the underlying heat is absent; and so the expression begins to look grotesque.

Gooseflesh rises on my body. My hands and feet are suddenly chilled. Stonily I say, "I was already happy, Alice. You don't have to make me an offer like that." I almost tell her to wipe the look off her face. Instead I say, in a gentler tone, "You understand that our deal is set, right? I have obviously already paid your rent. I am going to go on providing meals and transportation and any other comforts that occur to me. There's nothing you need to negotiate from me. I will follow through on our arrangement, right to the end. Understand?"

She lets her mouth relax. I gaze at her pretty face and into her green eyes.

"But if I keep making you especially happy," she says, "you might want to continue our relationship."

I blink. "Continue?"

She says nothing. With a gut-hollowing feeling I realize what she means.

"You mean extend our arrangement," I say.

She nods.

I let out a long breath. "This is for one month, Alice. I told you that at the start."

"But you might change your mind."

"I won't."

"But you might."

I might buy her for another month. That is her thinking. And admittedly, it is clear thinking. Logical. But she doesn't know how determined I am, how I set down these parameters at the outset for solid, intractable reasons. Offers of anal sex aren't going to dissuade me. The finite nature of our relationship is one of its key components.

I don't try to tell her any of this, however. Perhaps she has had success with this tactic in the past, stringing along a sugar daddy for some while. Let her believe I might have a change of heart; let her hope my libido will overcome any reason I have. Maybe Carrow, her stand, employs this same stratagem. It is hardly farfetched to picture him as the plaything of some female old, perhaps my age or even older; or, just as likely, playing the catamite to some lonely male old.

Alice doesn't know that I have entered into this relationship with her in order to address my own past--specifically my past with Sissy Anspaugh. Alice doesn't even know who Sissy is. I have never mentioned her.

Not once.

I clear the plates from the table. Alice wordlessly heads to the bedroom, to await my pleasure.

But Sissy is in my mind as much as Alice is. I will need to confront my history and my feelings regarding my onetime lover, my erstwhile mate. Sissy. Sissy. I can only think of you in our two stages. Before. Then after. The good times. Then the bad. Only in that way can I bring you wholly up from my memory.

CHAPTER FORTY-THREE

The Story of Sissy, Part I

Kyle Norris was a native San Franciscan, temporarily transplanted to the woodsy wilds of Northern California. He was attending Humboldt State University, and this was his third year. For a time, in the first months of his arrival, he had been uncertain he would survive this academic environment. College was challenging, in a way high school had never been. There would be no coasting, no last-ditch cram sessions to pull out a passing grade. He couldn't do this schoolwork in the traditional half-assed manner. This was adult time. He had to be personally responsible for his performance. It was a very sobering situation he had found himself in.

But by now the worst was over. The work wasn't any easier; actually, these third year courses were mental back-breakers. But Kyle knew how to apply himself. All those stupid aphorisms from grade school--like You get out of school what you put into it—had turned out to be true. It hadn't meant anything to him as a youngster. It was part and parcel of the whole schoolroom milieu, which had seemed as pointless as the silly blue uniform sweater he'd had to wear.

This was Kyle Norris at age twenty, with several years away from home under his belt. This was a Kyle who studied earnestly, who took his classes seriously; who also had worked several jobs in his "spare" time, restaurant gigs, as the town where the university was located had a lively if funky dining scene. He had started out as a dishwasher at one place, gone to bus tables at another, until finally, this year, he was actually waiting tables. And making pretty good money off tips.

It was a punishing schedule. He basically had no free time; or would have had none at all if he hadn't sacrificed an hour or two of sleep most nights, repurposing that time for some necessary socializing or simple down time. It was part of his self-management regimen. Early on at the university he had learned how to be an effective student. As a junior, he had also perfected the art of being a sane, not too stressed out human being. Or he'd almost perfected it.

He just didn't quite have the sex thing locked down, in a tidy orderly fashion.

Oh, he had gotten dutifully laid. In that sense he was like any semi-privileged university attendee away from home and parental supervision for the first time, and flooded as well with the customary tide of hormones, and fairly saturated with the expectations of libidinal merriment which a lifetime of horn dog college comedies had bestowed upon him. Kyle had had, in the vernacular, his share of pussy. Or if it wasn't perhaps a full proper share, it was a passable proportion. He'd slept with a small sample size of female students, as well as two co-workers from his various restaurants jobs.

But there had been no one truly steady, not even anyone he could reliably call a fuck buddy. He probably would have liked that: fuck buddy had a lovely ring to it.

He was hardly the only student from the Bay Area. There was also a great passel from the Los Angeles region. But Kyle didn't seek any of these out specifically; he felt no nostalgia when it came to San Francisco. The geographic change was a component of the great shift in his life. He had left home. He was engaged in an adult undertaking, the slow steady earning of a business degree. He was employed and nearing the point where he could actually get himself an apartment, albeit nothing fancy; but to have a place, a home which was truly and incontestably his own...that would be a worthy accomplishment, and a sure signifier that he was making something of his life.

Yet there was no denying that it would have been nice to have a reliable, consistent sexual partner.

* * *

* * *

Blowing off steam was a holy rite to some. There were those attending the university who were not so ardent about their studies or who were more adrift than Kyle, not quite fully focused on what they wanted to achieve, either at the school or in life. They nibbled at their courses; they sipped from the various scholastic cups being proffered to them. But when it came time to seek relief from the drudgery, they went at it like sailors on shore leave.

It was always a tribulation to attain alcohol, but students not yet twenty-one had found the timeworn workarounds—getting someone of age to buy it, fake IDs—and liquor or at least beer was often on hand at the weekend gatherings which popped up on and off campus.

Kyle wasn't particularly enamored of booze. Neither did the prevalent and just as unlawful underage pot culture much interest him. It was enough that he set aside time to socialize. Fighting through a hangover the following day or the spaciness that came of being high the previous night weren't obstacles he liked to put deliberately in front of himself. Humboldt County had a long, storied history with marijuana, well back into the dark ages of its total illegality. But even that didn't really tempt Kyle. After all, he wasn't trying to go local; he was just here to prepare himself for a life where he could earn a reliable living. There wasn't much that was romantic about that. His was a steady course, the needle pointing magnetic north and nowhere else.

Some had brought their artistic ambitions with them to the university. Kyle had already quietly and sensibly set aside his latent musical aspirations. Oh, he could still ring out the same chords as when he was a teen. But he no longer had illusions about himself and the guitar. The instrument was just something he had a passing knowing of. He also knew how a shovel worked, but that didn't make him a ditch digger.

A Saturday in early spring brought the usual raft of parties, and Kyle was invited to a few. Even in his third year at the college he didn't have a tight circle of friends, a small inviolable coterie, say; but he had what seemed to him a plethora of friendly acquaintances, people he could expend his social energies on.

He picked a gathering at random and set out that evening. The grueling week had left its mental marks on him. It was time to turn off his brain and squander a few hours. The party was off the campus, in the town proper, a house on a secluded street which was being rented by three students. Kyle's plans for finally moving out of campus housing were aimed toward solo living, a one-bedroom apartment where he wouldn't have to share a bathroom with anybody, where he could seal himself safely up just by shutting his front door. Another few weeks working at the restaurant and he could actively start looking for a place.

The party, when he arrived, didn't turn out to be a rager, which suited him. He hated gatherings with pounding music. He rang the doorbell, was let inside, and found chips and other snacks, along with the requisite bucket of beer. Since soda was on hand as well, he chose one of those.

About twenty people were strung through the rooms of the modest one-story house. The place was decorated in early college student castoff; or maybe the place came furnished this way, furniture that a given group of college-age tenants couldn't inflict much noticeable harm on.

Kyle greeted and was greeted by familiar faces. HSU was an amiable place, with a congenial student body. The current generation of burgeoning human adults was a good one, Kyle thought, when he had time to think about such matters. Politically the nation was presently living in a Vonnegut novel, but the people coming of legal age seemed to share a seriousness, a purpose, a vague but perhaps quite powerful collective will. They might, just might, change the bruised planet for the better. Stranger things had happened.

Of course, Kyle Norris wasn't prepping himself to be an activist or a revolutionary. Hell, he was lining up to be a part of the establishment—it was a word the local gray-haired hippies liked to throw around. He felt a general compassion for the human race, yes; certainly he was sufficiently woke to avoid any appearances of misogyny, racism or homophobia, not that he'd ever felt inclinations toward such backward thinking. He was, in a sense, of his time...just not as engaged with the world as some others around him were. Well, someone had to wear a suit and work in the financial sector. That would be him. In his way, he would play a part in whatever was to come, even if it was only to prop up the old economic pillars of the land. Nobody wanted the whole structure to fall, even those radicals who did want it all to collapse. They just didn't know they didn't want total fiscal failure. No one would want to live in that rubble.

Someone was smoking weed, and he did his best to steer away from the free-floating cloud. With his soda in hand he sidled into another room. It was a kind of foyer off the kitchen, and it seemed to lead to a backyard. An outside light was on, he saw through the dusty glass set high in a drab door. Normally it took him a good half hour to wander away from the main action of a party, into a yard or garage. But this time he saw movement outside. He pulled open the door and stepped out onto the little cracked concrete porch there. The cloak of night had dropped fully by now. Light pollution in the town was rather modest, and a vault of icy stars showed itself overhead. The air was chill. Spring did not bring immediate warmth this far north in California.

Only one person was out here. She strode one way across the yard, which was a mix of cement and wild grass, strewn with old broken pottery, a coil of garden hose, a couple foldout canvas chairs and nameless rubbish. When the woman neared the back fence, she turned on her heel and started back. She had a cell phone to her right ear. In her other hand was a cigarette—a plain old tobacco cigarette, trailing a thread of gray smoke. People smoked here. Kyle had been shocked at how prevalent the practice was, having grown up in San Francisco where the habit had been practically legislated and social-pressured out of existence.

But he barely saw the cigarette. The woman was coming right at him, on a dead-on heading. He had a perfect view of her, as if she were coming down a fashion runway toward him. The impressions hit him all at once, a glut of sensory data. Her hair was a cumulonimbus of red, great bouncy curls of frosty strawberry. Her brow was a slope of porcelain. Beneath were her big searching eyes. Her nose was miniature aquiline. Her jaw was fine, her mouth...well, that was a sensual mouth. No two ways about it. She had a long neck, loose bare arms, and her gait was at once easy and aggressive, as though she were a naturally easygoing person presently walking off some negative emotions. Her legs swung as a dancer's might, and her hips moved in a way that made Kyle want to stare and stare at them. It was not—none of this was—his normal response when he looked on a woman for the first time. He was always careful not to gawk or gape, even if the woman in question was undeniably attractive. His thinking had always been that conspicuously beautiful people didn't need his ogling to know what they were made of and how the world routinely beheld them. They had no doubt banked plenty of self-esteem before he had ever showed up.

But it was more than that with an attractive woman: he just didn't want to be that guy. The leerer. The male who would immediately start in with suggestive comments, who would claim it was all in "good fun" if confronted with his behavior. No. Not Kyle Norris.

Still, he was struck all in a giddy rush by her physical attributes. Only now did the cigarette and cell phone fully register on him as he stood there on the small stone step. She was speaking in a tight tone, pausing to suck smoke and blow it out.

She came right up to tiny porch and halted with the precision of a drill sergeant. Then she did five things in rapid succession. She said a curt, "Goodbye, Seth," stabbed her phone with her thumb, dropped the cigarette, stamped on it with the toe of her white tennis show, and looked straight up into Kyle's eyes.

Her irises were amber, flecked with minute sparkling highlights.

In a voice that suggested she and Kyle were resuming a conversation momentarily interrupted, she said decisively, "That's not my last goodbye to him. But it's close. It is very very close."

Normally he needed a second or two before he could utter his first words to a woman. He thought of it as a kind of mental processing pause. He never wanted to blurt something stupid. But words were already at his lips, and he heard himself saying, "Perhaps that's for the best."

"Perhaps. Actually there's no perhapsing about it."

"Seth won't know what hit him."

"Yes he will."

"Then let's assume he brought this on himself."

"No, this was a group effort mismatch."

"I can't help feeling you're in no way to blame." Dismay started to catch up with him just then. He had been snapping off lines like in a black and white screwball comedy; and that just wasn't like him. Where was this wit coming from? From where the confidence?

She was still looking directly up at him. But now a smirk intruded on her pretty face. She had freckles, he saw. A patina of them, quite light, across the bridge of her nose. This sent a prickling through him for no reason he could name.

In a more relaxed tone she said, "You're being nice. Don't think I don't recognize that."

He decided to dip his head at that. They didn't let anyone bow anymore, so he did the next best thing: head dip. A gracious acknowledgment of her statement.

But now he had to say something more, or she might go marching past him, through the door, maybe through the house and out the front, and he didn't know her name, and he would ask others at the party who she'd been, and nobody would quite be sure, and no one would know her full name, so he wouldn't be able to find her on social media, and certainly no one would have her phone number; only Seth had that, damn pigheaded Seth, who needed to be removed from this picture—

"Hi. My name's Kyle. Kyle Norris. Hi."

"Hi, Kyle. I'm Sissy." And she smiled, revealing a slight overbite she didn't attempt to hide and which—again, inexplicably—caused his heart to speed, as if these physical traits were all in the sweet spot of what he most liked in women. Except that this Sissy wasn't some personalized dream-come-true female. He'd never had these particular characteristics in mind before. Freckles? Overbite? Why would those turn him on?

It was, he realized with an inner blooming warmth, as though he were imprinting on these things in real time, because she was invested with these physical features.

"Sissy," he said. Then again: "Sissy. I like your name."

She tilted her head two degrees, keeping up the smile. He had said the right thing. Not That's a pretty name, which was analogous to You've got a great rack. (She did, by the way.) Instead he had said like. Maybe she was slightly self-conscious about her somewhat unusual name. Probably she had gotten her share of razzing on the schoolyard.

And the night froze there, right there. Vaulting stars, bracing night air. She wore a suede vest--the chill didn't appear to bother her--and purple jeans, a corduroy bracelet around her left wrist. This was the back yard where they had just met, and it would always be that place. Because they had met. They were still looking each other in the eye. And names had been exchanged.

Someone was going to have to say something further. Contact info needed to be swapped. He was drawn to her, and his first social feints toward her had been excellent. He had been witty, playful, sympathetic. And she was still smiling at him.

One of them was going to have to ask the other out.

Somebody was really going to have to do that, in the next few seconds.

* * *

That first date was lovely. Of course, it wasn't a date. No one liked going on one of those. Dates conjured images of awkward formality, throwback social rituals, boys in pocketless sport coats and bow ties; perhaps a corsage would be involved. No. It was much more pleasant--and far less fretful--to meet up with somebody, even someone you were interested in, and just...hang out.

So, Kyle and Sissy hung out at a coffee haunt. The place had art on the walls. The music on the sound system was eclectic. Kyle said that the staff—a cross-section of local hipsters and part time university students--brought in their own tunes and played them in rotation. He had been to the coffeehouse before. He liked it. You could study here. You could decompress. Or you could rendezvous with that woman from the party two nights ago who you couldn't stop thinking about.

He had worried that his wit would abandon him, that its confident appearance at their first meeting had been a fluke, a strange cross-circuiting of internal processes which had gifted him, briefly, with the ability to speak easily and intelligently to a girl he found particularly attractive. But his humor, his intellect, didn't fail him. And she was just as witty herself, just as sharp. They played nicely off each other, verbal thrusts going every which way. And each seemed to say the right thing at the right time with the right amount of emphasis or irony. He had maybe never enjoyed talking to a woman more in his life.

Having hung out for about an hour at the coffee place, they regrouped the following day and hung out for pizza. Then they hung out at a study hall and sat across from each other at a long table and did their schoolwork. They were mostly silent, because others were also studying, but they looked up regularly at one another, and her eyes seemed to twinkle for him. He got a warm feeling every time.

She leaned forward, elbows on the tabletop, and whispered, "I said my last goodbye to Seth."

He smiled, and the smile gained strength and became a grin. "Good," he said.

That same night they hung out again, this time at Sissy's housing unit on the campus. It was nicer than what Kyle had, and she didn't have to share the space with anybody, as he did. She put music on, and they talked. And laughed. And things got flirty, then they got physical. They kissed. He found that first kiss transportive as well as impossibly intimate. It wasn't like any hand shake kiss, something tossed off almost indifferently. It wasn't sport, and it wasn't impulse. He had the distinct sense she had been anticipating the kiss for roughly as long as he had. Now it had come, and time froze again; and he felt something close to joy. Maybe he would have known for certain it was joy had he ever experienced it before.

They didn't have sex that night. He was okay with that. They did have it two evenings later, and he was good with that as well. Like the kiss, it lived up to all expectations. By now she occupied a permanent place in his thoughts, and only when he was with her did the world feel properly balanced. He cautioned himself against getting overly attached, but the cautions felt brutish, even cowardly.

She was smart. She dabbled in meditation. She was great in bed, limber and spry and not at all fastidious. Freckles sprayed her shoulders, as light as those across the bridge of her nose. She had lovely firm breasts and a backside that was lovely and firm also. Sensuality radiated from her, a hothouse warmth. Having known her carnally, he could look at her and be bombarded by images and become aroused. There was a sweet, slightly comical intensity to his adolescent-like excitements. She giggled sometimes but always made him feel okay about it. For, she admitted, she got as turned on from looking at him.

There were no downsides with her. No burdens. No ordeals she felt compelled to put him through. He'd enjoyed casual sex at the school, yes, but it was never as carefree as he would have liked. Often some kind of mind game was being played; often there was a price to pay. But Sissy didn't need to be cajoled. She didn't have blind spots or annoying quirks. It was remarkable. Then he realized what it was: they were honest with each other. It was like they were both stripped down, putting up none of the usual defenses. He didn't get embarrassed around her because he didn't feel she was waiting to pounce on any little faux pas. She appeared to trust him innately, sharing things about herself without first feeling the need to secure his pledge not to laugh or ridicule what she might say. It would never occur to him to ridicule anything about her.

At this point he could only appreciate and cherish her, and count himself fantastically lucky.

A week in and he had lost interest in any other women, or even in the idea of other women. She was seeing him exclusively as well; she told him so.

Two weeks:

"Can I call you my girlfriend?"

"Yes." Pause. "Can I call you my boyfriend?"

"Yes. Oh, yes."

Life took on a kind of rosiness. There was a stability which had never been present before. It was as if his heart were at last in the right place. He could breathe with her. He could be, in the deepest sense of the word, with her. Their connectivity was intense but not dismaying. No desperation came with his feelings. Oh, their mutual passions were decidedly urgent; but panic did not underlie them, and this was new to Kyle Norris and it seemed new as well to Sissy Anspaugh.

They were glad--very glad--to have found each other, and they said so often and meant it every time.

* * *

She was giving up smoking. It was a process, she said. He was glad she was doing so. "I would miss you if you died of lung cancer," he told her. She was down to three cigarettes a day.

She had come from Minnesota, and the Californian winters didn't impress her. She had her own car, which he did not; and it was great being able to pile in her sturdy heap and drive about the area. It was a startling, pastoral region, with redwoods and Sitka spruce and deep woods covering the rolling hills. There were rivers, and there was the ocean. They took in these sights and experienced them together, and they were made more memorable and precious because of that.

Sociology was her major. She was a fierce reader of fiction, liked detective stories a lot, but would read anything. Her tastes in music were broad. Her family was big, but no immediate relations lived anywhere near. She kept in touch with her parents and mostly ignored her siblings, who never reached out to her anyway. This didn't seem to trouble her.

They spent as much time together as they feasibly could. School was demanding, for her as well as him. He'd been hesitant, even apologetic, the first time he had told his life's plan, how he meant to use his business degree to secure himself a stable niche at some financial institution. The ambient mood about the town and the college was decidedly progressive, with a reflexive hostility toward capitalistic organizations. It wasn't a very well thought out philosophy, in Kyle's opinion. But again Sissy did not needle him, didn't pass judgment. Theirs wasn't an adversarial relationship, where contentions simmered just underneath the surface. They liked each other.

When he was ready to move into his apartment, he almost asked her to move in with him. But it was too soon. Cohabitation was a mammoth leap forward; and yet he was sure--absolutely certain--that they could have successfully shared a living space, even after just these few weeks of officially being girlfriend and boyfriend.

She helped him move his stuff into the new place. He didn't have much. But it was glorious, after that afternoon of hauling furniture and boxes, to shut his door, lock it, and lead her to his bed, which was just a box spring and mattress on the floor. There they made a kind of soft solemn love. And he knew this was indeed lovemaking, not just sex, not merely a happy screw with a female to whom he was strongly drawn. They joined on every level. They were twin heats and identical energies, and the world crackled and coruscated about them when they became one. He wanted her. He needed her. He had lost some part of him in her but had gained it back in the product of their joining.

They whispered in the night, even in the safe confines of his private living space. She told him his thoughts, and he told her hers.

* * *

She had the car, so they often went grocery shopping together. They had gone in the afternoon, after their last classes for the day. Kyle kept teas stocked that she liked. Sissy stayed over at the apartment regularly but not so much that she was, by default, living there. If and when the two of them ended up cohabiting, he wanted it to be a mutually arrived at decision, soberly made and honestly implemented.

He could see it happening, in the future. The near future.

It was still so exciting to be with her. But the excitement came sometimes from simple domestic moments. Hearing her gargle her mouthful of toothpaste when she was done brushing; a habit she'd had for years, she said. Or trading texts in the day, abbreviated inside jokes or wonderfully lachrymose endearments.

Or...

Later that same evening, after the grocery shopping earlier, Sissy at her wheel suddenly turned them into the Safeway parking lot. They were coming back from an open mike comedy night at a club-- bad bad stand-up, but nonetheless great kitschy fun.

"Forget something before?" he asked as she pulled neatly into a spot.

She killed the ignition and turned to him, a kind of manic gleam in her amber eyes. "The lime."

"The...lime?" She had bought a lime earlier. She liked slices of lime in some beverages she drank. She was now down to two cigarettes a day.

"That funky one," she said. "Bumpy. Weird. I picked it up, but it didn't look right. Not gone bad, not moldy. Just unusual. And I put it back and got a different one."

"That's your prerogative, as a shopper." It was his attempt at wit. He didn't think the drollery had failed him, but his wry comment didn't appear to land.

Sissy was serious. "No one's going to buy that lime. It's going to get thrown out in the end, after having watched all its siblings get purchased. They will all get used and enjoyed. They'll become part of the great cycle. The ugly duckling will wind up in a dumpster, shunned and forgotten." She licked her lips, like she was about to jump out of the car at the start of a heist. "And I--will--not--have--that."

Kyle's mouth opened, but words didn't follow. Neither did the laugh he halfway expected. An ugly lime. Siblings? What was she on about?

But then it hit him, all at once, what she was really saying. She meant it all. Her motives were as simple and beautiful as an urge to keep a citrus fruit from feeling left out of the scheme nature had designed for it. Instead of laughter, tears suddenly stood in his eyes, even though he had thought he had long since lost the ability to cry. He blinked and reached for his door handle. He hoped only that they were in time to save the homely lime that deserved a better fate than the one in store for it.

They were in time. It had not yet gotten thrown out.

That was the night Kyle Norris realized he loved Sissy Anspaugh.

* * *

Actually the idea of loving Sissy--of being in love with Sissy--hadn't crept up on him, catching him unawares. He had in his most private thoughts already considered it. He had even, previously in his life, tried the words out on two other females. One was the girl he regularly groped in high school. The other was a woman he'd met on campus in his first year. She was the first woman at the school to take him to bed, and he'd enjoyed the experience; and after they had gotten together on three other occasions, he had felt particularly expansive in the afterglow and in a wry, "sophisticated" tone had murmured, "So, are we in love now or what?" The woman in question, who was also a freshman and whose skin was pale and pasty, had sat up on an elbow and looked at him with a kind of baleful dismay. "No," she had said. "We most definitely are not."

Twice he'd flirted with the ultimate phrase, the maximum expression of affection. Twice the words had gained him nothing, and now, in retrospect, he saw he hadn't meant them. Because he hadn't known what he was talking about. Because he hadn't known love. Not before this.

He told her one day when they'd gone hiking in the nearby national park, which was somehow within the limits of the town itself, full of looming trees, the hush of rampant greenery and many winding trails.

"You seem tense," Sissy said when they'd paused to sit on a log that had mushrooms growing on its far end.

He turned to her. "I've got something to say."

"Okay." Her voice was completely neutral.

He swallowed. "I love you."

She nodded. "I love you too, Kyle."

"For real?" he heard himself say. A grin split his face.

"For real." She smiled.

They kissed like they were sealing a verbal contract. That was what it felt like, actually. A promise that the words were meaningful, true, heartfelt. This wasn't some feint, some experiment. He was in love with this woman. He'd been nervous to say the words, but now they were said; and his heart soared up among the highest branches of the ancient trees.

* * *

They were still together a month later. They were together a month after that. They were Sissy and Kyle, lovers, in a committed relationship, and everyone who knew them knew this as well: Kyle and Sissy were in love. The real deal. If you wanted to see what a happy, healthy, honest relationship looked like, you could do much worse than study those two. The love was evident in how they treated each other, in the affection expressed, in the trust and respect with which they effortlessly treated one another. Take a look at them. That was love. That was love.

They went on into the summer, together. Both were taking summer courses, which were lighter than those of the regular semesters. They spent even more time with each other now. Some of their friends had gone home for the summertime. Sissy said she had no desire to return to Minnesota; Kyle wasn't going back to San Francisco. He had told his parents about Sissy. It was the first time he had ever mentioned anything to them about any romantic entanglement of his. This seemed something of a quiet milestone. Eventually, he hoped, he would introduce Sissy to them. Yes, his parents really should meet her. She was very important to him, and she might well be in his life for some time to come.

His feelings only deepened for her. Whenever the giddy bliss of the thing seemed to have reached a theoretical limit, he discovered new depths of sentiment, of affection, of pure human warmth. They were so very compatible. It bordered on the ludicrous how well they got on together, in all things, under all circumstances.

That was the summer that word first broke of a great medical breakthrough; or, really, the impending-ness of such a breakthrough. The official claim came out of Geneva, with the imprimatur of the World Health Organization to give it credence. The cure for AIDS was within measurable distance. It was nearly on the cusp. A laboratory had established a means of potentially sterilizing the long-vexing "latent reservoir" of HIV-infected cells. The nightmare disease, held over from the twentieth century, would likely soon be eradicated.

Celebration swept the land.

Kyle and Sissy had of course been scrupulous in their birth control practices. Nonetheless, as the elation reached its peak in the university town, they found themselves attending a party which, to their initial dismay, degenerated--evolved?--into an outright orgy.

They were both agog. At first. But the swiftly escalating scene was somehow not seamy, not sordid. It was an exhibition of unadulterated joy. One of the great bogeymen, cause of untold suffering, was about to be brought low, finally. Everyone at that party had grown up in the long shadow of AIDS. Everyone knew, from a young age on, that safe sex was the only permissible sex.

And so the clothes went flying, and the bodies piled on, squirming and squelching in a heap which spread from room to room throughout the party house. Pot smoke filled the air. It was a positively Roman spectacle.

Kyle had been utterly faithful to Sissy; she'd been likewise exclusively devoted to him. But she turned to him, her lovely face flushed, and mouthed the words: Just this once. And he nodded. And they went to join the great carnal display, feeling abandon, feeling as if the world would be a better place tomorrow.

It was the most sexually adventurous night of Kyle's life. He had never done anything like this before. He and Sissy separated early on in the orgiastic proceedings. It felt as though there were no limits, no taboos--and yet condoms were still used, of course, and no one of the thirty or thirty-five gathered was coerced into any act which she or he might find disagreeable. A vast spirit of carnal cooperation suffused the scene. Kyle caught sight of Sissy at one point. She was in a sweaty tangle with a man and woman he didn't know, and she saw him and grinned and rolled her amber eyes, as if to express how hilarious and wonderful this all was, this one-time-only departure from their conscientious practice of sexual fidelity. Kyle, for his part, following an instinct both unfamiliar and potent, anally copulated with a male for the first and only time in his life, a ferociously outspoken pansexual by the name of Winston.

They left the party and returned to his apartment, disheveled and shivering, giggling and holding onto one another fiercely. They showered together and got into bed. They didn't regret the experience.

* * *

Their enviable compatibility did not mean they agreed on everything. They retained distinctive tastes. There were books and films he liked which didn't move her. She had a fascination for ancient cartography that he found, at best, odd. "Old maps," was all he could mumble about it, despite the several coffee table-sized tomes she had on the subject.

Sometimes they wanted to do different things on a given evening. Their backgrounds were also dissimilar: she with her large family, he the only child in his household. She was more vocal about past romantic experiences than he would have preferred; but she was never goading him with mentions of ex-boyfriends, never attempting to provoke jealousy in him; it was just her way.

And that was how it went whenever the two of them didn't synch up perfectly: it didn't turn into an issue, a point of contention. No one sought to start a fight with the other. Their relationship wasn't a contest. No one needed to win because neither of them were contending.

It was unlike any partnership Kyle had ever experienced. Sissy felt the same way and said so, more than once. They communicated well. Their mutual honesty served them.

They spent the summer months very much in each other's company. Kyle's apartment was too small for two people, full time. He thought again about cohabitation. He checked local rental websites, just to see what a bigger place might run. Sissy got a decent allowance from home. She had mentioned she would be willing to work a job. He could probably help find her one in one of the eateries where he'd worked.

They could see out their senior year together as roommates. Well, more than roommates, of course. They would be living together as man and woman. It would be a serious commitment. But he wasn't daunted by the idea. He could see living with her. He could envision a long-term partnership, beyond the wonderful months they had already spent. He could see that.

He could see beyond even that extended time. They were both twenty years old. A good deal of future lay ahead. It was up to them how they wished to furnish it. They were compatible; perhaps their life ambitions could be compatible as well.

Perhaps Sissy was the one with whom he should spend all the rest of his days. Take the commitment to its ultimate level. It was possible--entirely possible--that she had thought along these same lines too.

Devoted to each other. Each had the other's back. No game playing, no pettiness. He would be content to know her and no other women. He could do that. Easily. She, after all, was his alpha and his omega. She was that. She really was all that.

He really could marry her.

But he had to ponder that, of course. He had to seriously and strenuously mediate upon that very grave notion. And he needed to do so before ever uttering a word aloud about the matter, before he ever let loose the slightest whisper on the subject to Sissy. He had to know he meant it before he would even begin to seek whether she felt that way as well.

Because she might not. She might never have considered

marriage.

But, also, she might have. She might have had these same thoughts, and was just as cautious about approaching him. That was a real possibility. And it kept Kyle in a state of giddy turmoil. He loved her so much.

* * *

It was a week before fall classes were to resume. Kyle's parents had plans to come visit later in the month, in part to meet Sissy, the girlfriend he had made mention of a number of times now. Kyle himself was still plumbing the depths of his feelings for Sissy, with a practical eye toward asking her to live with him.

He was on his break at the restaurant. He always took his break at the same time. His cell phone buzzed in his jacket on a hook on the wall near where he was sitting and sipping a cup of house coffee. He got out the phone.

Sissy was calling. "Hello."

"Kyle. Uh. Damn. I don't know if--" She sounded flustered.

"Sissy?"

"I don't know. Over the phone. Should I say this over the phone?"

He sat up, trepidation sending icy fingers through him. This didn't sound like her. She was level-headed. She was good in a crisis. Was this a crisis? What was she trying to tell him?

"Sissy, what's going on? Please tell me." His heart, instead of speeding with fearful adrenaline, somehow slowed, the beats individualized, the spaces between enormous.

In the last fragment before she spoke again he knew what she was going to tell him.

"I'm pregnant."

CHAPTER FORTY-FOUR

Final Week

It feels like I am staying home sick from grade school. Perhaps I am even playing up the sniffles into a low-grade fever, hoping my mother will take pity. I managed that subterfuge a few times as a boy; or just as likely, my mother knew I was faking, knew I needed a break from school for my mental health, and allowed me to get away with it. She was a kind, sturdy woman. I still miss her, sometimes explicitly and intensely.

I have had days at home now, days when I would normally go into the office, and while the hours aren't empty, I feel somewhat lost in them, wandering through time bereft of urgency, of responsibility. I've earned this vacation time; I feel no guilt about it.

But I have had to put it to some use, even if the use is passive and internal. I have also tidied up my home some, done a couple of small carpentry projects. Mostly, though, I have looked within myself. I have been with my memories.

Yes. I have been with Sissy.

I go to collect Alice. There is stubble on my jaw and cheeks. I have never in my life grown a deliberate beard or moustache, but I kind of like the roguish unshaven look on me. Of course I will scrape it all off before I return to work. I will go back to the office, to my old life, as Kyle Norris. The perfectly recognizable and familiar version of him.

He will go back unattached to Alice, the cold girl who might give the firm's clients pause. She will be gone, and he will be himself.

I feel a quickening when Alice gets in the car. Sounds and smells seem heightened. The evening chill has such a bite that I feel it rush inside in the time it takes her to open and shut the passenger door. I tap on the heater. But first I lean over and kiss her; of course I do that before anything else.

The flesh of her face is cold, but her lips are soft and welcome and responsive. I pull us away from the curb. I am the anomaly among all the self-driving traffic. The unpredictable factor. The other vehicles know I am guiding my own car. They keep an added distance. They are wary of me. This gives me a strange satisfaction as I take us out of the downtown. At home dinner is prepped. I will need only a few minutes before serving Alice a hot meal.

We have a week left. On this day next week our month will be over. I have been aware of this fact; it has been with me today, there in the background, even as I took myself down memory lane into another time, another era entirely. Still, I knew the day, knew what it meant.

Our last weekend together approaches. Then, just a handful of days will remain after that.

I guide the car through the streets.

"I know what I want to do this weekend. Where I want to take you."

It is not something she will respond to. She will sit and stare ahead and--

"Where, Kyle?"

I swerve a little in the lane. Then I tell her where. Early streetlights splash brightly across the windshield for a while, until we reach a block where several are black.

I ask, "You don't want to go?" Another question unsuitable for a cold. I know better. I have learned how to talk to her.

But I give her time, almost a full minute. She says, "I wouldn't go there on my own." There is of course no bitterness in her raspy voice. But it is a bitter statement, nevertheless. She wouldn't go on her own. But she'll let me take her there. Because it is what I evidently want.

I wonder...if she could, would she hate me?

Swiftly I back away from the thought. I keep the car aimed straight ahead, hands too tight on the wheel now. Alice does not hate me. She doesn't. She can't.

Just as I can't help what I feel for her.

Can't help it at all, at this point. I have, it seems, given in to the madness.

Together we soar through the dimming city, toward an aerie atop a hill, where I keep captive this beautiful young bird. She has stayed with me as if behind the bars of a cage. But a week from now the door goes up, and she will have no choice but to flap her way free. I won't let her stay.

I won't.

CHAPTER FORTY-FIVE

The Story of Sissy, Part II

Kyle Norris, about to start his senior year at the university, was...confused. That seemed to be the overriding emotion, the one he found himself steeped in, hour by hour. But was confusion an actual emotion? he wondered. As a boy he had been unwieldy with his own feelings, as though he couldn't figure out the smooth easy workings of them. Now, confronted with the most dramatic milestone in his life thus far, he felt only a dazed disorientation. It was like entering a strange room, one full of frightening decor and a ceiling that was about to come down on one's head, after having dwelled so comfortably and pleasantly in all the other rooms of a house.

He told this metaphor to Sissy when he saw her face to face the first time after that phone call. The call in which she had told him she was pregnant. She came to his apartment, her face wan, and he embraced her; and then he unpacked the metaphor for her. He had thought it rather clever, in that it pretty well explained his own current mental state.

She stepped back from his embrace. She sat on the red velvet chair. Her knees were together, and she'd burrowed her hands into her jacket pockets, which she hadn't taken off. She looked up, the freckled bridge of her nose pinching. "What fucking rooms are you talking about?"

Sissy sounded tired. Her manner was irritable. He had seen her weary and flustered before; but she had never directed those emotions at him, not like this. He stood awkwardly. He felt uncomfortable in his own apartment. That too was new.

He looked over at his mini stove. His kitchen was tiny, not even a separate room. Twilight seeped across the windows. "You want me to make you a coffee?" His tone was meek. That went with the confusion he'd been feeling all day as he had listlessly finished out his shift at the restaurant. He still hadn't fully absorbed Sissy's news: she was pregnant. That wasn't good news. It was an upheaval. And so far he couldn't get past the stark fact of it, the binary nature of her state. She had not been pregnant, and now she was.

She nodded curtly. She wanted coffee. He took a hesitant step toward the stove and froze. Something prickled the back of his neck.

"Uh, should you be drinking coffee?" he asked. It was that same meek voice, so defensive, so wary.

She shot her amber eyes at him, and now an outright glower overtook her face. "What--you think coffee's going to hurt the baby? Is that what you think?" Harsh tone, the words like a series of slaps.

He had no idea how to respond to her anger. If this was an argument, he was ill prepared for it. He'd never fought with Sissy, and right now he couldn't even define the parameters of the dissension between them. Was she upset because coffee wouldn't harm a fetus and he was being an idiot for suggesting so? Even though he was pretty damn sure pregnant women shouldn't have caffeine.

At that moment her features suddenly fell. She put her elbows on her knees and dropped her face into her open palms as color rushed at last into her cheeks and she heaved with sobs.

Kyle had seen her cry before. She'd seen him cry his newly rediscovered tears. The world had the power to move both of their sensitive souls. He knelt before the chair and put his hand on her bucking shoulder. For just a flash of an instant she seemed to flinch, but he might have imagined that. He squeezed her shoulder as she cried.

There would be further conversation, he knew. Certain questions would be answered. Was she sure she was pregnant? Was she certain he was responsible? Two dumb questions. Of course she was sure. Sissy was possessed of an admirable thoroughness; it showed in how she conducted herself academically. She would have done more than peed on a pregnancy test stick. She would have ascertained the unequivocal facts of the matter.

The second question was even more ludicrous. She'd had a period between now and that crazy orgy night. No one had impregnated her on that occasion. She had only been with him since. Of this he had no doubt. Her fidelity was as dependable as gravity.

A grimness settled over him as he crouched there, cupping her shoulder. In that moment the confusion began to lift, but rays of warming sunshine didn't break through the clouds. Instead a great heavy dampness came down on him, a thick not-quite-rain which gave him a bleak feeling at the pit of his stomach.

Her sobs ebbed. She hiccupped through the last few, then let out a long ragged breath before raising her head. Her eyes were swollen. The amber irises were like small lost islands surrounded by unforgiving bloodshot ocean.

She said, "We have to abort it. You know that, right? We have to abort."

* * *

In fact, he had known this. The realization had come without delay when she had told him the news on the phone. He had looked down at the mug of coffee he held, seeing the webwork of infinitesimal cracks in the ceramic, and he'd heard the steamy chug of the nearby dishwasher; and he had known: this baby would never be born. He and Sissy could not be parents, could not bring a child into the world and care for it. That was a logistical fact. Parenthood was beyond their capabilities, outside the realm of their own plans and desires.

That sure truth came through in the seconds after Sissy had breathed those tremulous words into the phone: I'm pregnant. It was his moment of clarity. It didn't last long, but it did occur. Confusion set in almost immediately after, and he wallowed about in this state for some while, even as he tried to digest the news in a less gut level, more intellectual/rational way.

Obviously they couldn't keep the baby. It would be madness to do so. In their time together they'd gone through hundreds of condoms. Their collective sex drive was potent; their intent to prevent conception was equally urgent. They were both twenty. It could be argued they were both still children themselves.

So the way was clear. This pregnancy had only one solution. It must end in a medical termination. It must be aborted.

Yet Kyle was--disappointed? Hurt? Maybe he just felt the tiniest bit left out by Sissy's unilateral decision, her blanket statement. They were going to abort. Any discussion at all was simply skipped past. There would be no debate. She had jumped over any intervening steps, and he had no choice but to keep up with her.

She stayed over at his apartment that night. But they didn't make love. Kyle didn't even undress all the way when it came time to get into bed. He started to peel his briefs down from his hips but checked himself. She was getting under the covers in a T-shirt and sweatpants, even though the night was warm. He felt a sudden self-consciousness about his near-nudity. He almost grabbed up a shirt from the floor. But Sissy had snapped at him several more times this evening, and he was suddenly afraid of doing much of anything. Her aggravation with him seemed free-floating, without underlying logic. He couldn't think his way around her new wrath.

And it was new, this exasperation with him. This outright rancor, even. She had never treated him like this over all these past months. Tonight she bit his head off repeatedly. He didn't know how to handle it. Should he snap back? It wasn't in his nature. It certainly didn't jibe with any previous behavior he'd experienced between them. Besides, he had the distinct impression that if he said a single edged word back at her, she would blow up.

This was a life crisis, the most serious one he had ever faced. He required comfort. But Sissy was the one to whom he would go for succor. And she was not, it seemed, in a receptive frame of mind.

She was, however, determined and organized. There was a Planned Parenthood in a nearby city. It was literally a ten minute drive. Kyle knew the city. It was an urban cess pit compared to the bucolic splendor of the college town. Methamphetamine had rotted the city, whose population was double that of the town. It was also bigger, uglier, and had always struck Kyle as a kind of failed state. The streets were dirty, poorly lit and pitted with potholes. It had an outsize number of homeless.

Sissy made the appointments, the arrangements. She informed

Kyle of everything after the fact. The procedure was scheduled for this coming Thursday. Procedure. She spoke that word a lot. She no longer said abortion.

She was only a small way into her pregnancy, of course. But changes had started. This most obvious one was a skewed and heightened sense of smell. She said she was craving certain odors and found others nauseating beyond measure. She carried a spray bottle of perfume--something strange and musky--and repeatedly splashed her inside wrist before jamming her nose against the skin. Her inhalations had an unnerving animal-like quality to them. Amazingly she didn't start smoking again. Maybe it didn't occur to her. She made no attempts to meditate. He wanted to suggest she try it but didn't say anything.

She was jumpy. Noises startled her easily.

She spoke of phantasmagorical dreams, monsters like something out of Lovecraft. Kyle had never read Lovecraft.

She continued to castigate him at every opportunity--and even when there was no opening, when he'd done nothing that could have possibly offended her. But she was more the victim here than him. So he told himself. She had a right to the bigger grievance. This debacle had been visited upon her body, after all. Nothing was growing inside him. Nothing was happening to his hormones or the other familiar functions of his physiology. He had merely squirted some semen into her and gone on his merry way.

He silently cursed whatever failure had occurred in their birth control regimen. Maybe the odds had simply caught up with them. A man and woman who screwed as much as they had should probably expect the roulette ball to drop on double zero eventually.

"I wish you'd gotten that vasectomy like I said." She uttered these words out the blue one afternoon at his apartment.

He was preparing lunch. Something ticked with a cool metallic force in his head. He set down the spatula. In a tight voice he said, "You never asked me to get a vasectomy."

He could feel her head whipping toward him, even without looking. Her strawberry curls no doubt bounced with the movement. "How do you know what I said?" she shot.

"Because I pay attention to what you say. And you never said that." He wondered how he might have reacted had she suggested the operation. The procedure, he should say to speak her current language.

He turned slowly and looked at her. His face felt hard. This was the first resistance he had offered her since the ordeal began. Would she fly right off the handle, throw a tantrum? Given her state, he wouldn't put it past her.

But tears suddenly overflowed her eyes. Her face contorted. She said, "IIIII'm soooryyy, Kyleee..." in a blubbering voice. So he went to her and held her and told her he loved her, and lunch burned on the stove.

* * *

Except that she wasn't erratic and irascible, not all of the time. Her old self shone through now and then. He hated to think of this as her old self, but there wasn't really any other way to label it.

On those occasions, when her face softened and she was gentle and sweet and even offered a little levity--albeit, gallows humor--his heart ached with a supreme joy. He wanted only to cocoon her in his arms, to make everything bad go away without upsetting her further.

A few times when these windows came along, they made quiet love. Kyle continued to use a condom, until one time when Sissy, lucid and loving in how she treated him, said, "Do it without, babe. I've never, y'know, felt it when you come inside me."

And so they had unprotected sex. Or sex that was protected because the unwanted eventuality had already occurred. He couldn't make her more pregnant.

It was a curious sensation, breathless and distant, until the intensity of the pleasure swelled, and he realized how tactile the experience was without the intervention of a latex sheath. His orgasm practically turned him inside out. Afterward, he wanted to say something about how it had been, but he refrained. Her moods turned quickly, and he already had the intuition of a coming storm. She reached for her perfume spray and snorted a line of musk off her inside wrist. She was muttering under her breath as she did so.

Kyle told no one what was happening. He asked his parents to delay their visit. He isolated himself from his friends, concentrating only on Sissy. He withstood everything she threw at him. Plainly she was scared and angry, and if she needed someone to vent at...

But it wasn't how it should have been, and he knew it. Sissy— the old Sissy— would never have taken anything out on him. She would have had too much affection, too much respect for him, to do that. She would have been aghast witnessing this behavior in anyone else; would further have pointed out to him how superior their own relationship was. They would never be so petty, so thoughtless. Never.

It was a misery. But Thursday was almost here. The procedure was imminent. It was a necessary move, and the results would be good. When it was done, she would be pregnant no more. The threat of parenthood would be removed from their lives. They could return to where they'd been, to who they truly were. Sissy and Kyle, lovers and friends, possibly one day mates for life. They could get back to that. They could.

In the night she woke him. She shook his shoulder and called his name, and he came up out of a stress dream in which he was trying to wait on every table at his restaurant by himself while the kitchen moved in literal slow motion and riotous customers demanded their food. His heart beat quick and anxious.

Sissy was sitting up beside him.

"Kyle, I need to tell you something."

She was going to tell him she was pregnant. It was going to be the worst news imaginable, short of a cancer diagnosis. Pregnancy would cut a ruinous swath through their lives. It would--

No. That had already happened.

"What is it?" he asked, throat scratchy.

The room was a sea of shadows. The bedside clock's glowing red digits sketched her profile. And even now she was lovely. Lovely still.

She said in a tired, dead tone, "This has happened to me before. I got pregnant in high school. I had to tell my parents. I begged them not to tell anybody else. But they were very upset and brought in my siblings on it. They said this had to be discussed as a family. It was like being put on trial. Everyone got to question me--about the boy, about what precautions we'd taken. But mostly they talked about what to do. Have the baby? Put it up for adoption? I didn't want to go through any of that. It was like I'd broken a leg and my family was engaged in a big debate as to whether or not the bone should be set.

There was only one answer to this situation. I knew it. They knew it too, I think. Even my parents. The pregnancy had to be aborted. A baby, even one I let get adopted, would rip my life to shreds. The experience was mortifying, having my brothers and sisters— some of them younger than me--and parents sit in judgment before they finally and reluctantly agreed that an abortion was necessary. I went through hell, Kyle. I went through hell."

A profound ache of empathy overcame him. He was sitting up on one elbow. He blinked a hot tear down one cheek. He reached a hand toward her.

"Don't touch me!" she yelped, a real raw hysteria in her voice, pushing out the weariness. She was suddenly like an exposed cable, there next to him in the bed.

He wanted to comfort her. She wouldn't let him even try. He lowered his head back onto the pillow. He turned away from her. His compassion turned to mist and dissipated, and a cool prickly resentment slowly replaced it.

It was hours before sleep returned, and it only brought more bad dreams.

* * *

They drove out on Thursday, taking the freeway, which connected them swiftly to the city. It had already been a tense, nearly wordless morning, but Sissy hadn't said anything harsh to him. It was a sad commentary that this seemed like a win; his girlfriend wasn't actively acting nasty toward him.

Sissy did the driving. He would take the wheel on the way home. She would stay at his apartment for a few days. She would want to sleep a lot, she told him. He had promised to take care of her. And he would.

All they had to do now was get through the...procedure.

He had never thought himself particularly squeamish on the matter of abortion. He lauded its legality and wondered with a kind of retroactive horror what it must have been like when the safe and sane medical operation was a criminal act. Barbarous times. A woman had the right to choose. How could that ever have been up for debate?

He thought of the familial tribunal Sissy had evidently had to face as an impregnated teen, and a shiver went through him. He felt bad for her about that. But some part of him also wished she had told him about it before this. She'd had an abortion in high school. They had shared so much about each other, volunteered so many secrets, eager only to know and be known by the other as deeply as possible. Why hadn't she told him this?

There was a separate life inside Sissy. Kyle didn't think that the life was a person, but it was some form of human. It wasn't an animal; it wasn't some anonymous protoplasmic glob. It was an early stage of life, human life, and it had come to be during an act of love between himself and this woman.

They got off the freeway, and she navigated the slovenly streets of the city. At a light at an intersection someone several car lengths back honked for no discernible reason. Sissy started sharply, straining against her seat belt. She was still oversensitive to loud sounds.

"Motherfucker," she snarled at the rearview mirror, just before the light changed and she fairly stomped on the accelerator. Kyle stayed silent.

They reached the clinic.

There was a small party of protesters. They had signs. They looked at Sissy--not at Kyle--with bored benevolent contempt. Kyle put himself ahead of Sissy, put up his arm as if to ward them off. He hadn't realized there would be a group like this. You would never have seen anything like this in the town of the university. They said things to Sissy which were vacuous and predictable. Sissy made a sound low in her throat, and he hurried her to the clinic's doors.

Inside it was cool, and there was a hospital scent of antiseptic. Kyle was going to lead Sissy to the reception desk, but she strode past him and told the person on duty who she was and what her appointment was for. Her words were clipped, tone unapologetic. Maybe in her mind she was addressing her family; this time not asking them, not submitting to their interrogations, but telling them. She was here to get an abortion.

Kyle handed over the money. Cash. Sissy had insisted on paying half, even though he said he could cover it. In fact, when he'd offered, it led to another fight. Only, these weren't fights, none of them. Because he wasn't arguing with her or deliberately contradicting her. He had no idea any longer what might set her off, and he was stung and bruised by her attacks.

They just had to get through this....

They settled in a waiting area. The decor was unnervingly banal. When he closed his eyes, he couldn't remember the color of the walls or the upholstery. Considering what went on in this building, it seemed the setting should be more dramatic. This could be a dentist's office or an airport lounge.

They waited with others. No one sat alone. Everyone was in pairs. Sometimes two women, sometimes man and woman, and sometimes the age disparity was extreme. Kyle guessed this was a parent or some older relative accompanying the young woman, because the women all looked young. Sissy's age. Younger. No smiles in the waiting area.

He sat and stared at nothing and said nothing to Sissy, because she was giving off that live wire aura once again. She fidgeted in her seat, the movements occasionally violent. He didn't reach over to pat her knee or offer any other physical reassurance. If she were to cry Don't touch me! here in this hushed sterile space, he would go find the closest high window and jump out of it.

Time dragged. It took a while before he realized this wasn't just his nerves. This was taking a long time. He didn't dare look at his phone to check the time. That would be like begging Sissy to flare up at him for some imagined affront.

But several people had been collected from the waiting area and taken beyond through another set of doors. He saw now that someone who had come in after he and Sissy was now being called by a woman wearing a white medical coat.

Sissy had been forgotten. Mislaid. He was stranded here with her in this reception lounge, and the clinic would carry on its business and just leave them here to—

"What is happening?" It was Sissy, beside him, her voice a whisper, a croak. She sounded choked with stress and sorrow.

Kyle realized he hated this place. He wished it had the decency to look like a slaughterhouse and to operate just as efficiently. At the moment he didn't care whatever other vital services the clinic offered. He needed it only for its most drastic function: to serve as a mill which would remove the unwanted life from his girlfriend's uterus. That was it. And the goddamn place was just letting them sit here.

He felt himself rise. Tension tightened his limbs. Another technician in white had emerged from the doors which led, no doubt, to the depths of the place. It was another woman, and she was calling out someone else's name— not Sissy's— and moving toward that person, and the woman in the white coat had a patient face and soulful eyes.

Kyle physically cut her off. He didn't know what expression he wore on his face, but she flinched a little when she halted and looked at him. In a calm, steely voice he said, "Look, we have been waiting quite a while now. People who have come in after us have been seen. I would like for us to be seen. The name is Anspaugh."

The woman sorted it out for them. Five minutes later Sissy raised her head when her name was called. Kyle stood, and when Sissy didn't stir, he put out his hand to her. She might have said something, might have slapped the hand away, but she didn't. She took it softly and allowed him to help her up from the padded chair. Together they went through the doors. He had already said he would be with her through the procedure.

And so he was.

He drove her car back. She leaned on him as he walked her to his apartment. She went straightaway to bed and to sleep. He sat down quietly in the red velvet chair and tried to work out what he may have lost.

* * *

It never came back. The feeling. The sonorous depths of it. The surety didn't return. Kyle had for many months relied on his love for Sissy. It was the most crucial landmark in his emotional topography. When he knew he loved Sissy and knew she loved him back, a balance had been achieved in his life, unlike anything he had known before. He had been more than merely happy. He had felt...safe.

But it didn't come back. Not all the way. Not far enough. She stayed on at his apartment a few days and did indeed sleep a great deal. When she was awake, she was groggy but affable. She smiled at him. He returned every smile. She was no longer spring-loaded, no longer run through with a dangerous electrical current that might shoot out at him at any moment.

But, still, the old feeling stayed away. They were cordial to one another. Sissy went back to her campus living unit. One would never have known anything had happened to her. She was suddenly vibrant, animated. She took up running and ran through the town's streets and forest trails. She didn't ask Kyle along; he'd never been a runner, anyway.

Classes resumed. He busied himself with the work, even though it all seemed hollow. Working at the restaurant felt more engaging. But he persisted with his studies, still made his grades. His plans hadn't changed. But he would just follow through on them by rote, strictly because it was the most obvious path forward.

He saw less of Sissy. They had physical relations a few times, but it felt so stilted that neither of them could look the other in the eye afterward.

She phoned him at the restaurant, when he was on his break. Before she could say much of anything, he said in a blunt, cheerless voice, "You want to do this over the phone or in person?"

They met up that evening. They said goodbye to one another.

* * *

Kyle sleepwalked through senior year and sleepwalked through his office apprenticeship when he returned to San Francisco. He did not stay in touch with Sissy. He had only seen her by chance, on campus, during that final year.

When the Cold Era began, when the facts about cold children being born had been thoroughly established, he did a few mental calculations and realized that the fetus he and Sissy had aborted might have been one of the last emotionally equipped children born to the world, had it been allowed to live. That thought would never entirely leave his head, not for the next twenty years.

CHAPTER FORTY-SIX

To the Facility

She doesn't want to go. That is the bedrock fact of the matter. Of course she does not want anything, not in the classical emotional sense, in the old way of wanting, in the bygone human way...but I have been with this woman for some time now, and that proximity has fostered an undeniable intimacy. I can almost conjure up a cold equivalent of what it means to want something. I can perhaps say her survival instincts are in play and she is responding according to the stolid urgings of her base brain chemistry.

But the truth is simpler, and it really doesn't matter how we arrive at this conclusion: Alice doesn't wish to return to the federal camp where she spent most of her childhood.

Do I fault her for that? Hell no. She has told me about the place, and there is probably much she hasn't told me, because I haven't prompted her with the right questions. But the institution must hold many negative memories for her. Nonetheless, we are going, because I insist that we do; and she will comply, hoping I still might change my mind about extending our arrangement. Another month's rent would benefit her. So would further free meals. She continues to earn money at her job. Her funds grow. She and Carrow are saving up to move into a real apartment together.

It has been a taxing week for me, more so than any typical

workweek. Odd that with this time off from the office I am wearier than if I'd worked sixty hours. Or not so odd. I have spent this solitary time revisiting my past, in stark graphic detail, opening up memories I had gladly left dormant for many years. This week I was with Sissy. Dear long-lost Sissy, who so touched my heart half a lifetime ago. I spared myself nothing. I plumbed the deepest joys we shared. And I forced myself to relive our ignoble fall, the luridness of the abortion, the emotional rubble in which we found ourselves from the moment she discovered she was pregnant. I put my whole being through it all over again, reviving every spark, polishing every surface to a high unforgiving gloss. It has drained me.

When I have touched Alice these past days, it has been docilely. I don't try to summon a violence of passion. She is still exquisite to me, but I have been weighed down with remembrances of my former love, who I knew in another time, in another world practically.

I still have said nothing to Alice about Sissy. Even I can't imagine what the information would mean to her. Probably nothing. Mere biographical statistics. She might find it interesting that two olds--though we weren't olds then, because colds didn't yet exist--could be so undone by a simple pregnancy.

But she has seen out the week, and tomorrow the weekend begins. And I will take her across the Bay, to the camp in the city of Concord, still very much in use, housing the cold offspring rejected by their parents. Alice, as a former official resident, has the right to visit this facility, even to return there if she so asks. She also holds the right to bring with her a counsel, who needn't have any legal authority, who only has to declare that he is along to safeguard her welfare. And that is what I will do. I will take her back into lion's den that spawned her, and I will protect her the entire time.

* * *

Alice lingers in the shower. The water runs and runs some more. After, I hear the hair dryer, and she uses it for several minutes, longer than she has before.

I allow myself a smirk. I am still unshaven, and the bristles of beard are thickening on my chin, but I too have showered. Alice, however, is stalling. I doubt I could make another old believe it, but she is doing this deliberately because she doesn't want to make this journey. It is not, at its heart, an emotional reaction, but the result is the same. She's dragging her feet because I'm making her do something that she finds disagreeable.

She is still knocking about in the bathroom. I go and rap the door with a knuckle. "Alice? We've got to get going."

"I'm coming."

I snicker silently. It does seem a little comical. I too am uneasy about this venture, but I want to know what her early life was like, so to better understand her. The sand is running out of the hourglass. I don't even have a full week left with her.

This delay is almost...childish. A kid reluctant to do something, who tries every passive resistance ploy, just to buy another minute, a further handful of seconds. I have only ever thought of Alice as an adult, her cold status notwithstanding. But this is Alice as a girl: not a twenty year old grownup but a twenty year old girl.

She is, of course, the age my and Sissy's child would have been now. If we hadn't aborted it. If it had been female. And what if the conception occurred on the nearer side of The Line, and she was destined to come into this world as one of the first colds, instead of as among the last of the olds? Lot of ifs there. I don't even apologize for the disturbing, distant incestuous implications of thinking of her as being the same age as the never-born child Sissy and I might have made.

Lover. Daughter. Cold. Old. It is a world of merciless definitions in which we all live. In time the word "old" as it is currently designated will be struck from the lexicons. We olds will have all passed from this earth....

I hear the lock on the bathroom door. She has picked up that habit from me, the practice of privacy. I wonder if she'll continue with it when she and Carrow are cohabiting, when they have taken the step which Sissy and I were never able to.

Alice comes out of the bathroom. She crosses to where I stand near the foot of the bed. She stares, then lifts a hand. To my surprise she traces a finger down my cheek. I am further surprised when I see the fingertip gleam with damp.

"What does this mean?" she asks.

How do I explain tears? How could anyone? I say, "It's just

something we do sometimes. My kind. Something we do."

It is time to go. She delays no more.

* * *

For whatever reason the Bay Bridge--the second of the two bridges leading into San Francisco--appears in far better repair than its more famous counterpart. The Golden Gate Bridge is a noble rusting ruin; but the more prosaic Bay, with its multiple lanes and two decks, endures with the impassive functionality of an ancient Roman road.

Traffic is light. Do people still go anywhere on the weekends? I can't say. I know that before Alice I hardly did anything exciting on the weekend, much less travel outside the city.

I won't get to take Alice over the Golden Gate--not unless I do it at night in the first few days of the coming week--but I can give her this experience, at any rate. Below, the water flashes blue and white. A number of sailboats are out. The sun shines like summer in some other city, with nary a cloud in sight. You can't know what the weather will do anymore. I shoot us across the span, heading east. The suburbs await, environs I thought unworthy as a native San Franciscan high schooler who was inevitably infected with a modest dose of hometown pride. San Francisco was a city, a metropolis. The surrounding suburban reaches were comprised of prefab plastic. Fake towns full of fake people. I didn't love San Francisco back then, just like I don't love it now, but it was in a real sense mine. I was glad not to have been born in one of these outlying communities, which seemed unsophisticated even to my unsophisticated sensibilities.

The bridge is Interstate 80. I will take it through Berkeley, then further eastward, eventually passing through Walnut Creek before gaining the outskirts of Concord. It is a deep foray into the hinterlands.

I settle into the comfortable stupor of driving. Certainly this is less scenic than the coastal route down to Santa Cruz, but there is still the rhythmic jounce of the car, the steady thumps where we cross the bridge's roadway joints. The gray suspension cables swoop past on either side. I guide the vehicle, and we eat up the miles. Alice is wearing her sunglasses. I wear a pair as well. Maybe they add to the scruffy bad boy image I fancy I am currently projecting. Check out the forty-year-old with the rakish stubble and his hot young girlfriend in the passenger seat. I wonder where they're going, what adventure they are on. I'll bet he's seizing life by the horns, wrangling every last possibility of joy from the time laid out before him.

But there are no envious looks from others crossing the bridge. They sit in their self-drivers, looking at their phones and other devices. None of them is on an adventure, so they can't conceive that anyone else might be.

This isn't an adventure, of course. It is one of the Stations of the Cross, something arduous I have assigned to Alice and myself. I think this excursion necessary, though it is certainly unlike the romantic getaway I tried to concoct for us in Sausalito.

She is not wearing one of the colorful tops today. These may be her own clothes, in fact, one of the outfits I first saw her in, springing down Powell Street on her bicycle. I don't think it's a coincidence that she is dressed like this today as we beat on, boats against the current, borne into her past. But if I asked her directly why she wore this nondescript ensemble, she wouldn't give a straight answer. She wouldn't admit to any considerations beyond the pragmatic. Yet she has spent so much time with me. And I, though maladroit in their use sometimes, do possess emotions, and I do make emotional decisions. She has some instinct toward mimicry. Those smiles she has tried to give me. Those hints of emotional infrastructure which have occasionally peeked through--or seemed to peek through. I know she is a cold. I know she is incapable of generating conventional emotion. That is a neurochemical and physiological fact.

But even without emotion she is not entirely cold. Some part of me remains convinced of this.

A question occurs. I ask it: "Are you wearing any of the underwear I gave you?"

She hooks a thumb in the waist of her pants and drags the drab fabric down over the protuberance of her hipbone. She has on blue panties. For some reason this feels like a small triumph. She may have reverted to her previous style of dress, but she still wears the underwear I gifted her.

We drive onward. The temperature rises significantly. San Francisco, a fingernail at the end of its peninsula, is exempt from the normal cycle of the seasons. It remains chill and often fog-bound and receives its summertime balminess in late September and through October. It is one of the city's eccentricities.

But these outer regions get their four seasons as nature intended; and even as badly as we humans have disturbed the environment, this is California at the end of July, and the heat fairly beats down. I let the air rush in the windows for a while, then raise them and put on the car's AC.

We're through Lafayette, into Walnut Creek. These places don't look fake to me now. They are just slightly sleepy communities. I wonder if they have lost residents, the same as in San Francisco; and if they have, where have those people gone?

There is still Pleasant Hill ahead, before we begin our final leg toward the city of Concord. These place names. They do sound a little phony, I have to admit. Alice gazes blandly at the passing scenery. If any of this reminds her of her childhood, she doesn't show it. Well, of course she doesn't. What would I do if she turned to me right now and said, "I don't want to go to my old camp, Kyle, because I had a hard time there and don't want to walk through those memories again. Please, would you take me back to the city?"

If she were capable of saying those words, I would obey. Gladly. But going to her camp with her is one of the last chances I will ever have of truly knowing her. I need to try to discover all I can, while I still can. When we part, I want to say I left no stone unturned. I knew Alice as best as any old could ever know a cold. I will need to believe I gave it my every effort.

* * *

Sunvalley Shopping Center. Or it was. I don't quite remember when the whole complex was razed. A lot was going on at that time. The world was frantically adjusting to the new reality of colds being among us. I was, even then, still in a numbed state; even after all that time away from Sissy; so the events occurring around me, as monumental as they were, sometimes felt staged, affected, as if it were all being put on for someone else's benefit and I was only a hapless witness.

But I recall hearing about the camps. They were inevitable, it seemed. Hundreds of thousands of unwanted children were being dumped into the system, and it couldn't possibly take on the overload. Parents, realizing that their children were effectively nonhuman creatures, rejected the abominations. It didn't happen all at once, of course. The truth of the cold phenomenon was a gradual thing, the case slowly building, the reality sinking in, until it was backed by indisputable scientific data.

Then the camps started appearing. A necessary step, most everyone agreed. But let the facilities be humane at least, others added. Even that early on there were some who felt empathy, even a ghostly compassion for the strange beings who were children and yet were not children. Not human children. Because there would be no more human children.

I have researched Alice's facility. It was necessary when I was finding a way to accompany her back there. I have seen images of the site.

And yet...when it comes into view, I halfway expect an Auschwitz. Or at least a Manazar. And perhaps the large fortified institution I see now is one of those, a camp that is also a blight on humanity, evidence of our worst instincts. The big drab buildings may yet house horrors or memories of horrors, but from the outside the place is not sinister. A long wide approach road is the only way to reach the main gate, and I have put the rental car on that straightaway and we are nearing the point of entry.

The security system seizes my vehicle and, the dashboard voice giving warning, squeezes my brakes to a gentle stop. I am instructed to respond to the communications beam. I tap open the channel and converse awhile with a voxsynth.

The approach road is paved, but it is also dusty. Pale swirls rise in the baking heat. I squint into the distance, wondering if long-range weapons are trained on us. A sufficiently powerful sonic device could permanently disable this car and leave both of us bleeding from our ears.

I have submitted the proper pixelwork, and sooner or later they will have to let us approach. Eventually the artificial voice tells me to do so. I move us forward at a modest speed. There is no one outside the looming gate. No bands of protesters. The camps, for good or ill, have generally been accepted as normal societal institutions.

We have to get out of the vehicle. I do so, halfway expecting Alice to stay in her seat, arms folded, pouty obstinacy on her pretty face. But that is what an old might do. She steps out into the bright day and heat. An underground ramp opens, and the car self-drives down into shadowy depths. We have been told to remain where we are. I feel like I should have my hands raised, palms outward, fingers spread.

A smaller gate opens in the bigger gate, and out comes an actual person at last. He is a husky man, in a uniform which suggests custodian more than prison guard. Nevertheless, a firearm is holstered at his hip. He addresses me by name, telling me he will now frisk me. So I do raise my arms, and he is quite thorough, though the matter seems purely routine to him, his jowly face remaining in a disinterested cast. I haven't brought along my shockstik, and he finds nothing objectionable on my person.

Alice receives a similarly complete and indifferent searching. I don't like the man's hands on her, though I know this is an absolutely necessary step to gaining access. But a thought nags: what if this is one of those guards to whom she once extended oral favors? But in my research I learned that personnel are regularly transferred between camps, so that fresh crews can see to the smooth running of operations. Such is the language on various websites. The truth is probably that the rotation is meant to keep down institutionalized corruption. The longer a guard--or caretaker or steward, or whatever other term is used--remains at a single location, the more likely the job will be abused. This way they don't have much of a chance to dig in.

He leads us back through the smaller gate, and we find ourselves in an anteroom, with a desk, chair, shelves. I expect a lengthy discourse on the dos and don'ts for visitors, maybe an electronic scan, but he simply puts forms in front of us for us to sign. Our chips verify our identities. He opens a door at the far end of the office, tells us maps are available on our devices, and waits for us to go through. He appears no more interested in our presence than when we drove up.

I walk ahead, and Alice follows. We go through the door, and the guard pulls it shut behind us. I don't hear a lock engage, but maybe I missed the sound. There is no one on the other side to meet us. We will have no escort, then. No doubt we are being surveiled, but our access to the facility appears unconstrained. It isn't what I was expecting.

I look to Alice. Her breathing appears deeper than normal, her breasts rising and falling with added drama; or I am projecting my own nervousness.

"Will you show me around?" I ask her. "Give me a general sense of the place?"

I have brought her where she does not want to be, and now I am making her my tour guide. I wonder again if she doesn't somehow hate me, in her own cold way. And this time I can't easily turn away from the thought.

Wordlessly she starts ahead, and now I am the one following. We have come out into a short corridor. No doors line it. She walks to the end. I follow and peer out into a larger space, which opens out and up, revealing tiers and railings on one side. The levels rise toward a broad ceiling, half a dozen stories up. From this angle I cannot tell what is on each tier, but the layout looks like a typical jailhouse. If so, the levels will be lined with individual cells.

The lighting seems just a touch dim. The colors are institutional grays. But the place already appears constructed with more care than the metaceramic barracks at Fisherman's Wharf.

Alice's head swivels back and forth, slowly. When I step up beside her, she says to me, "Left is eating area, exercise floor. Right is quarters."

The tiers are on the right. On the left is an open, warehouse-sized space. I hear noises now--the sounds of inhabitation? But it doesn't sound quite right. I nod right, and Alice starts that way.

There is a stairway going up to the tiers, but Alice leads me to the bottommost level. Long windows give onto unlit rooms. I peer through the glass but can't make out much. "What are these used for?" I ask her.

For an answer she takes me along until we reach a lighted window. I jerk to a halt.

The broad window reminds me of those in maternity wards. When there used to be maternity wards in hospitals. Inside, in fact, are bassinets, and I see that three are occupied. Newborns lie swaddled in these cradles. The sight astounds me, and I literally feel my jaw drop. I perceive movement within the bassinets, the tiny motions of infants; a minute hand waggles, minuscule fingers spread; a miniature leg kicks. They are so...small. Something hot and nameless rushes through me, like a burst of fever but with potent emotion attached. And yet I am uncertain of my feelings. Surprise, yes. Shock, most definitely. But beneath the startlement is some primal thing, perhaps a protective instinct. Or maybe something simpler: blunt wonder that beings can create other beings, and they start out this small and helpless.

A nurse in scrubs is attending the three infants. It doesn't seem a strenuous task. As I watch, he makes his short rounds, stopping at each bassinet, then returns to a desk off to the side.

None of the children cries. They surely make the goos and gurgles one might expect of any infant. But these aren't any infants, I remind myself. They are of course cold newborns. Olds don't get born anymore, not for the last twenty years. How these three babies came into the world really doesn't matter. Some old couple got careless, perhaps, and for whatever reason the pregnancy wasn't terminated. So the baby was brought to term and handed over to this facility. The birth would have been illegal, but the statute which prohibits breeding in this country does not include forced abortion. Maybe it's different in other nations. Maybe they have the right idea.

My head swims a little. For so long I haven't seen anything like this, aside from those awful mechanical babies people sometimes carry around. It is a dizzying experience.

But I note the empty bassinets and the darkened windows we passed. This ward was once far busier than it is now. The birth rate has plummeted, naturally; and yet a few are still getting through, and will no doubt continue to do so. The species will continue. Not my species, of course. But these human-like beings, such close cousins, will carry on.

I take a step and stumble. I steady myself and put my forehead against the cool glass. The nurse hasn't once looked our way.

When I'm ready, Alice leads me to the stairs, and we go up to the first tier. There aren't cells here, as in a jail, but the living units aren't so much different. Alice walks me to an open unoccupied one. There is bunk bed inside, along with toilet and sink. It is, I silently note, far roomier than the cage confinement of her own quarters in that metaceramic tenement.

Someone emerges from another of the units. It is a girl, eight or nine years old. She wears a faded smock and slip-on booties. Her hair is buzzed short, utterly without style. She appears well enough fed, and there are no sores on her face. That face is expressionless as she marches past us, toward the stairs. I watch her descend. They have freedom of movement, then. Maybe she's hungry and is going to go get something to eat. Do they not regiment the meals here? It is one more way this isn't like a jail.

We go up another level. The residents become older, and there are more of them; each successive age category belongs to a time when more breeding occurred. These are the products.

Facility personnel are on hand as well. No one questions our presence. They must know the facility has visitors today. The guards-- or maybe caretaker is, after all, the correct word--do not carry sonic pistols like the one who admitted us. They go about custodial duties.

By the time we gain the fourth level, I realize why the place sounds wrong to me. It is too quiet. There is no ongoing babble of voices, as one might expect with so many people. Several hundred must live here at least. But I hear little more than the shuffle of feet, perhaps the echoey murmur of something said by one of these younglings. No conversation, though. They have little or nothing to say to one another.

How eerie it is.

In some of the cell/units programs are projected on the walls. These, then, are the tutorials Alice mentioned. This is how she learned to read. But none of it is structured. The olds who are the facility's personnel do not intervene. The colds are left to their own lights, whatever those might be. However colds make their decisions, they can decide here whether or not they will gain a basic education.

There seems a certain neglect in that. Do any children, even cold children, truly know what is best for them? I imagine they all require some form of guidance. But then again, society--old society--does not accept total responsibility for these creatures. They are our collective offspring, yes; but the colds have, fundamentally, betrayed us by not being us. And so we warehouse them, because that is the human thing to do. Because we can't really care for them. We can't worry over their futures.

We can't love what won't love us back.

Alice is climbing the steel steps to the next level. I reach out and tug on her arm. She stops and turns.

"I appreciate what you're doing," I say. "I know--" You didn't want to come here. "--know you wouldn't be here if not for me. I want to tell you I'm grateful." I drop my gaze, shake my head. I am throwing emotion-laced words at her. Ridiculous.

She is silent; then: "You're welcome, Kyle."

My eyes snap up. Her face is placid, eyes neutrally cast. For the barest instant I see amber irises instead of green. And for that instant I am afraid another tear will slide down my cheek.

The tour resumes. She has been around me, intimately entwined with me, exposed to all my verbal habits. You're welcome, Kyle. Surely she has picked that up from me. Or else she knows the words, in a rote manner, and uses them bluntly, hoping to allure me further. I am an old. Instead of rationality and survival instincts I have feelings. I have stated that our relationship will end when our month is expired. But I might change my mind. In the abstract, she is correct. I'm an emotional being and might not mean everything I say.

In a strange way our coming breakup will harm her almost as much as it will me.

The uppermost tier is less crowded than the one immediately below it. Many units are empty. But these, according to the paradigm, should house those who are among the oldest of the colds, the first generation born, which was the most abounding of course. People still thought they were giving birth to normal children; so there were no checks on breeding.

"Where are the rest?" I ask Alice.

She walks along the rail. We're up quite high by now. I recall that plunging to one's death was a favorite way to kill oneself in prison. But colds don't traffic in suicide; Alice told me so, when we were held up on the coast road down to Santa Cruz where someone had evidently jumped off the cliff. Besides, whatever else this facility is, it is not a prison.

She glances back at me, replying, "They left."

Of course. The oldest colds, like Alice herself. Ready to face the world, they have gone from the camp, to take up jobs in the cities.

But not everyone has done so.

Alice reaches a closed door. Without knocking she pulls it open.

The unit, indistinguishable from all the others I have seen, has one occupant. She lies on the lower bunk, facing toward us. She wears the same worn smock and booties as everyone else. She doesn't appear to have just woken. She isn't reading. She isn't doing anything. Just lying there. She gazes impassively at us, as we intrusively fill the doorway.

Alice points. "I slept on the top bunk."

She told me once that she had left her camp two years ago.

The woman on the bottom bunk says nothing. Her gaze has moved away, and she exudes a blankness. She isn't bored. She isn't curious as to why we are here. Most shocking of all, however, is that she makes no especial note of Alice's presence. Alice, who must have been her unit-mate for some time. Perhaps they even moved up the tiers together, year by year, until Alice emancipated herself and this other...she, simply and inertly, stayed?

"Who is she?" I whisper. I stare. An angular face, an evident Asian heritage. She is stouter than Alice. She must get less exercise. I wonder if she chose not to learn to read and if that fact undermined her general motivations.

Alice says, "Nori."

I don't know what else to ask. Alice won't volunteer anything. She wouldn't understand why I would want to know anything more about Nori.

Still whispering--and a tremor in the whisper now--I say, "I'm done being in here."

I back out, shaking. Alice steps out as well and shuts the door with a soft metallic thud. All the doors are steel.

* * *

We come down from the tiers and reconnoiter the food area, which looks relatively sanitary. What they feed the residents isn't quite gruel, but it's nothing I would willingly ingest. Next we go to the exercise floor. No one is currently using it, but this must be where Alice played basketball against the guards. Where, I wonder, did she perform her other activities with those same guards? Did her custodians take her to a special room? Did they film the escapades, or did they make certain that nothing was ever recorded?

The other buildings comprising the facility are given over to administrative and maintenance needs. They are restricted. But one of the personnel informs me that I have seen all the areas where the residents themselves can go. The large showering area adjacent to the exercise floor is empty as well, but the residents I have seen appear more or less hygienic. Perhaps some sort of regimen is enforced and the cold don't take up lax grooming habits until after they are out on their own.

I want to be angry about the sexual abuse Alice suffered here-- even though I am seeing the situation strictly through an old's sensibilities and "abuse" probably isn't the right term, which only makes me want to seethe all the more. But the proper wrath just won't come. Alice survived here because she is a survivor. I may find her deeds unwholesome--and I very goddamn much do--but they were her choices. A cold can't be cajoled into something. A threat would do it, but I don't think children were forced into acts at sonic gunpoint in this place. In these recent, more enlightened years inspections have been conducted routinely at these camps. No doubt this curbed a good deal of the abuse, but had that abuse been epidemic and of a violent nature the truth of it would have come out by now.

The tour is done. Alice looks just as stoical as when we walked in, but once more I feel a subliminal buzz that I take to be her displeasure, her impatience. Or I'm projecting all that, keenly aware of my own emotional exhaustion.

Alice starts back toward the entryway into the facility. But I tug her arm once more. There is still a question I have left unasked. I didn't plan on putting it to her here. The babies in the bassinets flash in my mind.

"Alice...do you and Carrow plan on having a child one day?"

Such an intrusive question. It would have been so even in the Pre-Cold Era. Suppose at the height of our relationship, when all was bliss, someone had put the query to me and Sissy. How would we have responded?

Alice gives a slow blink. "Yes. We do."

Something gives way inside me. It is so strong a reaction that I can't even identify it. It might be jealousy again. It might be twisted regret over the child Sissy and I never had. It might just be that a future awaits Alice and her mate, and I will be no part of that future.

I say, "Let's leave this place. Let's leave now."

CHAPTER FORTY-SEVEN
Like a Red, Red Rose

We were in there awhile. Driving back, I am weary enough that I let the rental take the wheel. I slouch; I shut my eyes. I don't intend to sleep, but the next thing I'm aware of is the late afternoon light, the familiarity of my street. Alice has gently shaken my shoulder. Or maybe it wasn't gentle. For all I know she gave me a rough shove. I made her walk through her childhood today, and if that camp wasn't as dank and horrifying as the dungeon I might have imagined, it was still a cheerless place, and her ghosts all dwelt there.

I lumber out of the car. I feel groggy. We go into the house, and I am so glad to be home I could sob. But I don't. Enough emotion for one day. Enough of my old nonsense.

I go into the bedroom. I shuck off everything but my briefs. I'll just lie atop the bed, pull a single cover over me. Close my eyes because they feel grainy, like I should rest them.

It is dark when I come to. I go into the bathroom, and when I emerge, Alice is in the bedroom.

"Are you okay?" she asks.

It is yet another thing I would never expect a cold to say, but she has said it nonetheless. The emotion I held in check on arriving home now overtakes me. I feel such a warmth for her, such abiding affection. It's not how I remember it with Sissy. It couldn't be as it was with her. That was a different age. A different world. But the intensity is there, and all the worn middle-aged mechanisms of my passion are aimed now solely at this woman.

I smile. "I'm fine, Alice."

"We have usually eaten dinner by now."

"I lost track of time. Take my chip. Order us some delivery. Anything. The choice is yours." She has chosen before. She chose to heed the teaching programs at her camp. She later chose to leave the camp, to go out and forge an independent life for herself.

And she chose Carrow, and Carrow probably chose her. I try to picture the two of them, standing together, with a baby. Brave new parents, self-tasked with perpetuating their kind. Maybe they'll even matter in the coming cold world. There is no saying what sort of society this replacement species will ultimately form, once we olds are no longer so underfoot. And their child will live in that world. What will be its role, its fate?

She goes out of the room. The future is too far away to think about. I wonder what we'll be having for dinner.

* * *

I know time is slipping away, hour by hour, minute by minute. My interlude with Alice grows increasingly short, yet Saturday night we eat what she has ordered out of biodegradable cartons. It becomes a lazy night. I make a rum hot toddy with a slice of lemon and offer Alice a sip. She sniffs and leans away from the brim of the glass, the way a cat might when confronted with something it doesn't like the smell of. So, she has had coffee, but she will not imbibe alcohol. I can't give her every experience. And what would one do with a drunk cold, anyway? I chuckle at the thought.

I stream a movie. Why not? She has been exposed to my emotional behavior. Let's see what she makes of fictionalized emotional behavior, rendered for maximal dramatic effect. The film is Pre-Cold. As with the elegiac strains of modern music, I do not enjoy the current crop of visual presentations. What few movies are still made are brimming over with existential dread, replete with characters bemoaning the fate of humankind and staring down the loaded shotgun barrel of tomorrow. I don't find such motion pictures cathartic. Perhaps some olds do. But I'm already dealing with my own personal burden of existential angst, and I would rather be transported out of this time. Take me back to the old days, before we knew we were going to be olds.

The movie is clever, fast-paced, amusing. The problems the characters face seem ludicrously inconsequential, but I embrace the whole spectacle, nursing my hot toddy and laughing out loud where appropriate. I have my arm around Alice, and I like the feel of her; and I congratulate myself on having engineered this relationship. She has done all right by me, and I can say I never abused her. Considering the unorthodox parameters of our partnership, I have to call this a win.

She doesn't respond to the film. Her eyes track the movements on the flatscreen, but she could be watching goldfish. So what? It doesn't matter.

The fatigue is still on me, but it is soft now, enveloping, almost a comfort. I don't want to copulate. But I hold her to me in the bed, and again her presence, her fleshy reality, is so very welcome.

* * *

Sunday morning I wake up restored. I shave my face clean. I scour myself in the shower. This is the last complete day I will have with Alice, the last day when I won't lose a swath of hours with her to her job. Everything seems to glow with a fragile pale loveliness.

I make us a late breakfast. I am aware of the scent of her--aware that she has a scent, one I am likely to remember, a combination of body chemistry and the soap and shampoo in my bathroom. She has smelled this way here; she won't smell the same elsewhere. It is a personal fragrance unique to her time with me, in this place.

She is again casually nude this morning. I soak that up as well. It doesn't feel like prurient imagery, a private pornography to store in my memory files. Well...it is that, a little. But it's more as well. I want to know she was here, really here. I must always be able to convince myself of that fact, no matter how many more years pile up on me, no matter how age violates my body and perhaps even sabotages my mind. Let these remembrances stand all the tests of time. Let me take them with me, all the way, until there is no more of me. But let her be there, even at the end, when I wish to remember the good times of this life. And when I need to feel the pain of our parting.

"How about we go out for a walk," I say. "Around the neighborhood."

She goes to dress. I wonder if this counts as squandering the remainder of our time together. But no. I don't think so. I have no urge to do anything drastic, go anywhere that isn't convenient. I have taken her places--Santa Cruz and Sausalito, to restaurants and music venues. An unassuming stroll about the environs of Potrero Hill sounds just right to me. I am glad not to feel desperation or panic, the sense that I must fill up this time with frantic activity. There isn't even any urgency now, just her sweet presence, merely this gentle calm coda to what I have already known with her.

The streets of Potrero Hill are wide. The sky is as clear as it was yesterday, out in the suburbs, but the temperature still cannot struggle above 60. I wear a sweater. Alice is in a long-sleeved top. We hold hands. She moves in her easy gliding gait. The streets go up and down. There are old houses and newer ones. The colors all seem to pop for me, even the duller hues. It's like I'm seeing the neighborhood for the first time. It is charming. I like the greenery, the trees. It seems a separate entity from the rest of the city, a special place, a haven even. The birds sing a little louder here.

There is 16th Street and Cesar Chavez Street, Vermont and Mariposa and Channel. McKinley Park and Jackson Playground. Restaurants and coffee shops: Aperto and Cup of Blues, Dos Piñas and old reliable Farley's. We traipse all about, do Alice and me. If we receive nasty looks, I don't notice them. We're just a couple, out walking on a somnolent Sunday afternoon.

I tell her on the 300 block of Rhode Island Street. I finally tell her.

I squeeze her hand, and she stops. I am acutely aware of the asphalt underfoot, of the beats of my heart. This spot, this small patch of sidewalk, will now forever be the place where I spoke the words to Alice Felzien. Just as there is a back yard up there in Northern California which is the first place I laid my eyes on Sissy Anspaugh. These are the monuments in my humble little autobiography, the sites where my world turned. I beheld Sissy, with her great head of strawberry curls, smoking a cigarette, speaking tersely into a cell phone; and my life would change, because I had seen her, because she drew me right from the start. Because she would become everything to me, and later it would all be wreckage. A back yard at a party. What if I hadn't gone that night? But I did, and I am glad I did. Because, no matter the misery we eventually found ourselves in, Sissy was worth the trouble. I was ready to love, even if I didn't know it, and she was there for me. And loving her was worth it.

Alice looks up at me. She waits, without waiting, as only a cold can.

I say, "I love you, Alice. I want you to know that. I need you to. Even if those are just words to you--sounds, with intangible meaning attached...just remember them. Please. I love you. It's all you need to know."

It is not something she is able to respond to. I haven't prompted her to reply. I squeeze her hand again, and we resume walking, back to the house.

CHAPTER FORTY-EIGHT

Goodbye and Keep Cold

The fleeting moments are like discrete treasures. Alice comes toward the car with her origami bicycle over her shoulder. My brain freezes the image, catches her at the most artistic instant, with the composition just right, light on her narrow shoulders and glazing the line of her jaw. Alice at my kitchen table, eating the dinner I've made; she lifts a forkful of buttery mashed potatoes, cuts a slice of beef, stabs up a few spears of sautéed asparagus; repeats the same sequence, over and over, until the food is gone. Alice, joined to me, in the throes of physical fervor: the grasp of her, the faint slickness of perspiration on her body, her green eyes wide in the dim bedroom.

It is August. It is August, and it is not warm in San Francisco. The wind blows, and the fog comes. And there is something else in the atmosphere, an...undercurrent. If I had a trick knee, it would probably be throbbing by now. While Alice is at work, I stream a local weather report. The meteorologist is animated, saying something about barometric outliers. I can't figure out where he is going with all his data. The weather is crazy. I get it. We riled the planet. Well, like the cold, Earth need only outlast us. Which it most certainly will. Hell, it'll surely outlast the cold too. No matter what kind of run they ultimately have, they are a fragile species, just like we always were. Nature--or God--probably has something in store for them, perhaps a few tens of thousands of years from now. Or maybe sooner.

The calmness in me persists, even in the face of nearing calamity. A meager handful of days are left, no more. When Alice goes, she shall leave a furrow behind, a wound in the very pith of me. It cannot be avoided. I have come to love her, and so I am vulnerable. It's the ancient proposition. Emotion is still the currency in which I trade. I know no other system. If I were cold, if I were like her, I wouldn't be facing this approaching catastrophe.

Because make no mistake: even though I know it is coming, even though I have deliberately engineered this tragedy, I am wholly susceptible to it. Alice will soon no longer be in my life, and that will devastate me.

* * *

So I mark the passing instances. I take them up and set them carefully under glass as they occur. I am both in the moment and removed from all real time. I am the curator of my own experiences.

But Alice is still here, still achingly tactile. I see her. I touch her. She is my breath, my heart. I am not who I was when we first got together. I remember how skeptical I was, how cynical. I doubted I would even want her for the whole month--or only desire her intermittently. In my mind I was the creep.

I no longer think of myself as a creep. Yes, our relationship came into being because I bluntly paid for this woman; and yes, that is a dubious way for a romance to commence. But I perceive how my own feelings progressed. Looking back, the path is straight and true.

But...she is a cold. Yes. She is. But she is no biological automaton. She is possessed of an ability to make decisions. She believes in her own future. It is more than I would have expected of any cold.

I am not wrong to love her. This is the last great passion of my life. I don't mean I will become a celibate after this. Or even that I won't one day feel a genuine affection for some woman. My drives aren't going to go away overnight. I will probably retain an instinct for companionship to the end of my days. But I will be more judicious. I will be in no hurry to overspend the coin of emotionality. I'll be far less vulnerable, and I will use that to my advantage. And that is just what I will be seeking in a future relationship: advantage. Because it'll be a game again, a contest, and I shall maneuver and finagle, because I will want to come out the winner.

I will not reach the heights I have achieved with Alice. Suck in the rarefied air, Norris. You'll not taste its like again.

It is August, and we are almost done. It is August, and surely Alice still holds out the possibility that I will change my mind, that I can be used to gain another free month's rent. She wants that. Therefore, she wants me to want her badly enough to renege on my vow to end this.

There is nothing stopping me from extending our relationship. I could avoid all the hurt which is coming toward me.

I could.

* * *

I have begun to catalogue it all. I have these free hours while Alice is out doing the work of Sherwood Messengers. I don't begrudge her this time away from me; I agreed to this up front, and I will honor this clause in our contract.

But during this alone time I start on the archives. We have a history, she and I. A month is a short span. It is also an eternity. I create files and put memories into them. Here are the many movements of our beginning: when I first saw her, when she first stirred me, the first glimmer of my plan to procure her. There is a substantial prologue to our tale, I realize. How I fretted over all this. I am glad I did so. It shows I took the situation seriously, right from the start. Alice deserved every bit of that solemn consideration.

I take delicate care with our first kiss. My hands tremble as they take up the memory and gently, ever so gently, set it in its niche. I can view it through the glass. It is preserved for all time. Or at least for all of my time.

Our first lovemaking...I have to come back later for that one. It is incendiary, so fraught with emotion and heightened physicality that I am initially frightened to handle it. But its terrible beauty calls to me, and finally I gather it and set it in its place of honor.

I add cross references. In the future I will want easy access to all this material. I index the incidences, classify the episodes. I summon a graph and begin to plot my feelings. An x axis and a y. Time and intensity. The longer I was with Alice, the greater my emotional investment. It is a fairly obvious upward pointing line. Its trajectory seems inevitable now. My uncertainty at the outset never stood a chance against the desire I felt for her. Curiosity became passion, and passion became--

Yes. I shall mark the point, circle it in red. Here is where I fell in love with her. It is there on the chart now.

I did this same thing with Sissy, I realize after a while. But the exercise was far less deliberate. She and I had more time. There was no artificial ending imposed on us--just the rotten luck of a slip-up in our birth control. But Sissy's memories too are filed away. I know this because I so recently examined them, going down deep into the tomb of remembrance, exploring first all the good things which had occurred between us, then the bad.

I will not hide Alice's memories. I won't attempt to bury them. This archive will remain accessible, for I intend to cherish our time together. As much as it is going to pain me to part from her, the memory of her will be radiant within me.

* * *

Yet this archiving does nothing to slow the passage of time. I am startled to wake up one morning to realize that this is the last full day and night I will spend with Alice. I'll take her to work, then later retrieve her; then she will stay once more overnight; and then--

And then, tomorrow, we will say goodbye.

The startlement tries to turn to panic. A cold oceanic fear shifts inside me, the sort that could turn my guts to water. It is suddenly real. Time is finite. Everybody is mortal. I can't be with Alice forever.

If she knows that tomorrow is our day of parting, she shows no sign of it as I serve her breakfast. But what signs might I expect? Would she gaze upon me with grave longing? Might she murmur some endearment to me as she takes my hand and presses the fingers to her cheek? I would like that. I would like any overt demonstration of sentiment from her. Somewhere in her depths she cares for me. Even if that fondness is a purely mathematical proposition. I have benefited from this man. He has not been abusive to me. I have gained from our arrangement, and there will be an absence in my life when we are no longer together.

Yeah. It would be nice to hear something like that, to know such thoughts might be in her head. But I have faith that these musings are present within her, at some level. Huh. Imagine that: I have faith, after all. God isn't up there. But a spirit dwells inside a cold, this particular cold, anyway.

I love her. And if she could say it, she would tell me she loves me too.

And thus I take my final full leap of faith, right out over the yawning jagged chasm.

* * *

My archival efforts do me no good now. The operation is finished. I have already stored up my memories with Alice, and they are tidy and accessible, just as I wish them to be. All that remains is our finale, which hasn't occurred yet and which will no doubt sear itself into my soul when it does happen.

I have taken her to work. I am back home, alone. The day feels frail, precarious. Panic, raw and powerful, again menaces me. The floors feel like glass, and it is as though I will crash through with every aimless step I take. I need to leave the house.

Grab gym shorts. Lace up my running shoes. I fairly flee the ground floor of the Victorian. I hit the street, strides long, heart already pumping with that extra athletic vigor. The city blocks flash by. Soon sweat is stinging my eyes because I neglected to put on a headband. No matter. I wipe it away; I blink it away. I go on, legs growing heavy even as my feet continue to land lightly. I run, and I am not accustomed to running much. It is a wandering course. Gadding about the precincts of my neighborhood. No one honks at me when I step out into the street. The vehicles are self-drivers; they can avoid me.

I am pounding down the 300 block of Rhode Island Street before I know it, coming down the sidewalk, body strained, limbs beginning to feel leaden. Yet I push on, as if I'm training for a meet. Something wells up in my chest. I wonder if I am about to be sick. But what comes up is laughter. And it is a rather ghastly laughter. My eyes sting again. I could just as easily be running and weeping, making an absolute spectacle of myself.

The laughs are convulsive. They put a stitch into my side. An elderly woman is walking her dog, a labrador who itself appears quite advanced in years. The two are taking their time, coming up the sidewalk. They are very near the spot where I told Alice that I loved her.

The woman looks at me with bright intelligent eyes, and with an expression of such open sympathy on her creased face, that I want to fall to my knees and throw my arms around her middle. She would understand my pain, my grief. There is maternal nurturing in her; I can sense it at ten yards.

But I go pelting past her and past the patch of sidewalk where Alice and I stood together a short time ago. A raft of lifetimes ago. I hear my own words as I pass. Please. I love you. It's all you need to know.

The sounds are already fading behind me, as if they hang in the air over that tract of sidewalk, repeating over and over. But they are also in my archive. And inscribed on my soul.

* * *

I pick her up after work. I put questions to her that she can easily answer, so that there will not be silence in the car.

I am making dinner. Serving it. I sit across, picking at the food, unable to eat.

The bedroom. We are in the bedroom. The moments are slipping through my fingers. Her touch. Her texture. Her aroma, so exhilarating. I hang onto every heartbeat, every microsecond. I try to. But time is merciless. I had forgotten, because I am used to time being the enemy on the larger scale. The years advance, and there are more colds and less olds. The cycle is inevitable, and time is its vicious accomplice.

But this is that disaster writ small and personal. Alice is going away from me. Time wants her, and time shall have her. What will there be for me, then?

I gamely keep my focus, despite the dread running through me, vibrating with increasing current. I hold her body. I caress and kiss, stroke and nuzzle. I'll not leave her with a disappointing final night.

Not that she would be disappointed. But it is as she once told me: sex is necessary.

So I see to her necessities and, in the course of things, to my own. There is no fault in my performance, and she, as always, has acted the exemplary carnal partner. Whoever the luckless female old is who follows this act, I pity her in advance. She will not be as good as this cold girl. And I will probably be faltering and ambivalent, wondering where the familiar taut young body went, replaced by a sagging joke comprised of middle-aged flesh. Not that I'll be any great prize, physique-wise. Forty years can do brutal things to a man.

I want to go again. But I am spent. My body tells me, simply: no. Then I want to stay awake, to hold her consciously, to feel her breathe, to know the living splendor of her naked form against mine.

But...I am tired. The drag weight of my entire kind shackles my ankles together, and I am drawn down into the sad fading mass of olds; and though I clasp Alice tightly in my arms, she isn't really there. She has never been there. I have loved mist and shadow. But I have loved truly.

* * *

Morning. She showers. I make breakfast. It is the last time we will do these things together. I drive her to work. I lean across the seats to kiss her before she gets out and retrieves her bike from the trunk. The kiss lingers on my lips. I will pick her up at the usual time.

At home the day is surreal. At noon I stand at my kitchen counter trying to decide what flavor of coffee to make for my afternoon cup. The decision stalls in my brain. I take twenty-six minutes to decide, and every second of that crawls by with excruciating slowness.

Later, the time between three-ten and five past four o'clock simply vanishes. I find I am sitting on my couch, doing nothing, but that interval has elapsed without leaving any trace. I have no idea--none--what I have done for the past near hour. There is nothing in my memory but a faint static.

I am not tired enough to nap, but vague lethargy follows me from room to room. I don't go out. My calves ache some from yesterday's run. Maybe I should get more exercise in the future. But imagining anything beyond today is difficult. Tomorrow is unreal. It feels as though it might never come. And part of me doesn't want it to.

It is time to go fetch Alice.

I make the drive. I park at the curb on Clay Street. She is late coming out. She knows this is the day I have designated as our last. Perhaps she is preemptively taking her leave of me. The finale to our relationship might be messy; after all, I am an old. My reactions come from a place of emotion. She might think it prudent to simply slip away. I couldn't fault her. She has given me the month I paid for. These last hours don't necessarily belong to me.

But she does emerge from the underground garage, carrying her folded up bike by its strap over her shoulder, and spent adrenaline courses through my veins and leaves me slack for a moment. I have to consciously draw my breaths as she approaches the car.

I drive her back to my place.

I ask about her day.

I cook her dinner. We sit across, at the table. I have prepared a small roast, with tiny round potatoes and steamed Brussels sprouts. I pour her a glass of cranberry juice. I have a ginger ale with the meal.

When we finish, I clear the dishes. There is still some roast left, and I put it into a plastic container and put it in the refrigerator. No potatoes or sprouts are left over.

Alice watches me. Her hair has started to grow out, just a little, but the cut still looks good on her.

I say, "I have put your things into bags." The travel bags we used on our getaways. I have loaded them with the clothes I got her, the underwear, even the lingerie. Also all her toiletries from the bathroom. That is really all I accomplished during the day: I packed up her stuff.

She is still seated at the table in the kitchen. She looks up at me, says nothing.

I go into the bedroom and bring out the bags. She is standing now. She watches as I carry the bags to the front door and set them down, side by side, neatly aligned. Again I am breathing evenly but self-consciously, as though my lungs might stop if I disregarded them.

Alice has come out of the kitchen. Her green eyes are slightly narrowed, and it gives her lovely stoic face just a hint of wariness.

I wait until a breath has emptied from me; then I steadily draw another, and say, "The car will take you home. Don't forget your bicycle in the trunk." She won't forget. The bike is her livelihood. I will be gone, but she'll still have her job.

She comes toward me, and her movements really do appear reluctant now. She peers up at my face, as if searching for something.

She stands before me, by the front door, by her waiting bags. "Do you really want me to go, Kyle?" She speaks softly, which somehow accentuates the rasp in her voice.

"No. I don't." I have to pause to swallow. My throat is tight. "But you have to go."

Her lips start to move, and I'm afraid she is going to try another of her smiles. Perhaps she reads my trepidation, because she abandons the attempt. Her expression stays neutral. "Change your mind, Kyle. Please."

My hands goes to my pocket. I take out my chip. It zeroes in on the chip in her own pocket. I enact a transaction. "There," I say. "I've paid you another month's rent. But there's nothing attached to it this time. Our relationship is over." I want to wish her and Carrow well, but it is too far of a reach for me.

She doesn't check her chip. She continues to gaze up at me.

"We should kiss goodbye, then."

Incredibly, she is the one to have said it. This cold girl, wanting to kiss me one last time. My heart roils with warmth in my chest.

I touch my fingertips to her cheek. I lean in, and she comes up half an inch on her toes. Our lips meet, and the contact is sweet and poignant and brief.

I can say nothing more. I open the door, and Alice picks up both bags. There is a last--truly, last--moment of direct eye contact, when we are face to face and all the world seems to stream from her; then she turns and goes down the lavender paving stones to the car. She puts the bags on the back seat and climbs in on the front passenger side. The vehicle pulls away. How smoothly it moves, without any of the personality or unpredictability that comes of having a person behind the wheel. I watch it all the way up the street. I watch it until there is nothing left to see. It has crested a slope and gone on to the other side.

Standing in the open doorway, I put both hands to the jamb. I press firmly against the wood. This will hold me upright and in place.

And as if it is a physical act, I drop my emotional defenses. All the checks. All the curbs. The whole breaker circuit system I have been building since preadolescence, when I first saw that life would require investment from me, and I wasn't sure I could provide the necessary strength of feeling; and so I thought I would need to conserve my sentiments, mete them out when needed, when I could effect them in the most convincing manner.

I dash my protections to the ground. I cast off every barrier, every shield. I brace myself and let in the feelings. Alice is gone. The woman I love is out of my life for good. It doesn't matter that I have sent her away. It doesn't matter if this construct is somewhat artificial in nature. The heartache is there, seethingly present. It rushes over me with an awful heat and a stench of burning leaves. Alice. Alice. Never to see her again, never to know her. She is lost. She is lost.

And right behind that hurt, joined to it in sorrowful sisterhood, is all the pain which Sissy wrought in me. Only now, instead of being numbed by it, I feel. I feel it. The boiling cauldron of grief is upended over me, and everything I once avoided by sleepwalking through it abruptly scalds me. I silently cry out. The agony writhes me.

Above and around me I hear the great somber tolling: the funeral bells, resonant and deep, sounding all the misery of the world. Bong. Goodbye, Alice. Bong. Farewell, Sissy. Bong. Godspeed, human race. Bong. And for the colds too I feel grief and pity; I truly do. You will never know the ecstasy of such pain. You will never be so rawly and totally cabled into the universe as I am in this supreme moment of hurt, this final epiphany of sad, ridiculous, feeble, honest human heartbreak.

Bong. Bong. Bong. Bells. As night comes. Bells. As I wait alone for the next day's dawn. Bells, tolling for every last inhabitant on the planet. We wretched bunch. We band of noble fools.

I push off limply from the doorway. My knees are weak. I step back into my house and shut the door.

CHAPTER FORTY-NINE

And Leave Thee in the Storm

Norris had been surprised, last night, at how easily sleep came. He'd more than halfway expected a grisly dark night of the soul, with much tossing and turning in the empty bed, his mind torturing him with images of Alice.

Instead, he had felt the gravity of slumber overtake him in fairly short order. It had drawn him down into a soft private blackness, and he had slept so deeply dreams seemed unable to reach him.

Awake, he went through his morning routines--the old ones, before Alice effectively cohabited with him. He performed his ablutions, got some good coffee into himself, and considered the day. There was nothing urgent ahead. He could do his grocery shopping if he wanted. This coming weekend he should return the rental car. Perhaps today he could--

But something felt wrong. Something outside his own skin. Frowning, Norris breathed the air, as if it held some strange impurity. And there was an oddness. Perhaps not an outright scent but...

He went to refill the cat bowls outside his back door, the ones for the neighborhood strays. He looked up at the sky and recoiled. It was a curious color, both too pale and too vibrant at the same time. A wind blew, strong, as though with a sinister undercurrent. He recalled the weatherman talking about unprecedented barometric readings the other day.

Hurrying through the house, he reached his front door and flung it open. Outside, the apocalypse was visiting itself upon San Francisco. He stood rooted, there in the same place where only last night he had felt and accepted the full measure of his loss with regard to both Alice and Sissy. It had been a moment of exorcism, of surrender; and he knew it had changed him, for good.

But none of that mattered now. He looked out and saw, to the south and west, the most awesome natural phenomenon he had ever witnessed with his own eyes. It appeared centered on Bernal Heights, approximately one neighborhood over, on the great knoll of the park which crowned it. A vast funnel of debris-filled air was rising from the ground, spinning madly. At the same time a similarly shaped cone was reaching down from the grotesque mass of coal-black clouds above. The two churning forces stretched toward each other, coordinating perfectly, and when they met, the air--the whole atmosphere over the city--seemed to snap electrically with the contact. The sky was roaring. Norris heard it clearly now.

He gawked at the tornado, even as in the distance it ravaged the high ground of Bernal Heights. It must be doing untold damage. There were of course residences around the park. That such cyclonic phenomena had never before occurred in this part of the country-- much less within the bounds of San Francisco--was meaningless to the moment. Every reasoned argument against the appearance of a tornado was violently refuted by the sight, miles away, of the funnel sucking dirt and trees and all manner of rubble up into itself, whirling it high above the earth.

In fifteen seconds the cone fell apart. Such weather events should not occur here, and the sensibility of that overcame the tornado's brief reality. But it had happened. It had struck.

Norris turned and raced back through the house. He grabbed the first aid kit out of the bathroom and ran out through the open front door, shoes slapping his lavender paving stones. The medical kit in its plastic rectangular box felt immensely inadequate to the scope of destruction the tornado had doubtlessly wrought.

But he had to do something. Emergency vehicles would be responding, but they would surely be overwhelmed by the number of casualties. He could help transport victims to the nearest hospital. The injured would be both old and cold. The tornado wouldn't have discriminated. He meant to help whoever he could. He leapt into his rental.

Norris pulled out into the street, spun the car sharply about and jammed down hard on the accelerator.

CHAPTER FIFTY

Come the Cold

My days are orderly. My life is a calm sequence of habits. I am back at the office, doing my steadfast unremarkable work. I mull the idea of purchasing a car, though I do not need one. But I enjoyed driving myself about, while Alice was with me. I have all the memories of her; and they are not bitter; rather, they are tender and restful. I needed to love, one final time. And she was there. She was there.

Today I am accosted by a young-old. It happens just outside my office tower. He is garbed in masquerade finery, the outfit soiled and crumpled; the same state he appears in, in the dregs of an all-night spree. He is alone. He has wandered away from his pack. He gibbers at me. I smile blandly, a smile that says: One day you'll be my age, kid.

And so, bemused, I continue to dwell in my bewildered city. Here I will carry on, as best I can, accepting what is happening and giving to my fellow olds what emotion I can spare.

And all the while, behind us, come the cold.

THE END